W9-CED-185

ENTER IF YOU DARE

ALYSON LARRABEE

WHISKEY CREEK PRESS
www.whiskeycreekpress.com

Published by
WHISKEY CREEK PRESS
Whiskey Creek Press
PO Box 51052
Casper, WY 82605-1052
www.whiskeycreekpress.com

Copyright © 2014 *by Alyson M. Sousa*

Warning: The unauthorized reproduction or distribution of this copyrighted work is illegal. Criminal copyright infringement, including infringement without monetary gain, is investigated by the FBI and is punishable by up to 5 (five) years in federal prison and a fine of $250,000.

Names, characters and incidents depicted in this book are products of the author's imagination or are used fictitiously. Any resemblance to actual events, locales, organizations, or persons, living or dead, is entirely coincidental and beyond the intent of the author or the publisher.

No part of this book may be reproduced or transmitted in any form or by any means, electronic or mechanical, including photocopying, recording, or by any information storage and retrieval system, without permission in writing from the publisher.

ISBN: 978-1-61160-839-7

**Cover Artist: Gemini Judson
Editor: Dave Field
Printed in the United States of America**

Dedication

For Annie + Belen = Annabelle

"No man for any considerable period can wear one face to himself and another to the multitude, without finally getting bewildered as to which may be the true."
Nathaniel Hawthorne

Acknowledgements:

First, thank you to all the family members, friends, co-workers and students who encouraged me to follow my dreams, dream big and not give up.

A huge thank you to the first people who read the book in its entirety: Kathleen Sousa, Serena Shea, Samantha McGuinness, Lauren Hartman, Baileigh Martin, Ruksha Senthilkumar and Annie Larrabee. Also, thank you to Warren Lizotte who, five years ago, met me at my classroom door every morning to see if I had written another chapter for him to read, back when the story first began to form in my imagination.

Thank you to Ross Muscato, for his encouragement and knowledge about the Bridgewater Triangle. Thank you to Hazel Varella, Duncan Oliver and Ed Hands for their fascinating class about the History of Easton. Special thanks to Duncan and Ed for their informative pamphlet about Easton's graveyards.

Thank you to Mike Atwood for encouraging Annie Larrabee to do her English project on the paranormal legends of the Bridgewater Triangle.

Thank you to the handful of people who lent me their vacation homes so I could write in solitude and quiet: Rob Keleher, John and Terri Larrabee and Amy and Cliff Curtis.

Chapter 1

There's a New Kid in Town

Once again the new kid's sitting next to the only empty seat in the classroom.

And once again I'm almost late. Still panting from my sprint down the hallway, I slide into the last empty seat, crashing my elbows and slamming my knees. Two seconds later, the bell rings. A book topples off my desk and the new kid catches it midair, then hands it to me.

To avoid making eye contact, I stare down at the book and mumble, "Thank you."

Wyatt Silver leans over so I can hear him above the ruckus. "You're welcome, Annabelle. Did you study for the quiz?"

Pretending I didn't hear him, I open my notebook.
Damn.

It's my English notebook and this is History. I start rummaging through my book bag, looking for my History notes. I have a C minus average in this class and my parents will be pissed if I don't bring my grade up. Unfortunately, I had no idea there was a quiz today. I'm never prepared for tests or quizzes and I'm always late. Wyatt seems not to have noticed. He keeps trying to start conversations by asking about our History assignments.

He should be able to tell just by looking at me that I'm the wrong person to ask about anything.

Ten minutes ago I was still in the shower and my hair's dripping down my back. Even my body's still damp. Like an idiot, I didn't dry off enough before I yanked on my clothes.

I'm wet. I'm shivering. I'm dropping things. Obviously, I'm the most disorganized kid in the class. You'd think he would've figured that out by now but he hasn't.

As persistent as a bloodthirsty mosquito, Wyatt leans toward me again and asks in an even louder voice, "Did you study for the quiz?"

To which I reply, "What quiz?"

Finally, I locate the spiral notebook containing the right notes. Spreading it open on the desktop, I begin to read my chaotic interpretation of what happened centuries ago in the British Isles, I think. This is AP History and I'm sure I have the lowest average in the class. Everyone else is brilliant. If he's looking for a study partner he's chosen the wrong girl. If he's looking for *anything* he's chosen the wrong girl because I've sworn off boys. Not forever but at least until college.

Since the first day of school, two weeks ago, Wyatt has asked me at least fifty questions about our History assignments. Sometimes I provide an unhelpful answer. Most of the time I provide no answer at all. He still hasn't taken the hint. I've done everything but say, "Don't look at me. Don't talk to me." I can't do that, though, because my mother raised me to be polite. So I continue to stifle my rudest impulses and provide stupid answers to his questions. My stupidity isn't feigned, either. I'm really that big of an idiot.

Wyatt must be starting to notice, because next he asks me, "Do you own a hairdryer?"

I almost smile, but at the last second, as the corners of my mouth start to twitch up, I twitch them back down. I will not smile at Wyatt Silver.

He doesn't give up. "Do you have towels at your house?"

"Yes, we have towels." I push a clump of wet hair away from my face and a few drops of water sprinkle across my notes, blurring the ink. He laughs.

I'd like to ask him a few questions, but I have no desire to get to know him, so I don't. I'm curious about why he moved to Eastfield, though. Everybody is. He used to live in New Hampshire and now he lives here, with his uncle, not his parents.

Some people say that he got expelled from his old school for selling weed.

More Wyatt Silver gossip: he had to leave because he got a girl pregnant. My personal favorite: Every single person in his former hometown has an STD and he started the epidemic. That really happened on Lifetime TV, but it was in California. Not New Hampshire.

I've heard all the gossip and I don't know which story to believe. Who transfers to a new school for senior year? Nobody if they can avoid it, so there must be drama in his recent past. And I wish he'd leave me alone because I hate drama.

He's not your typical dangerously handsome bad boy type, but he's good-looking enough, in a tall, awkward, shaggy-haired way. Except he blushes like mad when he talks to me, even if he's only asking about the homework. No subject is too boring for him and every time he speaks to me, his cheeks turn all pink and his eyes darken. I try not to look at him, but whenever I do his unruly face is changing color.

He leaves me alone for the rest of History class. After flunking the quiz, I tune out a boring lecture about the Celts in the fifth century. Finally the bell rings and I can escape from him so I jump up to leave. About two feet away from the classroom door, I feel something fall out the bottom of my pants leg. When I look down there's a pair of my underwear, lying on the floor. Orange and black tiger print bikinis.

Ugh!

They must've gotten stuck inside my pants leg in the dryer. This morning I pulled a pair of clean jeans out of the dryer and yanked them on in a hurry. Should've checked inside the right leg for bunched up undies.

Damn.

I bend and swoop in one graceful motion. The panties are inside my bag within three seconds of hitting the floor. Nobody even noticed. Except Wyatt Silver, who's right behind me. Just in case his grin fails to say it all, he adds, "I'll catch your books when they fall, Annabelle, but I've gotta draw the line there. You're on your own with this mishap."

I love the word mishap, but I hate the burn that's racing across my reddening face. Even my dripping wet hair can't cool me off. Now the new kid knows a lot more about me than I want him to know: I own a pair of tiger print bikini underpants and they're in my book bag right now. At least it wasn't a thong.

I don't see Wyatt again until lunch and that's too soon. When I get to the cafeteria, I hop between two of my friends who are sitting on a long bench at one of the picnic-style tables. As usual I'm so hungry I'm salivating. After ripping my paper lunch bag open I tear into my first sandwich.

While slurping up a carton of milk, I glance around and see Wyatt Silver, once again checking me out. He's sitting four tables away and we almost make eye contact.

Quickly, I shoot my gaze down to the fascinating focal point of my straw. Then jiggle it around on the bottom of the milk carton, suck hard and make a loud gurgling sound as I vacuum up the last drop. I smile at my friends, Jen and Connor, on either side of me and then at Meg who's sitting across from us with her boyfriend, Ryan; we all eat lunch together every day, on the seniors' side of the school cafeteria.

Jen says, "I want to dive into his blue eyes and swim around naked."

I laugh. "Jen, you would never really do that."

"Would too. What is wrong with you, Annabelle? He's so hot!"

"Nothing's wrong with me. I know he's hot. I just need a break from boys. I want to stay single this year."

We all know who Jen's talking about, but we also know better than to look directly at the new kid.

Jen and Meg, individually, not together, glance in Wyatt's direction. We've worked hard to perfect the skill of checking out a situation without getting caught. We combine quick, well-aimed glances and peripheral vision; which can be used more casually and slowly.

Meg warns me. "He's *so* checking you out. He's staring. I think he feels safe being four tables away, like maybe you won't notice, but you'd have to be unconscious."

"He sits next to me in History class, first period. Kelsey told me that he looks at me a lot. Sometimes he even talks to me, stuff like, 'Did you study for the quiz'."

Jen spoons a bite of applesauce into her mouth, gives my damp hair the once over and frowns. "I'd get up at five in the morning to do my hair if he stared at me the way he stares at you. I'd get up at four if he talked to me."

"It's been going on since the first day of school. He always sits next to me. I've shut him down a million times. I don't know why he keeps trying."

"Because you're a catch, Annabelle. You're smart and

funny and gorgeous," Ryan says.

I don't like it when people compliment me, especially about my appearance. It makes me feel uncomfortable. They all need a visit to a good eye doctor, anyway. My nose and my neck are too long and my boobs barely fill an A cup. I snort at Ryan.

Who responds, "It's definitely not your laugh that turns him on."

I snort again, just to annoy him.

Meg says, "Shut up, Annabelle. You sound like a farm animal."

Ryan won't quit. "He likes you. He wants to get to know you. He asked me about you at soccer practice."

Jen and Meg start piling on the questions ten times faster than Ryan can answer them. "When was this?" "What did he say?" "What did you tell him?"

Wyatt could go out with any girl in the school and I've been playing mad hard-to-get. Except I'm not playing. I'm serious. I mean it. Why isn't he discouraged? What the hell's up with him?

I ask the most obvious question. "Why me?"

"He says there's something about you." Ryan's answer only makes Wyatt's interest in me seem even more mysterious.

Connor says, "There's a lot about you, Annabelle. Your face is gorgeous and the golf team voted you best butt in the whole school."

"Thanks, Con, I'm so glad the whole golf team has been checking out my butt."

"Silver would have to be blind not to notice you. I have an idea. Let's see if he gets jealous; a little experiment." Connor leans in so close to my right ear that his lips are touching it. We've always had kind of a flirty friendship. And he's definitely flirting with me now. Anyone watching us would think so.

His warm breath whispers against my skin as Connor gives directions to Meg and Jen. "Watch Silver and see how he reacts."

His chest presses against my shoulder. He rests his hand on the back of my neck and nudges my ear with his nose. "This could be interesting. Does he really care about you? Does he think he has a chance? What will he do, Annabelle?"

"Wow, he's staring straight at you guys and I swear his eyes changed color!" Meg's voice creeps out from between her closed teeth, like a ventriloquist's. She knows how to be discreet. "He just stood up!"

I throw my right elbow into Connor's stomach and then look across the cafeteria at my not-so-secret admirer. Wyatt Silver is indeed standing up. His formerly blue eyes have darkened to battleship gray. The grim line of his mouth stiffens. A muscle in his reddening face twitches.

I launch myself up, banging the backs of my knees on the edge of the bench.

"Shut up, you guys." My warning's unnecessary, though, because everyone has been stunned into silence. At least their mouths aren't hanging open. Not that it matters. Staring straight at me and only me, Wyatt Silver takes a step in my direction. I need to escape fast, before he gets to our table.

But as I try to climb out from between Connor and Jen I lose my balance and almost fall over. Grabbing onto Connor's shoulder, I effectively demonstrate how uncoordinated I can be. At least I'm not wearing a skirt. Awkward is what I do best, but flashing everyone in the school cafeteria would be extreme, even for me.

During my almost-fall, one leg flies up and my flip-flop catapults into the air, end-over-end, landing I know not where. When I finally I regain my balance, I can feel how disgustingly sticky the floor is because one of my feet is bare. Spinning around frantically, I try to spot my sandal, and finally succeed. It's lying a few feet away, next to another table.

I need to get away fast, before I end up having to talk to Wyatt. So I scoop up my books and then turn back toward the spot where I saw my sandal a second ago. It's gone.

A large hand with long fingers wraps around my forearm. Wyatt's hand is so big he can hold my arm gently, without squeezing, and still encircle it. I stare at his hand for a second before my gaze trails up to his face. He's smiling and his face and eyes have returned to their normal color.

In the hand that isn't holding onto my arm, he's holding a stack of books, on top of which sits my flip-flop.

"Lose something, Tiger?" He lets go of me, turns and stalks away with my sandal still resting on the cover of his Calculus book. Struggling to keep up with his long-legged stride, I jog after him.

"See you in Math class, Connor." Wyatt tosses this comment over his left shoulder like a live grenade.

When I catch up to him he grins. "What's up, Annabelle?"

"Give me my shoe. I'm barefoot on this slimy floor and everyone's watching."

"Only one of your feet is bare."

"Please." I decide to try being polite.

"I'll trade you."

Oh, crap, what now?

"Trade me what?"

"All I want is a conversation; a chance to get to know you better."

"It'll have to be a fast conversation. I can't be late for my next class."

"Which way are you going?"

"I have English upstairs."

"C'mon. I'm going upstairs, too."

We're in high school so a lot of kids are watching us. There's no way I can avoid walking to class with him without being outrageously rude and obvious about it, in front of everyone. Besides, he still has my shoe. So I walk with Wyatt Silver, through the hallway and up the stairs. I have to take two steps for each one of his and I'm wearing only one flip-flop. If he doesn't give me the other one soon, my foot will be filthy by the time I get to English class.

He asks, "So, Annabelle, what do we have for history homework tonight?"

And I don't know the answer. I refuse to look at him, but I can hear him and he's chuckling softly.

"I know what the homework is. Too bad for me if I didn't. You're never much help."

He takes a deep breath and blows out his next words fast. "You made a movie last year, about ghosts. Everyone still talks about it. I'd like to watch that movie with you."

Chapter 2

Make New Friends but Keep the Old

My head snaps up and I stare into his serious face.

"Who told you about the movie?"

"My uncle, Oliver Finn. I asked him about you and he said you were an interesting girl. You and your friend made a movie for a project last year and everyone still talks about it."

Mr. Finn was my History teacher last year. I liked his class a lot but I have no interest in getting to know his nephew. "I don't talk about it."

"Why not?"

"It happened last year. That part of my life is over."

"It's not over."

He's right, but how could he know? How could he have found out about the nightmares? I haven't told anyone. It's too weird and people already think I'm weird anyway. I don't want to make it worse. This is high school. I need to seem as normal as possible. I want to fit in at least a little.

That means forgetting about the movie and what happened last year, but there's someone who won't let me forget and he visits me in my dreams. Often.

"I'm gonna be late. Can I have my shoe back now?"

"The movie?" He's over six feet tall and he's holding the sandal up, just out of my reach; causing a small scene, right outside my English classroom.

I give in. "My house. Eight o'clock. Saturday night. Bring popcorn."

His smile dazzles me. All white teeth and sparkly eyes. Finally, he hands over the flip-flop; I slap my foot into it and rush into English class. Ms. Coffman's hardcore. She hands out detentions like mad and she hates tardiness.

I'm almost at my desk when someone comes up behind me and puts his hand on my shoulder. Turning around to see who it is, I find myself staring into Matt Riley's face. He's the reason I've sworn off boys.

I haven't seen or spoken to Matt since the first week of summer vacation, shortly before he dumped me. I can't remember any of the witty phrases I've been rehearsing in the mirror for this occasion, so I just warn him. "You're gonna be late."

"It's okay. I have gym next. Mr. Burke doesn't care."

"Coffman's gonna yell at you."

"I don't give a crap, Annabelle. What was all that between you and the new kid?"

"Nothing."

"Stay away from him. No one knows where he came from or why he's here."

"Thanks for the warning. Bye. I gotta look over my notes. There's a quiz today." I have no idea when the next quiz is but I want to get rid of Matt Riley. Fast.

"Are you and Silver gonna hang out?"

"Why do you care?"

"I still care about you."

"What happened to Liz? I thought you two were together now."

"Not exclusively."

That's so him. "Not exclusively" is Matt Riley-speak for: "I'm waiting for the next girl to come along because she might be hotter." I'm not good at interpreting Matt Riley-speak. I never did become proficient in his native language and I don't want to. Last summer, I could've used an interpreter, though. I might've been spared a lot of heartbreak if someone had told me what he really meant when he said he loved me. I still don't know.

"Matt, you're gonna be late and none of this is your business."

"Lots of guys you've known for a long time want to hang out with you. You don't need to hook up with a stranger, Annabelle."

"Thanks for your concern. But we're not hooking up."

"There's a party Saturday, at Colleen's. Her parents are at their Cape house. Are you going?"

"No, I have plans."

"With Silver?"

I hate lying and it feels awful, but I don't want Matt Riley to know anything about my life now that he's not part of it anymore. So I answer, "We're not together. We just sit next to each other in History class."

That part's true, but then I add, "He needs a study partner for a project."

"Okay, but be careful. The dude's weird."

Ms. Coffman glares at me over the top of her goofy-looking glasses. They're perched down near the end of her nose and the lenses are half the size of regular lenses. What's up with those crazy-looking things? I think she wears them just so she can stare at you over them. To creep you out and make you feel guilty even if you haven't done anything wrong.

I show her the smile I've been practicing for when I beat my personal record at the race this Saturday and all the kids on the team run over to congratulate me.

She stands down. Never underestimate the power of a friendly smile. I treat teachers like they're human beings from the same planet as me. And I always laugh at their jokes. It helps to have a good relationship with your teacher when you need an extension for a research paper.

Coffman heads toward my desk. "Boyfriend troubles, Miss Blake?"

I want to say, *neither of those douche bags is my boyfriend.*

Instead I say, "No. It's all good." Then quickly change the subject. "New sneakers, Ms. Coffman? Very fashion forward."

Laughing out loud, she says, "Same old sneakers. But thanks."

Then she walks to the front of the room and starts talking about Shakespeare.

Chapter 3

Dumped but Not Forgotten

I recently closed the door on an episode of my life that I want to forget because of the pain and humiliation. Matt Riley taught me all about rejection last summer. And I hated it.

Matt's a very chill, very popular guy. Last September, in Biology class, he started paying attention to me and then things moved along pretty fast. We had been together for almost ten months when he broke my heart on the first day of summer vacation.

Matt hooked up with the prettiest member of a clique called the Juicies. I don't know what that means. Maybe like a juicy apple is tastier than other apples or something. I don't care. I'm not nearly rich or popular enough to be part of their group anyway. And one of them recently stole my boyfriend.

Matt and I spent a lot of time together last year. Our favorite thing was watching movies at each other's houses: slasher horror movies at his house, classic thrillers at mine. My brother Clement's a film major at Emerson College and his enthusiasm's contagious. He's taught me a lot about film. When Clem's home, we watch movies over and over again, debating, theorizing, discussing. It never gets old for Clement and me. Evidently it *did* get old for Matt.

For his birthday, I bought him the deluxe edition DVD of *The Silence of the Lambs,* with lots of previously unreleased footage and commentary by the author, director and actors.

Shortly before we broke up he confessed that he'd never watched it. I guess it wasn't quite as exciting as *Saw 12.*

Last March, for my birthday, he bought me a t-shirt that said "Legally Brunette." I never wore it. After Matt and I broke up, I gave it to Jen. I hate t-shirts with cutesy expressions. How could he not have known that? I guess I realized early on that Matt and I were way different from each other, but we definitely had chemistry. My biggest regret: he dumped me before I could dump him, and I never saw it coming.

I was babysitting for my neighbors one Saturday night in late June. As soon as the kids fell asleep, I texted Matt a couple of times. I remember how happy I was. The kids were old enough so they were fun to play with, but young enough so I could still boss them around. They had Wii and we played games for a couple of hours. After an intensely competitive burping contest, which I won, they went straight to bed without arguing. I kept thinking about how much fun we'd had and how I was getting paid ten dollars an hour for fooling around and laughing.

I thought I'd share these thoughts with my boyfriend, but he didn't answer my text. I figured maybe his phone had died, even though, during our ten-month relationship, I'd always been able to reach him. We'd even texted each other at one in the morning sometimes, to share boring information about our boring lives. We flirted so furiously our phones should've caught fire.

On this particular night, though, he didn't answer my text. The next day, he finally texted me back. He thought we should try being *just friends* for senior year. When I sent him back a "WTF," he finally called, so we could have an actual conversation.

He explained, "If we break up now, before we start our senior year, we won't have to worry about a long-distance relationship when we get to college. I don't want to influence you if you decide to apply to schools that are out-of-state. And you shouldn't influence my college choices, either. We're too young to get into all that."

We'd never had a serious discussion about the future before, so at first I was impressed. Matt was thinking ahead and being logical. Even though I felt hurt, I saw his point, plus I thought I could easily change his mind when he saw me in person with my summer-time tan, wearing really short, faded denim shorts and the lily pad green shirt that matched my eyes. I'd just had my belly button pierced.

Summer was here. Why wouldn't he want to hang out with someone like me?

Because he had someone like her, that's why. Liz Mayer drives a BMW which is actually hers, not her parents'. But they bought it for her. The license plate says, "LizM."

Every article of clothing she wears advertises whoever designed it. I can't make fun of her for being a bimbo, because she has the brains and the money to get accepted at an Ivy League school. She's smart, rich and beautiful. It would be mean to say that whatever she wasn't born with, her parents buy for her. But it's true.

She has a great body, because her parents pay for her membership at an upscale gym, not because she participates in sweaty sports. Her year-round, golden-brown skin comes from tanning salon visits, not from helping with the yard work. From the roots of her perfectly highlighted hair to the soles of those two hundred dollar fur-lined boots she wears, even in warm weather, she advertises everything money can buy. And last summer she stole my boyfriend along with some of my self-confidence.

I scooped ice cream for minimum wage, went to the beach with my friends on my days off and sulked. I dealt with anger and jealousy by running. Senior year was going to be *my year* on the cross-country team. I ran my ass off; training seriously for the first time ever. I went to all of the captains' practices and sweated like a monster.

With each pounding step, I assured myself that *she* would never get sweaty. Work hard at a sport. Run every day; even in a downpour. I made varsity this fall and it feels good. I'm one of the top ten runners on the team now. The coaches were surprised. For my freshman, sophomore and junior years I'd just cruised along. Cheered on my teammates and helped struggling new runners build up their confidence. I never tested myself until this year.

I decided that senior year was gonna be my time to shine, even if I'm shining with sweat. My mother comes to every cross-country meet and my dad often leaves work early to watch me run. Clement even came home from college last week end and captured me on film, my ponytail flying back, like a dark, glittering flag and my fast feet barely touching down on the path. He calls the film *Run, Annabelle*. And he's entering it in a college film festival.

Take that, Matt Riley. You suck. Have fun with your rich, gorgeous, smart girlfriend, who'll never be able to run five sub-seven minute miles in a row. And I can do it without barfing, too.

No matter how fast I run, though, I can't escape the nightmares. Matt Riley couldn't keep them away and Wyatt Silver won't be able to either. I need a hero but I'll never find him. No one can save me from the cold presence of my midnight visitor. He's relentless and he seems so real that I wake up screaming.

Click, click, click. I hear the same sound every time. Frosty air seethes in from nowhere and wakes me up. Except I'm not awake. I'm dreaming but it seems real because I'm in my bed, right where I was when I fell asleep.

He brings the winter with him.

The window's closed. So a nocturnal breeze couldn't have lowered the temperature to below freezing. I watch as frost forms on the antique crystal doorknob. *Click, click, click.* An invisible hand turns the knob and the door opens, slowly. All on its own.

He crawls toward me, weeping quietly in the darkness. When he reaches the bed, the hairs on the back of my neck rise. His whisper feels like thousands of icy spider legs scuttling around on my skin. "Whhhhh…" no words, just white noise blown from between his frigid lips. Into my ear, along my cheek. "Whhhhh."

He won't leave me alone. I pull the bed covers up over my head. Grasping my blankets in a death grip, I imagine a cold-blooded hand as damp, dark and slimy as a salamander under a rotting log. What if his chilly fingers grab my throat and squeeze?

Huddling inside my cocoon of blankets, I try to scream but no sound will come out. When I start kicking my legs, I finally wake myself up, poke my head out from under the covers and look over at the door; it's open. I closed it right before I went to bed. I yell like a five year old. "Mom… Dad!"

My father rushes in to reassure me. "Annabelle, just keep the door open. I'll check the hinges again tomorrow when I get home from work, and the doorknob, too." The nightmares started about a year ago and my parents and I have been replaying the same scene again and again since then.

Dad has his own theory about the dream; it involves

one of our Blake ancestors. He explained it to me one night last winter, after I woke him up at midnight for the second time in a week. He spoke in the patient voice he uses when he's trying not to sound annoyed because I'm bugging the crap out of him. His story was boring and his voice was soothing, so I fell back to sleep again. Before I dozed off, though, I heard him say:

"The original part of this house dates back to the sixteen-hundreds. For four centuries, our family has lived here in Eastfield, at the edge of the Great Hockomock Swamp. Sometime during the mid-1600's Josiah Blake built a small and humble cabin, here on the driest section of his land. Gradually, through the generations, our ancestors updated and remodeled the existing building and built additions onto the original house.

"A few months before you were born, I finished remodeling your bedroom. I moved some old doors from another part of the house: the dining room addition, built by Zephyriah Blake in 1885, and used them to give your bedroom an antique look. I put one on your closet and one on your bedroom door. I wanted your room, which Grandpa Blake added in the fifties, to fit in better with the rest of the house. Plus, the removal of the old maple doors opened the dining room up to the kitchen, which made your mother happy. She always wanted an open floor plan."

I drifted off to sleep, picturing myself sipping a cup of hot, sweet tea in our cozy, safe kitchen with its big open floor plan.

Dad joked with me the next morning. "Old Zeph's annoyed and wants his doors moved back."

If that's the case, though, why now? My father moved the doors upstairs seventeen years ago. Why did Zeph wait so long to invade my dreams? And what about the crying? Why would Zeph be crying?

For most of my junior year of high school and then all summer long, I endured these nightmares. I like to sleep in a dark, quiet room, so stubbornly I closed the door every night when I went to bed but the dream kept waking me up at midnight. And when I opened my eyes and looked, the door was always open. Now I'm afraid to fall asleep because I know I'll wake up in the dark, alone and terrified. Only my parents know about my recurring nightmare. I'm not ready to tell any of my friends such a freakish story.

Finally I did the only sensible thing; I started leaving the stupid door open. For privacy's sake I hung a sign from the top of the door frame. "Do not enter. I might be naked." And he left me alone, for one night. I decided to take it a night at a time.

I still have the nightmare once in a while, but not nearly as often. I've begun to feel a little bit happier and more relaxed.

Except now Wyatt Silver has come along. He wants to see the movie and that's how the nightmares started.

Every fall, the students in the junior class have to do a big project on the history and literature of Massachusetts. Last year, Meg and I decided to make a movie about local paranormal legends.

"Do you know what would be fun? Grab a flashlight. Let's go find a ghost." It seemed like a good idea at the time.

Eastfield is located in an area of southeastern Massachusetts known as the Hockomock Triangle. It's like the Bermuda Triangle, but smaller and colder in the winter. Lots of weird things have happened here.

My last year's History teacher, Mr. Finn, who's also Wyatt's uncle, is an authority on the Hockomock Triangle. So he was one hundred percent in favor of letting us do the movie. He even helped us with our research. That's how Wyatt knows about it—but I still have no idea why he's so interested. I guess I'll find out Saturday night.

Chapter 4

Saturday Night at the Movies

Wyatt arrives exactly on time and I stay upstairs, hoping one of my parents will answer the door, so Wyatt will have to make awkward conversation while I keep him waiting. My plan is to stand at the top of the stairs and listen.

Dad lets Wyatt in and, sure enough, starts the interrogation. Where is Wyatt applying to college? What does he want to study? Is he thinking of playing a sport? I have to stop myself from running downstairs and hugging and kissing my dad for asking so many dorky questions and making Wyatt squirm. If it gets awkward enough, maybe he'll leave me alone.

After about ten minutes of listening to my dad grill Wyatt about his plans for the future, I hear my mother enter the kitchen. She takes Wyatt's box of microwave popcorn and begins popping it. Mom knows his Uncle Oliver because she's a member of the Eastfield Historical Society and Mr. Finn's the president. So she starts talking to Wyatt about the history of our house and the Blake family because we've lived here for so many generations. Wyatt's probably bored to death, but he has to act polite and listen.

Finally, I make my belated entrance, looking dazzling in a pair of SpongeBob pajama pants and my dad's old high school track sweatshirt. If my outfit for the evening could speak it would say, "Make this quick because I'm tired and want to go to bed."

But Wyatt doesn't seem to care about what I'm wearing. He looks happy and relieved to see me.

Mom hands me the bowl of buttery popcorn and I head down the stairs to the basement. Wyatt follows me, carrying two cans of orange soda and some napkins.

We sit down on the couch and in between bites of popcorn I explain some background information. "My brother Clement was away at school, which was good, because I wanted it to be *my* movie and it would've been too tempting to ask him for help."

"What, exactly, was the assignment?"

"In English class we were reading Hawthorne and Melville and some other boring authors. And then in Mr. Finn's class we were studying local history. So for the project we had to focus on New England culture, like literature and art and stuff. Suddenly I got this great idea. I decided we should make a movie about the ghost stories of the Hockomock Triangle."

"I've heard all about the triangle from my uncle. Isn't there an entrance to the Hockomock Swamp right near here?"

"Yes, just a few feet past our driveway. There are miles of swampland in back of our house, on the southwestern corner of the property."

"According to my uncle, the Hockomock covers about sixteen thousand, nine hundred and fifty acres of wetlands."

"It's big."

He laughs and then turns serious. "So which legends did you document in your film?"

"We narrowed it down to five ghost stories. First we shot some film at the Lizzie Borden Museum, in Fall River."

"She was found innocent of those murders, right?"

"Yes, but I think if they had forensics and C.S.I.s back then, they could've proven she was guilty. Most people think she did it. No one else was ever accused of the crime."

"Cool. Where else did you film?"

"We visited five main locations altogether; each of them was supposedly haunted. We got some pretty spooky footage at a few graveyards right here in Eastfield. Then of course, we went to the Wild Wood Psychiatric Hospital where we really got freaked out. Our goal was to see a ghost. We wanted to capture evidence of an authentic haunting on film."

"And did you?"

"I'll show you the movie so you can see for yourself. A lot of kids skipped out on their classes to sneak in and watch it. Everyone was talking about us. We generated a lot of hype—my fifteen minutes of fame."

After about a minute of skimming through the titles of the DVDs on the shelves under the TV, I find my film and slide it into the DVD player. Wyatt gets up and turns off all the lights. Then settles into the coziest corner of the couch. I sit back down, as far away from him as possible.

"I haven't watched this film since last year. It creeps me out too much. Sometimes I still have nightmares," I confess.

The shimmer of the TV screen casts an eerie glow on Wyatt's face. He raises his arm up along the back of the couch and gestures to me. "You can sit a little closer if you're scared. I won't let any big, bad ghosts get you."

"Dream on, Silver."

"Hey, you're the one with the nightmares. I'm just trying to help."

When he smiles his teeth flash white in the darkness.

"Thanks, but I'll be okay. I don't need anyone's help." The only thing that scares me more than the movie is sitting close to Wyatt.

I sneak a quick look at his profile. He looks dead serious even though he was joking around a second ago.

"For the first part of the movie, we decided on a slide show of pictures taken at the Lizzie Borden Museum in Fall River. We downloaded some photographs from the internet and used some pictures we took ourselves, for the other slides." I point the remote and click "Play." The images flash in quick succession to the raging beat of "Raining Blood" by Slayer. The heavy metal music matches the gruesome axe murderer's tale.

Wyatt laughs out loud. "Awesome. Great music! I love it, Annabelle. You're too hilarious."

On the screen of our basement TV, the camera zooms in on my face and I begin to narrate. *"In June of 1893, Lizzie Borden was tried for the brutal, bloody murders of her father and stepmother. She was found innocent. But was she really?*

"Someone bludgeoned her father to death with the blunt edge of a hatchet, while he was napping on the couch one steamy afternoon in August of 1892. The murderer swung the axe with such force that they broke Andrew Borden's skull and split his right eyeball in half. Then the unknown perpetrator hunted down Lizzie's stepmother, who was changing the sheets in an upstairs bedroom. They chopped her up, too; right here in this house, on quiet, sunny Second Street, in Fall River, Massachusetts."

The scene on the screen wobbles a little as Meg steps back and pans the camera around the room. I continue to narrate as she films.

"The museum is also a bed and breakfast-style inn. You can sleep in the second Mrs. Borden's bedroom for a hundred and fifty dollars a night and in the morning enjoy an authentic 19th century-style hot breakfast just like the one Lizzie Borden's parents ate on the day they were murdered."

As Meg moves in a little closer with the video cam, Wyatt and I are treated to a slightly tilted view of me from the waist up.

"These rooms are haunted by the ghosts of the victims, because the violent killings were never avenged. The jury acquitted Lizzie and no one else was ever arrested or tried for the bloody crimes. Welcome to the room where her father died."

I sweep my arm to the left and point. *"Right over there on that scratchy old sofa."*

The large brown couch has lace doilies on the arms and back. I ask the camera lens, *"It seems like we're alone here in this room, but are we?"*

I turn to Wyatt and explain, "The Lizzie Borden part was just a warm-up. Nothing scary even happened. When we visited the graveyards at night, it got a lot scarier."

Chapter 5

The Graveyards

I remember arriving well after dark, on the night when we filmed at the oldest cemetery in Eastfield. Statues of angels and obelisks stood tall, bone-white against the black, moonless sky. The small flags next to the veterans' final resting places stirred in the silent breeze and it was my turn to be the cameraman. After panning out to show a whole row of worn and crooked headstones, I zoomed in for a close-up of Meg's face.

Wyatt and I stare at the screen together, as Meg explains the gravestones' various shapes, sizes and styles. *"The oldest markers, from the 1700's were made of local slate from nearby quarries in North Attleboro and Braintree. Winged skulls and rising suns decorate these grave markers. The suns symbolize resurrection."*

She strolls down a path between two rows of graves.

"From 1810, through the Civil War and on into the turn of the century, white sandstone became popular." Waving her flashlight in a dramatic arc, Meg continues to narrate. *"The traditional willow and urn adorn most of these nineteenth century grave markers."*

I apologize to Wyatt for the boring parts. "We spent a ton of time researching everything, so our movie would at least be kind of educational. If it was too exciting and scary we'd never get the A plus we were hoping for. Fortunately, Mr. Finn and our English teacher ate all that boring crap up with a spoon. Meg and I both got A's."

He responds. "Yeah, my uncle loves 'boring crap' like History. Probably because he's a History teacher."

"No offense. He's a great guy. Definitely my favoritest teacher ever."

"Thanks. You should come over to our house some night. Get to know him better, as a person, not just as a teacher."

"Maybe."

Maybe on a cold day in Hell. I'm not spending any more time with Wyatt Silver after tonight. I agreed to show him the movie. That's all. I'm not going over his house to hang out with him and his uncle.

On the big screen, Meg's face is solemn and she lowers her voice for effect. *"In 1796, Edward Jenner discovered that people inoculated with material from a cowpox lesion became immune to smallpox. Before this discovery, smallpox was a lethal and widespread disease that claimed the lives of millions each year."*

The camera, operated by me, points to a cluster of gravestones.

Meg continues. *"Thirteen members of Captain Jeremiah Duncan's family were buried here during three separate smallpox epidemics. Captain Duncan himself succumbed to smallpox on October 23rd, 1757 at the age of 59.*

"Some brave midnight visitors to this burial ground have heard children laughing and a sorrowful voice calling out the name Emma. Jeremiah Duncan's three year old daughter, Emma, died of smallpox on May 22nd in 1750..."

Meg pauses but we hear nothing, other than the eerie hooting of an owl. Big disappointment.

On the saggy old couch in our basement, I stare at the TV and shiver.

Wyatt offers, "It's warmer over here, next to me."

"No thanks. I'm fine." I'd rather freeze to death.

"Here's the part about the Blue Mist." I direct his attention away from me and back to the movie.

"I've heard of it. Something to do with a plane crash, right?"

"Yes, we filmed this part at the old horse farm, across from Rocky Hill University. A plane crashed in a meadow there, right near the barn. Shh. Listen."

On the TV, I start the story while Meg films me.

"The ghost we'll be watching for tonight is called the Blue Mist. On November 6th, in 1932, a small plane flew over this field on its way north, to Boston. Shortly before the aircraft was scheduled to arrive at its destination, the cargo

shifted and the plane plummeted toward the earth. The pilot tried to bring it down safely, but his plane overturned during the emergency landing. The impact from the crash killed him instantly. Every year, on the anniversary of his death, if you walk down here after dark, a blue mist descends over the meadow; the plane takes shape in the fog and the pilot climbs out. It's now 10:30 PM on November 6th. Let's see what happens."

Wyatt and I watch a cloud sink down low and settle on the ground. The fog seethes around, just below my thighs, obscuring the camera's view of my feet. Everything on the screen jostles and shakes as Meg shifts the video-cam so she can hold it with one hand and clutch my hand in her other. For a split second, there's a skewed close-up of our tightly grasped hands. Then the camera jolts up.

About six feet away from us, an area of mist gathers itself into a ghostly density resembling the wreckage of an old-fashioned airplane. A blurry image, shaped like a man, drifts out and away from the transparent fuselage. I back up and step on Meg's toe. She yells, stumbles and almost falls. The camera angle goes all crazy and frantic as we run back to my old Chevy Prizm and speed away.

Wyatt turns his whole body sideways on the couch and looks at me. "November 6th, we're going there together, Annabelle. I gotta see it for myself. Wow. Your cinematography's kinda shaky but this is an amazing movie. Oliver must've loved it."

Wyatt's praise pleases me for a moment before I remember that I want nothing to do with him. "Yes, Mr.

Finn's an awesome teacher. I still can't believe he let us do this for our big junior year project. Most of the other kids chose totally boring topics."

Up on the flat screen, the last graveyard scene begins. The camera shows me squeezing through a narrow opening in the rusty iron gate at the historical cemetery on Prospect Street. As soon as Meg and I are both inside, I illuminate the first cluster of headstones with the beam of my flashlight. The sounds of nature halt for a second and a quiet voice hisses, "Who are you?"

I scream, squeeze back through the gate and sprint toward the car. Meg stumbles along behind me, still filming.

I turn to Wyatt. "When I peeled out of there that night, my tires left a black mark on the street. You can still see it. I'm never going back."

Reaching over, he lifts the remote out of my hand and clicks the replay button. Holding his breath so he can listen really hard, he watches the two-minute scene again. We hear the barely audible hiss. "Who are you?"

Turning the volume all the way up, he replays it three more times, so it sounds like a rapid-fire echo. "Who are you? Who are you? Who are you?"

Wyatt pauses the DVD. "Holy crap, Annabelle! What the hell was that?"

"I don't know. I think it might've been a ghost."

"I think so too." He lowers the volume, un-pauses the DVD and the movie continues.

"Are you ready for what comes next? It's the scariest part."

Wyatt laughs softly. "I think I can handle it."

"We saved the Lonesome Boy for last."

I saw the Lonesome Boy for the first time over a year ago. It was late in bleak November. At the Wild Wood Psychiatric Hospital.

I remember the full moon, trout-belly white against the dark sky, casting an uncanny light on our surroundings. Meg and I parked the car on a deserted back road and hiked across a big field and through a stretch of woods. Next, we had to climb a chain-link fence. As soon as we jumped down from the fence, Meg started filming.

Silent and thoughtful, Wyatt watches and listens to my matter-of-fact voice describe the mood set by the weather that night.

"The moon has risen high and pale in the black sky and casts shadows as distinct as those shaped by the sun, but colder; menacing and distorted in the dreary light. The ancient Celts called the November full moon the 'Dark Moon'. If sunlight is life, then moonlight is death. Something that comes after, a reflection, a phenomenon not possible unless real life and light have existed before it."

I explain. "My last year's English teacher loves Poe. She swooned when she heard that part."

Wyatt smiles. "You're very creative, Annabelle. *I* like that part, too. And I like Poe. His work is disturbing, but fascinating."

Next, Meg hands the camera to me and I pan it around to show off the eerie scenery as she recites the facts we researched.

"We're on the grounds of the abandoned Wild Wood Psychiatric Hospital. Founded in 1882, by Dr. Raymond Wilde, it quickly became a dumping ground for unwanted members of local families. Later, during the twentieth century, after Dr. Wilde's death, the government took over the hospital and it continued to serve the same purpose: a conveniently located facility where desperate families dropped off and then forgot about embarrassing *relatives who suffered from psychiatric disorders."*

Shining palely in the moonlight, the expression on Meg's face reveals her disdain for these uncaring relatives.

"We're walking through the institution's graveyard now. The stones are almost buried by the surrounding earth. Only names and dates were recorded on them, no epitaphs. Hundreds of patients are buried here." On the screen the camera sweeps across row after row of small white grave markers, some of them barely visible in the high, untended grass.

"To the left of the graveyard, lies the forest, leading down to the edge of the Hockomock Swamp, where many brave visitors have heard the pathetic sound of a young boy's weeping. According to a local legend, this sad voice belongs to the famous Lonesome Boy.

"No one knows who he was when he was alive. Everybody assumes he used to be a patient here at Wild Wood before his mysterious death."

Meg reclaims the camera and we head toward the hospital. She follows me as I climb inside the ruins of the enormous stone structure through an empty basement window frame. Rusted beer and soda cans, cigarette butts, shattered glass and a few candle stubs litter the grimy concrete floor. Graffiti decorates the walls. The smell, I remember, was damp, musty and unpleasant, like someone might have used one dark corner as a urinal.

I explain to Wyatt that we turned off the camera for a few minutes because on the ground level floor we found only offices. "The nameplates for doctors and administrators were still attached to the walls. Inside some of the rooms, we saw some old, rusty file cabinets with files still in them. But I didn't want to spend any time reading boring old documents. I was looking for realistic action shots of paranormal phenomena. I was looking for a ghost."

"Did you find one?"

"Wait and see."

Meg pokes the camera inside an examining room so our audience can see the high tables with thick, wide leather cuffs and dangling straps—restraints.

A mildewed straightjacket hangs from a hook on the wall of the dismal old room. I pinch a tiny corner of grimy fabric and gingerly hold up one sleeve.

"Some of the more violent patients were restrained in garments such as these," I report, staring into the lens.

We leave the ramshackle torture chambers and head toward a concrete staircase encrusted with years of filth.

Upstairs, in a dark corridor, lined with doors at regular intervals, I stumble into a wheelchair. There are straps dangling down from the arms, legs and back. It looks like a small electric chair on wheels. A bike helmet is lying next to it. I gesture toward it and stare into the lens, wild-eyed. *"The kid who wore this helmet never rode a bike."*

Then I hold up one of the wheelchair straps. *"Everywhere the patients went, they were restrained."*

Twisting the doorknobs as we arrive at each door, I demonstrate for the camera that all of the rooms on the second floor are locked. On my tiptoes, I peer into the small windows, while Meg holds the camera and films. Each room is similar to the others. All of the tiny cells contain two beds and no other furniture. A few rooms have padding on the walls. Then we find the door to room 209, the only open door. Because of a detached hinge it rests crookedly on the bare wooden floor.

Meg's trembling voice announces, *"Here is the infamous Room 209. According to the legend, the door is always open; it's the only open door on the second floor. Curious visitors, brave enough to venture into room 209, have heard all kinds of eerie noises, creeping out of the darkness. But the sound heard most often is the crying of a young boy. Many people believe that the famous Lonesome Boy spent most of his life locked up in room 209. Let's see for ourselves if this ghostly legend is true. Enter with us if you dare."*

Chapter 6

The Lonesome Boy

Sitting on the couch, Wyatt and I stare goggle-eyed, mesmerized by what's happening on the TV.

The scene's dark, mostly shades of gray and black, illuminated only by one small bobbling flashlight and a beam of light from the video cam.

I can recall every detail of the next few seconds when I reached up to push aside a curtain of cobwebs and walked into the dim chamber. *Click. Click. Click.* The doorknob behind me rattled, all by itself. And a heartrending whimper swished past, riding on a breath of cold air.

"What was that?" Wyatt asks. I shush him. He turns back to the screen and stares in silence.

I'm standing still, inside the hellish room, where someone chose to shelter disabled children. I pull a thermometer out of my pocket and hold it up. *"The temperature in room 209 is thirty degrees, fifteen degrees colder than it is outside tonight. Look. There's a thin layer of frost on the floor."* Meg points the camera down and I continue. *"You can see my footprints in it."*

Two beds lie at opposite sides of the dimly-lit room. Tattered sheets and blankets splotched with mildew cover them. At the head of each bed rests a filthy pillow.

That night I saw something I've never spoken about to anyone.

As I peered into the gloom, I could barely make out the shape of a huddled figure in one dank corner. I stepped closer and my flashlight revealed something which appeared for only a few seconds, but that was enough.

I glimpsed a shadow that wasn't dark as nature intended, but suffused with a pale glow. A quick, sideways glance at Meg's calm face told me that only I could see him. The camera didn't record the shimmering form.

He sat in one dark corner, on the cold floor, with his skinny knees tucked up under his chin. And spoke no words. But wept endlessly. As I watched, his closed eyes opened. I saw the madness within them and the solitude that caused it.

Then a flash of something else lit up those extraordinary eyes. Recognition. He knew I could see him. During that incredible moment, the Lonesome Boy realized he wasn't alone anymore.

I blinked my eyes once and he was gone.

Wyatt stares in amazement as the camera zooms in on one of the cots. An impression appears on the pillow, as if a heavy-headed person is lying there. The large, rounded dent deepens. We hear voices, but no words, just the groans of people who appear to be engaged in a struggle. The sounds grow louder and the ratty blanket shifts and tears. Spellbound, Wyatt continues to watch and listen.

Eventually, the noises fade into silence and the bedding stops moving.

My voice booms out of the surround sound speakers. *"Let's get the hell out of here."*

I bolt and Meg follows as we plunge through the darkness toward the stairs.

Meg tracks the hare-brained path of my escape with the camera as she jogs along behind me, struggling to keep up. I glance back a few times to make sure she's still there. We scramble up the chain link fence like chimpanzees on crack. When we land on the other side, our frantic pace resumes.

Finally we can see my old Chevy Prizm. Wishing out loud that it had keyless entry, I grope in my pocket for the keys. Panting, I open the passenger side first and Meg jumps in. Then she turns, points the camera at me and follows my flight around the front of the car. Quickly, I unlock the driver's side door and yank it open. Leap inside. Slam it. Lock it. Click my seatbelt in place. Safe! Revving up the engine, I shift into reverse.

Behind us in the back seat, someone cries out. Meg looks at me. Her mouth drops open. I didn't make that noise and neither did she. I shift into drive, flip on the headlights and pull out onto the deserted road. Meg switches off the camera.

In real time, in my basement, the screen on the TV is black and the surround sound speakers are silent for about two seconds.

"It was so cold in there," I whisper to Wyatt.

Suddenly, the screen lights up again. My friend Jen filmed the closing scene for us, right here in this room: Meg and me sitting on the couch, talking quietly. For once in our lives we're totally serious. Meg speaks first. *"I'll never go back to Wild Wood again."*

"Why not, Meg?" I ask as if I really want to know, although we wrote and rehearsed her answer.

"Because I'm too young to die of a heart attack and I almost had one on that horrifying evening. I still wake up in the middle of the night screaming sometimes."

"I have nightmares about it too. Will these memories ever leave us alone?"

"I don't know, Annabelle, will they?"

Then the credits start rolling to the eerie melody and lyrics of Death Cab's "I Will Follow You into the Dark."

As Wyatt and I listen, our eyes abandon the screen and we turn toward each other. Huddled on the far end of the couch, with my arms wrapped around my body, I tremble. Because I can feel the cold again, like I did that night. Wyatt clicks off the TV with the remote and slides closer to me. Gently, he pries my arms apart and holds both of my hands in his. Lowering his face so he can look into my eyes, he says, "We have to go back there together, Annabelle. I can help."

"I never want to go back."

"You have to. And I have to come. You need me."

"How can you possibly help?"

"I can stop the nightmares."

"How?"

"I'm not like everyone else, Annabelle."

"What do you mean?"

"We're the same, you and me. We're not like other people."

I pull my hands away and turn my head so I don't have to look into his chameleon eyes. "Your eyes are doing that thing again. What the hell is that?"

"It started happening when I was about thirteen. I can't control it. They change color when my emotions change. They darken."

"Why are your emotions changing?"

"Because I'm with you."

I stand up. "Don't say that."

"I'm not talking about those kinds of emotions. And I'm not talking about us, being together. Not really. Not yet." His face reddens. "Sometimes I can't look at you and talk at the same time. My thoughts dive into another time and place where nothing's clear, nothing's in focus. It's hard to explain."

"Is that why you always stare at me in History class?"

"You're the most beautiful girl I've ever seen but looking at you is the hardest thing I've ever done."

"You told me it wasn't about you and me getting together."

"It is and it isn't. I have to tell you something, Annabelle, but I don't know how to say it."

"Wyatt, this can't get any more awkward. Just tell me."

"When I look at you I see something else."

"What do you mean, 'something else?'"

"It's hard to explain."

"Try."

"We need to talk about room 209. What you heard. What you saw."

"I don't want to."

"You have to. What did you see, Annabelle? I know you saw something. Please tell me."

I don't want to tell him but I lose my grip on the words and they tumble out. I say it for the first time. "A ghost."

Then I say it again. "I saw a ghost."

Now I can't stop talking. "The camera didn't capture his image. Meg didn't see him. Only I did and now I can't forget him. He won't leave me alone. I dream about him. A lot."

It feels good to tell someone and I'm weirdly glad that it's Wyatt. It feels so good that I keep going. "In my dream, the door knob rattles and he opens my bedroom door. It sounds like the doorknob did that night, in room 209. When I wake up, the door's still open and my room's freezing. He brings the winter with him."

"We have to talk about it, Annabelle. He's not going to go away." Wyatt stands up and faces me. He takes hold of my hands again and his hands feel big and warm around mine. His irises darken into shards of smoky gray crystal. "I don't know if we can get him to go away, even if we try."

Suddenly an Arctic blast of cold tingles across my scalp, travels down the back of my neck and then my spine, all the way to the soles of my feet. Tears spring to my eyes and one trickles down my cheek. "Get who to go away, Wyatt?"

"The ghost. He followed you back."

"What the hell!"

"When you left room 209 at the hospital, Annabelle, he followed you back here."

The light bulb on the floor lamp behind the couch sizzles and explodes. The lamp crashes over, onto the rug. A surge of electricity snaps on the TV. The screen fizzes with static. An avalanche of meaningless noise hisses all around us. I jump into Wyatt's arms and they tighten around me, but it isn't romantic. We're scared out of our minds.

My mother comes racing down the stairs. "What's going on, you two?"

I push Wyatt away.

He thinks fast. "I sat on the remote and the TV came on really loud. Then Annabelle jumped up and knocked the lamp over. It's okay, though, only the bulb broke."

"You gave me a heart attack. Honey, you look all pale." She touches my cheek. "You're so cold, Annabelle. It's freezing down here. That's so weird. It's warm outside and upstairs. Close to seventy degrees still."

I attempt to explain why I'm shivering and Wyatt's lips are blue. "It's always colder underground."

"Not this much colder. Come upstairs, you two. I'm going to make you some tea. Let's go."

Tea is my mother's cure-all for everything.

Are you feeling down? Have some tea; it'll cheer you up. Feeling happy? Let's celebrate with a cup of tea. Are you feeling sick? Maybe some tea will make you feel better.

Suddenly there's nothing I want more than to sit in my mother's warm, bright kitchen and drink a cup of her hot, sweet tea. She matches teas with moods and circumstances, her special talent, and she's always spot-on, too.

Mom grabs a small bag of dried-up flowers from the cupboard and empties it into a round-bellied, ceramic tea pot. "Chamomile, it's very soothing." She smiles at Wyatt and me, as we sit silently watching her. "Let's add a pinch of lavender for luck and some lemon balm to calm us down." My mom releases handfuls of herbs and flowers into the opening at the top of the teapot. Next she pours steaming water over the fragrant mixture. Then she replaces the lid with a gentle clink.

Six minutes of steeping makes the perfect cup of tea. My mother never uses store-bought teabags and she won't pour anyone a cup until the six minutes is over. The two of us wait silently while Mom putters around the kitchen. Wyatt and I send each other meaningful looks over the steam feathering up out of the teapot's spout.

Finally, when the six minutes is up, she pours the steaming liquid through a small, hand-held metal strainer, into three mugs. My mother's tea smells beautiful, like a sunlit meadow, but it doesn't taste all that great. If you put enough honey in, though, it helps. Then the tea smells like a flower garden and just tastes really sweet.

I scoop spoonfuls of honey into my cup. Our neighbor, Mr. Long, is a beekeeper and my mother always sweetens her teas with his honey. Using plants she grows in her garden, she makes the wildflower and herb mixtures herself.

Tons of drying plants hang upside down from the hooks in our pantry. She won't pollute her tea with some impersonal honey from the supermarket. Only Mr. Long's will do.

I smirk at Wyatt as he blows on the steaming concoction and then takes his first sip. Grimacing, he rolls his eyes at me. I reach over and grab his cup, spoon in four blobs of honey, stir and hand it back to him. He sips again, nods and smiles, signaling that it tastes way better.

The scent of chamomile, lavender and lemon balm fills the kitchen and calms me down. In addition to the fragrant tea, two white pillar candles, with their flames flickering, sit on silver pedestals, infusing the air with their flowery smells. My mother always lights candles after dark. She makes them herself, from Mr. Long's bees' wax and the flowers and herbs in her gardens. You can see the soft colors of the leaves and the flower petals embedded in the wax.

"I'm going to send Daddy down to replace the light bulb. I don't want either of you cutting yourself on the glass."

"Mom, we're eighteen, not five. We can clean up a little glass," I argue.

"Wyatt may be eighteen, but you're still only seventeen, and you will be until March. Besides, I don't care how old you are. You're both a couple of klutzes. I've had enough excitement tonight. I don't need any more surprises." She rummages in the kitchen closet for a minute and then bustles out of the room, calling to my dad and waving a box of light bulbs.

As soon as she's out of earshot, Wyatt speaks. "Your mom's the best. She's all kindness and love. He quivers and shrinks in her presence. I think she intimidates him."

I know immediately who Wyatt means by "he." But I'm afraid to talk about what happened down in the cellar. Only Wyatt dares to mention it and he's whispering, as if he's afraid he'll stir up the ghost again if he speaks too loudly.

"He's still here, but he's hovering, over in that dark corner. I have this weird feeling that he doesn't like the candles. He's always with you, but sometimes closer than others. I saw him the first day I noticed you in History class. I was staring at the most beautiful girl I've ever seen and she wasn't alone. He follows you everywhere."

"You're creeping me out."

"It's true. You need to face up to it, Annabelle. He followed you back and he's not going to go away."

"What does he look like?"

"He's wearing ragged pajamas. And they're too short; I can see his bare feet and thin, white ankles. I think he was about our age when he died; he's almost as tall as I am, but thinner. I can't see his face clearly, but it's pale and transparent."

"Have you told anyone else about him? Did you tell Oliver?"

"Yes. And then he told me about the film. We watched it together. I thought I could find out more if I watched it with you. And I was right. When I saw your face, as you entered the room at Wild Wood, I knew immediately."

"Knew what?"

"I knew that you saw him. And Meg didn't. Annabelle, he wants something from us. He feels a connection to me, but he's obsessed with you. It's difficult to figure out. I can only get impressions of feelings, not words, but I can see some unclear images, in my mind's eye, not in front of me, with my physical eyes. He's angry about something and I don't know what. Maybe he's upset because you could only see him that one time, at the hospital."

"You're right. I haven't seen him since. I only heard him, tonight and in my dream."

"He's cringing over there now, in the corner of the kitchen, hating that he can't come closer. I think maybe he used up some of his energy with all that drama down in the basement. I'm not really sure. Everything's confusing and nothing's obvious."

"What else do you know about him?"

"He's been dead a long time."

"And he's obsessed with me?"

"Yes, I've seen ghosts before, Annabelle, but never like this."

"What? You should have told me that!"

"How could I? You haven't been very friendly and talkative. You wouldn't even give me a chance until tonight."

"This might be the only chance you get. Tell me what you know about ghosts."

"Usually, spirits stay in the same place. They don't stray far from where they died or where they're buried. They don't have enough power to leave and follow someone unless that person was with them when they died. But your ghost is different. He left the scene of his death and he's following you. He refuses to go away. My presence seems to make him stronger. The closer we get to each other, the more trouble he causes. Leave it to you to bring out another facet of my unusual talent."

"I'm scared, Wyatt. I don't want this. I didn't ask for it."

"Evidently you did, when you trespassed over at Wild Wood. It's been closed down for years and they have a security guard there round the clock to keep people away. You're lucky you didn't get tased or something."

"We didn't go anywhere near the guard. His trailer's next to the gate and we climbed the fence about a quarter of a mile away. It's a big place. Besides, the guard doesn't have a taser. We checked before we went over. Meg's mom knows someone who works for the state; she looked into it for us. The guard just carries a flashlight and a cell phone. And he stays in his trailer all night. I think he's afraid to go into the hospital."

"I think he's smart."

"We just wanted to investigate, get some spooky footage for our film. I never thought we'd find *him*. I never in a million years imagined that he'd follow me home."

"Not just home, Annabelle. He follows you everywhere."

"I'm never going back to Wild Wood."

"We have to. Otherwise, he might never leave. We need to find a way to send him back where he belongs and keep him there."

Wyatt barely finishes speaking these words when one of the candle flames grows taller, first a few inches, then more than a foot. The slender thread of fire stretches higher and higher. When the flame reaches the ceiling it disappears in a wisp of smoke, with a hiss that raises the fine hairs on the back of my neck. We both look up. There's a tiny black scorch mark on the ceiling where the flame touched it.

Wyatt's voice wavers. "I made him mad. He wants to stay here with you. There's nothing he's ever wanted more."

A whoosh of cold air blows past my face and extinguishes the flame on the other candle. Wyatt jumps to his feet; the chair clatters against the wall behind him. I shout out the first word that comes into my mind, "Mom!"

She comes running, just like when I was little and yelled for her in the middle of the night.

"What is it, Annabelle?"

"Nothing, Mom, I thought you and Dad had the door closed so I yelled loud. Can Wyatt take some tea home to his uncle? Mr. Finn's had trouble falling asleep lately."

She shakes the confusion off her face with a quick nod and then begins one of her favorite tasks, matching the tea to the person and his problems. "Hmm, does he have indigestion, Wyatt, or just insomnia?"

"I think both, Mrs. Blake. He's getting old."

"He definitely needs some lemon balm and let's mix it with a little apple mint and some dried chamomile blossoms." She's already walking over to the small pantry where she keeps her jars of dried blossoms and herb leaves. After about two minutes, she returns to the table with a baggy filled with the fragrant mixture. "Tell him to measure out two tablespoons of this into a teapot, pour one cup of boiling water over it and let it sit for six minutes. Then strain it into a cup and drink it hot, with a touch of honey. He does have honey, doesn't he? He needs local, organic honey." She hands the baggy to Wyatt.

"Yeah, he's a good cook. He has a lot of ingredient-type stuff around the kitchen."

My mother looks at the clock then back at Wyatt. He picks up her nonverbal message quickly. It's almost eleven o'clock.

"Good night, Mrs. Blake." Wyatt walks over to our back door, with the teacup still in his hand.

"I'll walk you out to your car." I'm afraid to be outside in the dark, but I have so many questions still buzzing around in my mind. I'm going to need more than some of Mom's special tea to help me sleep tonight.

Outside, in the warm night, I turn my face up and stare at the faint sprinkling of stars. The moon's waxing near to full, a gibbous moon, and the driveway looks pale in the wash of its mild illumination. I look back over my shoulder and see my mother's shadow outlined in the yellow rectangle of light framed by the living room window. For once I'm happy she's watching. She twiddles her fingers in a quick wave and continues to gaze at us. Normally I'd feel annoyed by the fact that she's spying on me, but tonight isn't a normal night. I shiver and Wyatt strokes my arm.

"I think he's afraid of your mother. I don't know why, but his presence shrinks when she's near."

"I wish I could sleep in between her and my dad tonight like I used to when I was little and I got scared."

"He'll leave you alone after I drive away. All this activity has weakened him. And he doesn't want to freak you out too much. He just wants you to know he's around, but he doesn't know how to go about it. This may sound weird, but I get this feeling he wants you to accept him. He doesn't know how to do it, though, without scaring you. But he's being careful, isn't he? Most of the time, anyway, until tonight. You barely even knew he was here before I told you. Maybe you were in denial."

"I knew he was here. Before, when I went to bed, I always closed the door of my room. In my nightmare, he opens the door and then when I wake up, the door's really open. Now I leave it open all the time and I don't have the dream as often. I mostly just have the feeling that he's here."

"Oh, he's here all right. And he's not leaving. I can tell."

"How can you tell?"

"Remember what I said, down in the basement? I'm not like other people. I have a connection with the next world, with the dead. I didn't ask for it. It just happened. I can see them. Sometimes I hear them. Just like you."

"I'm not like that. This is the first time and it'll be the only time. I'm not some kind of freak."

"You're not like everybody else, Annabelle."

"I want to be. I've always felt different and it's lonely. I don't like it."

"You can't change the way you are and neither can I. We're in this together now."

"Okay but we're not 'together-together.'" I give the expression air quotes. "We're not in a relationship. You can help me with the ghost, Silver, but nothing else. This is a business arrangement. Because I don't know anyone else who can help me. It's not personal."

"Just relax. I've never met a girl who's as hostile toward me as you are. Don't you think you should get to know me better before you start hating all over me?"

"I don't hate you. I'm just not interested in getting to know *any* boys right now. I don't want to go out with anyone, not you, not anyone."

"I never asked you out. I just wanted to talk to you."

"And now we talked. Besides, you told me I was beautiful. That's not *just* talking to me. So goodnight."

"What did he do to you?"

"What did *who* do to me?"

"Matt Riley."

"Nothing. He didn't do anything. I just want to be single for senior year. Who told you about Matt Riley?"

"Ryan. He said the guy's a douche and that he dumped you. That's all."

"Thanks for throwing me under the bus, Ryan."

"Did you want me to think the problem's me? Like I'm so repulsive you can't even look at me?"

"Sorry."

"That's better. That's actually the nicest thing you've ever said to me. And you're looking at me, too. Thank you."

"You're welcome."

"Look, Annabelle, you can stay single. I'm not gonna put the moves on you. Not tonight, anyway. I can't make any long-term promises, though. But as of right now, I just want to help you. We're most likely the only two people on this earth who've ever seen him. You need me. And he needs us."

"I'm afraid. I don't want to go up to my room. What if I have the dream again?"

"The dream doesn't matter. He's with you when you're awake, too. He's always with you."

"How can we get him to go away?"

"We need to find out what happened to him. Who he was when he was alive. How he died. We need to get to know him."

"How do we do that?"

"I have to think about it. Try not to worry."

After handing me his empty teacup, Wyatt gets into his car and backs away, down our long, winding driveway. I promise myself I'll try to be nicer to him. I need him. He's right about that. Shivering from a cold that has nothing to do with the weather, I jog back toward the house.

Chapter 7

Getting to Know You

Monday morning Wyatt was waiting for me, next to the only empty seat in History class. As soon as I sat down, he whipped out a towel and tossed it over my head. Laughing, I rubbed my damp hair with it.

Thus began our paranormal business association slash friendship. Since that Saturday night in my basement, with the movie and the Lonesome Boy, we've been spending more and more time together. Between classes, in the hallways, in the cafeteria, after school. We're constantly whispering about *him*. I haven't seen the ghost since that night at Wild Wood, so I always have to ask Wyatt what he's doing. The Lonesome Boy isn't with me all the time anymore. He follows Wyatt, too. We share him.

In our tiny little high school world with its huge social limitations, Wyatt Silver and I become a couple. Rumors fly around faster than they can be swatted down by the truth. According to those members of the senior class who are "in-the-know," we've hooked up on many occasions at many parties when, in reality, the only thing we have in common is our ghost. We've never gone on a date. We've never kissed. But at school, people have noticed that we're always together and the gossip goes wild.

Everyone's saying that we're dating each other exclusively and sleeping over at each other's houses all the time. That part's hilarious. Over my dead body. Like my parents would ever allow it. Like I would ever do that anyway.

Lots of girls have crushes on him and some of them are mean to me, but I don't care. The same girls were mean to me when Matt Riley and I were together. None of them have ever been my friends. None of them know anything about me.

Not everyone admires Wyatt, though. Some people believe the rumors about why he left New Hampshire and moved here. I still don't know the truth. We've been hanging out constantly for a few weeks now, but I haven't asked him yet. I've been trying to think of a way to bring up the subject. Maybe today after school I'll get an opportunity.

Leaning against my locker, sipping from a bottle of red Gatorade, I scan the crowded hallway. No sign of Wyatt yet. Because of his height he's pretty easy to spot. Finally, I catch sight of him, jogging toward me, wearing a huge smile. He stops his momentum by slamming his hands into the lockers on either side of my head, seriously invading my personal space. Then he grabs the Gatorade out of my hand. Half of it's gone before he stops chugging and burps; an inch away from my face.

"Wyatt! Ugh!"

A passerby yells, "Watch out! You don't want to catch anything, Annabelle."

"Is she a friend of yours?" Wyatt asks me.

"I don't even know her. She's not a senior. Maybe a sophomore or a junior."

"Why would she say that to you? Is she talking about me?"

"You know. There are some nasty rumors about why you left your hometown. There's one about you being a drug dealer."

He rolls his eyes. "I've heard that one. I swear I've never been arrested."

"There's also one about you spreading an STD around your old school."

"Completely false." He holds his hands up, palms out, as if he can stop the rumors with them. His face reddens and he looks away from me. While we're on the subject, I figure I should get the worst of the stories out there.

"Do you find that rumor more disturbing than the one about you getting a girl pregnant?"

He doesn't even laugh. "Yes! More disturbing and more false; where do people get this crap?"

"I think they start out wondering why you would transfer here for your senior year. Then people start coming up with ideas and they say them out loud. The people who hear these lies repeat them and your legend's born."

"Can't my legend be like Batman or something? Can't I keep my really cool car in a cave and drive around fighting crime? Do they have to make me into a drug-dealing pornographer?"

"Ignore it. Your real friends will believe only the truth about you."

He puts one big, warm hand on my shoulder and moves in so close I can smell him. He smells clean, like the first breath full of sunny air the morning after a rainstorm.

"Are you my real friend, Annabelle?"

I turn away and close my locker. "I'm late. I have to get to practice. Call me later."

Then I pivot and run out the door, toward the big yellow bus that'll take the team over to the Town Forest. As I run, I can feel his gaze on my back so I pick up the pace. Good thing I got voted best butt in the whole school.

At about ten o'clock, when I'm already in bed, Wyatt finally calls me. I'm practically in a coma because the coaches worked us so hard today. But I want to know why he really moved to Eastfield, so I make an effort to wake up and talk to him.

"Sorry, Annabelle. Were you sleeping?"

"Yes, but that's okay. I asked you to call me."

"So I did. What's up?"

"After school today, we were talking about why you moved to Eastfield. I know none of the rumors are true, but you've never explained the real reason."

"I'm not running away from anything bad. I just like living with my uncle better than living with my mom and he invited me to come to Eastfield."

"What happened between you and your mom?"

"Nothing awful. My parents are divorced. She has a boyfriend now and we get along and all, but, you know, he's in a relationship with my mom. It's awkward. Besides, my uncle and I like the same things. I love History and he's the head of the History Department and the president of the Eastfield Historical Society. He's fun. He's interesting. She's boring and she's in a relationship. Because she's my mother that's weird for me."

"What about your dad?"

"My parents divorced when I was fifteen and my father moved to California, remarried and started a new family. I don't want to live with my father and his twenty-five year old bride and their baby. I have a stepsister I've never met. She's almost two years old. Besides, Dad never invited me to live with him anyway."

Whoa, that's awful.

I don't know what else to say, so I change the subject.

"Is Mr. Finn your mother's brother?"

"Yeah, but it's hard to believe they're from the same family. They're so different."

"In what way?"

"He's less judgmental."

"Judgmental about what?"

"I'm interested in the paranormal, you know: ghosts. Uncle Oliver thinks it's cool. My mother gets annoyed with me because she doesn't believe in ghosts. She wants me to get serious about something like engineering because I'm good at math. I prefer history, philosophy, stuff like that. We're always arguing about my future."

"When Meg and I made that movie last year, your uncle sat through two interviews with us. He was an excellent primary source, really helpful. He never acted annoyed or anything."

"Yeah, he's a great guy. I think he gets kind of lonely sometimes. He's not married. He has no kids. He has tons of friends, but I'm family. He wanted me to live with him. He asked me more than once before I finally decided to come."

I believe him, but I have a feeling he's holding something back. I don't think he's told me the whole story. According to Wyatt he transferred to a new school for senior year because he wanted to try living with his uncle instead of his mother. I'm not buying it. There has to be another reason. But it's late and I decide not to push it right now.

Wyatt starts working a little too hard to convince me he's telling the truth. He goes on to explain that he's never felt more accepted than when he's with his Uncle Oliver. That part I believe because Mr. Finn really is an awesome guy but I'm still suspicious. Finally we hang up and I fall back into a deep sleep immediately.

* * * *

Saturday night Wyatt calls and wants to get together so we can talk about the ghost again. I don't have any plans because I've sworn off boys and dating, so I invite him over.

He wants to know if it's okay to bring a DVD. "Maybe we should pretend to be watching a movie, just in case your parents ask any questions about what we have planned."

He's right. They might ask and a movie would be a good cover. I'm not ready to explain to them that Wyatt and I are conducting a paranormal investigation.

When he arrives, we're both starved and I'm in the mood for pizza so we decide to go out first and then come back later to supposedly watch a movie together. Even my parents think we're dating.

Wyatt chooses a popular pizza place. We walk into the restaurant and it's crowded with groups of high school kids. From the moment we enter the warm, garlic-scented atmosphere, the stares from dozens of gawking eyes follow us. He orders a large cheese pizza and as soon as it's ready I grab it, along with some paper plates and a handful of napkins. Wyatt fills two big paper cups with root beer from the dispenser and we squish our way through the crowded room, looking for an empty table.

He leans down to my ear and whispers. "Shh! Listen! What do you think they're saying about us?"

I laugh then pause to listen.

Our classmates release a whoosh of gossip. Rumors about Wyatt and me fly all around the restaurant like birds heading south for the winter, squawking and pooping on all the surfaces below. I feel like ducking and covering my head with a pizza pan.

Wyatt steers me over to a table where six boys from the soccer team are devouring multiple pizzas and large heaps of mozzarella sticks. He says hi to them and for a couple of minutes they exchange noisy opinions about Friday afternoon's game, the yellow cards, the red cards and the blindness of the refs. Laughing, Wyatt squeezes my shoulder gently, to signal that we should move along and find our own table.

I spot an empty booth, over in a corner near the window, and sit down across from him, with only a small rectangle of shiny red and white checked table-top between us. Suddenly self-conscious, I edit the wideness of my smile down to a small grin. But then, when I look into his eyes, brilliant like a sunlit ocean, I give up and hit him with the real thing. Two thousand dollars worth of braces worn all through seventh and eighth grade have made my teeth even and perfect and they're framed by shiny, strawberry-flavored lips. Wyatt tilts his head back and laughs. It's not easy to chew and swallow pizza when you're grinning like a couple of dumbasses, but we're hungry and we manage.

Chapter 8

The Calm Before the Storm

When we walk through the back door into the kitchen, my mother's rummaging through a cabinet.

"Mom, Wyatt and I are going down cellar to watch a movie," I yell.

She pulls a box of microwave popcorn off a shelf.

"I was just about to pop some popcorn. Do you want some?"

"No thanks. We already ate. What're you and Dad doing tonight?"

"Watching golf on TV. Your father loves that classic sports channel. I'm just going to keep him company, read my book and try not to snore too loud when I doze off."

My parents lead such an exciting life.

"Have fun. We're going downstairs."

"Come on. Say hello to your father. You haven't seen him all day." My dad's in construction and he's building a huge new house for somebody rich, so he's been working a lot, even on the weekends.

When we walk into the den, Dad's stretched out on the couch. He puts down the remote and stands up to shake hands with Wyatt. No need to lower the volume when you're watching golf. Even when someone sinks a putt, the clapping is quiet and reserved. My dad makes us a tempting offer. "You kids should stay up here and watch a little of this. Phil Mickelson's about to win the 2004 Master's. He's the best professional left-handed golfer ever."

"Sounds great, but no thanks. Wyatt brought over a DVD and we want to play some ping pong, too; work off some of that pizza." My dad can be so lame sometimes. Why would I ever invite anyone over on a Saturday night to watch golf on TV with him and Mom?

"Have fun. Watch out for her, Wyatt. She's pretty quick with that paddle, beats her brothers all the time."

I grab Wyatt's hand and pull him out of the room before my father can embarrass me any further.

"Thanks. I couldn't think of a polite way to refuse his invitation and he *is* your dad. I didn't want to seem rude." Wyatt lets me tow him toward the basement stairs.

"Golf on TV, is there anything more boring, except maybe classic golf on TV, when you already know who wins?"

"Gardening shows."

"What?"

"You asked me if there was anything more boring than classic golf on TV. And there is: gardening shows. Not exactly fast-paced. You get to watch plants grow."

"That's what my mom watches! America's most boring couple."

"They seem nice."

"They are. They're pretty funny sometimes. Once in a while it's even intentional."

"Promise not to destroy my ego with your ping pong skills," Wyatt teases. He isn't far off, though. He stinks at ping pong and his air hockey skills are miserable, too. We give up and he puts in his DVD. Wyatt sits down on the couch first and then I sit down, leaving about five feet of space between us. He shows me the DVD he brought over: *The Silence of the Lambs*. Best movie ever.

"My uncle's really into film and this one's his favorite. He helps organize a local film festival every year."

"I know. My brother Clement won it when he was a senior. He made this amazing movie in the graveyard behind the old Unitarian church. He shifted the camera shots back and forth, zooming in on epitaphs and names carved into the gravestones. Then he created short, fictional scenes about the lives of the people buried there. He called it *Life and Death*."

"I'd like to see it sometime. Has your brother influenced your taste in movies?"

"Definitely, I don't know as much about films as he does, but I love them. When he's home we hang out down here sometimes, watching movies and talking, if I'm not busy beating him at ping pong."

"I know. I feel kinda humiliated. Ping pong isn't my sport, sorry. I wish I could've given you more competition."

"Is soccer your only sport then?"

"Yes, I play forward mostly. I'm not exactly a star out there, but the team seems to appreciate my size and speed. I think I grew so fast my coordination will never catch up, but I can point myself in one direction, run fast and kick a ball really hard. In the spring I'll probably run track, sprints. Do you run track in the spring, too?"

"Nope, I play tennis."

"That explains your dominance at the ping pong table."

Getting beaten game after game doesn't seem to annoy him at all. He puts his feet up on the lumpy old ottoman and settles back on the couch.

I'm exhausted so I turn lengthwise, slump down, rest my head on the arm rest, kick off my flip flops and put my feet up. Wyatt pulls them onto his lap. Rubbing my toes gently with his big warm hand, he says, "Your feet are freezing."

We start watching the movie, quoting some of the lines out loud and announcing our favorite parts as they come along. If we aren't careful, we'll give my parents some competition in the boring contest. But I don't feel the least bit bored, just relaxed. My feet are warm and cozy. Right when Clarice is about to ring the serial killer's doorbell, I doze off.

"Hey, Sleeping Beauty!" Wyatt tickles the bottoms of my feet and I wake up. "The movie's over. Everyone lived happily ever after, except that cheesy psychiatrist guy, Dr. Chilton."

"Sorry, I was really out. We have an early practice every Saturday morning."

"I'll leave, let you get to bed."

"No, that's okay. Stay. We haven't even talked about *him* yet." I want Wyatt to stay so we can discuss the ghost; I hate that I feel so sleepy.

Wyatt moves my feet off his lap and stands up. "I'm going. I'll talk to you tomorrow. Thanks. It was fun."

And he's gone, boom, no hesitation. Once I'm in bed, even though I'm exhausted, it takes me twenty minutes to fall asleep because my feet are so cold.

* * * *

Wyatt calls the next day, Sunday, and we talk for a few minutes. After that we get into the habit of calling or texting each other a lot; even more than before. At school, whenever something happens that's funny, he texts me and I text him just as often. Some of the teachers will take your cell phone away if they catch you using it in class, so we have to keep it under control. But if there's a substitute, they usually assign the work or start the movie and then ignore the class. You can get away with almost anything.

Today, there's a really clueless sub in Wyatt's English class. When I leave Physics and pull out my phone to check for texts, he's left me ten, mostly about other kids in his class and what they were getting away with because of the sub. Jen's in his English class and she actually took out a bottle of nail polish and did her nails. Wyatt said he was surprised she didn't take off her boots and do her toenails, too. I'm heading toward my locker, reading his texts, giggling, with my head down and my eyes on my phone, when I hit a wall. Except it's not really a wall; it's Wyatt's chest. Even quivering with laughter he's solid and immovable.

* * * *

On Wednesday he calls and invites me over to his house for Saturday night, to hang out with him and his uncle. I only agree to go because we might get a chance to talk about the Lonesome Boy. Maybe Oliver knows something about the history of the Wild Wood asylum. I'm sure I can find a way to bring up the subject somehow.

I don't get my chance, because there are too many people there. But it's fun, which surprises me, seeing as junior year, Mr. Finn was my History teacher. After a half hour or so, I don't feel awkward at all and he doesn't seem to either. Wyatt's uncle has invited a few friends over: Jackson Andrews, the pastor of the Unitarian church and some ladies from the Eastfield Historical Society who know my mother. He made a delicious vegetable and pasta dish and we all eat together and then watch *Gone, Baby, Gone*, one of my brother Clement's favorite movies.

The adults drink wine and talk about the movie and I'm happy because I read the book which is way different than the film and only one other person has read it—Mr. Finn. We get into an intense discussion about how certain characters are completely different in the movie than they are in the book. Wyatt's uncle insists I call him Oliver and I feel really mature because I'm holding my own in a conversation with an intelligent adult.

Finally, Wyatt and I say good night to everyone and climb into his car.

We still haven't made any progress in our investigation of the Lonesome Boy. His spirit has been quiet lately and I haven't had the nightmare in a while. But Wyatt says we need to be patient. He's always with us. Something will happen. I'm scared, but I want to know more. I want something to happen.

Chapter 9

Be Still My Heart

Rainy Sundays in New England can be awful, but a baking project cozies-up even the wettest, most miserable day. So Meg, Jen and I decide to get together at my house and bake something. Mom thinks it's a great idea and runs out to buy all the ingredients. Meg wants to be a chef, so she's in charge.

Soon after we start baking, Connor texts Jen, looking for something to do and ends up coming over. Just as we're putting the first loaded-up cookie sheet into the oven, Ryan calls Meg. She tells him we're at my house, baking cookies.

Then she turns toward me and says, "Wyatt's at his house. They want to come over."

Ryan plays keeper on the soccer team and they've been hanging out a lot lately.

I whisper, "Yes."

"Come on over. I'm cooking, so the food will be professional quality." Meg smiles and we bump fists. Ten minutes later Wyatt and Ryan are pounding on my back door.

As soon as the double batch of cookies is done, we start in on them, finishing off two dozen pretty fast, along with almost a whole gallon of milk. Then we all head downstairs to play ping pong. Meg and Jen challenge Connor and Ryan to a match. As they begin whacking the ball back and forth, Wyatt touches his finger to his lips to shush me, grabs my hand and pulls me out of the room. Together, we tiptoe into the unfinished part of the basement. After he eases the door closed, we move through the dark, hand-in-hand, past the furnace, into the middle of the room. We can barely hear the distant pop of the ping pong ball because the pelting rainwater's splashing so hard against the window pane. It looks like someone's spraying the glass with a hose. Wyatt turns to me and takes hold of both my wrists.

"They won't notice we're gone for a while." He leans in closer. "I've thought of a way to find out more about him."

I know Wyatt's referring to the ghost. But even though I'm anxious to find out more about him, I feel weird about sneaking off like this. "Everyone's right in the next room. What are they gonna think?"

"Why do you care so much about what they think? Let them think we're making out. Everyone in the whole school thinks we're hooking up anyway. Who gives a damn, Annabelle?"

"I do."

"Why? What would be so awful about hooking up with me?"

"I'm leaving." I pull away from him and start toward the door. I didn't sneak off to talk about our nonexistent relationship. I want to know more about the ghost.

He grabs my hand and pulls me back toward him. "Okay. I give up. For now."

"Thank you. Now what about the ghost? How can we find out more?"

"I want to try to communicate with him. If we hold hands and concentrate really hard, maybe something will happen. Kind of like a séance. Are you in or out?"

"I'm scared."

"That's okay. We don't have to try it if you're too scared. We can go back in there with the others." He cocks his head toward the door.

Curiosity sneaks in, overpowering my fears. "Is he here now?"

"He's always nearby, Annabelle. And right now he's very close."

"What's he doing?"

"Just watching and waiting."

"Waiting for what?"

"For us to make a move."

"What kind of a move, Wyatt?"

"A move that will empower him further. He grows stronger when we're alone together. But never speaks. I think he might be able to if we help him."

"How can we help him?"

"By staying in here alone together and concentrating really hard."

"It's getting colder." A shiver runs across my scalp and down my neck.

"That's because he's growing more powerful."

"How do you know that if he doesn't speak?"

"I can read his emotions. I feel them as if they were mine." Wyatt stops talking for a second and his eyes open wide. "The cold just moved into my hands."

His hand in mine turns to ice.

"My arms! My chest! I feel like I'm neck deep in a snow-bank...I'm freezing, Annabelle."

Wyatt drops my hand and holds out his arms to me, as if I'm his only hope on earth for warmth. But I hesitate.

Gently, he tips my chin up, with one icy finger, so I'm forced to look into his eyes. "Come closer. It won't work unless we're holding each other."

I take a deep breath. Then step into his arms. Immediately, he folds me in so I'm pressed solid against him. He lifts me up, until my feet dangle a couple of inches off the concrete floor.

"Shh, listen." His icy breath chills my ear. Even through the layers of both Wyatt's clothing and mine, I can feel the deadly cold temperature of his body. His heartbeat thunders against my chest. Slow but strong. Once. Twice. Powerful and hypnotic. The only warmth generated between us lies centered at the union of our pulsating hearts.

"Shh, listen," he says again. He rests the side of his cold face against mine. Then turns and presses a frigid kiss against my cheek.

A blinding flash of lightning explodes. Seconds later a blast of thunder shakes the foundation.

Wyatt's heart thumps once then stops. I can't feel it anymore.

Like an ice sculpture, we stand frozen together in our treacherous embrace. Frantic, I wedge my arms in between us and push at his chest. With a loud groan, he exhales and then finally relaxes his grip. My feet thud onto the floor. Then another flash of lightning sprays across the room. The burst of brilliance illuminates Wyatt's face. His eyes are rolled up with only the whites showing. He's trying to inhale but can't. I open my mouth to scream but only a croak comes out.

Finally he steps back, bends over, rests his hands on his knees, and starts choking. I whack him on the back. He coughs a couple of times and then starts to breathe normally.

When he straightens up, I grip his icy hand firmly between my two warmer ones. Trying to sound calm, I suggest, "Just relax for a second, Wyatt. I'll go up and get you some water."

As I turn toward the only exit, my eyes adjust to the gloom and our surroundings grow more distinct: the furnace, the fieldstone walls, the cement floor, the rusting oil tank in the corner, a bookshelf with cans of paint organized by size and color and an old wooden Adirondack chair my mother sanded down, but hasn't started to paint yet. The sight of this familiar junk, together with the damp, earthy smell of the ancient rock foundation, quiets my panic a little. I turn back toward Wyatt and point to the chair.

"You should sit down for a few minutes." He still doesn't move or respond. His eyes look wild with confusion, like he flew off somewhere and when he returned, he crash-landed here in the basement. I keep trying to sooth him. "As soon as you catch your breath, we better go back and join the others."

"Others?" His voice curves up, like he's asking a question; like he has no idea what I mean.

"Wyatt, do you feel all right?"

"Feel all right."

His response doesn't reassure me at all. I touch his cheek with my open hand. "You're still freezing."

As if he thinks that moving his head might cause it to fall off, he dips it uncertainly, down then up. "Freezing." He whispers the word. His eyes open wide and his lips part in wonder as the sound travels up his throat and floats out of his open mouth. His brow furrows in concentration and the echo of his voice reverberates off the stone walls before it finally dissolves like steamy breath on a winter's day.

"Do you feel sick?"

Slowly, he dips his head down then up again and says, "Sick."

"Maybe you're coming down with something."

"I have words." He stares into the darkness as if he could catch sight of them before they fade and disappear. His fingers drift up to touch his lips. Then move down to his throat.

"Annabelle." The quality and depth of Wyatt's voice sounds different; hoarse like he's unused to speaking.

"We need to go back to the others. C'mon."

"I can look at you with his eyes; speak to you with his voice."

"Whose voice, Wyatt?" I'm more terrified than I've ever been before in my life.

He reaches for me and I flinch and back away.

"I want to touch you." Suddenly, he shoots one long arm out and wraps his hand halfway around my neck, pressing his icy thumb into the hollow at the base of my throat. Tingles of panic slide down my spine and into my feet. I want to run but I'm paralyzed by fear. And something else. Fascination.

The shape of his hand and the texture of his skin feel normal, but he's freezing.

Shiny, deep and dead, his reptilian gaze mesmerizes me.

"You're not Wyatt!" I try to pull away, but he tightens his grip on my neck. I gasp for air and tears rush to my eyes.

Immediately dropping his hand, he whispers, "Sorry."

I stagger back, horrified by the sinister, disturbing creature before me.

"Come here, Annabelle. Please. I've waited so long."

I need to get away from him. Keeping my movements slow and my thoughts to myself, I start backing toward the door. I know I should call Oliver, but I don't have his number in my phone. So I stop inching away. Careful not to seem panicked, I hold out my hand. "Can you find Wyatt's cell phone?"

"It's right here in my pocket." As he digs around in the pocket of his jeans, an expression of pleased discovery dawns on his face. Pulling out the phone, he presents it to me, like finding it was an accomplishment.

I grab the phone and quickly find Oliver's number. He answers after the second ring. "Wyatt?"

"Oliver," I hurry to explain. "It's Annabelle. Wyatt's here and he's okay, physically, that is, but something's wrong. He's not himself." I can't think of another way to say it.

"I'll be right there. You're at home, Annabelle?"

As soon as I say "yes" he hangs up. I reach out my hand to pass the phone back to Wyatt and his knees sag. He lurches toward me. I cringe at the idea of touching him, but he seems like he's about to collapse. So I drape his right arm across my shoulders and help him move backwards until his legs bump the seat of the Adirondack chair. As he eases himself down into the dusty old thing, he looks up at me and the irises of his eyes lighten to fish-scale gray.

He clears his throat as if he's preparing to speak but just then, hesitant footsteps stop right outside the door. Two knocks announce someone's arrival.

"Come in," Wyatt croaks.

Ryan opens the door and stands at the threshold, peering through the gloom at us.

"Hey, Wyatt, I gotta get going. My dad just called and now that it's stopped raining, he needs help clearing the leaves out of the gutters."

"Okay. I think I'll stay a little longer. Annabelle, can you give me a ride home later?"

"Sure. No problem."

Ryan steps farther into the room. "You don't look too good, Silver. Are you feeling okay?"

Wyatt's slumped down in my mother's latest yard sale find. "Yeah, I'm fine. Just go ahead without me."

"Connor and Jen left about ten minutes ago. I'm gonna give Meg a ride home." Ryan moves toward the doorway. "'Bye Annabelle. Thanks for having me over. See you at practice tomorrow, Wyatt."

About a minute after he walks up the stairs, I hear his car start up in the driveway.

I'm feeling confused and pretty annoyed with Wyatt, but I'm too worried to act mad. As we head up to the kitchen, I hold on tight to his hand because he's still shaky and I'm afraid he'll stumble and fall down the stairs.

"Any cookies left, Mrs. Blake?" Wyatt asks as soon as we walk into the kitchen. My mother gestures to the counter top behind her where a hill of delicious smelling chocolate chip cookies sits on a platter.

"Would you like some milk, Wyatt?" Mom doesn't wait for an answer. She's already pulling the gallon jug out of the fridge.

Sitting at the kitchen table, with a huge glass of cold milk and a plate of cookies in front of him, Wyatt perks up a little and begins to eat and drink. His episode, whatever it was, hasn't affected his appetite; if anything he seems even hungrier than usual.

Rubbing my arms with both hands, I announce, "It's freezing in here."

My mother fills the tea kettle and puts it on the stove. As she turns on the burner we hear a car speed up the driveway and come to a screeching halt.

Mom looks out the window and announces, "Oliver's here. Why is he in such a hurry?"

Wyatt doesn't respond to her question, so I give him a sideways look, kick him in the shin under the table, and start a lie that I intend to pass to him after I run out of fake ideas. "Oliver's expecting company for dinner and they're due any minute now. He just called Wyatt to invite me and swung by to pick us up on his way home from the grocery store."

Wyatt reaches down to rub his shin and glares at me, but continues my story as if he's done it a million times before; tag team lying, our favorite sport. "Because Oliver's a vegetarian, he has to have really fresh, organic vegetables every day. He goes out to buy them right before he starts cooking. We have to run. Thanks, Mrs. Blake." He grabs my arm and pulls me out of my seat and toward the door in one rough motion.

"'Bye, Mom," I yell as Wyatt yanks me out to the driveway. My mother follows us and stands on the threshold watching, as Wyatt shoves me into the back seat of his uncle's car, whacks the door shut and then jumps into the shotgun seat.

Oliver rolls down his window on the driver's side. "Thanks for the tea. I've been sleeping like a baby."

"You're welcome, Oliver, any time."

Mom knows Wyatt's uncle pretty well because she's a member of the Eastfield Historical Society and he's the president. She always sells her teas and homemade, scented candles at the historical society's booth, during the annual Eastfield harvest fair. Also, my father's side of the family has lived here for generations and my mother donated their family diaries and Bibles and other artifacts to the Eastfield Historical Society Museum. She smiles and waves goodbye to us as Oliver backs down the long, winding driveway.

Wyatt's uncle drives pretty fast for an old guy. The scenery's streaking by, making me a little dizzy. I'm sure that we're traveling about twenty miles over the speed limit. Maybe cops don't give tickets to teachers because then their kids might flunk a subject at school, kind of like a small town educational mafia.

Chapter 10

Revelations

Stepping out of Oliver's car, onto his glistening driveway, I breathe in deep, hoping the extra oxygen will give me courage. The night air smells like wet rocks. Wyatt must've noticed my hesitation, because he reaches for my hand before leading me into the house.

In the main room, the flames of a huge fire celebrate wildly in Oliver's fireplace. Close to the crackling heat, a man with a powerful upper body and a halo of brown curls stares up at us from his shimmering throne. Backlit by the holy light, he resembles a renaissance painting of an archangel.

Many artists have labored to immortalize faces like his, but being alive adds so much warmth to his features that he steals my breath like no painting ever could.

This living, breathing work of art smiles at me and then holds out his right hand. "Nathaniel Flyte. You must be Annabelle."

Unruly curls frame his face, jaw and neck. The sleeves of a faded t-shirt stop right above his sculpted biceps. Beside his wheelchair sits a huge dog, with fur the color of an orangutan's. His long floppy ears, sad eyes and drooping jowls look like a bloodhound's. But he's a full size bigger than that breed. Sitting upright and alert on his haunches, his head's at the same height as Nathaniel's. He stretches out his neck, points his muzzle at me and sniffs the air.

After grasping Nathaniel's hand only long enough to seem polite, I sink to my knees at the feet of the handsome creature. It's true; there's such a thing as love at first sight. The dog begins licking the worried look off my face with kind of icky but very effective kisses.

"Meet Jeff, the best judge of character ever. I think you just passed the test. Annabelle." Nathaniel introduces us.

"You two look pretty cozy together." Oliver smiles, but then looks over at Wyatt and frowns.

Wyatt's pale, expressionless face droops out over his neck as he stands near the doorway, staring blankly at the wall behind his uncle. Oliver places a gentle hand on his nephew's back and nudges him over to a big, overstuffed chair, next to the fire.

"I'd just put dinner on the stove when you called, Annabelle. What happened? You seemed upset."

Oliver's voice sounds not quite sincere to me.

I relax into a cross-legged position on the worn oriental carpet beside Jeff, who lies down by my side. Like a furry guardian angel, the dog leans against me and lends me courage. I'm not used to standing up to adults, but I'm so pissed off that I let loose. For me anyway, it's letting loose. "You tell me, Oliver. You came speeding over to my house like a NASCAR driver. Why? What did you think had happened?"

"You used Wyatt's cell phone to call me. You said he wasn't himself. I panicked."

"Why?" I ask again.

"I thought he might be ill."

"But he wasn't, was he?"

"Maybe *you* should tell me, Annabelle. You were there." Oliver's voice remains infuriatingly calm.

I can see that he isn't going to reveal anything he knows about Wyatt's condition. It's a stalemate, so I relent.

"While Wyatt and I were hugging, he stiffened and grew cold. His heart stopped beating but then a second later it started up again. Finally, when he recovered enough to speak, his voice sounded different. As if he was someone else. He said, 'I have words.' Like he was surprised that he could talk."

"Tell me everything he said."

"No. You tell me what you think happened. Because I have no idea. I need information and I think you know more than you're letting on. So start explaining."

Lifting my chin, I challenge Oliver by staring bravely up at him as I scratch the top of Jeff's warm, furry head. The dog rolls onto his side so I can rub his belly. Then he moves his head into my lap and closes his eyes. I risk a sideways glance at Nathaniel and he's sending a grin my way that's the equivalent of a thumbs up. Someone else is on my side, not just the hound.

"Nathaniel's a medium. He's had a lot of experience with the supernatural. I think he might be able to help us. You and Wyatt are relatively new to this," Oliver begins.

"New to what?" I ask.

"Channeling. It's one way for the dead to communicate with the living. Wyatt told me about the ghost that followed you back from Wild Wood. He thinks this presence has been trying to communicate with you for almost a year now," Oliver explains.

"So you know all about that?"

"Yes. I've watched your movie multiple times. I'm not one of the skeptics who thinks Clement helped you add special effects. I could tell the work was all your own by *The Blair Witch Project* style. Actually, it was even more amateurish than that awful film." Evidently, despite the serious subject of our conversation, Oliver can't resist making a joke about my unskilled cinematography.

"Thanks, Oliver. Get to the point, please."

"Fair enough. I know you had a paranormal encounter at the hospital last fall. And I know it was real. Then Wyatt told me that whatever materialized in room 209 while you were filming has attached itself to you. Recently, it seems this ghost has connected itself to Wyatt, too. Because my nephew has experienced episodes like this before, I'm concerned. I'm worried about both of you."

Wyatt had mentioned he could see ghosts, but he didn't go into detail. "What kind of episodes did Wyatt experience?"

Oliver looks down at his feet then walks over to a chair and lowers his tall, lean frame into it. The firelight glimmers on his neatly-clipped silver hair.

Placing a forearm on each of his spread-apart knees and folding his hands together in between, Oliver leans forward and starts talking.

"It all began when Wyatt was about fifteen years old. I invited him to stay the weekend here in Eastfield because my friend Jackson Andrews had witnessed an unexplained phenomenon. He's the pastor of the Unitarian church and on several occasions Jackson had heard whimpering in the hallway, near the back door of the church, late at night. Every time he went to check it out, no one was there."

"Did Jackson think his church was haunted?"

"Yes. He thought it might be. He called me because he knew that Wyatt and I shared an interest in the paranormal And he knew I was familiar with the history of the church. He thought there might be a legend or a ghost story. I asked Wyatt to help me investigate and we went over there together. That night we experienced something unusual."

"What?"

"At about ten o'clock, Jackson, Wyatt and I crept into the church hallway, using only a flashlight to guide us. Jackson heard again what he'd heard on several other occasions: a woman crying softly. I heard her too, but only Wyatt could see her. She was a young girl, a bride. Her long lace veil was folded back, revealing her beautiful face. As Wyatt watched, she wept into a white linen handkerchief embroidered with blue morning glories and the initials M. C. M. Before she faded away, she turned her face and looked directly at him."

Goosebumps crawl across my scalp. "Then what happened?"

"As Wyatt stared, the girl's quiet weeping turned to loud sobs. She covered her face. Her shoulders heaved. Soon she grew soaked through to the skin. The hem of her dress was dripping onto the stone floor of the church. Jackson and I couldn't see the apparition, but we watched a puddle spread across the floor until it touched the tips of our shoes. Then the water receded and disappeared. And so did she."

"What were you able to find out?"

"We did some research on wedding fashions and Wyatt's description of the bride's clothing helped us estimate a date. Then I looked through the archives of some local newspapers and read all of the engagement announcements from the most likely years. We found initials that matched those on the handkerchief and an engagement photograph of the young woman. Wyatt identified her as the ghost in the church. Further research revealed that she never married the young man to whom she was engaged."

"Who was she?"

"Her name was Mariah Catherine Marshall. She was supposed to marry Colin Lynch III on June twenty-first in 1942, in the Unitarian Church here in Eastfield. The wedding never took place. We couldn't find any record of the marriage in the church registers or at town hall, but I did find her obituary and a record of her death certificate. Two days after her scheduled wedding date Mariah's body was found in a pond, in the woods behind the church, face down, wearing her bridal dress and veil."

"Was her death accidental?"

"At first it was difficult to get any information about the drowning. There are direct descendants from the Lynch family still living in Eastfield, but no one would talk to us. Finally, we found Mariah's sister, Serena, though, and she told us the whole story. Serena was twenty-one years old at the time of her sister's death, a year younger than Mariah. She's in her eighties now. According to her, about a week before the wedding, after a three-year engagement to his childhood sweetheart, Colin broke it off. He'd met someone else. And she wasn't from a respected New England family. Colin Lynch's new paramour was a professional dancer; from Paris."

"Mariah was heartbroken."

"Most definitely. It turns out that young Colin was quite a partier. He met a French beauty in a nightclub and married her a few days later, in Mexico. When Mariah heard the news, she put on her wedding dress and veil. She didn't even leave a note. She simply took a long walk through the woods and never returned. A search party found her the next day, floating face down, in Langwater Pond, about a mile from the church."

In spite of my annoyance at being kept in the dark about all this, I can't keep the enthusiasm out of my voice because I can't wait to hear more.

"Were there more incidents?"

"Yes, the most recent was just a few months ago. It

happened in New Hampshire. This summer, when Wyatt was training for soccer, he was running through an old burial ground adjoining his mother's property."

"Go on."

"One calm, sunny day, Wyatt was jogging through the graveyard, slowing down because he was almost home. Suddenly, a wind whipped up, propelling leaves and dirt into his face. Blowing in a circular pattern, all around him, the wind formed a small tornado called a dirt devil. He blinked the grit out of his eyes, spit it out of his mouth and sprinted for home. When he glanced back over his shoulder, he saw a five foot-tall funnel of swirling leaves and dirt a few feet behind him. As he peered at the rapidly moving debris, he saw two pale arms. And then above the arms, the transparent outline of a woman's face. Gradually the dirt devil died down and collapsed into a pile of crumbled leaves and soil. The real problems began that night."

"What kinds of problems?"

"Similar to your experience, Annabelle—the ghost followed him back to his house, which is highly unusual. However, unlike your ghost, she couldn't get inside. We think she must have died near my sister Rowena's house. Maybe in the street out front, in a car accident. People drive pretty fast down those back roads in New Hampshire. And she's probably buried in the nearby graveyard, the one Wyatt was jogging through when he saw her. But your ghost is even more powerful than she is. He follows you everywhere, inside, outside, miles away from Wild Wood, where you found him, where he probably died."

This pronouncement makes me shiver with fear, despite the blazing fire and the dog's warm body beside me. But even though I'm scared, I want to know more. "What else happened?"

"After leaving the cemetery, Wyatt never saw the strange apparition again. However, he heard her. She wouldn't leave him alone. Screaming and wailing outside his bedroom window, she begged to be invited inside. But he wouldn't let her in."

"Thank goodness." I glance over to where Wyatt's sprawled in the chair by the fire; pale and exhausted.

"Every night, when Wyatt went up to his room, that thing clawed and banged at his windows. Her piercing wails seemed like they might shatter the glass. She shook the house with her horrible shrieks. Wyatt couldn't sleep. He couldn't even think. The relentless demon gave him no peace."

"I believe you." Oliver's story is so strange that it must be true. He couldn't be making this up.

"Wyatt's mother, my sister Rowena, didn't believe him. She never heard any of the noises. She thought Wyatt was hallucinating. She had him tested for drugs. The tests, of course, came back negative. She brought him to a psychiatrist who wanted him to take antipsychotic medication. They wanted to hospitalize Wyatt in a residential facility, on a locked floor."

"But she didn't do that." I keep looking over at Wyatt, who has dozed off in the middle of this incredible tale.

"No, because Wyatt called me and I jumped in the car and rushed to New Hampshire. The whole experience was causing a huge rift between him and Rowena. They were fighting and arguing constantly. I didn't think I could solve the problem alone, so I brought Nathaniel along."

"Who ya gonna call?" Nathaniel smiles.

Oliver ignores him and goes back to telling his story. "I thought maybe Nathaniel could help us banish the ghost. When we arrived, though, I realized that if I told Rowena about Nathaniel being a medium it would hurt our chances of helping Wyatt. She doesn't believe in ghosts. She would close her mind and not listen. So Nathaniel played the role of a good friend who was merely offering support."

"How did you two save Wyatt from getting locked up in the mental hospital?"

"That was tough. Rowena insisted that Wyatt needed psychiatric treatment. We had to get him away from her fast. We downplayed the whole ghost angle and went with a different strategy. Our paranormal situation had to take a back seat to rescuing Wyatt before his mother could lock him away."

"What did you do?"

"Nathaniel and I convinced Rowena to let Wyatt move in with me. We talked her into believing that a change of location would do him good. I promised her that my friend Jackson Andrews would counsel him. Jackson's not only a Unitarian minister; he's also a practicing psychologist. She agreed."

"What about the ghost?"

"We weren't able to discover anything about her. My sister refuses to believe that Wyatt can communicate with spirits. So we had to be very careful. Maybe one day we can go back to New Hampshire and find out what was really going on, but solving the mystery had to come second to rescuing Wyatt."

"So Wyatt's mother agreed to let him go."

"Yes, Rowena finally folded and let Wyatt come to Eastfield. She was dating someone new and I think she didn't want him to find out about her 'unusual' son. She decided that a son who lives with his uncle sounds preferable to a son who's locked up in a psychiatric hospital. Nathaniel and I helped Wyatt pack up his car and the three of us headed back to Eastfield. Fast."

"Where he met me and my ghost."

The expression on Oliver's face grows even more serious. "Wyatt's experience with you changes everything. This is the first time he's seen a ghost that was able to follow a person everywhere. Usually, a spirit haunts the place where it's buried or the scene of its death. On rare occasions, it can follow someone, but this can't happen unless the spirit and the person he's haunting had a close emotional connection when it was alive. Your ghost breaks all the rules. Annabelle, he attached himself to you, traveled miles away from the scene of his death and he's still with you. He has no boundaries."

Nathaniel frowns. "Even I've never heard of such a thing and I've been doing paranormal investigations for several years now."

Oliver explains. "Nathaniel is an experienced medium. He can communicate with the dead. I invited him to dinner tonight to consult with him about Wyatt's part in all of this and it looks like he arrived at just the right time."

Nathaniel adds, "Your ghost really concerns us, Annabelle. He waited a long time for the right person to come along. For years he fed off the fear of every amateur ghost hunter who visited the abandoned hospital. Panic and chaos can nourish a ghost. The spirit soaks it all in and it makes him stronger, more able to reveal himself to us. As we grow weaker, more frightened and more confused, he grows more powerful. The Lonesome Boy has orchestrated the most formidable haunting that I've ever heard of."

"Powerful. Formidable. You're really scaring me." I can't think of anything I did to deserve this. "Lots of people try ghost hunting. Lots of people have visited the asylum, looking for the Lonesome Boy. He never appeared to any of them. He isn't stalking any of them. Why me?"

"The spirit of the Lonesome Boy waited in room 209 at Wild Wood, hoping someone like you would come along."

"Someone like me?"

"Someone very special. Someone with a gift."

"I don't have a gift. I'm not a medium. I'm not like you and Wyatt, Nathaniel."

"You saw him, Annabelle. And no one else did."

I don't like what I'm hearing, but I have to listen. I need to know what happened tonight. I need an explanation.

Nathaniel continues. "By the time you finally showed up, the ghost had gathered enough power to stalk you, to stay with you for months. He left the asylum. After he followed you home, he hid in the shadows, in your dreams mostly. He was hoping someone would come along to empower him further."

"And that someone was Wyatt."

"Yes. The ghost remained reasonably quiet until Wyatt arrived in your life."

Wyatt opens his sleepy eyes and speaks up. "I'm so sorry, Annabelle."

Staring at me with a puppy-dog face which would rival Jeff's in an adorable competition, he looks pathetic and exhausted. Maybe I should lighten up on him.

"Okay, I forgive you, but I need to know the whole truth. You have to tell me everything, no more secrets or half-truths, please."

Wyatt smiles weakly. "I promise."

Nathaniel goes on. "I can't help you unless you tell me every detail. I'm not sure if you and Wyatt are in danger, but you could be. Everything about this situation's unusual."

I'm not going to tell him anything until I find out what he knows. "Nathaniel, you need to tell me what happened to Wyatt tonight. I know you're hiding something important from me."

"Before I can figure it out, I need more details. But there's one thing I do know for sure. This thing doesn't belong here with the living. And, unlike other spirits, it seems to know no boundaries. We need to send it back where it came from."

A loud snore from over by the other side of the fireplace interrupts Nathaniel. We all look over at Wyatt, who's lying with his long legs splayed out in front of him and his head sunk into the back of the overstuffed chair. His mouth's opened wide and he's drooling a little.

Nathaniel's forehead furrows with concern. "Oliver, he's sound asleep." He turns to me. "Annabelle, was he unusually hungry after you called Oliver?"

"He's always hungry. But he devoured about a dozen chocolate chip cookies and two huge glasses of milk right before Oliver arrived. That's a lot, even for Wyatt."

"This isn't good." Nathaniel reaches down as if to pat his dog, but smoothes my hair instead. "Please tell me everything that happened. Start at the beginning."

I look at Wyatt's slack form; he's tall and strong, but also vulnerable. My doubts collapse. I need to trust Nathaniel if I want him to help me, so I begin to reveal the whole story of my trip to Wild Wood. I start with the pale, ghostly form that only I saw. Then I tell them about the crying Meg and I heard in the car afterwards. Finally I describe the nightmares.

With my voice trembling I explain about the night Wyatt and I watched my movie together. The same night Wyatt announced that something had followed me back from the asylum.

"And as soon as Wyatt finished telling me, the light bulb exploded and the lamp tipped over. The TV came on loud and the screen was all static. When we went upstairs, my mother made us some tea and we were sitting at the table, talking. Suddenly the candle flames went out. The ghost extinguished them."

Nathaniel finally speaks up. "He's more powerful than any spirit I've ever encountered."

"I'm scared. Today, in the basement, Wyatt's heart stopped beating for a few seconds." I look up at Nathaniel, hoping that he can reassure me.

"That's not unusual for a medium who's channeling the dead. His heart started right up again, didn't it?"

"Yes, but afterwards he was different. Disoriented and cold; unbelievably cold."

"Annabelle, today the Lonesome Boy's spirit was able to enter Wyatt's body and speak, using Wyatt's voice."

"That's what I thought might have happened. But I was afraid to say it."

"It's called channeling. They've both been exhausted by this experience. I've done it a lot of times, at séances. Every time I've channeled for someone, I did it voluntarily, though. I consciously opened the door to my soul and let someone else in. But today there was no séance. Wyatt acted recklessly. He shouldn't have done what he did. I think he realizes that now. I think he even scared himself."

"Well, he sure as hell scared me."

"This is uncharted territory. We're learning as we go."

Oliver volunteers, "We need more information about what happened at that hospital, specifically, what happened in room 209. Who is the Lonesome Boy, or rather, who was he?"

"How can we find out?" I ask.

Oliver answers me. "You and Wyatt have seen what he looked like. If there are some old files that were left behind at the hospital, we might be able to find a photograph of him."

"That would be a good start," Nathaniel says.

"We need information about the patients at the hospital. Files and old newspapers, that's my department. I'm the historian. I'll lead the research team," Oliver announces.

"Meg and I saw some files when we were there. The offices are all creepy and dirty, but there are rusty metal file cabinets with files still in them. I'm afraid to go back, though."

"You have to, Annabelle, but we'll be with you every step of the way. I don't suppose it's wheelchair accessible." Nathaniel frowns.

"We climbed a fence to sneak in." I don't know what Nathaniel can do to help if we revisit the hospital. There's no way for him to get inside. "There's no electricity, no working elevators or anything like that. We saw a few ramps, but nothing to help you travel from one floor to another. And no way for you to get over the fence."

"Let's sit down and eat while we talk about it. I have all this food and everyone must be hungry. If we can wake Wyatt up, I'm sure he'll want something." Oliver's suggestion is the best I've heard all evening.

I go over, nudge Wyatt's shoulder with my hand, bend down and speak softly into his ear. He stirs and smiles lazily. Then he turns his head so that his lips almost touch mine. I move my face away quickly and shake his shoulder. The dog starts barking.

"What?" Wyatt sits up straight in his chair and looks around. "Nathaniel? Hey, good to see you."

"Hi, Wyatt. How are you feeling?"

He still looks disoriented. "I feel okay, thanks. Just tired. And hungry. That smells great, Oliver. What is it? I'm starved."

Chapter 11

Nathaniel's Story

I'm starving, but it's hard to eat because Wyatt keeps dozing off and leaning against my right arm. When he slides to the left, Oliver elbows him awake and I do the same when he heads back in my direction. If he falls forward, his face will end up in his dinner, so we have to stay vigilant at all times.

"The poor kid needs a couple of thick, juicy cheeseburgers. All this tofu stuff isn't good for a growing boy. If you fed him right, Oliver, maybe he wouldn't be so tired and weak." Nathaniel grins at us from across the table.

Oliver smiles and gives it right back. "That tofu disappeared pretty fast from your plate, Nathaniel. Would you like some more or are you feeling too tired and weak to lift your fork, because you're eating vegetarian food tonight?"

He passes the steaming platter, heaped with tofu, vegetables and rice, over to Nathaniel who says thank you and spoons a ton more of the delicious food onto his plate.

We're all shoveling in Oliver's tofu concoction. I want to compliment him, because he's a really good cook, but I don't want to seem like a kiss-up, so I just smile and put some more food onto my plate.

Finally Wyatt stumbles off to bed and Oliver and I clear the table.

After I load the last dirty dish and close the door on the dishwasher, Nathaniel calls out to me from the living room.

"Annabelle, come in here."

Oliver nods at me. "I just have one more pan to scrub. Then I need to run upstairs and check on Wyatt. Go ahead. Nathaniel has something to tell you."

Before I step into the living room, I stand still in the doorway for a second, to admire the view. Nathaniel looks like an artist posed him. The light from the fire plays with his shimmering curls and scampers over the muscles of his bare arms. Jeff's massive head is resting on his paws and he stares up at me without shifting his relaxed position at all.

"Come here, Annabelle. You've had a rough day. Sit by the fire with Jeff and me."

"You're right. What happened today was pretty disturbing."

I lower myself onto the rug, next to Jeff and settle in. Nestled at the foot of Nathaniel's wheelchair, leaning against the dog's furry side, I feel safe, full of good food, and cozy. Jeff's a living, breathing security blanket.

"Your day's about to get even more upsetting. But soon your confusion and fear will give way to understanding and acceptance."

"What do you mean?"

"You're upset. Oliver obviously annoyed you by not warning you about Wyatt's paranormal talent. It was kind of funny."

"Funny?"

"Is there an echo in here? Yeah, I thought you were funny. No one ever stands up to Oliver like that. You challenged him. Demanded to know what was going on. You surprised him. And it's hard to surprise Oliver. He thought you'd back down without an argument and accept what little information he was willing to share."

I like Oliver a lot, and Nathaniel, and even Wyatt. But I'm tired of being patronized like I'm some little kid who has to go to bed earlier than the grownups.

"It wasn't fair. Someone should have warned me. I was alone with Wyatt when he was possessed by that ghost."

"It was your ghost to begin with."

"But Wyatt took everything so much further."

"You two are both in way over your heads. You're going to need my help."

"Doing what?"

"Channeling spirits. I let them enter my body and speak, using my voice. I'm a medium, an experienced one. Wyatt's an amateur. Tonight was his first time."

"And his arms were around me! He was holding me when the ghost took over!"

"And here you are, back from your encounter with the undead. Safe and healthy. Yelling at me."

"You deserve it!"

"Annabelle, you're unbelievably special and Wyatt senses that, even though he doesn't know all the facts yet."

"All what facts?"

"You're even more unusual than you realize and you'll find out tonight about your own talent. But that's your story. First you have to hear mine, because we're all connected in the end."

"I have no clue what you're talking about."

What does Nathaniel know about me that even I don't know?

"Sometimes the dead can't let go of the living until we make it possible and this can be very hard to do."

"I'm still confused."

"Be patient and listen to my story."

"Okay. I'll try."

"Let's start with Jeff, because he's always been there for me. He had my back right from the beginning."

I stroke the warm fur on Jeff's side and he lifts his head for a second, to lick my hand. Nathaniel begins.

"When I was a college student. Before the accident..." He pauses and looks down at his immobile legs. "...I devoted my strong body to every good cause. I worked hard, got good grades and donated lots of time to organizations like Amnesty International, the local animal shelter and Students Against Drunk Driving, among other charities. I wanted to save people, save animals, save the whales, the rain forest, everything. If something needed saving, I belonged to an organization that was trying to save it. I didn't really have a girlfriend, but I guess you could say I had a different girlfriend every weekend."

I roll my eyes and snort. Nathaniel pauses to smile at me, flashing his white teeth.

"Charming laugh, Annabelle. Very ladylike." Then he resumes his story. "One day my best friend, Ted, called me, to ask a favor. Someone had stolen a puppy and wanted to bring it to the animal shelter, where I volunteered. Ted asked me to adjust the paper work so it all looked legal. I refused, of course, but he begged me to meet the dog, just once, before I made up my mind. I said no again and he played his ace. Two beautiful sisters had stolen the dog and they had a good reason for stealing it. My desire to obey the law weakened, for selfish reasons, and I agreed to meet the girls and the puppy."

"And the puppy was Jeff?"

"Right. The puppy was Jeff, but I haven't gotten that far yet. Be patient."

Jeff's sleeping peacefully, supporting my weight with no complaints. Taking no interest in his own part of the story, he's snoring a little and twitching his tail in his sleep.

Nathaniel continues. "Ted brought the two girls and the puppy over to my house one fall afternoon. I was home alone that day. Mom was out grocery shopping; my father's been gone for about twenty-five years."

"I'm sorry for your loss." I feel like I need to say something, because Nathaniel looks so sad right now.

"My father didn't die. He disappeared when I was a baby. We tried to track him down a couple of times, but it's expensive. We ran out of money before we could find him. He probably changed his name, took on a new identity or something. I have no idea. After a while we stopped caring and just accepted the situation. Anyway, it's ancient history. I never knew him and I got used to not having a father around. Mom and I have managed very well on our own."

I don't know what to say so I just nod and hope he'll go on with his story. And he does.

"Now, back to the part about meeting Jeff for the first time and meeting Holly. My friend arrived on that fateful day with the most irresistible puppy I'd ever met and two of the most beautiful girls I'd ever seen. They were sisters. The older one's name was Holly. She was my age: twenty one. I immediately agreed to help them, even if what they asked me to do was illegal. The first time Holly smiled at me, I decided I'd rob a bank for her if that's what she wanted."

I giggle, picturing Nathaniel all bug-eyed over a girl. Jeff stirs in his sleep for a second.

"I fell hard. Did a face plant and never got up. She had a sarcastic smile, like she was thinking, 'Yup, I really look this good, but do you care about what's inside? Am I smart? Am I funny? Do you even want to know?' I just kept staring at her until that smirk widened into something genuine and rare, with dimples, too."

"I get the point. She was gorgeous. Now what about the dog?"

"Okay, okay. Sorry for digressing. Holly's family had just moved to Eastfield. We were practically neighbors. She had recently dropped out of college but was thinking of taking a few courses at River Wind. My dream-girl lived in my town and would be going to my school. I couldn't believe my good luck."

I give him an "Ahem."

"Okay, Annabelle. Back to the dog."

"It's just that the romantic part is a little boring."

"Aren't you kind of young to be so cynical about romance?"

"I'm not cynical. I just think it's boring."

"Right." Nathaniel shoots me a close-lipped grin and then continues. "Before she moved to Eastfield, Holly lived next to a very sketchy guy whose dog died under not-so-mysterious circumstances. This neighbor kept his dog outside, all the time, tied on a short rope, with only a ramshackle old dog house for shelter. Holly had knocked on the guy's door a couple of times and begged him to stop neglecting the pathetic animal, but he only insulted her and he threatened her, too."

"What did he say?"

"He didn't just say it. He did it. One spring day, Holly's mother came home from work to find that someone had uprooted the flowers from her garden. They suspected their creepy neighbor, but they couldn't prove it. So they knew they'd have to handle the situation themselves."

"What did they do?"

"They called the animal control officer, but he told them there was nothing he could do. The dog hadn't been obviously beaten and it was fed and given water."

"That's horrible!"

"It gets worse. One cold winter day, Holly had just stepped out of her house early in the morning. She looked over at the neighbor's yard, to check on the dog, and his rope was lying slack on the frozen dirt. No dog attached. There was a mound of fresh dirt in the neighbor's backyard where he'd buried the poor animal. He must've had to chop through the frozen earth with a pick axe. The bastard worked harder to bury his dog than he did to take care of it. Holly cried herself to sleep that night."

I squeeze back my tears and swallow them. I love dogs.

"Winter passed and spring arrived. One day Holly looked out her bedroom window and saw a puppy tied with the same rope, lying beside that wreck of a doghouse, hopelessly lovable, but with no one to love him."

"Oh no!"

"Oh yes. She knew she had to take action. Her mother had just started a new job in Boston and they had decided to move to Eastfield because it was closer to the city. They had already found a condo, bought it and started packing."

"But what about the puppy?"

"A couple of days after the move, Holly and her sister waited until after dark and dressed themselves all in black, like ninjas. Armed with nothing more than a sharp pair of sewing scissors, the girls drove back to their old neighborhood. They snuck into the mean neighbor's yard, cut the dog's rope and tiptoed back to their car. The poor puppy never even whimpered or barked. He seemed to understand that his very life depended on his silence. They brought him home to their new 'no pets allowed' condo, where, of course, the neighbors discovered his presence after only one day."

"So Holly had to get rid of him."

"Yes. Because Holly, her sister and her mother were so kind and sweet and the puppy was so adorable, the condo association gave them two weeks to find a new home for him."

"And they found you."

Nathaniel nods his head. "Holly's sister knew my friend Ted and he thought of me because I worked at the animal shelter. I'd no sooner finished listening to Holly tell her story when I offered to take the puppy right away. She asked how she could possibly thank me enough. I had pretty specific ideas about how she could thank me, but I decided to be patient and not rush things. She was worth waiting for. I didn't want to come on too strong."

"Again with the romance, Nathaniel. What about the dog?"

He laughs. "I turned to the dog and asked him what his name was. The girls found this pretty amusing, which was my intention. However, to my surprise, the dog answered."

"What did he say?"

"Some dogs bark and they make a 'woof' or a 'ruff' sound, but he distinctly said 'Jeff.' We all heard him. His previous owner had never called him anything but 'Stupid.' He deserved to be consulted about his new name. On that special day, four years ago, my dog named himself. We've been inseparable ever since."

"What happened between you and Holly?" Despite my aversion to romance, I'm a little curious.

"She came over to visit Jeff a lot. We brought him on long walks together. He'd jump into the back seat and we'd drive over to the state forest, or the Eastfield Country Club, at dusk, when most of the golfers had finished up. Jeff knew I had a pocket full of dog biscuits, so even though he was still a puppy, I could let him off the leash and he'd come back. He ran like joy fueled every muscle in his awkward, gangly puppy body. Long-legged, big-pawed and beautiful. Overflowing with clumsy enthusiasm. He chased after birds, bunnies, chipmunks, squirrels. You name it. He'd try to tree it. Jeff always returned when I whistled, filled with gratitude for the dog cookie and our friendship."

"Good boy." I pat Jeff's head and he licks my cheek with his enormous, rough tongue.

"I'll always remember this one day." Nathaniel smiles. "Holly and I took Jeff to the state forest, so he could run free and terrorize the squirrels. We unclipped his leash and walked for a while, holding hands. Then we climbed a grassy hill and stared down at the meadow below. It was kind of hot out. The sun was setting. Jeff was running around. Chasing butterflies. Trampling wild flowers. A breeze blew across the nearby pond and ruffled Holly's hair. She smoothed it back with one hand. And smiled. I kissed her for the first time. She tasted like she belonged to me, like I'd been waiting for that kiss my whole life."

"Yeah, it was a great kiss. I get it. What happened next?" I can't resist giving Nathaniel a hard time. He punches my arm and continues with his love story. I keep hoping that it has a happy ending. Like they're married now and Holly's waiting at home for him tonight.

"We saw each other every weekend and sometimes during the week, too. One Saturday night, I was home alone, waiting to hear from Holly. A friend of hers had just gotten engaged and they were having a girls' night out, celebrating. Holly told me she'd call me when she got home. When she was with her girlfriends something ridiculous always happened. I knew she'd have some funny stories."

"How long had you been going out?"

"About six months, but I already wished that we were announcing our engagement. I was trying to be patient, though. We were so happy just hanging out. We had saved Jeff's life together. Our bond was intense, but at the same time we felt comfortable with each other. Anyway, she went out with her girlfriends that night."

Nathaniel hesitates.

I prompt him. "And?"

He breathes in deep and exhales fast, puffing out his lips in a frown. "She called me really late, from a bar near River Wind. Everyone else was still drinking. She'd gone beyond her limit and felt sick. So she told her friends she was leaving. She knew I'd come and get her, no matter how late it was. On the phone she was slurring her words and I got worried. I jumped in the car, with Jeff, of course, in the back seat. We headed out to rescue our girl."

Nathaniel's face is so sad that it's hard to look at him while he's speaking, but I do. He turns away and bows his head. I stare at his drooping profile, backlit by the flames.

"When I got to the bar, I found her and she was wasted, almost unconscious. I carried her out to the car, sat her down on the passenger's side and buckled her in. Jeff whimpered at us from the backseat. Holly mumbled something about how sorry she was. I told her, 'Don't worry. It's okay. There's no one else in the world I'd rather rescue.'"

He pauses and clears his throat.

"Do you want some water, Nathaniel?" I stand and rest my hand on his arm.

"Okay."

I run out to the kitchen and fill a glass with ice and then water from the tap. When I hand it to him he gulps down half of it before he slows to sipping for a few seconds. Finally he sets the glass down on the floor next to his wheelchair and I resume my cozy position beside Jeff. Nathaniel continues.

"On the way back to her house, shortly before one o'clock in the morning, Holly said she felt sick and opened the car door, while the car was moving. I pulled over so she could lean out of the car and throw up. Then she closed the door and told me she was all right. I was frantic, though. I wanted to get her home, where she would be safe and I could take care of her."

Nathaniel reaches down, picks up the glass of water and finishes it.

"I drove too fast, screeched to a halt at a red light and waited impatiently. I watched the other light turn yellow, signaling that my light would soon change to green. I lifted my foot off the brake and let it hover over the gas pedal. The second the light flashed green, I shot out."

I close my eyes, as if I'm there and can't bear to watch.

"His car was traveling seventy miles an hour. The impact spun us around. Then we slammed into another car that had just entered the intersection."

"Nathaniel!" I rest my hand on his.

"I don't remember anything beyond stomping on the gas when the light changed. Everything else is black." He tilts his head back and closes his eyes as if to revisit that world of total darkness.

"The other driver was trying to beat the red light. He sped up when the light turned yellow. Caved in the passenger side of my car. Spun us into another car. I woke up in the hospital. Two days later. Spinal injury. Couldn't feel my legs."

I can't think of anything to say so I squeeze his hand. He doesn't squeeze back.

"When I opened my eyes for the first time in two days, my mother was sitting beside my hospital bed, crying. A doctor came in and explained that I might never walk again."

He pauses then continues. "Jeff was completely okay. A miracle."

I'm afraid to ask about Holly, but I do it anyway. "What happened to her, Nathaniel?"

"The first impact killed her. Instantly."

I can't find any words. Nathaniel turns his face away and stares into the fire.

"My soul fled from my body. For a long time my feelings were as paralyzed as my legs. I barely ate or slept."

Eventually, Nathaniel turns back toward me and looks at my hand, still resting on his. His beautiful archangel's face remains expressionless but a tear slides down one perfect cheek.

"The driver who hit my car died the next day. The driver of the third car was fine. He and Jeff survived intact."

"Nathaniel." I stand up and put my arms around him. Jeff stands, too, and lays his giant head in Nathaniel's lap. Nathaniel hugs me back and pats Jeff's furry head as if he's comforting us.

"I'll always regret every decision I made and every action I took that night. But I'm past obsessing about it. I barely ever think about it anymore. When I do stop to remember, the worst part is I still miss her."

I don't know what to say to Nathaniel. I'm not sure that I can listen to much more. She died so young. Nathaniel loved her so much.

"In a way, Annabelle, the end of this story was really the beginning of my life. The dawn of my purpose here on Earth."

"What do you mean?"

"Holly's ghost was the first ghost I ever saw. And I saw her everywhere. Tapping on my shoulder from behind. Pulling the bed covers down or up. Every morning when I opened my eyes, she'd be looking down at me with a sorrowful expression on her beautiful face. Lit by a light from within. At first I wanted to join her. I wanted it more than I had ever wanted anything before. But she wouldn't let me."

I sit back down on the rug and Jeff settles in beside me. Nathaniel's dog has heard all this before. He lived it.

Nathaniel continues. "One night, I tried to pull out all of my IVs and tubes and Holly pushed the call button. The nurse came running in."

What can you say to someone who's just told you he wanted to die? Nothing. So I sit there, mute.

"I'd lost my place on earth. The book mark had been yanked out of the story of my life and I didn't want to start over. I didn't want to look through the pages, chapters and experiences to find out where I'd left off. I wanted to join Holly. But she wouldn't let me."

He picks up his empty glass and tries to take a sip of the water that isn't there. Gently, I take it from his hand and refill it in the kitchen. When I come back, Nathaniel accepts the full glass and sets it down beside his wheelchair without drinking any. I guess he forgot that he was thirsty.

"On my first night home from the hospital, Holly kept tapping on my bedroom window. I couldn't get up to open it. I screamed for my mother. She came running in and opened the window, letting in the cool night air and my dead girlfriend. Then Mom went back to bed, oblivious."

The fire's waning and it's getting cold, so I get up and throw two more logs on.

"That was the night I grabbed the painkillers on my

nightstand, intending to swallow the whole bottle. Holly freaked out. She rocked my dresser until a lamp fell over. Jeff went crazy howling and barking. My mother woke up and rushed in again."

He pauses and I have no choice but to wait for him to continue.

"An unseen hand bumped my arm and I dropped the open bottle of pills. The tablets scattered all over the bed. My mother picked them up and put them back into the bottle. Then she shook one pill into her hand and looked around the room. As she righted the fallen lamp, the curtains moved, blown inward by another rogue wind. The light bulb in my bedside lamp dimmed then brightened. My mother gave me one pill and a sip of water. Then she carried the rest of the pills away with her. Holly had gotten her message across."

"Unbelievable."

"I know. Holly saved me. All I wanted to do was die and she kept saving me. Still, Jeff didn't like her. He adored her when she was alive. But after she died, he knew that her spirit had no rightful place on this earth; she belonged somewhere else. He tried to send her away with his relentless barking, but she wouldn't go. Even though he howled like a hound from hell, Holly's spirit kept coming back."

I scratch the dog's head and his voice rumbles, deep in his throat, like a lion's purr.

"Then one day, Holly's sister came to take Jeff for a walk. She thought it might bring her some peace; a feeling of connection. Because together, she and Holly had saved Jeff's life."

Nathaniel seems to suddenly remember the glass of water and he takes a few sips.

"We didn't have an electric wheelchair yet; I just had an ordinary one. With the visiting nurse's help, my mother got me into it and they wheeled me outside. I hadn't been outside in weeks. It was a beautiful sunny day and my mother thought I should get some fresh air. Why do mothers always want you to get fresh air?"

"Because it's good for you. Aside from the obvious uplifting emotional benefits, sunlight increases your vitamin D supply, which helps with depression."

"God, Annabelle, in addition to being beautiful, you're wise beyond your years. Remind me to tell Wyatt he's a very lucky guy."

"Yeah, but we're not dating."

Nathaniel smiles for the first time since he began telling this part of his story. "Okay, honey, keep telling yourself that."

"I will. Because it's true. But this isn't about me. You were telling me *your* story, Nathaniel."

"Ah yes, I digress. Again. Back to my story."

"Yes, back to your story."

"I sat outside, in the sunlight. My mother left to do a quick errand. The nurse was in the house. Holly's sister had Jeff. So I was by myself. Except for my recently deceased girlfriend."

"What happened?"

"She spoke to me for the first time. Not in words, though; it was like her voice was inside my head. She blamed herself because I was paralyzed. Her overwhelming feelings of guilt were keeping her here with the living. Here with me, where she didn't belong."

"Is that why she couldn't let go?"

"Yes. And I couldn't let go, either. I blamed myself for her death. We both needed to stop feeling so guilty. We needed to forgive ourselves. Then Holly would be able to rest in peace. And I would be able to go on with my life. I had to live with the truth; I still loved her and always would. And she had to die with that truth. We couldn't be together. We both had to accept it."

"How did you get her to leave?"

"I told her there was nothing to forgive. And she told me the same. We convinced each other not to feel guilty. People make split-second decisions all the time, but as long as they're made with good intentions and love, we can't blame ourselves for the outcome. Sometimes you're in the wrong place at the wrong time and something horrible goes down. Sometimes you're trying to be a hero and circumstances make it impossible. Sometimes you call for help because you know you need it and everything goes tragically wrong."

"And that's what happened the night she died."

He nods his head. "Holly did the right thing. She knew she'd drunk too much and she called for a sober ride home. Everyone she was with kept on partying, drank a lot more. They all lived to attend her funeral. I missed it. Because I did the right thing, too. I went out to rescue her. When they buried Holly, I was still in the hospital. I couldn't even go to her funeral."

I touch Nathaniel's hand again.

He turns it palm up and closes it around mine. "That day, sitting in the wheelchair, in the sunlight, I got my chance to say goodbye to Holly. Forever."

"I'm so sorry."

"I'll never forget her. What can you say about a girl who dresses up like a ninja and sneaks into someone's yard to steal a puppy? Goodbye, Beautiful. There will never be anyone else like you."

I sit there for a minute, thinking, stroking Jeff's fur. Finally I break the silence and ask, "You've seen other ghosts since then, haven't you?"

"Whether I want to or not," he answers. "If a person asks me to reach out to someone they've lost, I can usually channel the spirit, or at least communicate with them in some way."

"You channel them?"

"Yes, I meditate, freeing my mind of earthly concerns. Then they enter and speak through me for a short time. I can even remember what they've said, because I can hear them speak while they're speaking through me. I'm always starving and exhausted afterwards."

Nathaniel reaches down and grips my shoulder. I look up at him. "Annabelle, Wyatt channeled a spirit tonight. The ghost of the Lonesome Boy climbed inside his mind and spoke, using his voice. Both of you have taken on more than you're ready for. By the way, I can see your ghost, but barely. He's scrunched down in a dark corner over there, keeping his distance, so he won't upset Jeff. But he definitely belongs to you two lovebirds and he's a weirdo. Good luck with him; I'll help in any way I can. But you have a long, rough road ahead of you."

Ignoring the lovebird comment, I stand and bend over to hug Nathaniel.

He hugs me back. "C'mon, I'll drive you home. I know your parents, by the way, so I'd love to come in and say hello if it's okay with you. Your dad did the renovations on our house, to make it accessible."

"I suppose that's cool, as long as Jeff's included."

"Ahhh, another woman who's only interested in me because of my dog."

"He's a lot better looking than you are," I lie.

Chapter 12

My Father's Story

We say goodnight, leaving Wyatt in Oliver's capable hands. And I get to ride home in Nathaniel's pimped-out van. He can control everything with the remote on his keychain. There's a hydraulic lift in back for the wheelchair. Once he's back there, he secures the wheelchair and hoists himself up like a gymnast, through the two captain's chairs and into the driver's seat.

There are hand controls for everything and it's all digital. When I'm safely belted into the passenger's side, Nathaniel turns to me, smiles and points his thumb toward the back where Jeff's snuggled into his king-sized doggy bed, beside the empty wheelchair.

"Cool ride, huh?"

"Way cool."

"Turns out that the guy who hit me was drunk, speeding and ran a red light. His family didn't want a lawsuit and neither did I. We settled out of court and I was able to buy this van and hire your dad to remodel the house. So I have total freedom and independence."

"Sweet." I rub my hand over the leather upholstery.

"I have side airbags, too. I'm more of a safety freak than a lot of old geezers and I'm only twenty-five."

I glance in the back of the van where Jeff is resting his huge head on his paws. "I'm surprised you didn't name him Scooby, not Jeff, you know, with the van and the ghost hunter thing and all."

"Master of the obvious, Annabelle. That *did* occur to me, but there's nothing goofy about Jeff. He's *so* not a Scooby. Jeff is very Sphinx-like; mysterious and wise and all-knowing. He possesses the size and power of a king. Look at him."

Sure enough, Jeff lifts his head up and snorts disdainfully at us. When the van stops, though, his face breaks into a doggy smile and he wags his massive tail. We're at my house. I don't have to help Nathaniel with anything. He has a small portable ramp and places it over the three stairs leading up to our door. Because my father's family has been here for almost four centuries, a lot of elderly people have lived in our house and it's pretty accessible anyway.

My mother's waiting for us. Oliver must've called her, because she already has the table set with mugs ready for tea and a plate of Meg's homemade cookies.

"It's getting late, Annabelle, and you have school and track tomorrow, but you can sleep in. I'll write you an excuse note."

Now I'm suspicious. My mother's the queen of "Suck it up and go to school." And she just offered to write me a note when I didn't even ask for one. She nods to a chair at the table and I sit down. Then she bends and kisses Nathaniel's cheek. "Hey, there."

"Wonderful to see you again, Susannah. As always, you look amazing."

She laughs like a girl. This is getting weirder by the second. They seem to know each other pretty well.

Mom leans over and lights the two pillar candles in their heavy silver pedestals on the kitchen table. A teapot, a jar of honey and four ceramic mugs rest next to the glowing candles. Smiling at Nathaniel, my mother begins to serve tea.

"He's peaceful, now, Susannah. I don't think he'd harm her. But you already realized that."

Nathaniel's know-it-all attitude is starting to annoy me. "What's up, you two?" Swiveling my head, I look from my mother to Nathaniel and back. Everyone knows more than I do. Even my mother seems to be in on a big secret.

"It's time to tell Annabelle everything, Susannah," Nathaniel announces. "I know you were going to wait until she turned eighteen, but she needs to know now. Something's happened. A spirit from the Wild Wood asylum is stalking her."

My mother pulls out the chair next to me and sits down. "I knew there was a ghost involved. You're a bad liar, Annabelle, and Wyatt's no better. It started with the nightmares and then it got worse the other night, when the light bulb broke. Something big happened this afternoon. Didn't it? I could tell."

"How could you tell, Mom?"

Nathaniel jumps in. "Annabelle, you're the child that broke the Blake family curse. You have an important legacy. I knew when Wyatt came here he'd find you and he did, with no help from me or Oliver. I didn't count on the ghost, however. Even though I saw your film last year, I had no idea how intense the situation had become."

"What the hell's he talking about, Mom?"

Ordinarily, she would yell at me for my disrespectful language, but these are not ordinary circumstances. Nathaniel knows more about me than I know about myself and Oliver showed him my film. I look to my mom for reassurance, for an explanation that makes sense. She reaches over and covers my hand with hers.

"Annabelle, honey, I waited a long time for you and I risked a lot along the way. I was planning to explain everything on your eighteenth birthday. But I can't wait any longer."

"You can start anytime now, Mom."

Ignoring my sarcasm, she begins. "We'll start with the Blakes, because we live here, on their land, in their house. Nathaniel, help me out here." My usually serene mother seems totally discombobulated at the moment. I didn't think this night could get any weirder. But I was wrong.

"Okay, I'll start at the beginning." Nathaniel folds his hands around the warm cup in front of him and stares through the steam, into the distance. "During the 1670's the local settlers and the Wampanoag Indians waged war against each other, over land ownership, of course. The Blakes' property was at the center of the violent dispute. The white settlers won, killing almost all of the Wampanoag tribe in the process, including the Indians' leader, King Philip, in 1676. The war only lasted eighteen months, but it was a bloody and brutal conflict, especially for the Indians. Your mom can tell you the Blake part of the story, which is more legend than actual history."

My mom sighs, takes a sip of her tea and begins. "Nathaniel's right; no one's ever written the whole story down, but every member of the Blake family is familiar with it. Evidently, back in the 1670's, the Blakes had a very rebellious young daughter named Isabelle."

She pauses as my dad strolls in and grabs a mug out of the cupboard. Mom pours him a cup of her special brew and he smiles at her.

"The Pats are killing the Ravens and the game's pretty much over. Boring. But it sounds like you're discussing something pretty exciting out here: a story about my ancestors. Am I right?"

"Go ahead, Bill. Your daughter doesn't know that she's the girl who ended the Blake family curse." My new friend Nathaniel continues to flabbergast me with his outrageous pronouncements.

Dad reaches across the table to shake hands with everybody's life-long buddy, good old Nathaniel, who knows more about my family than I do. Then he begins in his deep, calm voice.

"Isabelle Blake, somewhere around her eighteenth year, as the legend's been told, had a Native North American lover."

Whoa, I've never heard my dad say the word "lover" before and it's kind of creepy. This is getting stranger and more awkward by the second.

Dad takes a sip of tea then continues. "Isabelle fell in love with a Wampanoag warrior. They broke the rules and conceived a child together."

"Why have I never heard this before?"

Mom reaches over and pats my hand. "Drink your tea, honey."

It's going to take more than herb tea to calm me down right now, but I follow her advice anyway.

Dad continues. "The father of Isabelle's baby was known for his bravery in battle and his uncanny ability to survive serious injuries. He was related to Metacom, whom the white settlers called King Philip. Metacom was the son of Massasoit, the most famous Wampanoag chief. Historians have portrayed Massasoit as a wise leader who maintained peace between the English settlers and the Native American peoples. He was chief when the Pilgrims landed in Plymouth Colony."

"But his son Metacom was a different kind of leader," Nathaniel adds.

Dad nods his head in agreement. "Unlike his father, Metacom fought viciously for the land which rightfully belonged to his tribe. The white settlers answered the tribe's violence with more violence. They wounded Metacom many times, but he always recovered. Again and again, he came back. Furious, strong and lethal. Both the whites and the Indians believed Philip was immortal. The settlers feared they might never be able to kill him. My family believes that the father of Isabelle's child was Annawan, a brave warrior who fought alongside Metacom."

"So we're related to the Wampanoags?"

"Yes, Annabelle. A fierce Wampanoag tribesman fathered young Isabelle Blake's child, a girl baby. Isabelle died giving birth, right here in this house. As she was dying, she begged her family to name the child Annabelle, a combination of her name and that of the baby's father. The family complied because it was their daughter's dying wish."

"I'm named after Isabelle's and Annawan's child?"

My dad continues the story. "You are. The Blakes raised baby Annabelle, ignoring the rumors that sprung up because she didn't look like the rest of the family. The other Blakes were fair-skinned, with brown hair and blue eyes, like me and your brothers."

"But I'm not."

"No, you're not. According to the Blake family's oral history, you resemble the first Annabelle Blake, born sometime during the 1670's. She grew into a beautiful young woman with dark hair and eyes and golden brown skin. She looked like you, Annabelle, and she was the last daughter ever born into the Blake family for over three hundred years and sixteen generations. Until you came along."

I have a mouth full of tea and most of it spurts straight out of my mouth and all over Nathaniel. He grabs a napkin and starts mopping up the tea. My mother jumps up and begins slapping my back because I'm still choking a little. After we calm down and Nathaniel dries off, my mother continues telling the story.

"Now for the part about the curse. During King Philip's War, the blood from the horrifying rage and the tears of the survivors soaked into the ground near the Great Hockomock Swamp, which lies at the southwestern border of the Blakes' property. The Indians named these wetlands after Hobamock, their spirit of low-lying places. He appeared in sacred visions as a huge serpent. The Wampanoags associated him both with honor and with death."

My father speaks again. "Like King Philip, the father of Isabelle's baby was eventually captured and beheaded. The English settlers wiped out most of the Wampanoag tribe. Those who didn't die in the war were sold into slavery. The male slaves were shipped off to the West Indies."

"The Wampanoags must've hated the white people."

"Yes, the Indians regarded the relationship between Isabelle and Annawan as a catastrophe, not a bond that might inspire a peace treaty with the settlers. But the baby, little Annabelle, was half Wampanoag, descended from and named after one of their bravest warriors, so they didn't harm her. Instead, they cursed the Blakes."

"They cursed us? I can't believe what I'm hearing."

Solemnly, Dad meets my eyes. "Summoning their spirit god, out of the swampland, the few surviving Wampanoags asked his help to ensure there would never be another girl-child born to the Blakes."

"Until me?"

"Yes. Until you, Annabelle, the curse hel*...*ue. Now it's time for your mother's side of the story. She can explain why we were able to break the curse."

I don't realize that my mouth's hanging open until Dad reaches over and nudges his index finger under my chin to close it.

Turning to Nathaniel, I ask, "How do you fit into this? You knew all about me before you even met me."

Jeff walks over and places his huge furry head under my left hand. Stroking his soft fur calms me down a little.

Nathaniel smiles at his partner in crime. "I've been mentoring Wyatt since he saw his first ghost. Oliver doesn't have any paranormal talent. He's just interested, open-minded and ready to help whenever he can, but my gift is pretty extraordinary. Unlike Wyatt, I can control the whole channeling thing. Wyatt's an amateur, so Oliver had to ask for my help. His research skills and passion for local history could only get them so far. They needed me."

"Okay. How did you meet my parents?"

"I met your dad when we hired him to make our house wheelchair-accessible. I got to know both of your parents because they're friends with Oliver and involved in the historical society. Ghosts, curses and History all fit together."

"I'm beginning to notice. Okay, let's hear your side of the story, Mom. How did you break the curse?" I can't get used to the idea, but saying it out loud helps. "Do Clement and Joe know anything about this?"

"They know you're the first girl born to the Blake family in a long time. That's about it."

Dad leans toward me. "I'm surprised you never noticed."

Now I feel like a dumbass, thinking about my relatives and realizing I have no aunts on the Blake side except the ones who are married to my father's brothers. Of course, I know I have no sisters. Stating the obvious, I announce, "I have no girl cousins on the Blake side. I've never even thought about it before. Tell me about breaking the curse, Mom."

Rising slowly from her seat at our kitchen table, my mother goes over to the sink with her empty mug and runs some water into it. Then she takes a crystal goblet down from a cabinet, opens the refrigerator, grabs a bottle of white wine, uncorks it and fills the goblet to the brim. After drinking deeply, she goes back to her seat. Settling down into her chair, she begins to speak.

Chapter 13

My Mother's Story

"The night you were born, your father and I realized everything was changing. I went into labor and we called Uncle Johnny. He came over and got the boys, so they could stay with him, but your father and I never made it to the hospital that night. You were born here at home."

"Isn't that dangerous?" I can't believe I'm hearing this for the first time. No one ever told me I was born at home. No one ever pointed out to me before that I'm the only girl on the Blake side for centuries.

"Not for us that night. You were born at the very moment of the vernal equinox, on March 21, the date when the night and the day are of equal length. Everything felt right. It was magical."

"How so?"

"I felt very calm and peaceful, even when I realized we'd never make it to the hospital. Dad called the midwife and she got here as fast as she could, but she wasn't in time.

Your father delivered you, here in this house, in the same room where the first Annabelle was born. The midwife showed up about fifteen minutes after you arrived and pronounced everyone healthy. She didn't stay long. We called Johnny and he brought the boys back. Our family was complete and the curse had finally been broken."

"But that's not the end of the story, is it? Why me? What was different about you and Dad together? Why did you break the curse when no one else in the Blake family ever could?"

"My family's story will answer your questions. And it begins at the beginning of time. We've had to keep a lot of secrets because of centuries of persecution. One generation of my family had to tell the next. We couldn't write it down. The details might get into the wrong hands and more of us would die. One of the earliest historical accounts of our existence took place during the time of the legendary King Arthur."

"King Arthur? Camelot?"

"Yes. But I need to begin even earlier than that. Before Christianity became the dominant religion in Great Britain, druids and priestesses worshipped the gods of the earth and the sky, fire and water. This ancient faith was the religion of my ancestors. Arthur kept one foot in the pagan religion and one in Christianity. He and his wife Guinevere were Christians. But Merlin, who was a powerful pagan wizard, advised the young King Arthur."

"So Arthur couldn't make up his mind?"

"He was under a lot of pressure to embrace Christian beliefs. The Knights of the Round Table were Christians and their sacred mission was to search for the Holy Grail, the cup from which Jesus drank at the last supper. It had disappeared and the Knights Templar strove to find it by charging forth on dangerous journeys called quests."

"Go on. What was your family's part in all this?" I'm upset because no one has told me anything until tonight, but I'm also fascinated.

My mother takes another sip of her wine and then continues. "The Grail wasn't originally a part of any Christian ritual. It belonged to Great Britain's pagan priestesses, my ancestors. Their own personal smith, Trebuchet, forged it. These women drank from the grail in their ceremonies, honoring the seasons. The autumnal equinox is the exact time every year when day and night are equal, the beginning of the path that leads to the dead of winter. The winter solstice marks the longest night of the year. The vernal or spring equinox, when day and night are of equal length once again, represents the rebirth of all life which renews itself. Spring then leads to the summer solstice, the longest day of the year."

"And I was born during the vernal equinox."

"Yes, this makes you very important, very blessed. The door to one season closes and another opens. The grail was a significant part of these pagan rituals."

"What happened? How did it come to be known as a Christian icon?"

"A mysterious thief stole it from the high priestess and it ended up in the hands of Jesus' followers, even though the grail originated in pagan times."

"Stolen?"

"Yes and my ancestors were desperate to get it back. The pagans used the grail in their rituals and its powers helped them as they sought to redeem the human condition. When Jesus Christ drank from this holy goblet, he did so with the same sacred intentions as the pagans; he died a horrible, torturous death so he could save the souls of the whole human race. After the last supper, the grail became a Christian icon. But Jesus' followers strayed from their savior's beliefs. They excluded women as spiritual leaders and began persecuting us."

"So you had to get it back."

"Exactly. The Christians, using stealth and deceit, had stolen the Holy Grail. And the pagans had to steal it back. But that's not all. My ancestors needed to make the grail disappear. Too many of the Christians sought only to glorify themselves and persecute others. Their actions led to worsening the human condition, not improving it."

"So how did you get it back?"

"Trebuchet, forger of the grail, dwelt on an island in the middle of a lake, near Wales in Great Britain. The lake surrounded the legendary island of Avalon. Magical mists usually hid this island from nonbelievers. The master smith lived there, with the famed lady of the lake, the high priestess of the ancient religion—Nimue. Fate. She who lives forever and embodies the collective memories of the whole human race."

"What part did Nimue play?"

"One of her handmaidens, Olwen, a whisper of a girl, who caused flowers to spring up wherever she went, used her own charms and magical slight-of-hand methods to find the grail and steal it back. The priestesses hid it on their island and Avalon disappeared once again into the mist."

"But the grail still wasn't safe?"

"The pagans became worried because the Christian knights searched for the grail so relentlessly. The priestesses didn't want it to fall into the wrong hands again. They convinced Trebuchet to melt down the grail. He blended the molten silver with other precious metals and then cast the mixture into twenty-six candle holders. Each of the thirteen priestesses took possession of a pair of candle holders. They planned to pass them down to their daughters from generation to generation. Our family's silver candle holders sit before you, Annabelle. One day they will belong to you and after that to your daughter. My ancestry is very powerful and I needed a daughter so I could pass along what's left of the Holy Grail to her."

The silver candle holders have always sat in the center of our kitchen table. They look the same yet different to me tonight. When I reach one hand out and tentatively touch one of them, the metal feels warm, as if it's glowing with a life of its own. None of my surroundings seem familiar to me anymore.

Nathaniel sips his tea thoughtfully and then sets down his cup. "You'll never be ordinary, Annabelle, so get used to it."

"There's more," my mother continues. "The surviving members of the ancient pagan coven had to go underground to stay safe from the Christians. The candle holders were kept as family treasures, but we never spoke of their existence outside of the family. We had to keep our heritage a secret for centuries, because the Christians hunted down and persecuted the pagans. However, we each carried the candle holders with us, hidden by our promise not to speak of them.

"Now, in the twenty-first century, the danger's gone. No one wants to execute us, but it's still to our advantage to be careful." My mother nods in Nathaniel's direction. "Who would believe us now anyway? Those who doubt us would ridicule us and those who believe us might cause too much excitement. We don't want the candlesticks to be sold at antique auctions for thousands of dollars. We shy away from attention. We've learned to keep everything on the down low."

"Down so low that I didn't even know about my own family?" I'm feeling somewhere in between thunderstruck and pissed off at the moment. My mother drinks a little more wine and continues. She doesn't look like she feels at all sorry for keeping so many secrets from me.

"I have to laugh at the thought of Arthur's knights. They all charged toward the East, the holy land, ready to do battle and die in their grand pursuit of the Holy Grail. But it didn't even exist anymore because a young girl had stolen it. Then a humble smith had melted it down and made the grail unrecognizable."

"It's a phenomenal story, Mom, but I need time to get used to all this."

"Are you ready, Annabelle, to live up to your heritage, on both sides?"

"I don't know. I need time to think. Time to adjust."

"You don't have time. Whether you're ready or not, the circumstances you've placed yourself in demand that you step up, grow up, be brave, realize your special talents and use them wisely."

"I have special talents?"

"We don't know the extent of them yet, but let me finish the story and you'll learn more about yourself."

"I guess I have no choice." I really do want to know more, even though it's all very overwhelming.

"During the seventeenth century, some of our female ancestors from England traveled to America toward a life where they could have more freedom, where they could escape religious persecution. They made a huge mistake. Take a wild guess! They settled in Salem, Massachusetts."

"No!"

"Yes. Annabelle, you and I are direct descendants of Martha Corey. She was hanged to death as a witch in 1692; insisting on her innocence with the last breath she drew. Her husband, Giles Corey, was pressed to death with stones. He was quite a few years older than Martha, and like her, proclaimed his innocence with his dying words."

"And we're related to her?"

"The candlesticks you see before you were hers."

"And she died during the Salem witch trials."

"She did. Even though she wasn't really a practicing pagan. Giles and his wife Martha *were* innocent. They were followers of the Christian religion, together with the pagan healing tradition. I don't know for certain what Martha's special talents were, just that she was a descendant of the high pagan priestesses from King Arthur's time. She possessed the candlesticks to prove it, too. But she didn't cast spells like the citizens of Salem believed."

"What did she do?"

"She practiced the ancient healing arts and there's nothing magical about them. Healing with herbs and positive thoughts is scientifically possible. And holistic practitioners still have success with these methods today. The only thing Martha was guilty of was helping her fellow humans. Fortunately, she was able to protect the life of her young daughter. Otherwise, you and I wouldn't be sitting here today, Annabelle."

"How did she save her child?"

"No one knows for sure. Once again, a written account would've endangered the lives of those who survived the witch trials. We do know that Giles Corey, her Christian, Caucasian and elderly husband, wasn't the father of her baby. Martha's daughter was a child of mixed race. Some historians believe the infant's father was Native American." My mother looks over at my father who gazes back at her. It's all starting to make sense now.

"We've had to rely on oral tradition, not written documents, which would have been way too dangerous, so no one knows the whole truth. After they hanged Martha, everyone grew even more secretive. It's a strategy that's worked for my family, so we've stuck with it. It's kept us alive."

"And we're all thankful for that, Susannah." My dad nods at her and sips his tea.

"Anyway, after Martha's execution, a friend kept her baby safe. The residents of Salem brutally murdered both Giles and Martha but the silver candle holders somehow remained in the family, passed down to Martha's infant daughter and then to her daughter and so on, through the years, eventually ending up here on our kitchen table."

We stare into the twin flames together.

"Miraculously, they survived and stayed in the family. Someone raised Martha Corey's child and she lived to raise daughters and sons of her own and the line continues, down to us, Annabelle."

"So you're a witch?"

"I'm the descendant of a woman who was accused of witchcraft and executed for it."

"Nathaniel said you were a witch. What spells can you cast?"

"I'm not that kind of witch."

"Okay, what kind of witch are you?"

"Even though I'm descended from pagan priestesses and a woman who was executed for practicing witchcraft, I'm no kind of witch at all. But certain talents prevail, traditionally and genetically."

"What kinds of talents?"

"I can heal with herbs in combination with my thoughts and touch. Unfortunately, I can't cure cancer or anything miraculous like that, but common headaches, anxiety, ordinary stomach aches, insomnia, back and neck pain brought on by stress: piece of cake, or I should say, 'cup of tea.'"

"And the candles?"

"Similar, but instead of making tea from the herbs, I imbed them in the candles and use them for aroma therapy; a few positive thoughts, a fragrant candle, a cup of tea with honey and you're on the road to recovery. I like to think of myself as putting the natural back in supernatural."

Nathaniel speaks up at this point. "There's one more important thing."

"What would that be?" I ask my mother. I feel I'm meeting her for the first time, even though I've known her since I was born.

"I have more intuition than most people, but I can't read minds, predict the future or anything weird like that."

"What a relief, you're not an extreme freak of nature, you just lean a little in that direction."

"I'm not a freak at all, Annabelle. I'm a lot like other moms, just a little more intuitive and I have a green thumb. I'm quite a gardener."

"There's one more thing." Nathaniel casts a meaningful look at my mother. My dad's tipping his chair back, smiling proudly like he's caught a fish that's much bigger than anyone else's.

"Okay, Mom, I'm dying to hear. What else can you do?"

"I can ward off evil," she reluctantly admits, rolling her eyes first in Nathaniel's direction and then in my father's.

"That's all? Meg's mom's a lawyer. Jen's sells real estate. Mine can ward off evil."

"Actually, both Jen's and Meg's moms could use someone like her." Nathaniel hits me with the full brilliance of his gorgeous smile.

Laughing out loud, I forget, for a moment, how pissed off I am. Then I look at my mom and realize none of this is easy for her either. She stares back into my eyes.

"Honey, I have to tell you one more thing and it's a good thing. Nathaniel doesn't even know this. Your brothers don't know. Only your dad and me."

"What?"

"You're a healer."

"I can heal people? How?"

"You can't heal other people. You can heal yourself."

"What?"

"Think about it. Remember the time you jumped off the roof with an umbrella for a parachute when you were a little girl?"

"I sprained my ankle."

"You broke your ankle. I knew it was broken the moment I looked at it, but by the time we got to the emergency room and the doctor x-rayed it, the fracture had already healed itself."

"How do you know that?"

"The doctor looked at the x-ray and told us your ankle was only sprained. He said you had broken the ankle before, but it had healed well. He could see evidence of a former fracture on the x-ray. He told us whoever had set the bone had done a great job. You could hardly tell it had ever been broken."

"And it wasn't an old fracture?"

"No, you had never injured that ankle before, not even a slight twist. There never was a fracture until you jumped off the roof and then your broken bone healed on the way to the hospital. The same thing happens when you cut yourself. The bleeding stops quickly and it heals quickly. You're not immortal and you *can* get seriously injured, so don't do anything stupid or reckless. You just heal faster than other people, a lot faster."

"What about you, Mom?"

"I don't have that gift. Only you do."

"What about Dad and his side of the family?"

"Only you. We have a theory."

"I'd love to hear it."

She ignores my sarcasm and continues. "Your ancestors from both sides of the family tree probably had a similar genetic trait. King Philip was hard to kill. He was shot several times and lived. When the great warrior chief finally died, the English settlers didn't take any chances. To make sure he was dead, they cut off his head and dismembered his body. They displayed his head on a pike at Fort Plymouth for twenty years, to prove to everyone that he was really dead this time. They were worried he might come back to life again, so they went into overkill. Annawan was even more indestructible. He outlived Metacom and continued his violent attacks on the white settlers for months. When they finished him off, they beheaded him, just like they did to Philip."

"To make sure he was dead."

"The great chief Metacom and his tribesman Annawan had the same talent you were born with, Annabelle. Like you, however, they weren't immortal."

"And what about the witches?"

"The witches were also harder to kill than ordinary humans. And the Christians caught onto this. They would test those suspected of witchcraft by holding the accused witch underwater, with her hands and feet tied, for a long period of time. If the woman drowned she was innocent. If she lived she was a witch. Then they'd execute her by hanging her or burning her or both. It was a lose/lose situation."

"All done in the name of Christianity."

"I'm afraid so. Giles Corey was pressed to death beneath piles of stones. When they arrested Giles, the torturers placed him under a wooden plank and piled heavy rocks on top of it. They kept adding more stones. They knew from experience that sometimes the accused witch continued to live and breathe long beyond the time when any normal mortal would have died. It was another test; how many stones would it take to crush them? More than it would take to kill an ordinary human."

"Amazing!" Nathaniel shakes his head. "No one else has this trait. Only Annabelle. It has to be because she broke the curse and the gene is present on both sides of your family."

I'm stunned, exhausted and having difficulty organizing my thoughts enough to speak, but I need to ask, "Why us, Mom? Why did our particular branch of the Blake family end the curse?"

My mother hugs me. "Because my ancestors suffered persecution similar to the Indians' and because we possess unusual powers related to our ancestors' religious beliefs, like the Wampanoags."

"The pagans and the Wampanoags." It's taking a while to sink in.

"The witches and the Indians," Nathaniel adds.

My mother keeps one arm around my shoulders. "People like us, Annabelle, can't perform a purely selfish or evil act, which makes us natural-born martyrs, but it also makes us strong; death can't finish us. Our spirits, our ideas and beliefs live on forever, influencing every generation that comes along. So we were able to break the curse. You were born, the first female Blake in over three hundred years. I have a daughter to inherit the silver candleholders."

Dad walks over to stand behind her and rests one hand on her shoulder. Nathaniel covers my hand with his. My mother tries to reassure me.

"Annabelle, I know it's a lot, way too much to absorb in just one night. Sleep on it. Go into school late tomorrow. We'll talk again any time you want."

I blurt out, "I don't want to be loved because I'm some miracle, because I'm the end of the family curse! I want to be loved because of my ordinary, human qualities."

"Everyone loves you. You're brave and funny and creative. Those are all ordinary, human qualities. When life kicks you in the butt and knocks you over, you get right back up and start running. It's your way of kicking life back." My mom smiles and pats my dad's hand where it still rests on her shoulder.

Dad doesn't return her smile. He looks serious. "Annabelle, not even Joe and Clement know anything about this. Your mother and I kept these secrets because we wanted you to grow up strong and know yourself before you started messing with the supernatural."

My mom joins in. "That's exactly why we waited to tell you. Your father and I wanted you to understand your ordinary human side before you developed your paranormal talents. But now something we didn't anticipate has happened. You met Wyatt and the two of you got involved with a ghost. We have to deal with it and I can help. I've helped Nathaniel before."

"Knowing someone who can ward off evil comes in handy when you're dealing with ghosts," Nathaniel assures me. "I never go into any supernatural situation without consulting your mother first. Imagine channeling a spirit, letting it enter your body and speak with your voice and not being certain whether its intentions are good or evil. I couldn't do it."

My mother shrugs. "That's why they pay me the big bucks."

"When have you been doing all this?" I've always thought she was a stay-at-home mom with a gardening hobby. I know she's quirky, but I never suspected anything like this.

"When I joined the historical society, I met Oliver. He knows all about your dad and his family history. He's been following your story since you were born. He realized right away that you were the first female child born to the Blake family in centuries."

"I feel like everyone knew but me."

"That's a good thing, honey," my dad reassures me. "You weren't ready to hear any of this. You still might not be ready, but now you have to accept it."

My mother continues. "Oliver and I became good friends. He was all over the King Philip's War angle of the story, the history, the truth and the legends. I told him some of my family's story. Oliver introduced me to Nathaniel and I started to accompany him to some of his séances, kind of like a spiritual bodyguard. Is that an oxymoron?"

"I don't know. I'm exhausted. I can't take anymore. I'm going to bed."

I kiss both my parents and Jeff. And then I hug Nathaniel, even though I have mixed feelings about all of them, except Jeff. At least his intentions are pure. Even though I know everyone cares and wants the best for me, I'm still annoyed about all the secrecy.

"There's one more thing you should know," Nathaniel explains. "Annabelle, you and Wyatt have experienced an unusual paranormal connection."

"What are you trying to tell me?" I ask.

"You looked for and found the ghost of the Lonesome Boy, Annabelle. Then Wyatt allowed the dead boy's soul to enter his body. It could happen again, too. Wyatt isn't experienced enough to control the situation. I only hope that when the ghost takes over again, I'll be there to help."

Chapter 14

My Nightmare Becomes a Hero

Monday night, just as my parents and I are getting ready to eat supper, my phone starts vibrating. I dive my fork right into the serving plate of steaming macaroni and cheese and shovel in one quick delicious mouthful. Mom puts her hands on her hips and glares at me. I chew, swallow, grin at her and then whip out my phone.

Dad warns me, "Make it quick. The food will get cold."

"Don't worry. I'm starving. I'll be right back." I duck into the pantry off the kitchen and close the door. "Hi."

Wyatt gets right to the point. "Annabelle, I know you're freaked out by what happened Sunday. Promise me we're still in this together, no matter how crazy it gets."

"It's okay. I need your help. I know that. Just warn me next time. If there *is* a next time."

"I promise I'll ask you first before I channel the ghost.

147

No matter what. We'll talk about it."

"Okay. That's all I'm asking."

"Sorry, I was trying to help."

"I know. Part of this is my fault, anyway. I found this crazy ghost to begin with."

"I feel like I've made things worse instead of better."

"It was pretty scary."

"I'm so sorry."

"No worries. It's all gonna turn out fine." I'm not so sure about this, but I say it anyway. Wyatt sounds completely miserable and genuinely sorry.

"Nathaniel's going to help us, too. He's been through stuff like this before. He knows what he's doing."

"He explained all that to me. Now I gotta go. My mom made supper. And I'm starving. I'll see you tomorrow."

"See you tomorrow."

I click my phone off and join my parents at the table. My mother's mac n' cheese is the best and I eat about three platefuls. Afterwards I watch a little TV while I'm pretending to do homework and then stumble off to bed at eight-thirty.

As the week passes, my only face-time with Wyatt is in school. We find it impossible to be alone together. Then Friday finally arrives and Wyatt has a night game: soccer under the lights. Because of my own busy schedule, I haven't seen a game yet and the soccer team's undefeated. The whole school's going, so when we finally get together in person Wyatt and I will be at the soccer game with a huge crowd of other people. Once again, we won't be able to talk about the drama that's been taking over our lives. For most of the night I'll be in the stands and he'll be on the field. I'm actually relieved we'll be able to act like a couple of normal teenagers at a high school sports event.

Before the big game Jen, Meg and I meet at Meg's house and decorate t-shirts. Meg bought three plain, bright orange t-shirts and some fabric paint. We're going to make super fan t-shirts for ourselves. Meg writes Ryan's name on the front of hers, in huge letters. I write his name on the back of my t-shirt, in small letters, along with a couple of other players' names. But then, in huge capital letters across my chest, I paint the word "SILVER." I outline the letters with black and fill them in with shiny silver paint. Underneath I write his number, "7." Then I carefully print out "Go Tigers!" It looks awesome.

The three of us get into Meg's car and drive over to Connor's to pick him up. When we get there, Meg blasts the horn and Connor runs out wearing a fake fur tiger blanket and a hideous pair of day-glo orange golf pants. His face and bare chest are painted with orange and black stripes. He's got the full tiger goin' on.

When we get to the game, I wave to Oliver and Nathaniel and Oliver's friend Jackson Andrews who are sitting with a lot of teachers, parents and other adults. The Eastfield fans fill the bleachers on our side of the field, right behind the players' bench. It looks like a sea of orange. Everyone's wearing orange sweatshirts and t-shirts with black stripes and letters. Cheerleaders don't cheer at soccer games, so we super fans have to sit together and make a ton of noise.

Over six hundred students are sitting on the Eastfield side, all yelling their asses off, all dressed in orange and black. I forget about my problems and scream and jump up and down with everyone else. The stands shake and the air's filled with roaring and cheering.

The game begins and right away, the opposing team moves the ball down toward our goal. Someone takes a shot and Ryan jumps three feet into the air to make an incredible save. With one arm, he hurls the ball back into the game. No one scores during the first half. I find it hard to breathe because I'm so nervous.

The second half begins and the whistle keeps blowing over and over again. Players from both sides get yellow cards, but no red cards yet. Wyatt's an incredible player and I feel so proud to know him. What he lacks in coordination and sophisticated foot work he makes up for with size, speed, fearlessness and incredible force. During the tensest moment of the game, Ryan blocks a shot and rolls it over to the left defender, who passes it to Wyatt. As soon as the ball touches his foot, he charges all the way down the field. No one can touch him. When he gets within range to shoot, he fires the ball into the goal, his body jackknifed into a V shape, four feet off the ground.

Toward the end of the last quarter, he bounces a shot off the keeper's ear and the poor guy goes down, as the ball whacks against the center of the net, over five feet off the ground. When I can breathe again, I scream his name and hug Meg and Jen on either side of me. All three of us jump up and down like crazy.

Defense does their jobs, too. In the goal, Ryan shuts the opposing team out and Eastfield wins a 3-0 victory, remaining undefeated. When the ref blows the whistle to end the game, I spot Wyatt on the field and run as fast as I can, never taking my eyes off him so I won't lose him in the crowd. As soon as I get close enough, I launch myself and throw my arms around his neck. He hugs me and lifts both my feet off the ground. We stay that way for a few seconds, hugging each other in the middle of a screaming mob of fans.

Then Meg and Jen run over to us with a bunch of other people and we form a massive group hug.

"Are you going to Carolyn Allen's party?" Wyatt shouts into my ear.

"I don't know. I have practice early tomorrow," I yell back.

"C'mon. You have to go, Annabelle. Don't take your own car. Meet me there and I'll drive you home. We'll leave early. I promise."

I hesitate and he makes a puppy-dog face which looks absurd on someone his size. A few minutes ago, he almost amputated someone's ear with a soccer ball, but right now he's melting me with an adorable puppy face.

"Okay, I'll meet you there. But I think I should go home and get my own car. You might want to stay late and celebrate with the team."

"No, no, no," he starts to beg. "I need you to meet me there, Annabelle, and leave with me and wear that t-shirt, pleeeez."

I look down at my chest. There's the word "Silver" spelled out in big, capital silver letters. I crack up laughing. "Okay, if it means that much to you. You're the hero tonight. I guess I can't say no."

He leans down, close to my ear. "I was afraid that if you knew my choices this summer were Eastfield High School or the locked floor of a psychiatric hospital, you wouldn't want anything to do with me."

"Wyatt, you dumbass. It's not that. Only one thing keeps pissing me off. I don't like all the secrets. No more surprises, promise?"

He smiles. "I can't promise that, but I promise only good surprises—only surprises you'll like."

I nod in agreement. It'll have to be enough of a promise for now. Then he hugs me up into a giant bear hug again. I notice, at this point, a lot of people are heading for their cars and the noise has died down. For the past few seconds, we've been able to speak without shouting at each other. I glance around and spot Meg, Jen and Connor glaring at me. Connor rolls his eyes.

"I have to go now. Meg drove me to the game and she's waiting over there."

"See you at the party. I need to head home for a quick shower." Then he runs off to join the rest of the team. They're jumping around pouring Gatorade and water all over each other. Wyatt's kicking his heels up behind him, both fists raised in the air. When he reaches the team someone takes a giant orange jug and tips it upside down, over his head. Gallons of water drench him. Sputtering and laughing, he shakes his head; drops fly all over his team mates. I stare at him and smile, sending Oliver a telepathic "thank you," because Wyatt's here with us and not locked up in a hospital somewhere in New Hampshire, pumped full of powerful antipsychotic drugs.

"C'mon, Annabelle." Connor yanks me back into the moment by pulling on the sleeve of my t-shirt. "Let's go. You'll see Wyatt at Carolyn's. Are you riding with us or not?"

"Yeah, I'm riding with you guys. Race you to the car." I win easily. As I cruise toward the car, my gait smooth, not even out of breath, I think about Wyatt, running for the goal like an unstoppable missile. Against him, I wouldn't have a chance, but running toward the car with my friends behind me is a breeze, a walk in the park. Just as I reach for the passenger side door handle, I feel my phone vibrate. It's a text. From Matt Riley.

R you going to Carolyn's? it reads.

"Yes." I reply.

See you there.

Just then Jen and Meg walk over. I'm in such a good mood that even Matt Riley can't ruin it.

Meg yells, "Let's party! Get in the car!"

Chapter 15

The Party

In addition to me, Jen and Connor, Meg picks up two other kids and we all crowd into the car. The second she switches on the ignition, the music blasts on, super loud. We all start singing along even though no one knows the words. Meg opens the moon roof and Jen sticks her head through and screams at everyone standing around in the parking lot, "See you at Carolyn's!" Then she sits down and we pull out onto the road, singing and dancing as maniacally as we can from sitting positions in a crowded car.

When we arrive at Carolyn's I can see that things are already crazy. At the speed of about a dozen people per minute, kids are heading across her backyard, down into her basement through the open bulkhead doors in back of her house.

Word's gotten out. Her parents aren't home. Connor, Meg, Jen and I use the front door and I end up hanging out in the kitchen for a while, talking to my friend Nicole, who's on the cross country team. There's some pretty good dip getting passed around with potato chips and nachos. So I grab a couple of sodas for Nicole and me. We sit down at the table together and start eating and gossiping about who's dating who on the team and whose race times have been really good so far this season.

After about a half hour, I head for the basement to see if Wyatt's here yet. Maybe he came in through the bulkhead and I missed him.

The chaos in the Allen's basement is generating some serious heat. At the foot of the stairs, a sweaty mosh pit of bodies jumps and jangles and twists to wicked loud rock and roll. Carolyn and her boyfriend are off in one corner stooping over an Ipod dock. I can feel the bass line of the music throbbing in my stomach. Carolyn loves to party and knows what kind of music's best for dancing. I squish my way over to her and say hello. She smiles and nods back at me, her head bobbing to the beat. Trying to talk in this noise would be futile unless you're a good lip reader so I just smile and look around until I spot Jen and Meg.

They're a few feet away, dancing with Connor and Ryan, in the middle of a bunch of people. Wiggling past a few dancing couples; I duck and dodge the waving arms and kicking feet. I'm almost there when someone grabs my arm from behind and yanks on it. I tumble into Wyatt's rock solid chest as he hugs me, kisses my cheek and yells into my ear.

"C'mon, let's dance!"

Wyatt turns out to be a fun person to dance with. One second both his hands are up in the air; the next they're around my waist, turning me so my back's to him, then twirling me so we're dancing face-to-face again. He dips me and spins me until I'm laughing so hard I almost pee.

After about a half hour of dancing madness I scream into Wyatt's ear. "I have to go to the bathroom. Wait for me. I'll only be a minute."

Shoving my way through the crowd, I run upstairs. There's a bathroom in the basement but I figure that's where everyone will go. I don't want to wait in line, so I head for Carolyn's parents' bathroom on the second floor. Sure enough, after hustling up two flights of stairs and running down a short hallway, I find their bathroom and it's unoccupied. They have really good soap in there too, the kind that comes out all foamy when you pump it and it smells like melons.

I can't lollygag though; Wyatt's waiting for me on the dance floor. Flinging open the bathroom door, I come face-to-face with Colleen Foley, the queen of the Juicies. And she doesn't have to use the bathroom. She's looking for me. If I had a nickel for every time Colleen Foley went looking for me, I'd have a nickel. Only tonight. Only now.

Why does she want to talk to me?

After Meg and I showed our movie last year for the big project, Colleen and her friends called me "Ghost Girl." They pretended they were joking with me, but they said it kind of mean. Like they were saying "weirdo" or "outcast" or "girl who'll never be as popular as we are." I don't even care. Who'd want to be friends with them anyway? Not me.

She doesn't call me "Ghost Girl" tonight, though. She calls me Annabelle.

"So, Annabelle, are you and Wyatt Silver together?"

"No, we're just friends." We're not really even friends. We're paranormal business associates, but I'm not going to explain that to Colleen Foley.

"Oh, good. I thought you two might be together because I saw you dancing and stuff and you're always with Wyatt in the hallways at school."

"Nope. Just friends. He sits next to me in history class. And his uncle is friends with my mother. So I have to be nice to him. You know how that is."

"Yeah, the parental connection, totally awkward. Thanks for the info. Have fun!" And she's off.

I head downstairs. In the kitchen, I run into Ryan and Meg who're getting ready to leave.

"Let's get out of here. I'm exhausted. Plus, the booze has appeared," Ryan says.

Looking around, I notice that lots of the kids near us are holding bright red and blue plastic party cups.

"Hurry up and find Wyatt, Annabelle. It's wicked noisy and tons more cars have arrived, just within the last ten minutes." Ryan sounds worried.

"Carolyn must've posted an invitation on Facebook." I actually think I saw it last week.

"Cars are parked all over the place out there."

Every room on the first floor of the house is swarming

with kids. Peeking down the stairs, I notice the basement's packed, too.

"What if one of Carolyn's neighbors calls the police? If the cops show up we could all get kicked off the team," Ryan warns.

It occurs to me that it's not just the soccer players who'll get in trouble if the cops arrive. Tons of people from the cross-country team are here, too; if we all got arrested that would be the end of the season. Plus, my uncle's a cop and he'd be pissed if I get arrested. I'd have to deal with his wrath in addition to my parents'.

"We'll get Jen and Connor. Annabelle, you go find Wyatt and tell him we need to leave, ASAP," Meg says.

Ryan adds, "Hurry. Let's get the hell outta here."

I rush down the steps, telling any cross-country kids I pass along the way, "The cops could show up any second."

People start leaving in herds.

When I reach the bottom of the basement steps, I look around for Wyatt.

Finally, I spot him, over in a corner, talking to Colleen Foley.

Her hand's on his bicep and she keeps rubbing it and smiling up at him. My mouth drops open and I close it quickly. Just then Wyatt looks over at me and even from across the crowded room, I can see the thunderheads rolling into his eyes.

He turns back and smiles at Colleen, bends down and says something into her ear. She kisses him on the cheek and they hug. When they finally let go of each other, he starts shoving his way through the crowd, toward me. I run up the stairs, hoping to catch Meg and hop into her car so we can speed away from here and I never have to see him again.

Colleen Foley! How could he? What's wrong with him? I confided in him. I told him everything about my ghost! I trusted him! I painted his name on my t-shirt! He's just like Matt Riley, only worse!

I spot Ryan and Meg standing at the kitchen door and head toward them as fast as I can. But before I reach them someone grabs my arm and yanks me to a full stop.

Matt Riley. In one hand he's gripping a red plastic party cup and in the other, he's gripping my arm. Fumes of vodka and Axe are wafting off of him and up my nose, so I try not to breathe in too deep.

"Hey, Annabelle, you look really pissed-off."

"Cuz I am."

"About what?"

"Guys like you."

"Hey, lighten up. Let's party. C'mon I'll get you a drink."

"Matt, I really have to go. My friends are waiting for me. Maybe I'll see you around." I try to pull my arm away, but he holds on tight. He's so drunk, he's wobbly but his grip's still strong, almost as strong as his breath.

"Stay, have a drink with me."

"Can't. Gotta get home. I don't wanna get caught and kicked off the team. I'm having a good season."

"Partying's way more fun than running, c'mon. It seems like forever since we hung out."

"Thanks, but I really have to go."

Maintaining his death grip on my arm, he pulls me closer so he can say something into my ear, but he never gets to speak the first word. Out of the darkness behind him a massive hand appears. As it comes down forcefully on Matt's shoulder, he lets go of my arm and spins around. His plastic cup tips and liquid sloshes over the side. Wyatt's face looms above Matt's.

"Read the shirt."

"What?"

"Can you read? Read her shirt."

Matt looks at my shirt and weakly pronounces the word printed across my chest. "Silver."

"Nice job, Matt. Now what do you suppose that means?"

"Sorry, dude, I didn't know she was with you."

"Well she is. Annabelle's my number one fan, so hands off."

Raising both his hands in a gesture of surrender, Matt stumbles backwards. "Okay, okay. I get it."

Because Matt's pretty drunk and he's walking backwards, he trips over someone's foot, bumps into another partier and almost goes down.

I turn to my self-appointed rescuer. "I could've handled that myself you know, Batman."

"Yeah, but we're in a hurry, so I expedited the situation."

"'Read the shirt.' Nice one."

"I think so...I like that shirt. Now let's go. I already told your friends you're coming with me."

"Not a chance."

Wyatt lowers his face until his lips bump against my ear. "Listen carefully, Annabelle, because I'm going to give you a choice."

I can't see his mouth because it's smooshed up against my ear, but he sounds like he's speaking through gritted teeth.

"You can take my hand peacefully and follow me out of this party right now. Or I'll sling you over my shoulder and haul you out of here. I'll announce to everyone that you're too drunk to walk and I'm giving you a sober ride home."

"That's a hell of a choice." I back away from him and stare bravely up into his gunmetal gray eyes. He wraps one of his huge hands around my right arm, ducks his shoulder and aims it toward my waist. I make up my mind.

"Okay, okay. I get it. You can stop going all Neanderthal on me."

Seething hotter than the inside of a parked car in July, I wriggle my arm out of his grip and place my hand in his. He straightens up to his full height, turns around and tows me through the crowd. When we finally reach the door, Wyatt yanks me out into the night.

I wrench my hand out of his and push him away. "I'm not going anywhere with you."

He takes one step toward me. "Why not, Annabelle? I thought we were *friends*."

He pronounces the word "friends" like it tastes bad in his mouth and he needs to spit it out.

"Well, we're not. We're business associates. We're conducting a paranormal investigation together. After it's over, our association is, too." I stand my ground and face off with him from about six inches away.

Wyatt's complexion darkens to the shade of an over-ripe pomegranate. The whites of his full-blown eyes stand out in startling contrast to his slate irises and reddening flesh. His hands are clenched into pale-knuckled fists. If he were thirty years older I'd worry that he was having a heart attack. Aiming a thunderous stare at me, he grits his teeth so hard that his right cheek starts to twitch.

Finally he sucks in a deep breath and blows it out slowly. His face cools to a healthier color. He widens the space between his clenched teeth just enough to speak.

"You told Colleen Foley that we're friends and that you're only nice to me because my uncle and your mom know each other."

"They *do* know each other."

"And that's why we're always together? Because your mother *makes* you *act* like you're my *friend*?"

"All right, so that's not entirely true. We really are friends and it's not just because my mom knows Oliver and it's not *only* because of the ghost any more. We're really friends, but *just* friends. Now can I go find Ryan and Meg before they head home without me? Then you can hook up with Colleen and give *her* a ride home."

He grabs my wrist. "No, Annabelle. You're not getting off that easy. You're gonna talk to me and we're gonna straighten this out now. First of all, we're a hell of a lot more than friends, whether or not you admit it."

"Bullshit."

He ignores me and keeps going. "Second of all. Colleen's been coming on to me since the first day of school. But I *don't* want to hang out with her. And I have *no* plans what-so-ever to hook up with her. The only reason she's left me alone lately is because she thought you and I were together. Now that she thinks we're..." He drops my hand, shoves his face down close to mine again and air-quotes "'*just* friends,' she's never going to leave me alone. Colleen was all over me tonight thanks to you!"

"You loved having her all over you! You kissed her!"

"*She* kissed *me*! On the *cheek*, Annabelle! I was being polite and trying to get away from her."

"Bullshit!"

Wyatt's jaw drops open and he guffaws. Then he shuts his mouth and puts his hand over it. When he uncovers his mouth, an obnoxious smile creeps across his face. I liked him better when he was gritting his teeth and turning red.

"Damn it, Annabelle! You're jealous!"

"Why would I be jealous? On a good day, we're..." I shove my face up close to his and air-quote "'*just* friends.'" I'm not jealous! You're free to make out with Colleen anytime. I'm leaving right now with Meg. So get the hell out of my way!"

But Wyatt doesn't step out of the way. He grabs me by the shoulders and sneers into my face. "D'you know why everyone thinks we're together? Because we're always together! We do everything together!"

"We do not!" Even to myself I sound like a whiny, mad little kid in a playground fight.

"Yes, we do! We do everything together except this…" His hands loosen so they're cupping my shoulders gently, as he stoops down and presses his mouth against mine.

Wyatt's lips feel remarkably soft considering that they were clamped together in barely controlled rage less than a minute ago. He tastes deliciously warm and sweet. I've never been this close to him before. His skin smells like clover and mint growing in a sunlit meadow. Gently, he grips my waist and pulls me closer.

My arms reach up and around his neck even though I didn't tell them to. Our lips stay connected as he hugs me against him and lifts my feet off the ground. Moving backwards, Wyatt slowly staggers over to one of the Allen's lawn chairs, sits down and gathers me onto his lap. I sink into the incredible melting heat of him, better than the first warm spring sun on your face, better than a bubbling Jacuzzi. Body and soul, Wyatt Silver surrounds me. And I can't think anymore. I can only feel.

He's worse. A quiet sound, like a sigh, rolls around deep inside of his throat for a few seconds. Shifting sideways, he nudges me off his lap and we stretch out together, on the lounge chair. I strive to move all of me closer to him, like everything green grows toward the sun.

Gradually, his mouth breaks free from mine for the first time since this madness began and he kisses my cheek, my earlobe and my neck before going back to my lips. The smell and feel and taste of him tumble over and around me, like clothes inside a hot dryer.

Finally, I realize that the night dew from the Allen's lawn has soaked through my pants. At some point we must've rolled off the chair onto the grass. Wyatt's sprawled beside me, still holding me and kissing me. It's a miracle I didn't break a tooth. Gently, I disconnect my mouth from his and he finds his voice, but it's hoarse.

"Friends my ass, Annabelle."

And I smile. My ass is resting solidly on the damp ground but my heart shoots up into the night sky and soars over the moon. We kiss again—but only for a minute because we have to escape before the cops arrive.

Chapter 16

The Surprise

Hand in hand, we run across the street, to where Wyatt's old, white Land Rover's parked. He opens the passenger's side door for me and I jump in. Then he runs around and hops into the driver's seat. Laughing, he leans over and steals one more quick kiss. Then he starts up the engine and a quiet, acoustic tune floats out from the radio. Easing my seat back a little so I can relax, I exhale in relief. Tonight was fun, but the excitement's over now and we're alone together, peaceful; no loud music and dancing mob, no party cups filled with vodka and worrying about the police. No Colleen Foley. No Matt Riley.

"It's still early. Let's go to my house," Wyatt suggests. "We can talk to Oliver. He's been researching our ghost."

"Everyone keeps saying he's my ghost. It's a relief to share him. 'Our ghost,' I like the sound of it."

"I don't think we have a choice. He belongs to both of us now. Anyway, Oliver has some information and some ideas about how to find out more."

"Okay, but I'd like to be in bed by midnight. We have practice at eight tomorrow morning and we're taking the bus into Boston so we can go over the course for the race next weekend—the Coaches' Invitational in Franklin Park."

"Maybe I'll come to the race. Cheer for my girlfriend."

His girlfriend.

That happened fast, but I don't argue. Instead, my lips widen into a smile that surprises even me. I kind of like being referred to as his girlfriend. I could get used to it.

"Don't you have soccer practice on Saturdays?"

"Yes, but I haven't missed one yet this season, so I can skip it. This is important. I've never seen you run, except for just now, dodging the cops."

"Not really. I didn't see any cops. We escaped early enough."

"Just as I was opening the door for you, I saw a flashing blue light over on Prospect Street, heading toward Carolyn's."

"No way! We really were dodging the cops?"

"Yup, sweet little Annabelle Blake, varsity athlete, honor student, running from the law."

"Not quite an honor student."

"That's right. I've noticed how you never know when there's a test or a quiz in History class, which probably means you don't study much."

"See, I'm a real bad-ass…poor organizational skills and caught on video tape fleeing the scene of a crime."

"Try *no* organizational skills. And lucky for you there's no videotape. I'm the only eye witness. And my lips are sealed." He lets go of the steering wheel with one hand and draws a finger across his lips. Then smiles. "We're here."

Wyatt pulls into Oliver's driveway, shifts into park and turns the engine off. Before I can open the door, he puts his hand on my shoulder. "Hold on a minute, Annabelle."

Half a second after his lips form these words they're on mine like he's starving. Like he hasn't kissed me in a year. I hug my arms around his neck and pull him as close as I can in the cramped front seat.

He leans over me and at the same time, reaches down with his left hand and pushes the lever to lower the back of my seat. It plummets down with a jerk and he lifts his mouth up to laugh before he places it back on mine again, melting me like a chocolate bar in someone's pocket on a summer's day. I move a few inches to the right, to make room for him beside me. He tries to climb onto my seat, struggling to find a comfortable position.

All through this whole time he's still kissing me. Our lips hardly ever lose their connection. He can't get his arms around me or find a place to put his legs. We readjust ourselves a couple of times, but it's way too difficult for someone who's six foot three to make out in a vehicle. Either Wyatt's butt or his foot or something hits the horn and we jolt apart.

Oliver's front door opens and Jeff runs out of the house, barking his head off.

"Nice one, Romeo. Try explaining this to your uncle."

"Hey, even Oliver thinks we're together. Which means he won't be surprised if he catches us kissing."

"Yeah, but a simple kiss doesn't blast the horn like that."

"Good point. I guess I better cool it when we're in the car."

"Right here in the driveway, too. What will the neighbors say?"

"They'll say that Oliver Finn's nephew is one lucky dude."

I punch him in the arm.

"Ouch." He rubs his arm for a second, grins and points toward the house.

Oliver's standing on the front walkway with Jackson and they're both laughing their asses off. They wave to us then turn and walk back in with Jeff following, wagging his humongous tail.

I push my tousled hair back, away from my face, and we both get out of the car. Wyatt helps me smooth my damp, rumpled clothes back into their rightful places, picks a couple of blades of grass out of my hair and chuckles. Putting his arms around my waist, he steals one more kiss.

While we're walking through the front door together, he says, "I have a little something planned for tonight. Nathaniel's going to help me. It's all gonna be good."

"What's all going to be good?" Nathaniel calls out, from inside the living room.

"You know, Nathaniel, tonight. We're going to try it out—the séance."

"*What?* I'm not ready for this." Shoving Wyatt's hand off of my waist, I try to turn around and run back outside. But he stops me by blocking the doorway to the hall.

"Just hear us out, Annabelle. Come in and talk to Oliver and Nathaniel. It's not as weird as it sounds."

I'm having trouble denying him anything tonight; especially when I look into his face and read the history of his loneliness.

"I'll listen, but I'm not promising anything."

Nathaniel speaks up. "We talked to your mother. She'll come over if you want her to."

"No, I'll be okay. I just need a minute. You guys really sprung this on me. I feel trapped. Like all of you were lying in wait and everyone knows everything except me. Even my mother's in on it. You can start explaining any time now."

Nathaniel begins. "I promise nothing bad will happen. I've done this kind of thing tons of times before. We'll all sit right here."

I look around Oliver's ordinary living room and see five comfortable chairs, arranged in a circle. One of the chairs is Nathaniel's wheelchair and he's already sitting in it. Jeff's lying over by the fire, snoozing.

Nathaniel continues. "We don't need to hold hands or sit around a table or anything like you see in the movies. We can even keep our eyes open. All of us will focus, however, on the boy from Wild Wood Hospital, the ghost you saw in room 209. Oliver can give you some background. He and Jackson have been researching the events surrounding the closing of the hospital in 1986. They think they've uncovered some information related to what you've been experiencing, Annabelle."

Nathaniel nods in Oliver's direction and Oliver starts in.

"I remember when the hospital closed, although there wasn't a lot in the newspapers. It wasn't a big story. There were some problems with government funding in the early eighties. I searched the archives of the local papers from around the time the hospital closed down for good. About a month before the official closing, a patient died; a thirteen-year-old boy. There was no investigation into his death. He must have died of natural causes. Only his young age made his death unusual and noteworthy."

"He was only thirteen?" It seems so tragically young.

"Yes. The obituary was short and pretty uninformative, though. Probably because his family had abandoned him at the hospital. That happened a lot. Families just dumped their mentally-ill relatives off and never visited them. Never saw them again. We think this boy's parents admitted him to the hospital and then neglected him, even leaving him to be buried by his caretakers when he died."

"I remember reading about stuff like that when Meg and I were doing the research for our film."

"Anyway, I assume the poor boy had no connection with his family anymore, so there was no one to kick up a fuss when he died. The event of his death wasn't considered newsworthy. The hospital probably tried to keep the whole thing pretty low key. Jackson and I looked at all of the local papers' online archives. We only found one article about the incident. Evidently, an anonymous source leaked something to the press. Someone who worked at the hospital contacted a reporter and told him the dead boy had shared a room with a violent patient who may have killed him."

"That's pretty shocking and I would think newsworthy."

"I know. This one reporter latched onto the story and tried to make something out of it. But he couldn't prove much of anything. There was no record that the dead boy had even had a roommate. The article ended by revealing the only officially documented fact about the child's death. He had died during an epileptic seizure, a condition for which he was being treated at the hospital. The seizure could have been the result of a violent encounter with another patient. But nobody could find any evidence or proof. The dead boy's name was Daniel Warren."

"Do you think that Daniel Warren is our ghost?"

"Hold on, Annabelle, let me finish."

"Sorry. I know I get too impatient sometimes."

"It's okay. We're all anxious to uncover the facts. Shortly after Daniel's death, a writer from *Boston Magazine* decided to do a story about New England's psychiatric hospitals and he visited Wild Wood. He exposed the overcrowding problem and the administrators' disastrous solution. The hospital was housing nonviolent patients and violent patients in the same rooms. The whole situation had been kept pretty quiet until then. Whether this practice directly contributed to Daniel Warren's death or not, the article drew attention to the hospital. State investigators stepped in and found out that somebody in charge had made some bad decisions. As a result of the investigation, Wild Wood lost a lot of its government funding, along with some grant money, and the hospital soon closed."

Oliver's story makes sense when I think about what's been happening with Wyatt and me and our ghost. So I try again. "You still haven't answered my question, Oliver. Do you think I found the spirit of Daniel Warren?"

The Lonesome Boy might finally have a name.

Nathaniel answers me. "We want to contact the ghost and ask him. Oliver, Jackson and I have been talking with Wyatt and we want to try channeling his spirit through Wyatt again, here tonight in a controlled setting. We want to ask your ghost some questions."

At this point my curiosity wins out. Fascination with the paranormal got me into this predicament and recent events have turned my passion into a love/hate relationship. But the love side still thrills me. I've never felt so enthusiastic about a school project before or since Meg and I filmed at Wild Wood. And now I want to know more about the haunting. My mother feels okay about me participating in the séance and I trust Oliver. He and Jackson make an excellent research team. Nathaniel has a lot of experience with the paranormal and he's a good mentor for Wyatt. I know Oliver would never let his nephew do anything truly dangerous, so I decide I'm in.

"Okay, let's try it. Let's contact Daniel."

"Great." Nathaniel smiles. "First I have to put Jeff out in the van. He hates ghosts."

Jeff lifts his head and growls suspiciously at Nathaniel.

"It's okay, buddy. Nothing bad's gonna happen."

After this reassurance, the dog stands up and starts barking. Nathaniel shushes him and gestures for him to go with Wyatt.

"Go on, boy. Follow Wyatt."

Jeff obeys and together they lope out to the van, which is parked under a single streetlight, next to the curb in front of Oliver's house. Standing at the window, I stare into the darkness and watch as the giant beast climbs into the van and offers one more bark of protest before he quiets and Wyatt comes back inside.

Behind me in the living room, Oliver turns off the lights. The fire's our only source of illumination. Enthroned in his electric wheelchair, Nathaniel sits with the flames at his back, Wyatt to his right and me to his left. Oliver and Jackson complete our circle. The logs in the fireplace crackle and shudder as the hellish spikes devour them. Lit from behind by the glowing flames, Nathaniel's curls form a halo around his shadowed face. He looks like an angel from Hell.

In a solemn voice he begins.

"Wyatt, focus inward and think about how it felt to let someone else in. Where did you go?"

"I was here but not here, gone but not completely gone.

174

Even though I possessed none of my five senses, I was aware of what was happening and what was being said."

"How did you feel?"

"I wasn't inside my body. I felt like fog. Like an icy mist. Then finally like snow. But the cold didn't affect me because I wasn't inside of my skin. *He* was."

Wyatt's pupils roll up and disappear. I lean across Nathaniel, coming part way out of my chair. Nathaniel touches my wrist and warns me with his eyes, so I sit back down but still lean forward, toward Wyatt.

His eyes open wider. With only the whites showing, they look like small shiny half moons in his ashen face. Wyatt's mouth grows slack and falls open. Then he slumps down in the chair, completely limp. His head lolls to the side. I realize his soul has left his body and I jump up. Nathaniel grabs my wrist.

Alarmed by the sight of this horrifying transformation, I start toward the door. I'm desperate to quit this nightmare. Nathaniel's grip tightens, reminding me I can't abandon Wyatt. Wherever he is. When Nathaniel finally lets go of me, I collapse back into the chair.

Suddenly, he speaks. Rather *it* speaks, using Wyatt's voice.

"I want to touch her."

"Annabelle, switch seats with Oliver. It's okay. You're safe and so is Wyatt."

Nathaniel gives instructions with an assuredness I suspect he doesn't feel.

With a nod of his head he sends a calm look at Oliver

who appears to be very freaked out.

Oliver and I follow his directions and trade seats. Now he's on Nathaniel's left and I'm on Wyatt's right, except Wyatt isn't Wyatt anymore. He turns to me, his eyes sunken into the dark hollows of their sockets. Thousands of prickly goose-bumps swarm over my skin and I shiver. Wyatt reassures me in a voice that seethes up from his throat and out of his mouth.

"I won't hurt you, Annabelle," he hisses.

Feeling like I'm in the presence of a monster, I'm both revolted and petrified at the same time. I want to run so badly that my feet are twitching. But then I remember the tragic story of young Daniel and strive for self-control.

"I know, but I'm still scared." Seeking reassurance, I look at Nathaniel. He looks intensely serious but still calm.

"He wants to be near *you*, Annabelle, so you should ask the questions. It's all right. I'm here to protect you and Wyatt."

My voice quivers. "Is your name Daniel Warren?"

"In life I couldn't speak."

I try again. "Is your name Daniel?"

"I didn't know any words or names."

"What did you know?"

"Nothing. My world was nothing but a storm of random sounds."

"What was it like to live in your world?"

"Torture. Confusion. Hell. My world was hell."

"I don't want you to feel like you're in hell. I want to help you. I want to know what happened to you when you were alive. Can you remember ever hearing the name Daniel?"

"Daniel," he repeats. "I have Wyatt's words because I'm inside Wyatt's mind, but it's all completely new. And confusing."

"Try to remember."

"I'm trying, but that day with you, Annabelle, in the basement, was the first time I have ever spoken to anybody."

He pauses. A grimace contorts the ghoulish version of Wyatt's face.

"I think I've heard the name Daniel said aloud, maybe once."

He grows silent for a moment and I observe how he looks like Wyatt, but different than Wyatt, in a subtle way.

Daniel's eyes are darker and set in hollows of gray. His face looks thin and pale with no trace of Wyatt's healthy tanned complexion. Sharp, slanted lines define his cheekbones. When Wyatt is Wyatt, even his face looks well-fed and muscular, but with Daniel hiding inside of him, he looks gaunt and hungry. Staring at the dead boy, I become lost, imagining what life must have been like in room 209.

Suddenly, he springs up to his full height, like a monstrous jack-in-the-box, and lunges at me.

Grabbing my arms, he pins me to the chair. Literally frozen in place by his icy grip, I sit like a statue, paralyzed with shock. Oliver shoots up like a rocket and Nathaniel zooms closer to Wyatt's other side. Both men grab his arms and attempt to pull him away from me.

I call out, "No, it's all right. I'm okay, just cold." My teeth are clicking together uncontrollably.

Daniel moves his hands up to my shoulders, stares into my face and speaks. "You're my only hope."

I can barely get the words out, my teeth are chattering so hard. "I want to help you but I don't know how."

"Go back to the hospital."

And he's gone. Wyatt's hands move down. As he caresses my bare arms, they grow warmer and he hauls me up, out of the chair, into his arms. Staggering backwards, he collapses into his chair and pulls me onto his lap. Cradling me like a child, he kisses my hair and whispers my name.

Chapter 17

We Plan a Field Trip

Oliver speaks first. "Are you two all right?"

My hand trembles as I smooth my hair back and feel drops of moisture; Daniel's tears. Or are they Wyatt's?

"I'm freezing." I stand up and look down, into Wyatt's disoriented eyes.

Jackson pulls his sweater off and tugs it over my head before I can protest. It feels warm from having been worn by an actual living person who isn't as cold as a corpse. Plus it's huge on me and really cozy. "Thanks so much. This feels really soft."

"It should. It's cashmere. Nice shirt by the way, Annabelle. I hate to cover it up."

I crack a weak smile because now I'm thinking about how silly I must've looked, with Wyatt's name painted on my chest during the whole dramatic scene of the séance.

"Don't knock it. I love that shirt." Wyatt speaks aloud with his own voice for the first time since we dimmed the lights and began.

Jackson grins. "Is that what you were doing out in the driveway earlier, showing Annabelle how much you like her shirt?"

Oliver changes the subject. "Everyone must be starving. Jackson, there's a plate of sandwiches in the fridge. We should put on water for tea, too. We all need something warm." Then he adds, "I'm going to run upstairs and get Wyatt a sweatshirt. I can see the gooseflesh on his arms from here and he's shivering. I'll be back down in a second. So we can make some plans."

We're now sitting in a much different circle around the kitchen table, sipping hot tea and eating cheddar cheese and alfalfa sprout sandwiches on whole grain bread. Even after a close encounter with the undead, Wyatt's uncle insists on healthy and organic food. Nathaniel makes a bunch of wisecracks about needing a cheeseburger and fries and Oliver good-naturedly shrugs them off, as usual. Wyatt's half way through his third sandwich before he finally joins in the conversation.

"So what's the plan?"

We all know he's referring to our field trip to the psychiatric hospital. Oliver suggests, "How about next Saturday?"

I say, "I have a race, in Boston, in the morning, but it'll be over by noon."

"I'm skipping practice to go to Annabelle's race. After that I'm free."

Nathaniel announces, "I'm in. I wouldn't miss this for anything. Besides, you'll need me even though I'll have to wait by the van. I'm the paranormal expert."

Jackson adds, "I wouldn't miss it either. I can help Oliver look through those files. Besides, I'm a psychologist and Wild Wood was a psychiatric facility. My background might come in handy."

I'm the only one who's been to the hospital and seen everything first hand. "It's as if everyone fled in the middle of the night. The bedding is still on the beds. There are curtains on the windows, and yes, file cabinets that might have files still in them. Everything has been sitting there for over twenty years."

"Just waiting for us to come along and investigate." Oliver smiles.

"My uncle's feeling a historian's enthusiasm for firsthand exploration and discovery. He loves the *story* part of history," Wyatt says.

"Wyatt's right. This has really piqued my interest. Let's meet here at three in the afternoon on Saturday. We'll take Jackson's SUV and Nathaniel's van. Bring flashlights in case we end up staying until after dusk. The days are getting shorter and we don't want to be fumbling around in the dark. I'll bring a camera. Don't be late."

"C'mon, Annabelle. It looks like you'll be needing a ride home." Nathaniel points his thumb in Wyatt's direction. He's sprawled across the table with his head resting on one outstretched arm, his face beside his empty plate. He starts to snore. Jackson and Oliver rise at the same time, so they can wake Wyatt up and help him climb the stairs.

When we get to my house, Nathaniel doesn't come inside. It's late and we're both exhausted. I kiss him on the cheek and Jeff on the top of his head and run up the driveway and into the house. The kitchen's dim, silent and empty. Standing at the window, I watch Nathaniel drive away before I turn off the outside light.

My parents are already in bed, so I don't wake them. Mom will be up before me tomorrow, like always. She'll pack me some snacks and Gatorade for practice and we'll talk for a few minutes before I leave, running late as usual.

Thinking these reassuring thoughts I head up to my room, which is a mess. There's a small TV with a built-in DVD player in my room. I like to watch movies sometimes before I fall asleep. The last ten movies I watched are stacked on my dresser and their cases are all over the floor.

As I kick aside a bunch of empty DVD cases, my foot gets caught in the strap of a sports bra. I disentangle myself and flop onto the bed, still in my clothes. Peeling off my jeans, I keel over onto the bed. I'm so snug and warm inside Jackson's sweater that I decide to sleep in it. Pulling the soft garment down as far as it will go, I tuck my bare legs under the quilt, and conk right out.

During the blackest part of the night something wakes me up out of a dead sleep. The sound of plastic clicking against plastic. Someone's shuffling through all those empty DVD cases. The fine hairs on the back of my neck perk up and I shiver, even though I'm still bundled up in Jackson's sweater and covered with a soft, thick quilt. The glowing numbers on the clock tell me it's midnight.

"Mom?" I ask, even though I know it isn't my mother tiptoeing across my mess, toward the bed. I know I'm the only living human in the room.

"Daniel," I beg. "Please, you're scaring me. Let me sleep. I have to get up early. I promise I'll see you next Saturday."

He stirs the curtains hanging on either side of the closed window. Then silence and cold fill the room. With Jackson's sweater pulled down over my butt and the quilt up around my ears, I fall back to sleep.

Chapter 18

Truth Night

I dream that Wyatt's holding me. He reaches under my shirt and places his palms against the skin on my lower back. One hand feels warm and alive, the other is deathly cold. He kisses me and his lips feel cracked and dry. The taste of dirt fills my mouth and a handful of plump, thin-skinned maggots, ready to split from the pressure of their oozing guts, squirm across one cheek and down my chin to my neck. I push him away, gasp for air and wake up screaming.

My mother runs in, with Dad right behind her. When they realize there's no intruder trying to haul me out my bedroom window, my father goes back to bed. I tell Mom it was just a nightmare.

"I'll stay here until you fall back to sleep, Annabelle. What were you dreaming about?"

"Just a generic nightmare, nothing specific or memorable." What am I supposed to answer? "I dreamed that while I was kissing Wyatt, he turned into a decomposing corpse."

I don't think my mother's ready to hear that. She's no fool, though; she knows me well and can probably tell I'm holding something back. But she keeps quiet and doesn't pressure me. Instead, she sits on the edge of the bed and watches over me until I drift off. When I finally fall back to sleep, I dream of nothing.

My alarm goes off way too early. My mother apologizes over breakfast on Saturday, before I even leave for practice. She makes no excuses and promises me that in the future she'll share with me any plans for séances and other assorted supernatural adventures that Oliver, Nathaniel or Wyatt dream up.

I need the truth and I need everyone to stop deciding when they should tell me stuff and how much they should tell me. From now on I want to know everything right away, as soon as everybody else knows it. I need to be an equal partner in this paranormal adventure; after all, I found Daniel in the first place. If it wasn't for me, we wouldn't be in this situation.

Nobody has actually lied to me, but nobody's been telling me the whole truth, either. I'm ready to demand the entire story from everyone. And I'm going to start immediately.

During Saturday morning's cross-country practice, Wyatt texts me, asking me if he can come over. *Do you want to hang out tonight?*

On the bus ride home from Boston I finally get a chance to reply. *Only if we can talk and you tell me everything.*

I promise. No more secrets or surprises. I'm sorry.

Be there at eight. And bring popcorn, with real butter.

After a long, hot shower, I put on my favorite green sweater and a pair of soft, worn-out jeans. Then I blow-dry my hair, straighten it and flick on some mascara. Next I choose a flavored lip gloss from my impressive collection: honey-vanilla, delicious. Wyatt arrives right on time, carrying a box of popcorn and a half stick of real butter. We pop the popcorn in the microwave and I melt the butter in a small pan on the stove. Wyatt pours it evenly over the bowl of popcorn. Grabbing a salt shaker and a couple of Gatorades, we head down the stairs to the basement.

Because I want to talk seriously with him, I choose a movie I've seen before, *Pride and Prejudice*, based on the novel by Jane Austen, who's my favorite author. Wyatt deserves to suffer through the ultimate chick flick, British accents and all. Plus, Keira Knightly is gorgeous, brunette and flat-chested. She gives me hope.

Wyatt is either too gentlemanly or too remorseful to complain and he sits through scene after scene of drama and witty conversation, waiting patiently for even a moment of sex or violence which never happens. Finally, as Mr. Darcy awkwardly begins to make his feelings for Elizabeth Bennett clear on the big screen, I begin my cross-examination.

"We need to talk."

He responds by lying down and pulling me over beside him. I push him away and sit up.

"Wyatt. Get up. I'm serious."

"So am I." He's still lying down and he pulls on my arm, attempting to persuade me to cuddle with him.

"We can't talk if our lips are smooshed together."

"Damn. I love it when our lips are smooshed together."

"C'mon. I mean it."

"Okay, okay, go ahead. You want to talk. So talk." He sits up.

"The day that you channeled Daniel for the first time you didn't tell me everything."

"What do you want to know?"

"What did you see? What did you feel?"

"Let's start with what I *did* tell you. When I saw you for the first time in History class, I saw Daniel, too. I felt a powerful connection to you both. I kept trying to talk to you but you kept blowing me off. Then that day in the cafeteria, I watched Connor touch you and I had to make a move. After that things got even more complicated."

"Complicated? How?"

"I wanted to tell you how I felt about you. More importantly, though, I needed to tell you that I could see Daniel. But I didn't want to scare you. Most of all, I didn't want you to think I was a freak."

"I had a ghost following me around. Doesn't that place *me* in the freak category, too?"

"Not quite as freakish as me. At least that's how I felt at the time. Now I realize you're a huge freak."

I punch his arm and not playfully. "Stay serious, Silver."

"Okay, okay, I'll stay serious. Just don't hit me again. I think you left a bruise."

He rubs his arm and continues. "That Sunday in your basement, I let Daniel in."

"What do you mean by you let him in?"

"I had a feeling that if I held you in my arms and opened my mind and my soul to him, he'd take over. And he did. I'm sorry I didn't warn you. If you're still mad, I know I deserve it."

The fact that Wyatt doesn't qualify his apology with any excuses makes me feel better. After all, how could he have explained? It's all so farfetched. I'm still having difficulty understanding, but I'm getting there. I know that I really want to be in this together with Wyatt.

"Promise me one thing."

"What?"

"I need to always know if it's really you or if it's Daniel taking over. Don't ever surprise me again like you did the first time."

"I promise I'll never do that again, Annabelle."

"Thank you. At least now I'll be able to tell the difference as soon as you touch me."

"How?"

"When you're you, you're warm. Incredibly warm all over. You're like a human Jacuzzi. I sunk into your lap last night and felt this wonderful melting feeling."

"Here, sink into it right now." He tries to pull me into

his lap and it's tempting, but I push him away.

"No, we're talking. This is serious. When you channeled Daniel, you felt unnaturally cold. Last night, when we were kissing, you felt really warm."

"This is torture, sitting here with you, talking about kissing and looking at you and not touching you. You look so cute. Mmmmm." He breathes in. "You smell like butter and salt and vanilla, like a popcorn flavored sugar cookie. I need to cuddle with you, just a little. C'mon, Annabelle."

"No, because I'm trying to make an important point here. *You* were in control when we were kissing. Daniel didn't take over. We can't be in this relationship and kiss and be close if I have to worry about Daniel taking over. I need to know that it's *you* I'm kissing, not someone who's been dead for more than twenty years. And last night I knew. You didn't let him in. I would've felt the cold if you had."

"You're right. I kissed you, not Daniel. Both times I let Daniel in, it was a conscious decision. He can't just take over, not when I'm kissing you, not any other time. I'm in control and I'll never surprise you again. Don't worry."

"That means when he *did* take over, you had to allow it. You had to *let* him, maybe even invite him. Tell me more about last Sunday, when you channeled Daniel during the thunderstorm."

Wyatt sighs and starts confessing everything. "I wanted it to happen. I staged things so it would happen. I purposely got you alone and held you and thought about it. I focused on letting Daniel in."

"What did it feel like?"

"It scared the hell out of me. I felt like I was dead, but I wasn't really dead. I still knew what was happening but I didn't perceive it with my five senses. Daniel had those. He controlled my body and my mind, the actual gray matter of my brain. I sort of half-traded places with Daniel. He got to be me, but I wasn't him. I was still myself, but without my body. I'm doing my best to explain."

"You're doing a great job."

"Without physically hearing or seeing anything that happened between you and Daniel, I still knew everything. I felt aware and I remembered what happened afterwards. When Daniel finally left my body, I felt hungry right away and about an hour later I was exhausted. Nathaniel told me that would happen every time, so I have to be careful; like I shouldn't drive when the exhaustion sets in."

"No operating heavy machinery?"

He grins. "Right, any more questions?"

"Can you take back your body whenever you want to?"

"That's the tricky part. Nathaniel and I are working on it. Both times I let Daniel in, he left on his own. I don't know if I could reclaim my body, just because I really want to. Nathaniel thinks I can, but I haven't had the chance to try it yet."

"You're scaring me now. I need to know if you can. It's important. Doesn't it frighten you?"

"Of course. The worst part was how cold I felt, cold like the grave, cold like death, freezing cold through and through, down into my bones, down into my soul."

I shiver just thinking about it, because I, too, have felt the cold. Afterwards, only contact with people who care about me could warm me up: Oliver, Jackson, Nathaniel, my mother, contact with the living. When he notices I'm shivering, Wyatt wraps me in his arms. "We're in this together, right, Annabelle?"

"Yes, we're in this together, as long as you keep telling me the truth, no more secrets and no more surprises."

"I promise." And we seal the deal with a kiss, while on the TV screen two lovers from another century kiss, too.

Chapter 19

Room 209 Again

The weekdays pass by quickly because I'm busy training hard for the race on Saturday. Wyatt's soccer schedule's crazy, too, and we're both exhausted from all the fresh air and exercise. Every afternoon, I tear through the forests and paths of Eastfield, releasing all of my pent-up feelings. While my feet thump the ground in a fast rhythm, I imagine Wyatt kicking the crap out of any soccer ball that comes near his size twelve feet.

During school, we walk to class and eat lunch together, but we're always in a hurry. Every night we talk to each other for about a half hour on our cell phones but it never seems like enough. We won't have any time to spend together until the weekend and I miss him so much.

* * * *

At the race on Saturday, finally seeing Wyatt face to face pumps me way up. I tie my personal record and fly into his arms, practically knocking him over, because I don't slow down even after I cross the finish line. My parents are both at the race, as usual, but I'm surprised to see Oliver and Jackson. Oliver congratulates me on a great race and makes sure to talk to a lot of other kids on the team, too, because he knows them from one of his History classes or the student film club he sponsors.

No one says anything about the trip to Wild Wood that's scheduled to happen later.

Finally the track meet ends and we all head for the parking lot. Oliver's ahead of us, walking toward his car with Jackson and Wyatt. Turning around to wave at me, he calls out, "Great race! See you at three, Annabelle."

As I wave back, my stomach jumps with anticipation. Usually I feel calm after a race, especially when I'm pleased with my performance. But there's nothing calm about my mood right now.

At home, while my mother and I are eating lunch together, Mom asks if she can come to Wild Wood with us. The fact that she asks and doesn't tell me she's coming makes me think it'll be okay. So she calls Oliver to run it by him.

"I'll stay near the van with Nathaniel and Jeff. I don't want to crowd Annabelle. I just want to be close by and offer support. I'll only give advice if someone asks for it."

She aims a meaningful look at me and I nod yes.

Shortly before three, my mother and I pull up to the curb in front of Oliver's house, behind Nathaniel's van and Jackson's hybrid SUV. We organize ourselves into two groups. Mom rides with Oliver and Jackson, in Jackson's car, and Nathaniel, Jeff, Wyatt and I follow in the van. I love riding in the back with Jeff because he's the best cuddler in the whole world.

When we arrive at the deserted back road, Nathaniel parks in the same exact spot where Meg and I parked almost a year ago. After bolting out of the van, Jeff lifts his giant rear leg against a nearby tree trunk and releases a minor flood. Then he starts pacing back and forth, twitching his ears, sniffing the air and keeping watch. My four legged wingman is ready for action. Jackson sets up a canvas soccer-mom-style folding chair for my mother and Nathaniel cruises over to her side in his wheelchair. They settle in to wait and my mom waves her cell phone in the air, reminding me to call if there's any trouble.

Nathaniel warns us one more time.

"Remember, Daniel's spirit will be very powerful here because it's the scene of his death. Be alert and careful."

Jeff, Oliver, Jackson, Wyatt and I head across the huge meadow and then through the woods toward the chain-link fence. Oliver's and Jackson's lightweight backpacks hold the minimal equipment we'll need and leave their hands free for climbing. Both guys are in their fifties, plus neither is exactly a fitness freak. But they make it over the fence okay. As Wyatt reaches for my hand, to lead me toward the fence, I pull away, turn back, rush over to Jeff and hug his big neck. He starts to whine and he never whines. I don't think he wants me to go, but I have to.

Wyatt puts his arm around me and leads me away from my canine buddy. We jog over to the fence together. After Wyatt climbs over, he reaches up to catch hold of me as I jump down and land, on the property of the Wild Wood Psychiatric Hospital. Once again.

Daniel travels on the wind. The late afternoon air lies still and unseasonably warm all around us, until he speeds by, bringing the winter with him.

I lead everyone across the fields and through the rows of abandoned graves in the cemetery. Finally we duck into the basement, using the same window Meg and I used a year ago.

On the first floor, the waning sunlight streams through the broken windows and elongates our shadows in the narrow, intersecting halls. Wyatt grips my hand tightly and clicks on his flashlight, to illuminate the dark corners the fading daylight can't reach. We find the first office and walk in. Oliver looks so excited I expect him to shout, "Eureka!"

But he doesn't. He just smiles.

Jackson and Oliver set up shop and begin pulling open the metal drawers of the file cabinets, searching through files and folders and taking notes. They're looking for any information they can find about the life and death of Daniel Warren. Wyatt and I make weak attempts to help, but it isn't the type of research we're really interested in. Thirsting for action, we both want to head upstairs to room 209. I try to be patient.

Jackson finally finds several folders with Daniel's name on the tabs and opens one. "Look, here are some records and notes mostly written by a nurse: Mary McGuire. She was assigned to take care of Daniel from 1981, shortly after he was admitted to the hospital, until his death in 1986."

He hands the papers to me.

"We didn't look through any of the files when we were here last fall. Meg and I were in a hurry to go upstairs and find the Lonesome Boy."

I give the papers back to Oliver who holds onto them carefully. Then he begins to skim through the neatly-printed words. As Oliver scans the papers in his hands, he summarizes the contents out loud for us.

"These are some very detailed notes regarding his day-to-day routine. Not only did Daniel Warren have epilepsy, but he couldn't speak and was also being treated for anxiety and insomnia."

"Wow." I can't believe we're finally finding some real information about the legendary Lonesome Boy.

Oliver continues. "Just weeks before his death, they moved him from the pediatric wing of the hospital to room 209 on the second floor. According to Mary McGuire's notes, his seizures had become more frequent and more violent, upsetting the already agitated patients in the children's wing. Plus the patients on the second floor were older, not young children, but teenagers and adults and Daniel was thirteen, closer to adolescence than to childhood. The hospital was crowded so he had to be placed in a room with another patient. Some of the patients on the second floor were violent and often wore restraints, including Daniel's cellmate, whose name isn't mentioned in Mary McGuire's notes."

Oliver comments, "During the investigation, no one could find any evidence that Daniel had a roommate. Someone must've hidden these files when the authorities were looking into Daniel's death."

Jackson offers his opinion. "Back in the eighties, not all data was stored on computers. The first search engine wasn't invented until the nineties. It was much more difficult and time-consuming to do research then. Maybe the people conducting the investigation couldn't go through *all* the files. There's so much here: tons of file cabinets, a lot of offices. They couldn't read everything. Some of these documents probably got overlooked. This is just a daily log, kept by a nurse; not Daniel's doctor."

I can see his point. I'm already tired of standing around in the office, looking through files and listening to Jackson's and Oliver's theories about Daniel. I would've given up easily if I had to read through all of this boring stuff.

Oliver's not bored, however. He photographs the contents of each file meticulously, while Jackson takes notes. The camera flashes about every two or three minutes, as we read the contents of each folder, then step back so Oliver can take more pictures. Writing rapidly in handwriting so messy only he's able to read it, Jackson scribbles indecipherable lines in a spiral notebook. We stack the documents we've already read on a nearby desk, intending to put them back in the files after we finish. Not until then will we move on to the next office. It seems to take forever; there's information about every bite of food Daniel took and every dosage of every medication. Wyatt and I keep shooting each other looks. We're dying of boredom.

Two tall stacks of folders and documents are heaped on the dusty old desk when Oliver announces it's time to move on. Wyatt picks up one precariously piled tower of paperwork and takes two steps toward the file cabinet. Suddenly, a cold wind swirls through the small office and blows open the top folder on Wyatt's pile. A yellowed slip of paper, folded many times into a tiny, two-inch square, falls out at his feet. I glance over at the room's single window. It's closed. The withered, disintegrating curtains hang listless and silent in the stale air.

Shivering and looking at the others, I announce, "The window's closed and it isn't broken, either. Where did that draft just come from?"

"Daniel," Wyatt answers.

Oliver stoops down and picks up the tiny, folded paper. He opens it carefully and begins to read aloud.

"On the day of his death, February 10, 1986, Daniel Warren followed his typical routine. As usual, the boy didn't speak a word. Compliantly, he took his seizure medication and an additional sedative in the early evening, because he'd been agitated recently and suffered from anxiety and insomnia. His official cause of death has been reported as suffocation, due to the effects of a particularly severe epileptic seizure. I'm a nurse, not a doctor, but I believe that given the timing of the administration of his medication and the amounts and nature of those medications, he couldn't have had a seizure severe enough to cause his death. It is my belief that he died at the hands of his roommate in room 209, a boy with a history of violent episodes, who never should have been placed in a locked room with another patient. I believe that Daniel was forcibly suffocated by his violent roommate.

"I've hidden this message in one of his files, because I don't want to lose my job, or worse, and because I have no authority in this situation. The administrators of this hospital don't want to be blamed for Daniel's death. They're at fault, though, because it was an administrative decision to place Daniel in room 209 with a patient known to be violent. I also made an anonymous phone call to the press, suggesting that Daniel's roommate facilitated his death. The doctors who placed those two boys in the same room are ultimately responsible. I fear for other patients as well, because they've been assigned to the same rooms as violent patients. Daniel wasn't the only one. Signed: Mary McGuire, RN. Dated: February 12, 1986."

We all stand there, flabbergasted. Jackson finds his voice first. "We need more information. Let's get these files back into place. Oliver, we should keep the note. Do you have a baggy or something?"

"Yes." Oliver shuffles through the contents of his backpack and produces a zip-lock sandwich bag. Then he folds the note back the way he found it, places it inside and seals it. He puts the fragile document into the backpack and begins to give directions.

"I thought we had thoroughly searched this office for information related to Daniel's life and death. Then Mary McGuire's note turned up. Before we move on to another office, we need to search through all the folders again to see if there are any more hidden documents tucked away inside them. We missed this one. We might've missed another."

Before I can stop myself, I heave out a loud sigh. Too late, I clamp my hand over my mouth as if a burp just escaped. "Excuse me. I'm sorry, Oliver."

Wyatt comes to my defense. "We're just bored with all the paperwork. I want to go upstairs to room 209 before it gets too dark. I know we have flashlights, but I want to see the whole room in natural light. The way it looked when Daniel lived there. I promise we'll be careful."

Oliver warns us, "Go ahead, just call my cell if anything happens and I mean *anything*. Jackson and I can be up there in less than a minute. Be super cautious. Don't try something stupid."

"Don't worry. Nathaniel taught me how to keep Daniel out and let him in when I want to. I'm in control. Let's go, Annabelle."

He snatches my hand and hauls me out of the office, before Oliver has a chance to reconsider.

I don't need any persuading. Finding the hidden note written by Nurse Mary McGuire is the only exciting thing that's happened since we entered the hospital. I've mostly felt bored to death up until a few seconds ago.

Chapter 20

The Open Door

Wyatt lets go of my hand and we race each other through the hallway and up the stairs. Anything's better than reading through all the stuff in those dusty old files. I'm so ready for action that I forget to be afraid. Plus, we have our cell phones. Oliver and Jackson can be with us in an instant if we need them.

Upstairs, most of the pale green paint flaked off the mangy walls years ago and now this sad confetti litters the floor. All kinds of crap crumbles and crunches under our feet as we jog along. Cobwebs hang in every corner. Cruising past the many closed doors, we head toward the only open one. As we slow down, our breathing echoes through the emptiness. I've never heard a sound so hollow.

"Here it is, Annabelle, room 209. Are you sure you're ready?"

Mutely, I nod yes.

Hand-in-hand, we step inside the room which has haunted my dreams and waking hours for almost a year now.

Behind me the doorknob rattles. "He's here."

"Did you expect any different? This is where you found him. Where you saw him for the first time."

"I know." I inhale deeply, as if the musty air were loaded with courage. "I'm ready."

Wyatt gives me a one-armed hug and asks again. "Are you sure you want to go through with this?"

"Yes. Let's do it." I survey the small, dismal room. "Where should we start?"

"Where could you hide something? There's no closet, no furniture, only the beds."

"You think he hid something?"

"Why else would he insist that you come back? There *has* to be something here—something that'll help us find out how he died."

"Okay, you take that bed over there and I'll take this one." I drop to my knees, on the floor next to the twin bed on the left and peer underneath. "Nothing under the bed."

I straighten up and look at Wyatt. He's lying full out on his front, scrutinizing the underside of the ratty mattress on the other bed. I decide to do the same and lift the mattress. It's thin and doesn't weigh much. Puffs of dust cloud my view. I sneeze a couple of times.

"God bless you." Wyatt's automatic response.

If God did bless me right now, it would be the first time he visited this room and blessed anyone. No one should ever have been forced to live like this.

There's no box spring underneath the mattress, just a criss-cross pattern of flat metal strips, each attached to the rusty iron bed frame by a squeaky metal coil. Poor Daniel, no wonder he had insomnia. These beds weren't built for comfort or pleasant dreams.

Through the dust motes, I squint up at the bottom of the mattress, near its center, and find a ragged tear, just big enough to reach my hand inside. Fearing that I'll encounter a family of mice or worse, rats, I feel around carefully until my fingers touch something hard. A book. I pull it out and peer at the cover in the gloom. It's a filthy old copy of *Robinson Crusoe*. I reach into the depths of the yucky mattress again: *Gulliver's Travels*. I keep digging out books: *The Adventures of Tom Sawyer*, *Huckleberry Finn*. All of my favorite books. Stuff I've read and reread countless times since I was a little kid. As I touch each grimy volume, I feel closer to Daniel.

He hid books under his bed, which means he could read. It doesn't fit in with what he said about himself at the séance: He not only said that he couldn't speak, he specifically said he didn't have words; that he didn't understand language.

One more grope into the nasty old hidey-hole brings forth the last book, a journal. I drag myself out from under the bed, sit down cross-legged on the bare, wooden floor and open it. Glancing over to see what Wyatt thinks about my discovery, I can see that he's flat out on his front, turned away from me. He appears to be feeling around, under the other bed to see if one of the floorboards might be loose. While he continues to concentrate on his search, oblivious to my amazing discovery, I begin to read.

> *It is January 20th in the year 1986 and I've been here, locked in this room with the raging boy for exactly one week now. My name is Daniel Warren and I'm a patient here at Wild Wood Psychiatric Hospital.*
>
> *The boy frightens me, but I pity him at the same time. His wordless screaming is beyond his control, but the staff here don't seem to think so. They speak harshly to him and place him in restraints with no sign of gentleness; as if they think he deserves to be punished. They haul him away and hours later bring him back. He's usually subdued and quiet for at least twenty-four hours after one of these absences and sleeps most of the time, not even waking up to eat.*
>
> *I've been in this hospital since I was very young, because of the seizures, which didn't start until right before my eighth birthday. After the third seizure, my parents packed me into the car and dropped me off here, at Wild Wood. I've been locked up ever since. My mother and father evidently felt repulsed by me, plus they didn't have enough money for my medical care. Most likely they were also afraid that my seizures might frighten my two younger siblings, or*

worse, I'd get so crazy that I'd harm one of them. They didn't want their deranged, epileptic son to damage one of their normal children.

My medical doctor referred me to a psychiatrist because after the seizures started I stopped talking for days at a time. Our family pediatrician couldn't find a physical reason for my silence, so he told my parents I was insane. The psychiatrist, Dr. Peterson, recommended an experimental program for epileptics.

Hospitals such as this one receive grant money for programs like the one I'm part of now. The doctors here study me as they try different medications and treatments. Their research is funded by the government and by a well-known pharmaceutical company. Basically, the doctors make more money because of me and other patients like me. And my parents don't have to pay. I receive free treatment and medication, plus a place to live. My family got rid of me at no cost. And I became part of a very profitable medical experiment. It's a win/win situation for everyone but me.

As you can tell, Dear Diary, I listen and I learn. I just never speak. Here, in this hospital, only my psychiatrist, Dr. Peterson, knows that I had a voice and once used it to express myself when I was younger. He seems not to have shared this information with the rest of the staff and patients. He encourages me to talk again, like I used to, but I've refused, letting my silence and blank facial expression communicate how I feel. My parents have never visited, nor do I expect them to. I was eight years old when they locked me away. I am 13 now.

January 25th, 1986

My usually furious and frantic roommate is sleeping. They must have given him a powerful sedative. No one else is around, so I can write. I need to record the events that led up to my relocation into room 209. It is important that my diary not get into the wrong hands. I may be in danger because of recent events. I can talk but I choose not to. I express my thoughts by writing in this journal and only in secret. Also, I steal books from the Wild Wood library and hide them. It's better that no one knows I'm literate. I'll be safer if I can keep my secrets and everyone underestimates my intelligence. Only Dr. Peterson has any understanding about my ability to communicate, but thankfully even he doesn't know the extent of my intellectual aptitude. And he has no idea what I saw.

Up until about a week ago, I was free to wander the corridors and fenced-in grounds of this institution. During one of these excursions I saw something I shouldn't have seen. I witnessed a crime.

Enter If You Dare

I was walking down the hallway that leads to the locked medication room. There's always a nurse in there, at the desk, to make sure drugs are dispensed correctly by authorized employees only. At 5:00 PM, though, she goes off duty. She locks the door and leaves. Her shift is over and the medication room is unstaffed until the night nurse comes on duty at 9:00 PM. She stays until 6:00 AM. The room stays locked and empty again until 7:00 AM, when the next nurse comes on duty. During the few hours when the drug room isn't staffed, it's always locked.

Evidently, one employee, a man called Mike, knew where to find the keys. I squatted behind one of those wheelchairs with the restraints and watched him unlock and enter the room, carrying a canvas duffle bag. It was about 8:30 at night. Most of the patients are in bed and asleep before 8:00. No one was around but me. Because I'm one of the older pediatric patients and I'm cooperative and quiet (understatement!) I have a little more freedom. As I hid and watched silently, Mike moved fast. About five minutes later he emerged, still carrying the bag.

Careful to stay far enough behind him so I wouldn't be seen or heard, I followed. He must have been anticipating a speedy return, because he didn't lock the exit door behind him. So I was able to leave the building. I trailed him all the way out to the fence, where I watched Mike take a key out of his pocket and insert it into the padlock that secures the gate to the employee's parking lot. As soon as he turned his back to me, I did something crazy. (After all, I am a patient in a psychiatric hospital.) I tiptoed over to a distant section of fence. In absolute silence and with remarkable agility, I climbed over. The metal did not clink even once as I scaled the chain links like a four-legged spider.

In a silent crawl, I passed between a row of cars and crouched down behind a nearby vehicle to spy on Mike. He opened the trunk of what I assumed to be his own car, but it wasn't. After he placed the duffle bag into the trunk of the car, another man emerged from behind some cars that were parked one row away. He walked over to Mike who handed him the car keys. The man gave Mike a large roll of paper money, which he quickly stashed in his pants pocket. Mike walked over to the gate that leads to the road and unlocked it. After the man got into the car and drove away Mike relocked the gate and headed over toward the other gate: the one that opens onto the hospital grounds.

While this was happening, I stayed carefully hidden behind one of the cars, but as I began to worry about how I'd get back into the hospital after Mike locked the door behind him, my medical *condition betrayed me. I should've known. Whenever I'm really anxious, I have a seizure, especially lately. I think I need my medication dosage increased because I've grown. Anyway, as I was squatting in the parking lot, scared and worried, my jaw began to twitch and I started grinding my teeth, like I always do right before a seizure. That's the last thing I remember.*

When I regained consciousness, Mike was leaning over me, along with another orderly who heard me go down. I think I probably yelled or cried out in some way, right before I fell. Thankfully, the other orderly had just entered the parking lot. If I had been alone with Mike, he probably would have harmed me. He might have made me disappear right then and there.

The next day they moved me into room 209, with my new roommate, the screaming boy. They locked the door, forever probably. Dr. Summers explained that I was getting too old to stay in the pediatric wing. My nighttime wanderings were agitating the patients and inconveniencing the staff. I had climbed the fence; a huge breach of trust and then I had a seizure in the parking lot. When Dr. Peterson found out they'd moved me and I didn't like my new accommodations, he tried to make a deal with me. He promised that if I decided to talk I would get a limited version of my former freedom back. He gave me this book and a pen and told me to write down the words I couldn't say; he thinks it will help. I've hidden the book because I don't trust anyone, not even him. If anything happens to me at least one written account of the events leading up to my death exists, even if no one ever finds it.

Dumfounded, sitting cross-legged on the dusty floor, with the open journal in my lap I stare at Daniel's lost words and in my mind I hear his voice. Someone believed they'd silenced him forever. But they were wrong. After a few seconds, I shake off Daniel's world and the present settles around me like snow. I'm freezing. The room has grown colder and dusk is falling fast. The last few pages were difficult to read without a flashlight. Wyatt and I should go downstairs so I can tell Oliver and Jackson about the diary.

I yell over to him.

"You won't believe what I found!"

Wyatt rises to a kneeling position and looks at the books piled on the floor all around me. "You found some books?"

"Not just any books. I found a diary."

"You're kidding!"

"No. I'm not. This bed must have been Daniel's. He hid all these books in his mattress because he loved to read but he didn't want anyone to know. He was afraid. The last book I found in there was his journal." I hold it up.

"Daniel's journal?" Wyatt drags himself up off the dusty floor and starts brushing his knees off. He's frowning.

"Yes. And it's beautifully written. His style is formal and old-fashioned like the books he loved. The journal entries don't seem like the writing style of a teenager from the eighties. It was like reading a classic novel from another century."

Wyatt blinks at me, from where he's standing near the other bed. He takes one step toward me. Then pauses. "Annabelle, our ghost never talked."

"I know."

"He told us that he'd never used words until I channeled him."

"It just doesn't fit, does it?"

"He didn't even know his own name."

"So how could he read the classics?"

"How could he write in a journal?"

"Maybe our ghost isn't Daniel." As I utter these words I realize what they mean. I jump up to warn Wyatt.

"He's the violent roommate!"

Wyatt and I stand frozen in place, staring at each other. He takes one step toward me, but then falters.

A high-pitched sound, like steam escaping from a kettle, whistles through the dark room. But nobody's making tea. We both turn toward the source of the eerie noise.

A weak stream of unearthly light seeps through the window near the corner of the room and pours onto the floor. Its consistency seems to lie somewhere between a liquid and a solid, like mercury, only blue. Out of the gleaming, wobbly puddle, a phosphorescent vapor rises up.

The ghost we thought was Daniel materializes and looms over us for two seconds before he lunges and wraps his hands around Wyatt's neck. My boyfriend's face flashes white then blue and finally a corpse-like shade of gray. His eyes roll up so only the whites are showing.

I'm watching the boy I love fight a losing battle for his life. The arms that used to be Wyatt's reach out and his body lurches toward me as he screams my name.

I spin around and bolt out the door.

Fighting the urge to turn and look behind me, I aim my body forward in a full-out sprint. Through the hallway. Down the stairs. I can't lose this race.

Because I'm running for my life; in a race against death.

It's pitch dark on the first floor. After slamming into a closed door, I fling it open and tumble outside. I've never seen this part of the meadow before, but I race through it as if my feet know every step by heart. Tears spring to my eyes, but I speed on, terrified of the boy who had no voice. So he stole Wyatt's.

Finally the fence looms ahead and I can't slow down. In mid-stride I leap. The toe of my sneaker slams through a hole in the chain links. Reaching high, I clutch a fistful of cold metal and hoist my weight up. Grabbing again and again; hand over hand. Frantic. Higher and higher, I scramble like a hyperactive gymnast. Finally, gripping the top with one hand, I vault over and pivot in mid air. Crashing into the other side, I cling fast to the clanking metal. Scale down two toe-holds. And jump from eight feet up. At the last second, I remember to bend my knees, right before I hit the ground and roll. Then I spring to my feet and speed away.

Before me lies my element as a cross-country runner: the forest. I don't have time to search for the cemetery and the old dirt road where Nathaniel's parked. So once again I race full tilt, aimed straight ahead.

My footing holds true as I plunge down an overgrown trail. Briars tear at my jeans. After wrenching one pant leg free from their thorny grasp, I scoot along the narrow path, made slippery by layers of pine needles. Sprinting toward my goal: anyplace far away from the nameless, raging boy.

The quickly-darkening forest is my only route to safety.

The Lonesome Boy already killed once. As I run, I imagine poor, helpless Daniel's death. Fear fuels my frenzied pace. And I start to feel weightless. Speeding over the ground, my sneakers barely touch down on the path.

"Noooo, Annabelle!" A horrible howl rises up from the boy's miserable soul. Then he sobs just once before his voice fades to a whimper. He won't quit until he catches me and he's closing in fast.

Even I can't keep up this pace for long and I begin to weaken. My soles start slapping crazily against the earth. I can feel the impact in my knees and hip joints now. My breathing grows ragged and choked. As I try to estimate how far I can go, my strength begins to fade. I already ran one 5K this morning. What if my legs give way and I collapse?

I begin to slip and slide as the path grows slick with mud. My sneakers make suctioning sounds as the muck becomes thicker. Sinking a little with each step, I strive to maintain a fast pace as I speed through a puddle. Nothing looks familiar. But I can't hesitate. The path forks and I head left. I can hear the dead boy's sobs heaving up out of Wyatt's lungs. The sound of his voice grows closer and closer.

I know I'm doomed but I can't give up. Down the slippery trail. Panting. Gasping. I have to slow down soon. Finally the path grows drier then widens. The hoards of trees begin to thin out as I whiz by them.

Where are my mother and Nathaniel? I need to find the road. The van. My feet fly down the now hard-packed lane. Toward a bend. Hope lends much-needed speed to my pace. But still I hear his quickening whimpers. No time to stop and catch my breath.

His wails echo through the darkness once again and suddenly he bumps into me, almost knocking me over.

Grabbing a fistful my shirt, he yanks hard. I flail my fists and pound them against his iron chest.

Staring up into his wild eyes, I swing one fist, as hard as I can, straight toward his nose. He lets go of my shirt and leaps back. A huge red-brown blur flies out of a nearby thicket, leaps over the brambles at the edge of the path and skids to a stop between us.

Jeff! Barking and howling like a wild beast, he snaps his jaws at my attacker. Then bares his teeth and growls as if he's standing guard at the gates of hell. Because he is.

Wyatt's body towers over us both for one second before he flops down onto one knee in the dirt. His head bows low. When he raises his face to stare at me, I'm looking into my boyfriend's familiar, clear blue eyes. They're not crazed with fury anymore.

Jeff calms down and grows quiet. I take one wobbly step toward Wyatt. His face grows hazy and my hand shakes when I reach out. A small, bright circle of golden light frames him but there's dark all around it. As I struggle to bring him into focus, the glowing circle shrinks to a tiny, bright hole. A pinpoint of light. Then the world turns black.

Chapter 21

Recuperation

When I finally regain consciousness, all I can see is the faded orange cotton of Wyatt's t-shirt because my face is pressed against his chest. He's carrying me through the woods.

"You can put me down now. I'm okay."

"Not a chance."

I struggle, but Wyatt only tightens his grip on me. My feet are dangling in midair and I kick them, but it's futile.

"Cut it out, Annabelle. I'm not putting you down."

I relax for a second and turn my head to see where we're going. Wyatt's following Jeff down the path. Eventually, I see a meadow of yellowed grass and then beyond it, the road where Nathaniel's van and Jackson's SUV are parked.

"C'mon. I can walk now. Think how hysterical my mom's going to get if she sees you carrying me."

"Good point, but I'm keeping my arm around you for support and if you so much as stumble once, I'm carrying you. You scared the crap out of me!"

Ahead of us, Jeff looks back, barks at me once and then wags his tail, as if he's expressing his agreement with Wyatt. My human protector hugs my waist with one strong arm and we continue to walk toward the van in silence.

I scared him.

That's ironic, seeing as his body was possessed by the spirit of a homicidal maniac and he was chasing me through the woods behind an insane asylum.

Even though I'm moving just fine, with just a little help from Wyatt, the second she spots us, my mother races over. She never runs and she never panics. It's weird to see my normally unflappable mother flapping wildly. Strands of her hair fall loose, making it look even more messy than usual. She's all breathless.

"Annabelle, what on earth happened? We've been worried sick."

"I fainted, that's all. I was running through the woods and I ran out of energy. I'm fine now."

"Fainting isn't fine. You've never fainted before in your life. Come to the car and sit down. You already ran one race today. Why on earth were you running again?"

She sounds exasperated. Nathaniel's beside me by now and he hauls me onto his lap so I can ride back to the van with him, in the wheelchair. I try to get up and walk, but he holds me down with his right arm and directs the wheelchair with his left. I'm getting fed up with being bossed around, manhandled and carried in one way or another. So I continue to squirm and kick.

"Annabelle, sit still."

Finally, I concede, mostly because I have no choice. His biceps are made of iron.

"Calm down. I have some Gatorade in the van. You probably just need some electrolytes."

Jackson and Oliver are jogging toward us. So it's five against one; six if you count Jeff. I know I'll never win. I relax and start to enjoy my spin in the pimped-out wheelchair. When we get to the van, Nathaniel opens a huge cooler and starts handing out drinks. I thank him and proceed to guzzle down half a bottle of Gatorade in less than sixty seconds. Wyatt stands beside me, slugging one down, too. He stops for a second.

"I don't think I've ever felt this thirsty before. I'm starting to feel really tired and hungry, too." He looks over at Nathaniel, who hands him another Gatorade.

"Hang in there, Wyatt. It's gonna be okay, buddy." Nathaniel's words are reassuring but his face looks worried.

I hop up and sit on the hood of Jackson's car and Wyatt opens the passenger side door so he can flop down onto the seat. Oliver and my mom hover over us as if we're invalids about to breathe our last.

Nathaniel puts his hand on my mother's shoulder. "Susannah, they're okay. They just need to rest."

Finally everyone calms down and Oliver decides it's time to talk about what happened.

"Okay, you two, we need to hear everything."

Wyatt and I take turns relating the details of our misadventure. Then Oliver tells us what was happening while we were gone.

"Jackson and I finished looking through a few more files in another office and discovered some important information. We tried both of your cell phones and got no answer so we went upstairs to find you. Room 209 was empty. I called down to the van on my cell and Susannah and Nathaniel hadn't seen you either. I'm sure you can imagine, Annabelle, how much your mother began to worry."

He shoots me an accusing look. Then continues. "As I was speaking to her on the phone I spotted the books scattered all over the floor and the journal lying open. It was obvious that you two had left in a hurry. Jackson and I stopped for a moment to read Daniel's diary. We realized you were in danger but tried not to panic."

"At least you're safe now," Jackson says.

"Thanks to Jeff." I rub his ears for him. He loves that.

"What did you think of the journal?" I'm interested in Oliver's opinion because it seems like he might have come to the same conclusion I did.

"Our ghost, whoever he was, had no mastery of language during his life. According to what he explained during the séance, he never possessed the ability to speak. When Wyatt channeled him for the first time the spirit expressed surprise at having words and being able to talk. During the séance he told us that when he was alive, he had a very limited understanding of what others were saying. Based on the facts recorded in the journal, Jackson and I deduced that our ghost couldn't be Daniel, because Daniel could obviously read. And he wrote beautifully; with skill and creativity. That journal was written by a very literate and intelligent child who'd completely mastered the English language, not someone who'd never spoken or used words."

Jackson offers his professional, psychologist's opinion. "I believe that Daniel was a selective mute. Because of psychological trauma, he either chose not to talk, or he actually couldn't talk, but it happened after he turned eight. After he'd learned to read and write."

Oliver continues. "I tried not to panic when I realized our ghost wasn't Daniel, but more likely his violent roommate."

Jackson adds, "When this dawned on us, we ran downstairs and attempted to figure out which way you'd gone. But we couldn't see any trace of you, so we hurried back to the van, hoping you'd arrive soon."

Oliver joins in again. "After Nathaniel and Susannah quickly read the journal, we stood around for a few minutes trying to decide what to do. I called Wyatt's cell again and got no answer and your mom tried your cell phone, Annabelle, multiple times, with the same results. Then Jeff started to act agitated. He kept sniffing the air and pacing back and forth."

Nathaniel takes over. "Suddenly, Jeff took off like a bat out of hell. None of us could possibly have followed him. Maybe a minute or two later, you guys came traipsing along, safe, but obviously a little worn out."

Wyatt explained, "Annabelle found the journal inside the mattress and read it. She started to tell me that the ghost wasn't Daniel and *BOOM*, he took over. I couldn't stop him. You were right about the power-up, Nathaniel. The dead boy took control. The force of his presence squeezed me out of my own body. I tried to stop him, but it was too late. Annabelle was off and running. And my body, possessed by a homicidal maniac, was after her. I didn't have a chance."

"Then what happened?" Oliver asks.

"I chased her until Jeff intervened. As soon as the dog started barking, the spirit's will collapsed like a punctured balloon. I think he's exhausted himself now. We're farther away from his stomping grounds and I don't feel any threat from him at the moment. What do you think, Nathaniel?"

"Wyatt's right. I can sense the spirit's despair. He had no strength left; no power. For now you two are safe."

Wyatt rests his elbows on his knees and covers his face with his huge hands. "What if it happens again? Annabelle, how can I protect you from the enemy when the enemy's me?"

I have no idea what to say to him.

"I don't just see dead people. I *am* dead people." His face is still hidden in his big hands.

I make a weak attempt at comforting Wyatt. "Only one dead person, so far."

My mother enters the discussion. "You're all forgetting something."

"What's that, Mom?"

"I can ward off evil."

"So if he was evil, you'd know."

"That's right, Annabelle. Nathaniel always consults with me before attempting a séance. More than once he's walked away from a situation because I sensed something wicked, something dangerous and repulsive."

"And that didn't happen today?" Wyatt asks.

"No, nor any other day. Annabelle's ghost has been around her for almost a year now. And I haven't felt anything."

"If he was evil, you would've known!" I can't believe I didn't figure this out before now.

"Yes, I would've known if he had bad intentions. I'd have felt nauseous and sick whenever he was near. And then I would've driven him away. However, I felt nothing. If Annabelle hadn't told me about the rattling doorknob and the opening door in her nightmare, I never would've suspected he even existed."

"So we're safe?"

"Honey…" She takes my hand and her soft eyes gleam. "He means you no harm. He needs our help. I don't think he murdered Daniel."

Wyatt gasps. "Annabelle!"

I hurry over to him. He stands up and reaches for me, pulling me close. Framing my face with his hands, he tilts it up and stares into my eyes. "He's trying to tell me something."

Everyone falls silent. "He needs us. He ran after you because only you can save him."

"Wyatt, do you think he'd hurt me?"

"Never."

Abruptly, Wyatt removes his hands from the sides of my face. "Annabelle, why the hell did you take a swing at me? Next time you take a poke at someone, think first."

"You were chasing after me like a murderous lunatic." He has no right to be annoyed.

"You would've broken my nose if that punch had connected. Damn it, Annabelle!"

Nathaniel's laughing. "I wish I was there, Wyatt. I'd love to see you knocked on your ass by someone half your size."

"No one knocked me on my ass. I jumped back and she missed. Then that rabid mutt tried to kill me."

Still laughing, Nathaniel explains. "Not you, Wyatt. Don't take it personally. The ghost still had control of your body and Jeff hates all ghosts. When he senses a ghost, he turns into a raging beast from hell. He doesn't know harmless from evil. He doesn't care. He just hates them all."

"Good to know!" Even my mother's giggling now. "Let's get you two home so you can rest and we'll meet tomorrow to discuss what the next step should be."

Nathaniel speaks up. "Wyatt, you're coming with me and I'm making you a huge, juicy, fat cheeseburger. I know what it feels like to come back from where you've been. You need something high in calories and fat. Broccoli and tofu isn't gonna do the trick."

"Okay, Nathaniel, you can have him and you can feed him. When do you think you'll be bringing him home?" Oliver concedes with a tired smile.

"Right after he eats. He'll probably fall asleep in the van and I'll never be able to manage him. He'll need your help, Oliver, and probably Jackson's too. You guys will have to get him into the house and up to bed."

My mom's smiling with relief now that she knows I'm safe. "Annabelle, you look exhausted. Let's get you home so you can rest."

What a day! I saw my mother run and heard her giggle; my confident, levelheaded mother, brewer of magic teas and enemy of evil.

I turn to the others. "One more thing; after Wyatt and I went upstairs, did you discover anything else of importance in the files, Oliver?"

"We found a written record of which patients were kept in which rooms during the time surrounding Daniel's death. After he died, the hospital staff attempted to place other patients in room 209, but no one ever stayed more than twenty-four hours. That means from the day Daniel died until the closing of the hospital in mid-February of 1986, no patients were ever housed in room 209."

Jackson adds, "And the hospital was overcrowded. Why couldn't they put anyone in the room?"

Oliver answers his question. "The Lonesome Boy was still there. That's why. Our boy died on February 10th. But his spirit never left the room."

"It's the only open door on the second floor. Maybe he kept opening the door." I'm thinking out loud.

"And the patients who were assigned to room 209 kept getting out," Wyatt adds.

"Plus it's always freezing in there."

Wyatt and I keep finishing each other's thoughts.

"So they couldn't put anyone in room 209."

"Even though the hospital was overcrowded."

Jackson glances down at his horrific handwriting. "Now we have some names from the files. Maybe we can locate someone who worked at the hospital during the winter of 1986."

Oliver peers over his shoulder, trying to decipher the hieroglyphics. "Strangely, there's no mention of Daniel's mysterious roommate anywhere, in any of the files, with the exception of Mary McGuire's unofficial, hidden note. And even she never mentions his name. Let's see if we can find out more about him. Maybe the names we *do* have will help."

Jackson reads aloud from his notes. "Dr. Peterson: Daniel's psychiatrist, Dr. Summers: Daniel's pediatrician, Nurse Mary McGuire and the mysterious Mike."

As we're preparing to leave, Oliver announces, "I think it's time to talk to the living."

Chapter 22

What's Your Name? Who Are You?

As soon as we get home, my mother makes me eat two bananas, because she thinks all the running depleted my potassium and that's why I fainted. Then she brews me one of her teas and loads it up with honey. What I'm really craving is something more substantial, though. So Dad takes pity on me and grills up some burgers and hotdogs. Afterwards, we watch a couple of old *CSI* episodes together and then I head up to bed early.

In my room, I grab Jackson's cashmere sweater off the floor. He hasn't asked for it back yet and wearing it makes me feel warm and safe. When it comes to stealing other people's clothes, I have no conscience. Nobody should ever lend me anything. I guess I like wearing my friends' stuff because sometimes I miss them when they're not here.

Jackson's gesture, on the night of the séance, was very sweet. When I wear the sweater he lent me, I feel his kindness all over again. It's kind of like the sweater's giving me a hug. I feel safer, like I'm not alone.

As I drift off to sleep, my mind cruises through all the discoveries we made this afternoon and all the unanswered questions we unearthed.

At midnight I wake up shivering, even though the covers are snuggled up around my neck.

He gives the doorknob a half-hearted jiggle. The door's open, but he rattles the doorknob anyway, to let me know he's here. But he's not inside of my dream this time. He's really here. Drawing some icy-cold air into my lungs, I sit up, to make sure I'm really awake. His frigid breath hovers around my face, causing me to shiver. But I'm not afraid, just freezing.

When I realize that Wyatt's still asleep, inhabiting his own body, safe in his own bed, I experience a sense of relief. The lost soul of the unnamed patient isn't seizing control of him. My nameless companion has drifted in to visit me while I'm alone. And I'm not afraid because my mother explained that he would never harm us.

Collapsing back down onto my pillow, I pull the covers up to my chin. "Hey, if you're going to keep hanging around, I'm going to have to give you a name."

His voice rises up, out of the cold, and into my thoughts. "I think my first name is Anthony."

"You have a voice! Without Wyatt, you have a voice." His frigid breath floats over my skin as his name echoes inside my head. We inhabit this moment together: Anthony and me. He has a name.

"What is this, Annabelle? I've found myself and my voice. If not for you and Wyatt it never could've happened. In life, Daniel *chose* not to speak, but I couldn't. Speech was impossible for me. I remember someone yelling 'Anthony,' just once, perhaps hoping to discover some sign of humanity within me. Someone screamed out my name."

"Who said it?"

"I can only hear it in my memory, which has never had words before. When I was alive, I didn't understand words, but for some reason, at that moment in time, I suddenly knew the difference between speaking and inarticulate screaming. Someone yelled, 'Anthony.' It was my name and somewhere, inside a deeply buried part of my soul, I knew it. Maybe, when I was really young, I heard someone say it and that memory emerged somehow."

"Then what happened? Try to remember."

"I had that one moment of clarity. I recognized my name. That's all. I've only recently been able to think in language; since I found you and Wyatt. I don't know whose voice spoke my name. I can't envision a face, just the name Anthony, screamed out loud in that horrible room. I can't remember words, but I can remember feelings: fear and hurt and sorrow, from both physical and emotional pain."

"Pain! They hurt you?"

"They dowsed me with freezing cold water to shock me into submission. But sometimes they strapped me into a tub of warm water to try to calm me down. When I wasn't thrashing around in that godforsaken hell-hole of a room with poor Daniel quivering in a corner, I was always restrained in some way. They bound me with leather straps and shot bolts of electricity through me as I howled and screamed and writhed like a wild creature."

"You weren't a wild creature, Anthony. You were a boy and someone gave you a name."

"I'm only human because I know you, Annabelle, and I've discovered my humanity too late."

"No, the part of you continuing on after your death has a purpose. You have a mission. We need to discover more. I know enough from talking to Wyatt and Nathaniel to realize there are facts that need to be revealed before you can leave us. You have a very important story, Anthony. Tell me more. Tell me everything you can remember. If we figure out what happened to you, maybe you can finally leave this earth and find someplace where you belong."

"I don't want to go anywhere. Now is all that matters. I don't care about my life, my past. I only want to be here with you. In life I heard only noise and felt only pain. I experienced confusion and rage. I acted out my impulses and reacted to others by screaming, hitting, kicking, biting. I grabbed whatever I could get hold of. I dug my fingernails into human flesh and tore at it with all my strength. I remember the restraints and the shots, the injections that sent me away. My consciousness disappeared."

"You acted out your emotions because you couldn't express them any other way."

"Exactly. I lived a life without the connections language helps us form. All I heard were sounds and I screamed and howled in reply, trying to drown out the hideous racket. I heard everything at once, crashing into my ears, exploding my senses. I heard many things on earth: disembodied noises and creatures, not all of them human. I heard countless sounds from hell. When I tried to end the unbearable clamor, only incoherent noise rushed up; through my throat and out of my mouth."

"And what about Daniel?"

"Daniel was silent. He never spoke or cried out. He shrank into corners, trying to disappear from life; he didn't rage against it. He felt petrified of everything, even me. Who can blame him? He was also scared to death of the way his body convulsed sometimes."

"He had epilepsy. He suffered from seizures. He was a selective mute, capable of speech but unable to speak, for psychological reasons." After I explain this to Anthony, I decide to ask the most important question of all, hoping he'll be able to remember and make some sense out of his experiences. "What happened that night, Anthony, the night Daniel died?"

"I don't remember. Think about it, Annabelle. I can only speak at all right now because I've visited the incredible library that is Wyatt's brain. When I was alive, my mind wasn't like that. As soon as you met Wyatt, everything changed for us. So much more became possible. I felt a connection with him immediately, but he hesitated, even though I suspect he knew all this was inevitable. I could feel his loneliness, how his talent isolated him from others, from his family, from his mother and his father. Like my parents, his mother wanted to lock him away, except he was older when it happened, and his uncle helped him."

"But you never had anyone like Oliver to help you."

"Nobody cared about me. I think that when my family sent me away, I must have been no more than a helpless baby. They locked me up in Wild Wood Hospital and there was nothing I could do to stop them. Everyone knew I'd grow up and grow even more repulsive, more uncontrollable."

"No one tried to understand."

"There are so many parallels between Wyatt and me. The way we feel about you is our most important connection."

"Anthony, I care so much about you and Wyatt. *I* feel that connection, too."

"When he finally got you alone that Sunday afternoon, he held you and your heart beat with his. I pushed at the door of his consciousness and he opened it for me."

"You took over Wyatt's body for the first time."

"I looked around in his mind, but not with my eyes. I became aware of his thinking process, like a waking dream. I had access to his memory. If I felt an emotion or had a thought, the right words materialized. And I could make the words come out his mouth. But the best thing was watching your face when my words reached your ears, watching the light in your eyes intensify as you understood what I said."

I want to hug Anthony, but he's only a disembodied voice.

"I'm able to inhabit Wyatt's body, Annabelle, but I only come close to being human because I know you. Wyatt and I both see you for what you truly are, someone whose beauty shines through from the inside to the outside like no other. The bond was formed. We three can't be separated; not until we know the truth."

"What truth, Anthony? The truth about the night you died?"

"Annabelle, what if I killed Daniel that night?"

I have to answer honestly and struggle to find the words. "I don't know. But Anthony, you need to believe that you wouldn't have done it intentionally. I know you would never have deliberately hurt Daniel. I truly believe that. We'll help you. We won't stop trying 'til we know for sure what happened. I promise."

"I can't think any more. I'm losing strength. Go to sleep. I have a little energy left. Let me use it to watch over you. Just leave the door open. I hate closed doors because I spent my whole life locked up behind them."

That's why he rattled the doorknob and opened the door!

"I'll leave every door open from now on, Anthony."

"In my life, in that horrible place, I hated to be locked up, restrained. I loathed being touched by those people. Now I exist only because I hope to be touched by you. When I'm in Wyatt's body, I live and breathe and speak only so I can be close to you. Sleep, sweet angel. No one can hurt you while I'm here."

After decades of waiting, watching and hoping, Anthony found me and now he's experiencing something he never felt during his short tragic life. I'm his only hope. I keep thinking about this until I finally drift off to sleep, thankful that I'm loved by my family, by my friends and now by Anthony. When he lived and walked on this earth, Anthony never felt loved by anyone.

Chapter 23

We Make Plans

I don't know if I can wait for the meeting at Oliver's house because I'm about to burst. But I have to wait, so I do. I haven't even told my mother about my early morning visitor. I only want to explain it once and answer everyone's questions all at the same time. Plus I'm picturing the drama my announcement will cause and I'm enjoying the anticipation. By the time we're finally sitting down around Oliver's kitchen table, though, I'm ready to explode. I'm squirming in my seat like a five-year-old.

Somewhere deep inside myself I find some self-control and let Oliver speak first. He informs us that yesterday, on the way home, Wyatt almost passed out from exhaustion. After he downed three bacon double cheeseburgers and a vanilla milkshake at Nathaniel's, he came straight home and went right to bed. He hasn't had a lot of time to research any of the information we uncovered in the hospital yesterday. But he does have a couple of things to report.

Oliver and Jackson pass around tea and sandwiches and we all settle in. Jackson goes first. He's one of those bald guys who embraces the hair loss and shaves the rest off just to show he doesn't give a hoot. Rising steam from his tea cup veils his features and, with his dark eyebrows and intense expression, he looks demonic. But he's one of the kindest, sweetest men I've ever met and a minister, too. He explains the results of the limited research he did last night, in bed, on his laptop, before he fell asleep.

"I found office addresses for both of the doctors' names we uncovered. Lucky for us, neither of these gentlemen has retired. Both of them have private practices now and they both stayed local, too. I think Oliver and I should make appointments with Drs. Peterson and Summers and conduct these interviews. Maybe one of these gentlemen remembers a hospital employee named Mike. I have the psychology background, so I should definitely be in on the meeting with Doctor Peterson."

I'm curious to hear Jackson's opinion. "From a psychologist's point of view, what do you think about our experience yesterday?"

"From what we've discovered so far about the unknown, violent roommate, I'm going to speculate that he was severely autistic. This could explain his mutism. Autistic children have difficulty communicating and they can have devastating meltdowns when they feel over-stimulated. In addition to autism, he might have suffered from a mood or a personality disorder, such as schizo-phrenia. His frustration with being unable to communicate was probably a contributing factor to his violent behavior. With the right medication and counseling, a skilled therapist might have been able to help our Lonesome Boy."

"But the doctors at Wild Wood didn't diagnose him correctly?" Wyatt asks.

"I doubt it. But, then again, it's hard to say unless he's your patient. A psychiatrist would need lots of time with him and careful observation and analysis to accurately make any of these diagnoses. I don't have a medical degree, only a Ph.D. Plus, he's not my patient. And he's been dead for over twenty years. So…" Jackson shrugs.

Oliver adds, "Of course, Jackson's information about the boy is limited. He's just making an informed guess. He also discovered something else that'll be helpful to our investigation."

"Thanks, Oliver." Jackson goes on to explain, "Not only do I have the psych credentials; my research skills aren't too shabby either. I also found Nurse Mary McGuire. Guess where?"

No one attempts a guess, because when people tell you to guess, they don't really expect you to. They just want to tell you outright. I decide to take a stab at it anyway, to humor him. After all, I still have his really expensive sweater. "Online newspaper archives, the obituaries?"

"Nope, somewhere way more obvious and she's still alive. Think again, Annabelle."

"I give up." Actually I really want him to finish telling us his news quickly, so I can tell mine and blow everyone away.

He smiles proudly and lowers his voice for dramatic effect. You can tell he must be an excellent preacher. "In the Eastfield phonebook."

This news is pretty cool, but not better than mine.

Jackson's smile is a mile wide. "Very low tech. Mrs. McGuire doesn't have a cell phone or a computer. I simply looked her up in the phone book and I spoke with her this morning. She's in her eighties now, and retired, but manages to stay pretty active. She's widowed for the second time and lives alone in the home she and her second husband owned together. She was raised in Eastfield and has lived here her whole life: a townie. Like many elderly people who live alone, she was happy to have someone to chat with."

"What did you say?"

"I told her I was helping some high school students with a History project about the Eastfield area in the 1950's and 60's. I said I got her name through the local Senior Citizens Association. I didn't want to make her too suspicious about our interest in the closing of Wild Wood Hospital, so I avoided mentioning your imaginary project about the 1980's. Right now, Oliver and I think you should focus on getting in the door, getting to know her. Open the lines of communication. Too many direct questions would alarm her. Feel out the situation and be friendly. Maybe you'll get invited back."

"When did you and Oliver decide all of this?" Wyatt sounds a little annoyed.

"Soon after I found her phone number, I figured out a basic plan. Then when I spoke with her, I could tell by her voice she was lonely and happy to shoot the breeze about a lot of subjects. She eagerly agreed to meet with two young people and I told her to expect your phone call today or tomorrow. So, Annabelle, you or Wyatt should call and set something up for early this week. We don't want to waste any time. I think Nathaniel should accompany you. We can say he's part of a mentoring program at the high school. We'll give her Oliver's number so he can back up your story. What do you think?"

"I think you've given us some little old lady to interview because you feel like she's the least threatening prospect on our short list. And we're supposed to talk to her about a subject that isn't even related to Daniel Warren or the closing of the hospital. Plus you're sending Nathaniel with us as a babysitter. You want us to stay out of trouble and you think we can't handle anything big." Wyatt's full-out pissed now and not bothering to hide it.

Oliver looks tired. His face is nearly as gray as his close-snipped, always tidy hair. But he finds enough energy and enthusiasm to stand up for Jackson.

"We always want you to stay out of trouble, Wyatt, but you've done a poor job of that so far. This is an important task. You need a subtle conversational touch. She's likely to open up and talk the most out of all three of our prospects.

Also, based on what we found out from reading the files at the hospital, we know she came into close contact with Daniel Warren on a regular basis. And her hidden note contains the only mention of the violent roommate we could find, besides the ones in Daniel's diary. She's key."

"Okay, okay. Maybe you're right." Wyatt manages a close-lipped smile and tilts both hands up in a gesture of surrender.

Jackson asserts himself. "She's an important source, even though she happens to be a little old lady. So brush that chip off your shoulder, Wyatt, and be a team player. You and Annabelle have a valuable part to play in all this. And you get to go first. Jackson and I won't get an appointment to meet with two busy doctors right away, but Mrs. McGuire is eager for company and not likely to postpone anything."

I don't care about any of this. I'll interview anyone they want me to interview about any subject. What I really want is to talk about the Lonesome Boy. I'm practically exploding because I'm so excited to tell them about last night. I was planning on a low-key introduction leading up to an explosive announcement, but instead I just blurt it out, "His name is Anthony."

"What the hell are you talking about, Annabelle?" Wyatt asks.

"The violent roommate. He visited me last night. At midnight, actually, which is always the time in my dream. He rattles my doorknob if the door's closed and now I know why."

My mother looks annoyed. "Annabelle, you should have woken me up."

"But, Mom, I wasn't afraid. You're the one who told us he isn't evil. He doesn't mean anyone any harm. And you were right."

Everyone's attention is super-glued to me and I explain how Anthony can communicate now because of what he learned from being inside Wyatt's mind. I tell them about his memory of someone calling out, "Anthony!" After I finish describing every detail, I hit them with the part about the door needing to be open.

"It all makes so much sense," Jackson says.

"Annabelle, you need to wake me up if this happens again," My mom warns me.

Nathaniel offers, "You can borrow Jeff. He loves you, Annabelle, and he'll bark loud enough to raise the dead if the ghost shows up. I've never offered to lend him to anyone before, but I'll do anything to help you. It's my fault this ghost has gained so much power. If I hadn't coached Wyatt in channeling, this would never have happened."

Oliver frowns. "I feel responsible. Before Wyatt ever even met Annabelle, I encouraged him to use his talent."

Jackson folds his hands on the table in front of him, as if he's about to lead a prayer and announces, "Wyatt and Annabelle aren't children any more. They're talented, brave young adults who are curious about everything. You have to let them explore and learn. Oliver, the world is their classroom now. It has no walls and no door to close and lock. If you worry too much about them, you'll undermine their confidence. Susannah, Oliver, you've done a great job with Annabelle and Wyatt so far. They have lots of confidence and courage. Don't feel guilty. Give yourselves a pat on the back."

I reach over and take Jackson's advice. "Good job, Mom. I haven't turned out all that bad."

She smiles a small, reluctant looking smile, but a smile nonetheless.

The best thing for Wyatt and me would be for Jackson's message to sink in. And for us to have the freedom to see this adventure through to the end. I'll sneak my friend the minister a hug later.

"Hey, you know what? I agree with Jackson." Nathaniel raises his tea cup. "I drink to your health, Jackson. May you live long enough to preach a million sermons and may everyone who hears them follow your advice."

Wyatt and I raise our mugs and drink, too.

"Amen," Oliver says as he sips from his cup.

No one likes to be proven wrong, especially an intelligent grownup like Oliver, who's used to being right. But he's being a good sport.

Nathaniel smiles. "We're the best damn ghost hunters ever."

Oliver corrects him. "Poor Anthony, we aren't hunting him. We're helping him, uncovering his story. We aren't ghost hunters. We're paranormal explorers."

I put one hand on Wyatt's forearm and rub the top of Jeff's head with the other. If these two behemoths have my back, how can any harm ever come to me?

Chapter 24

Talking to the Little Old Lady

Just like Oliver and Jackson predicted, when we contact Mrs. Mary McGuire, she's eager to meet with us and talk about her life as a long-time Eastfield resident. Wyatt and I duck out of our practices early and meet Nathaniel in front of her little cottage on one of the side streets near Main Street, not too far from Jackson's church. In this part of town the houses are pretty close together and have small yards. Most of them were built in the late 1800's.

Sandwiched in between two large Victorians with wrap-around porches, Mrs. McGuire's home looks like a dollhouse. Rose vines past their blooming season cling to a weathered but well-kept fence. Due to an unseasonably warm fall, rows of chrysanthemums, sedum and giant marigolds still brighten both sides of the flat stepping stones leading up to her front door. Enchanting.

The door itself is exceptionally quaint and unusual. It has a rounded top and a small rectangular window with six tiny panes, right at eyelevel.

"Awesome," I whisper to Wyatt. "My dad's a builder so I can ask about the architecture of her house. And my mother's a gardener so I'll be able to complement her flowers and name them all. I have good conversation starters so I won't sound stupid."

"Oh, you'll probably still manage to sound stupid, Annabelle."

I punch him in the arm and he rubs the spot and laughs.

Before we start up the walkway to ring the doorbell, the door creaks open. I expect a chubby little, hunched over hobbit lady with a wrinkly smile to peep out and greet us, but she's tall and slim with excellent posture. She looks more like a retired business woman than a character from a fantasy tale.

Stepping into her front yard, Mrs. McGuire smiles, extends her hand and greets each of us. Wyatt places Nathaniel's portable ramp over the two front steps and the four of us enter her humble abode. Outside, Jeff lies down for a late afternoon snooze in the dwindling sunlight.

Inside her domain, crocheted doilies and hand-knitted lap-blankets adorn every surface. If she were a character in a movie, I would cast her as the former president of a successful corporation. But her looks are deceiving. Even if she didn't invent cozy, she's bringing it back in a serious way. Her home is cluttered with knickknacks and crocheted covers for everything and she chats with us and fusses over us like we're royalty.

Just like a little kid, I ask to use her bathroom, only because I want to see what it's like. And it's awesome. She has one of those rugs that covers the toilet lid and it's a lovely shade of lavender. There's a fluffy piece of carpet on the floor, also lavender. Lavender shades and drapes adorn the single window. A ruffled lavender shower curtain hangs over the tub and she has lavender-scented candles, potpourri, soap and room spray, too. I know because I smelled everything.

Best of all, she keeps an extra roll of toilet paper on the back of her toilet and it's inside a decorative little doll. The hand-crocheted skirt of the doll's lavender ball gown fits over the roll of toilet paper which helps the doll stand up. I wish I knew our hostess better, so I could ask her to make me one. I'd ask for day-glow orange to brighten up the upstairs bathroom. Meg and Jen would kill to have one of those dolls on their toilet paper.

When I come out of the bathroom and compliment her on the décor, our cheerful hostess offers us tea and I help her serve it in delicate china cups with saucers. Each cup has a different flower on it. Mine is lily-of-the-valley, which is a highly poisonous plant. I decide not to point this out. She uses regular tea bags from the supermarket and sugar. I put three teaspoons of it in my tea and a ton of milk. It tastes delicious, even if it isn't as healthful as my mother's brews.

We all sit down within reach of doily-covered side tables supplied with plenty of crocheted coasters for our tea cups. My personal table is a deep brown, polished mahogany piecrust-style table with a sunshine yellow lace doily and matching coaster on it. When I place my fragile china tea cup on its lacy coaster it looks like a photograph in an antiques magazine.

Both of my male companions seem overgrown and out of their element. Their large hands look comical lifting the dainty tea cups made of china so thin and delicate it's translucent. I'm afraid Wyatt might break his, because his hands are huge and he's not very coordinated, but he's careful and Mrs. McGuire's dainty china lives to see another tea party. Our hostess places a small plate of homemade snicker-doodle cookies on the coffee table and Wyatt and I finish them off in less than five minutes. Nathaniel only eats one and Mrs. McGuire doesn't eat any.

Wyatt downs his tea in two gulps and looks around. I know he's scouting for more cookies. Mrs. McGuire smiles at him, remarks on his appetite and brings another plate of warm cookies out from the kitchen. When she isn't looking, I wink at Wyatt. He flashes a quick grin back and then takes a huge bite of a cookie. Nathaniel glowers at both of us and mouths the word, "Behave."

Ever my mother's daughter, I begin to throw around the charm and display my legendary manners. "Your flowers are beautiful. My mother would love your yard. I hope when she's your age she's still fit enough to garden the way you do."

"My son helps me with the heavy lifting, but I manage to do all of the planting, watering, fertilizing and dead-heading. My husband, may he rest in peace, built me a little cold bed out back with some old windows and a few railroad ties, so I can gather seeds after the blossoms fade and raise my own seedlings every year."

My mom has a small greenhouse attached to an ancient gardening shed my dad renovated for her out back. It has a gravel floor and an antique, soapstone sink, but I don't want to top-dawg Mrs. McGuire. That would be rude, so I just compliment her on her stunning flower beds again.

Then we shoot the breeze about how she always crocheted and tatted her own lace before the arthritis in her hands started to make the process too painful. I would never wish any kind of pain on anyone, but it's probably just as well she stopped making the doilies and blankets, seeing as how she ran out of surfaces to put them on about two decades ago and now she has to double up, stack and layer everything. We had to move stuff aside before we could sit down in the chairs in her living room. Glancing at Wyatt I daintily place a delicate, pale yellow, hand-knitted blanket across my knees, smile at our hostess and announce, "I feel a little chill."

She smiles back and comments that the color of the blanket suits me. "Pastels always look so pretty against dark skin. What nationality are you, dear?"

"My mother's family came over from England some time during the 17th century, but on my father's side we're part Native North American."

"Lovely, that's where your coloring comes from, just lovely."

"Thank you, Mrs. McGuire."

"Why, you're welcome, my dear."

We aren't seated around a table, which is a good thing, because Wyatt would probably kick me under it. He and Nathaniel are both taking turns giving me the evil eyeball, which is supposed to be a signal to stop slinging around the bull and get down to business. Mrs. McGuire seems like she would be happy to go on discussing flowers, crocheting and my lovely skin tone all afternoon into the evening, though, so I steer the conversation toward the past.

"Were these flower beds here when you moved into your home as a young bride?"

"Oh no. First of all, I wasn't a young bride. I was a widow with a teenage son. Mr. McGuire married me and bought this house for his ready-made family. He helped me with the flower beds and the cold frame. We used to love to do yard work together."

Nathaniel weighs in. "It must've been a lot of work, though. Your yard's impressive. Every inch seems to be artfully landscaped. Did you have time for a career?" Maybe this question will lead our hostess toward talking about her job as a nurse.

"Oh, yes. I was a nurse. Two incomes are better than one and Mr. McGuire was happy to have the extra money from mine; he would've done anything for me. Back in the seventies it wasn't as common as it is now for a woman to have a career and a family, but I managed both."

Here it comes. She's going to talk about her job at the hospital. Even if she doesn't, we can coax her in that direction now without being too obvious.

Maybe she won't need any more prompting.

"When I was a bride for the first time, back in 1952, I chose to go to college and study nursing, instead of starting a family right away. Even when my son was born in 1965, I kept working. My first husband, Mr. Donahue, may he rest in peace, supported my decision one hundred percent. Like many truly good souls, he died young. Your school report is about Eastfield in the fifties, right?"

Wyatt continues to lead the conversation toward Mrs. McGuire's job as a nurse. "Yes, Eastfield in the fifties and sixties. Annabelle's particularly interested in women and their careers during that time frame."

I hope she'll start talking about Wild Wood.

"I can certainly help you with that. Like I said, not many girls chose the college path and certainly not many married women. I worked over at the Wild Wood Psychiatric Hospital for many years, until they closed down in 1986."

Bingo.

I encourage her to stay on this topic. "Wow, Wild Wood. That must've been interesting."

"Yes. And I was very fortunate to have that job because I found myself a widow and a single mother, when my son turned twelve."

Bingo again!

We're finally on the right track. She brought up Wild Wood without too much prompting from us. Jackson and Oliver made us promise we'd just let her talk and not ask too many leading questions about Daniel and his mysterious roommate. I think they were afraid that Wyatt and I would arouse her suspicions and therefore, they sent Nathaniel along as a watchdog to make sure we followed the rules. He shoots me a meaningful look and clears his throat. Then he asks the next question.

"That must've been a demanding job. My mother's a single mom and a nurse and her life hasn't been easy. How did you manage?"

"Fortunately, a year after my first husband died, I met Mr. McGuire at a pot luck supper hosted by a mutual friend. He fell in love with my baked ham in raisin sauce and then I guess with me, too."

I think of a subtle way to nudge her back toward the topic of Wild Wood. "As a working mom, you must've been exhausted. Don't nurses have to work the nightshift sometimes?"

"I always worked the day shift, mostly patient care. Then I'd be home before dinner so we could eat together as a family."

I'm dying to ask her if she ever got emotionally attached to any of her patients, but I can't think of a way to casually transition into that area, so I dive right in. "Did you ever feel a special connection to a particular patient?"

Nathaniel shoots me a look that could kill, but my clumsy conversation pays off. She starts to talk about Daniel.

"I did become very close to one of my patients. His name was Daniel. He couldn't speak, but we both enjoyed our quiet time together. I used to read to him when I wasn't too busy with my other duties. He seemed to like The Hardy Boys series, but also some more advanced literature. I remember reading him *Oliver Twist*, the whole thing, chapter by chapter, and he sat silently, hanging on every word. My own son didn't care for reading, or listening to stories when he was little, but my favorite patient loved books. Too bad the poor, sweet little boy couldn't talk, or learn to read himself. Unfortunately, they moved him to a different wing in the hospital and we didn't see each other after that."

"Why did they move him?"

"I'm not exactly sure. In addition to his mutism, he was an epileptic. Maybe the seizures had something to do with the move. I didn't ask. The hospital was overcrowded and I had so many other duties. We were understaffed, so I didn't pursue the matter. Shortly after he moved to a new room, the hospital closed."

"Did they move him because of overcrowding? Did he suffer because of the poor conditions?"

"I told you. I don't know. Why are you asking so many questions about the hospital? That's not the topic of your report."

We're getting too close to the answers we need. I try to be patient, but the big bucketful of self-control I walked in with is leaking. My goal's in sight. "Do you know anything more about why the hospital closed?"

"They lost most of their state funding due to an investigation."

"What kind of an investigation?"

"I thought you were interested in talking about the fifties and sixties. The hospital closed in 1986. Aren't we getting off track? What about your school project?"

"I think the most interesting ideas surface when you're digressing. Don't you?" I can tell that she's getting annoyed because I'm rattling her cage with all of my off-topic questions. I'm afraid to look over at Nathaniel.

I keep hoping she'll get going on the subject of why the hospital closed; then we can make some progress. In 1986, she was interested in the investigation, interested enough to write that note and hide it in the files. But she seems unwilling to discuss it now.

"The hospital closed a long time ago and I don't see how the investigation fits in with your research topic." She puts down her teacup and it clinks against the saucer.

"I'm just curious about your career as a nurse. When the hospital closed, did you find another job at a different hospital?"

"No, I was sixty years old when the hospital closed and I retired. My husband had developed heart disease, so I stayed home and nursed him. Only a few months later he died and then I had his life insurance settlement. I could live off of that and my retirement money. I'd been working as a nurse for over thirty years by then. It was time."

Then Nathaniel speaks up and redirects the interview back to neighborhood life in 1950's Eastfield, and I pretend to take notes. When I try to ask more questions about Daniel and the hospital, Nathaniel interrupts me and asks me to go check on Jeff, who's still out in the yard. I walk to the front door and call out his name. Jeff gets up and lopes over to me, but refuses to enter the house.

Mrs. McGuire comes to the door, to see what I'm up to. As she reaches down to pat Jeff, a low rumble vibrates in his throat. He backs up, turns and trots over to his place on the grass to lie down again.

Jeff doesn't like her. I look back into the living room to see if Nathaniel noticed Jeff's growl.

He raises his eyebrows and shakes his head at me, as if to say, *don't bring her attention to it.* I don't want to piss him off, so I keep my mouth shut. But I can't help wondering why Jeff doesn't like sweet, elderly Mrs. McGuire who's willing to chat on and on forever about every topic known to mankind except the closing of The Wild Wood Psychiatric Hospital.

By the time we rise to leave, I'm frustrated and disappointed. I help her collect the tea cups and carry them to the sink. She declines my offer to help her wash them. Politely, we say our goodbyes and I thank her. Nathaniel and Wyatt go out to their cars, but I linger at the door.

"You know, my dad has a friend who used to work at the hospital. I wonder if you knew him. His name is Mike. I can't remember his last name, but I'm pretty sure he worked there right around the time the hospital closed. Do you remember anyone named Mike?"

"Mike, that's a common name. I don't remember anyone named Mike off the top of my head, but my memory isn't what it used to be."

Her memory is amazing, but the amiable chatterbox has disappeared and a closemouthed, unfriendly old woman has taken her place. As soon as I step outside she closes the door so fast she almost whacks me on the ass with it. I definitely won't be invited back, which is a shame, because there's a lot more I want to know about the closing of Wild Wood and an employee named Mike. Mrs. Mary McGuire, however, isn't willing to supply me with any more information.

I traipse back to Wyatt's car, thinking about today's botched interview. But perhaps the fact that I failed to uncover any further information about our ghostly patient is valuable information in itself. What's she hiding? Why doesn't Jeff like her? And, who's Mike? I think she knows him but doesn't want to talk about it for some mysterious reason.

Nathaniel has already driven away by the time I finish talking to our hostess. Wyatt's standing outside the Land Rover, waiting to open the door for me. "I'm guessing we won't be invited back anytime soon; thanks to you. Nice job pissing off the old lady."

I bless him with my most dazzling smile. "Why, thank you for that lovely compliment, Wyatt."

"Get in the car, Nancy Drew."

Chapter 25

Mom's Ability to Sense Evil Is Put to the Test

Just a few hours after our visit to the retired nurse's fairytale cottage, I decide it's time for bed and head upstairs early; before ten o'clock. Because it's pretty warm outside and because I'm a fresh air freak anyway, I open my bedroom window halfway, to let in the night breeze. Standing there, enjoying the quiet, I stare out over the moonlit landscape for a few minutes, and breathe in the cool, clean darkness. It's a good night for snuggling up under the quilt.

The cold that awakens me around midnight isn't from outside, though. He covers me in winter and startles me awake and alert in the same instant. Immediately, I recognize the iciness that follows Anthony everywhere.

"Wake up, Annabelle!" His frozen breath raises the hackles on my neck. Then he's gone.

I hear an unfamiliar noise outside and concentrate on the rattling sound.

What the hell is that? Is a squirrel climbing up the downspout that hangs from the rain gutter outside my window?

I creep out of bed. Instinctively, staying a few steps back from the window, I peer out over the rooftop of the screened-in porch my grandfather built fifty years ago, long before he and Grandma retired and moved to Florida.

Many times, I've climbed out of my bedroom window, onto that gently sloping roof, to read, or talk on my cell phone, or sometimes just to lie on my back and gaze at the clouds. But tonight it seems like a dangerous and creepy place. I look out, across the moonlit roof tiles, to where the gutter ends in the downspout. The damn thing's shaking and thudding, as if a full grown man's shinnying up it. No sooner does this petrifying thought enter my brain, than the top of his dark head appears, right at the edge of the porch roof.

Immediately, I find my voice and scream. Then pivot and run. All hell's breaking loose right outside my bedroom door. Dad's speeding down the stairs with a rifle under his arm and I chase after him.

My mother yells, "Annabelle, get back here!"

But I ignore her.

Dad shouts, "Susannah, call the police. Johnny's on duty tonight. Hurry!"

Mom races back into their bedroom to grab her phone.

My feet ripple down the stairs, skipping steps, in an

effort to keep up with my madman of a father. He can sure move fast for an old guy. And since when does he own a gun? I'm only a few feet behind him, so I see him plunge out the back door into the darkness and I follow.

As a sharp crack slices through the silence of the night air, I feel a sudden burn on my left shoulder. Like it's been stung by a wasp the size of a great horned owl. I try to suck in some air but can't catch my breath. Staggering backwards, I almost fall over. In the gloom, I watch my father's black silhouette raise the rifle to its shoulder. Then Dad cocks the gun and fires. He does it again and again before he finally runs into the woods to get off a closer shot and I lose sight of him in the dark.

The stranger in the woods shoots again. It's a smaller sound than Dad's rifle, so he must be firing a pistol of some sort.

"Dad!" I scream. Forgetting about the pain in my shoulder, I fly barefoot across our backyard and into the forest.

"Dad!"

He doesn't heal like I do. What if he's been shot?

Wild-eyed and barefoot, he charges along the path, toward me. "Annabelle, get the hell back in the house!"

I'm overjoyed to hear his voice, even though he sounds pissed off. Bending over, I put my hands on my knees, to hold myself up and catch my breath.

Dad takes a few steps closer.

"Shh, listen."

Rapid, faint footsteps scuffle away in the distance. I can barely make out the sound.

"Damn! He got away." Dad turns and looks down at me. "Annabelle! What the hell are you doing out here? You could've gotten shot."

He obviously hasn't realized yet that I did get shot.

Like an idiot, I begin to quiver and suck in deep breaths.

His tone softens. "Honey, are you all right?"

I have a sudden urge to say, "I've been hit," like they always say on TV. But this is no time for joking.

"I'm fine, Dad." I sniffle and try to stop shaking. "It just felt like a big bee sting."

By now my mother has turned on the outside floodlights and we can all see a little more clearly. Dad finally notices the blood soaking through the shoulder of my t-shirt.

"Holy shit! Oh my God!" He tries to scoop me up in his arms to carry me, but I wince at the contact and shove him away.

"I can walk, Dad. It's my shoulder, not my leg, and it only hurts a little." I'm lying. The stinging feeling has evolved into a horrible throbbing sensation.

"Get in the house. What the hell are you doing out here?"

"I had to know. I couldn't stay inside."

"You've always been like that. Worse than your brothers. When you were little, I was always fishing you out of some pond. Or helping you climb down from the highest limb of the tallest tree in the yard."

"Sorry, Dad."

"Shit, Annabelle. The lunatic had a gun."

"I'm aware of that."

He gently rubs the back of my head, puts his arm around my waist and supports me as I stumble into the house. I could probably walk fine by myself, if I wasn't shaking so hard.

My mother greets me with that mixture of anger and worry I know so well. I've been inspiring these two emotions, simultaneously, in her for as long back as I can remember.

She doesn't know whether to say, "You poor baby, you're hurt." Or "You idiot, why the hell did you do that?" So she says both.

We go into the bathroom together and she takes off my t-shirt, wraps me in a towel and cleans up my gunshot wound. It's superficial and easily patched up with some antibiotic ointment and a big square bandage. Still, it stings and hurts like hell when she touches it, even though her hands are gentle.

"That's Joe's UMass t-shirt, isn't it?" she accuses me.

"Go, Minutemen!" My weak attempt at a joke.

"Not funny, Annabelle. Not funny at all."

"Yeah, it's Joe's shirt, but even though there's a hole in it now and you might not be able to get all of the bloodstains out, he'll think it's cool. He'll probably still wear it." I'm still shivering really hard, so my mother runs upstairs and gets one of my dad's old flannel shirts. She helps me into it and buttons it up the front. It would hurt too much if I tried to raise my arms to get a sweatshirt over my head.

When we enter the kitchen, Dad's already back outside, pacing back and forth with the rifle; making sure we're all safe. I can see him through the big window because the lights are still on out there.

My mother makes me sit down and yells at me to stay put while she goes into her little pantry and measures out handfuls of lavender, Echinacea and golden seal. Then she brews me a cup of tea designed to speed the healing process and ease the nerves, plus it's nice and hot and I can't stop shivering. The night's grown a lot colder since I went to bed. The whole ordeal has really shaken me up. That happens when the adrenaline surges then ebbs. You feel cold and shaky.

Mom makes sure that I finish the whole mug of heavily-honeyed tea and then she pours me another. "Later, I'll make a poultice for your wound by soaking a clean cloth in cooled-down tea made from speedwell and yarrow blossoms. I'll put one on your shoulder every night until the scab falls off. Even though you heal more quickly than most people, you've been shot and that's always serious."

She lights her candles and we sit at the kitchen table together, both clutching mugs of hot, sweet tea. I put my face down near the cup and breathe in the steam. It warms me down into my toes.

"Wait 'til your father comes in, Annabelle. Then you can explain everything to both of us at the same time."

"What do you mean: 'explain'?"

"Don't you think you owe us an explanation? I suspect

you have some idea why someone was shooting off a gun in our backyard in the middle of the night."

"I suppose I do have a theory."

My mother eyes me. "I'm slowly starting to figure out what happened, based on the information Nathaniel told me about your visit to Mrs. McGuire's. You've been holding back. I don't know exactly what you said to her, Annabelle, but we need to know everything and so does Uncle Johnny. You just visited her this afternoon, so tonight's attack has to be connected to her somehow. I hope the police can find this guy."

"Me too."

"I still don't understand why you ran outside. That was so dangerous."

"I had to know. You and Dad were in danger and it's my fault. I did something stupid. I couldn't just sit in the house and wait. Everything happened because of me."

"Why did it happen because of you? What did you do, Annabelle? What did you say to that old lady this afternoon?"

I avoid answering my mother's questions and instead try to distract her by explaining tonight's sequence of events as best as I can.

"Anthony woke me up. Then I heard someone shinnying up the downspout. When I got out of bed and looked out the window I saw the top of his head. You and Dad must've heard something, too. By the time I ran out of my room, Dad was already in the hallway with his rifle."

"I figured out you were in danger through a different sense, not hearing: a sixth sense. When any kind of evil is close by, I feel sick: dizzy and nauseous. The feeling was so strong tonight; I woke up out of a sound sleep and grabbed hold of your father. He knew immediately, just by looking at me, that something horrible was going down. He ran for the gun and I screamed for him not to go, but he headed out back anyway. The old fool."

So, not only can my mother sense and ward off evil, my dad provides back-up, with a loaded weapon. And I always thought they were boring.

"That's amazing! He saved our lives tonight."

"Him and grandpa's old rifle."

"It was pitch black and he was barefoot!"

"That's a Blake thing. Your dad and his brother can move through the woods like animals. They don't make any noise. They have super-keen night vision. They're surefooted and stealthy even in the dark. His dad and granddad were the same way."

As if they know we're talking about them, my dad walks in with his brother, my Uncle Johnny. Both of them look pretty grim. Through the big bay window overlooking the backyard and the woods, I can see a handful of police officers searching everywhere with flashlights. They won't find him though.

The intruder's gone. I can tell by looking at my mother. She's composed and calm, not nauseous and agitated. There's no evil close by.

Dad starts in on me. "So, Annabelle, can we assume your intruder wasn't some random bad guy looking for an anonymous victim?"

Uncle Johnny and Dad sit down with us and my mother sets cups of tea in front of them. My dad's younger brother is obviously not pleased and I can guess why. A close family member's at the center of a giant heap of commotion in our small town. He'll have to think fast and perform a lot of damage control. Everyone in Eastfield will want to know what happened.

Why was someone on the Blakes' property firing a gun in the middle of the night? That'll be the question of the day tomorrow, in our close-knit, gossipy community.

My mother announces that my gunshot wound should remain a secret. I don't require a doctor, so we don't need to report it. We certainly don't want all the attention it will draw. Uncle Johnny agrees and delivers some directions into his crackling walkie-talkie. He manages to keep the other police officers outside and at bay, while we continue to have our private conversation in the kitchen. He even quells the flashing blue lights and sirens. My dad turns off the floodlights and the cops aren't using any huge, brilliant searchlights in the backyard, or adjoining woods and swampland. Only a quiet handful of police officers explore the dim shadows of our property with their crisscrossing flashlight beams. The circles of pale yellow light look like inflated fireflies floating here and there in the darkness.

Uncle Johnny goes outside and we watch him through the window as he converses with the other officers. Then he comes back inside and reports to us that the intruder got away. He ran through the woods, through the shallow end of the swamp and then disappeared. A cop with a bloodhound on a leash tried to follow his trail, but it ended at the edge of the pond. The police investigators have by now concluded that the culprit arrived and escaped by boat, somewhere farther into the swamp. Out there the wetlands open up into a small and isolated pond we call Deep Water.

The Morse family has owned Deep Water Pond and the surrounding land for centuries. Mr. Morse is quite elderly now, so he doesn't spend much time at the pond. But he always lets us fish out of it in the summer and ice skate on it in the winter. He won't take kindly to someone borrowing one of his boats in the middle of the night to sneak over and shoot at his closest neighbors.

"Old man Morse and his wife probably slept through it all. The intruder didn't go near their house. So they won't be able to tell us much about him. Most likely, he parked on the street at the edge of the woods and snuck out to the pond to steal the Morse's boat. Then he rowed it quickly across the water, got out and jogged through the woods into your backyard," Uncle Johnny explains.

"How did he know which window was Annabelle's?" my mom asks.

"My officers found a couple of snapped lower branches on one of the pines out back and a few cigarette butts under it. I think he sat up in that tree with binoculars and checked out the house for a while."

"I remember standing at my window, looking out before I turned off the light and went to bed."

"Then that's it, Annabelle. He saw you in your window, right near the porch roof, saw the downspout. Bingo. He made a plan and executed it."

"He almost executed Annabelle." Dad's calmer now but he still looks worried.

My uncle continues to question us so he can put together the facts.

"Bill, what the hell were you doing, shooting that damn thing off in the middle of the night? What the hell were you thinking?"

"He shot first."

"Then just call us. Let us do the damn shooting. Where the hell did you get the damn gun?" Uncle Johnny runs his hand through what's left of his hair but there's not even enough to mess up. His gray-blue eyes are wide open and wild.

There are a lot of damns and hells getting thrown around in my mother's kitchen. But she won't get mad unless someone lets loose with an F bomb. She won't care who's shooting off guns and running through the woods at midnight. My mother refuses to tolerate the F word in her home.

"It's Dad's old gopher-shooting rifle," my father answers. "I haven't fired it since we were kids. Remember how Dad used to set up those tin cans for us to aim at, down at the dump, before it became the landfill and recycling center?"

"It's a wonder you didn't blow the guy's head off, or shoot someone's pure bred poodle, out for a midnight pee."

"I aimed a foot above the guy's head. I guessed that he might be about average height, so I aimed about seven feet up just to be sure, although I wanted to blow his head off. I was always a way better shot than you and it all came right back to me as soon as I raised the butt to my shoulder and sighted down the barrel. Just like riding a bicycle."

"Very few people die from getting hit by a bicycle. And you were never a better shot than me."

"I'm calling Dad down in Florida. He'll remember."

"Okay, okay, no need to bother Dad. He and Mom go to bed at seven. Right after they get back from the early bird special. Let's not give him a heart attack. You're an excellent shot. I admit it. But that thing hasn't been fired in years. You're lucky it didn't explode and blow your face off."

"I haven't fired it in a long time, but I keep it cleaned up and in good condition just like Dad taught us. Also, it's licensed to me and always kept in a locked closet. I'm the only one who has a key. None of the kids even know it exists, except for tonight. Now Annabelle knows."

"It's a damn pain in the ass, Bill. We got people calling the station saying they heard shots. Susannah called me all hysterical to tell me you were headed out the backdoor full speed ahead carrying a loaded rifle in the middle of the night like some damn lunatic militia man."

"He's after Annabelle, Johnny. We can't have that." My dad's statement silences his brother.

"Now why would anyone be after Annabelle?"

"It's a long story, John. Like a lot of stories involving the Blakes, it's complicated."

I can't think of a good way to tell my uncle, the cop,

about Mary McGuire's hidden note and Daniel's journal without revealing that we trespassed at the Wild Wood Hospital. I'm hoping Dad or Mom will think of something. Also, I'm sure Uncle Johnny isn't ready to hear about the ghost, but then again, he's a Blake and they all know about the family curse and how I'm the one who broke it. I was the last to find out about all that.

"Johnny, maybe you should come back when you're off duty if you want to hear the whole story." Dad saves the day again, this time without a loaded weapon.

My uncle looks at his watch. "That'll be in about ten minutes."

"So call off the troops. Sit and finish your tea. In ten minutes I'll break out the Jack Daniels and we'll talk about the whole truth. Until then I'll give you a version you can use in your official report."

Chapter 26

Uncle Johnny Hears the Truth

I walk over to the big window in our kitchen and look out into the night, at the dark and dangerous world that used to be my backyard. Now it's a crime scene. Three or four police officers are still poking here and there with flashlights, looking under shrubs and in between the tall herbs in my mother's raised flower beds.

My dad and I go out with Uncle Johnny, to show him approximately where I was standing when the bullet grazed my shoulder. I whisper in my uncle's ear so no one will know that I actually got shot. Dad and Uncle Johnny look around but fail to find the bullet anywhere. There isn't much evidence out there. No one, not even my uncle's fellow officers, needs to know I got shot. At the first light of dawn, when no one else is around, Uncle Johnny and my dad will look around again, to see if they

266

can find the bullet that grazed my shoulder. The three of us go back in the house, and I watch the torch beams through the window.

Behind me I hear someone knocking at the back door. I assume it's one of the cops and continue to gaze out the window, facing away from the small group at the table. My mother opens the door to let the officer in. I feel pretty humiliated because I caused all the trouble, so I don't turn around.

As I hang my head and marinate in my own disgrace, two strong arms circle me from behind. Wyatt bends down until his lips are next to my ear. "What have you done, you stupid girl?"

I don't answer him.

"Thank god you're okay." Then he turns me to face him, but I can't look up and meet his eyes.

When he pulls me closer, I wince.

"Annabelle, are you hurt?"

My mother answers him. "She has a superficial bullet wound on her shoulder. But that's a secret, Wyatt. She's going to be fine physically. However, I think right now she just might die of remorse. Her recklessness has caused everyone a load of trouble, but worst of all, she's in danger."

No one knows what I asked Mary McGuire right before we left her house and it's time to confess. What I want to do most is stand here with Wyatt and hide my face against his chest. He seems willing to grant my wish, too, but my uncle interrupts.

"I don't think I've ever met this young man, Annabelle. I'd like to know what he's doing here in the middle of the night during a police investigation."

Wyatt lets go of me and steps forward to shake hands with Uncle Johnny. He introduces himself and then explains why he's shown up in the middle of the night.

"Marc Adams lives over there, to the left." He points out the back window. "We're on the high school soccer team together. He knows Annabelle and I are going out. Anyway, he heard the shots and his dad has a police radio, so he ran and turned it on. When the dispatcher mentioned Annabelle's address he called me to see if I knew anything. I answered 'No' then pulled on some clothes and raced over. Oliver's probably coming, too. He was moving too slow for me, though. I couldn't stand it. I had to see if Annabelle was all right."

"The cops outside just let you in?"

"I told them Annabelle called me and Mrs. Blake knew I was coming."

"You lied to the police?" My uncle looks pissed.

"Sorry, I had to, sir. I couldn't stand it. I was going crazy with worry. Plus I'm involved in this whole mess. I might be able to help in some way."

Feeling miserable, I stand quietly by Wyatt's side as the tears dribble down my cheeks. In a quiet voice, I beg my parents, "Can I please talk to Wyatt alone? It will be easier for me to tell him everything. Then we can talk to all of you together."

Rolling her eyes, my mother sighs and looks to my father and uncle for their opinions. When they nod their heads in agreement, she gives us permission. "Annabelle, count yourself lucky that your uncle and father feel uncomfortable in the presence of a crying female. You and Wyatt can go into the den for a few minutes, but we expect you to return soon and tell us everything."

So Wyatt and I head into my father's sanctuary. I turn on a table lamp and the glow reveals the familiar and comfortable furniture, along with everything hanging on the walls: my dad's framed prints and photographs of sports teams and stadiums mixed in with pictures of us kids in various poses. There are a couple of action shots of Joe and me playing soccer and tennis and one of Clement accepting an award at a college film festival in Boston.

On top of my parents' bookshelf filled with mysteries, thrillers and the biographies of famous people, sit about ten trophies the three of us have earned throughout the years. I feel a little less shaky just from seeing that nothing here, in this room, has changed. It reminds me that my parents will always love me and be proud of me even though I'm an idiot at times, like now.

Putting his arms around me, Wyatt lets me lean against him for a few moments before he speaks. "So, Annabelle, tell me everything."

Standing there silently, in the warm, strong circle of his arms, I imagine how I must feel to him, the small shaky figure of a ridiculous girl who got herself shot because of her own stupidity. Who put her family in danger because she can't use good judgment and control her curiosity.

"I should be shaped like a question mark, all hunched over in a curve. Even I don't know what I'm going to do or say next. Why am I like this? Why can't I stop myself? Why don't I even want to stop myself when I get going? Why am I so stubborn and stupid?"

"I don't know the answers to any of those questions, but I know you aren't shaped like a question mark. You're shaped like a girl." He hugs me closer. "And I love all those things about you, even the stubborn and stupid stuff. Except it's frustrating as hell sometimes."

"Remember all the stupid questions I asked Mrs. McGuire about the closing of the hospital?"

"Yes." Wyatt quietly waits for me to continue.

"When you were over by the car and I was standing at the door with Mrs. McGuire, I told her my father had a friend who used to work at the hospital right before it closed and his name was Mike, but I couldn't remember his last name. I asked if she knew him and she said no. She didn't remember anyone named Mike."

"But she does remember Mike and she knows him. She sent him over here to shoot you." Wyatt's rubbing my back but he's being careful of my shoulder.

"It appears to be that simple."

"Let's go tell the grownups." He doesn't let go of me just yet, though. He tips my chin up and kisses me, first gently and then when I don't complain or flinch with pain, he deepens the kiss, holding onto me tightly. When he finally raises his lips from mine his voice sounds a little breathless. "I'm so thankful you're all right. You have to stay safe. I can't lose you."

"Anthony woke me up and my mother saved us, too. She sensed the guy's presence and my dad went racing outside with his rifle. Then Mom called the police. Like an idiot, I raced outside. I followed my dad."

"Annabelle, you dumbass!"

"I know. I know. Come help me tell them the whole story. Uncle Johnny doesn't even know the beginning. He's family, though, and in my family that means accepting as truth what other families might consider to be really farfetched. He's off duty by now, so we can tell him everything."

Together, Wyatt and I walk into the kitchen to face my family and the others. Oliver, Jackson, Nathaniel and Jeff have all arrived. Jeff comes over to sniff at me and make sure I'm okay. After I hug him and kiss his muzzle, he settles down by Nathaniel's feet with his head on his paws. Only the perky posture of his ears reveals that he's still on the alert for danger and not to be messed with.

All the humans look pretty solemn and Wyatt puts his hand on my unwounded shoulder, to offer moral support. He tells everyone present what I said to Mrs. Mary McGuire about "Mike." Nobody yells at me or anything. They all obviously feel sorry for me, maybe because of my bullet wound, or maybe just because I'm a dumbass who's too stupid to live.

I took a reckless chance and now we all have to face a dangerous situation. We need to find out who Mike is fast and put a stop to his nighttime activities. As it turns out, though, his next move happens in the relative safety of sparkling daylight and much too soon for the cops to get a good handle on the situation.

Chapter 27

After the Drama, More Drama

I arrive at school on time, to avoid starting any rumors about last night's drama. As usual, Wyatt meets me in the parking lot and walks me into the building. I'm exhausted, but thanks to my ability to heal myself, my shoulder doesn't hurt much and I make it through my morning classes just fine. Word has gotten out that the police were at my house last night. Word always gets out fast in a small town like ours.

Before Uncle Johnny left, our small group of con-spirators concocted a story about my dad shooting into the air to scare off a dangerous pack of coyotes that were cruising too close to the house. The cops who showed up at our house with Uncle Johnny have agreed to keep everything confidential, so our real story's safe for now. Even the cops on the scene don't know everything. They all went back to the station before we revealed the preposterous truth to Uncle Johnny.

At lunch Connor, Ryan, Meg and Jen ask about my ordeal and Wyatt and I skillfully field the questions they throw at us. After I manage to get through my afternoon classes, Wyatt meets me at my locker and we talk for a few minutes before leaving for our practices.

He tells me I look tired and asks, "How're you going to be able to run? I've never seen you looking this awful."

"Thanks for boosting my confidence."

He smiles. "You're welcome."

"I'll just take it easy. I'm sure the coach heard something about last night. He'll know I was up late. I can run with the first-year people. Don't worry. I'll be fine. Running always helps me deal with stress and I need that more than ever right now. My uncle's going to be lurking around the woods, hiding behind trees and bushes, keeping an eye on me. I hope he can keep up with my pace. He's getting kinda old and the five mile loop might be too challenging for him."

Wyatt laughs. "He looks pretty fit to me. Be careful. Call me later." He kisses my forehead and squeezes my uninjured shoulder. I wish he could come with me, but he has to go to soccer practice. Besides, that would be weird. He lopes off toward the door opening out to the playing fields in the back of the school. I head out to the big yellow bus that'll bring the team to the town forest where we'll run along the winding paths in the woods.

About a dozen trails of different lengths meander through the acres of Eastfield's Town Forest and I usually look forward to any time spent on this beautiful conservation land. Today, however, I feel tired and scared. The police didn't find any good fingerprints on our downspout or Mr. Morse's boat. They found shoe prints, but the intruder wears a common size and he had on a popular brand of running shoe. Uncle Johnny was going to question Mrs. McGuire this morning and I'm anxious to find out what she had to say.

Oliver and Jackson will be moving ahead with their plans to talk to Dr. Summers and Dr. Peterson. I hate waiting on the sidelines while Oliver, Jackson and Uncle Johnny meet with key people and ask important questions. Maybe I haven't learned my lesson after all. I still yearn to be in the middle of the action despite the danger. Here, at track practice, however, at least I can keep moving. The exertion of running helps keep my focus off all the anxiety building up inside of me.

My jogging companions today are agreeable and I have no trouble keeping up with their pace. I'm running with two ninth-grade girls, Amy and Leah. This is the first time they've kept up with a varsity runner and I think they're acting a little shyer around me than they might act with their own friends. When we were stretching and warming up, Amy, the more talkative of the two, asked me if I was going out with Wyatt Silver. When I answered yes, she told me she thought he was hot.

After we started down the path, I jogged along at what for me is a relaxing pace and they matched my speed. I was left to my own deep thoughts because my side-kicks, flanking me, were too winded to chat. But they kept running and didn't complain…

Every few meters, I glance over my shoulder, expecting to see a dark figure aiming a gun at me. But I don't see anything, not even Uncle Johnny. Wyatt's under strict orders to stick with me at school, but I feel like I'm on my own right now with two fourteen-year-old girls in the middle of a forest. If my uncle would peek out from behind a tree and wave to me now and then I'd feel safer.

What if Mike the Bad Guy, as I've begun to think of him, has followed me here? There are tons of trees he could hide behind. Uncle Johnny's not the only one who's good at sneaking around the forest. It's no secret I'm on the cross-country team and lots of people know we run in these woods every day. The branches moving with the wind and the dry leaves crunching underfoot spook me until I'm almost as out of breath as Amy and Leah. So much for the relaxing qualities of long-distance running.

The coach divided the team into thirds and each group's running a different route. The other people in our group are either way ahead of us or way behind and I begin to fret silently about the solitude. I listen for crunches and thumps not made by our three pairs of sneakers. My head swivels left and right as I scan the forest on either side of the path for movement or shadows that don't belong. Patting the right-hand pocket of my shorts, I feel the reassuring presence of my cell phone. It's bouncing up and down, but still there.

A twitch of movement and an impression of something large catches my attention a few feet ahead, where the trees open into a large field. Shooting my arms out to either side, I effectively stop Amy and Leah in their tracks. "Shh," I warn as if they could control their panting. I point left into the distance and the three of us focus through the trees and peer at the meadow beyond.

A huge deer with his white tail stuck straight up races across the open field with four others close behind him. Leah gasps and Amy whips out her smart phone. She aims, fires and shows us she got a couple of decent pictures for *Instagram.* We stand still and watch the deer disappear into the woods before resuming our jog through their forest, being careful to tread as quietly as possible.

After we finish our five-mile loop we join the rest of the team. Everyone's sitting and chatting and guzzling water and Gatorade while we wait for the stragglers. Finally, the bus can leave and we head back to Eastfield High. In the school parking lot, I spy a familiar van and I'm happy and relieved to see Nathaniel, big, solid and reliable in his wheelchair, with Jeff by his side, sitting at attention, ears perked up, sniffing the air.

"I'm on duty to make sure nobody takes any potshots at you while you're getting into your car. We figured someone should be here just in case you got out of practice before Wyatt. The soccer coach is keeping the team later than usual."

I bend to kiss the fuzzy flat space between Jeff's ears. "Thanks, I appreciate it."

"No problem. What, the dog gets a kiss and I have to sit here all lonely, ready to take a bullet for you?"

I laugh and bend to kiss his cheek.

Rubbing my thumb against Nathaniel's stubble, I tease him. "Shave much?"

"Actually not today and not yesterday, either. I'm going for the 'drunk guy who slept on a park bench' look."

We share a laugh but then I get down to business. "Have you heard from Oliver or Jackson? Is there any new news?"

"They're meeting with Dr. Peterson as we speak and they have an appointment with Dr. Summers tomorrow. We figure that everyone should sit down with your uncle the cop tomorrow night and go over what we've found out. Maybe your dad's heard from him already. Anyway, the parking lot here's pretty peaceful. I got here fifteen minutes ago and nothing suspicious has happened. You probably should've parked in the middle of the lot, though, not over there by those trees."

He points at my car, which is squeezed into the very last space, right at the edge of the woods.

"I was running a little late this morning. You have to get here wicked early to get a good space. So I had to park over there."

I jog toward my car then stop as I get close enough to see it clearly. "Nathaniel!"

He speeds over, Jeff at his side. Together, we stare at my car. Jeff begins sniffing all around the ground surrounding it.

In the grime on my back windshield someone's written *Next time I won't miss.*

Nathaniel whips out his cell phone and calls Uncle Johnny.

Chapter 28

Can Anyone Keep Me Safe?

Nathaniel shouts into his cell phone, "It had to be him!"

After glancing left and right and then behind us, he softens his voice. "No one at the school knows she got shot. It could only be the guy from last night. Good idea to keep that detail quiet. Come in your own car, not a black and white, and no uniforms. Annabelle doesn't need a lot of attention. She's stressed out enough. As soon as you get here I'm bringing her home."

Nathaniel tells my Uncle Johnny what to do, a pretty bold move. My medium friend's used to taking charge and ordering people around.

He pockets his phone and looks up at me. "Try not to worry about it. The guy's a first class creep. We can keep you safe. I promise."

I don't believe him for a second, but I don't feel afraid anymore, either. My fear and anxiety have evolved into anger. Whoever "Mike" is, he probably killed Daniel and Anthony and now he's literally gunning for me. This has to stop. I desperately want him to pay for his crimes. I want it with all my heart, more than I've ever wanted anything before in my whole life.

The student parking lot's sparsely populated with only the cars belonging to kids who are involved in after school activities. My Uncle Johnny makes a low key entrance in his silver Honda Civic and heads right for my old Chevy Prizm, which sits alone in a row of spaces near the woods bordering the parking lot. Large oaks and pine trees curve around behind the parking spaces at the forest's edge and form a big arc around both the playing fields and the tennis courts. When I got here this morning, I could barely maneuver my way into a space because the lot was so full. Now most of those cars are gone.

My uncle might be out of uniform and driving his own car so he won't attract attention, but there's nothing low-key about his mood. He hops out and rushes over to where I'm standing, in between Nathaniel and Jeff.

"No wonder I didn't spot him creeping around the town forest. He was right here in the parking lot. Damn. Don't worry, honey. We're going to get him. We know who he is now. There's no way he's getting away with this."

"Who is it? Who's doing this to Annabelle?" Nathaniel's tone of voice is quiet but urgent.

"His name's Mike Donahue."

Why does the last name Donahue sound familiar to me?

Before I can place the name or ask my question out loud, Uncle Johnny answers it.

"He's Mrs. McGuire's son from her first marriage."

That's why the name sounds familiar. I remember the way her prim, old lady voice sounded when she said it. "My first husband, Mr. Donahue, may he rest in peace."

A discreet duo of police officers in jeans and polo shirts is examining my Prizm quickly and efficiently while Nathaniel, Uncle Johnny and I discuss the newest information about our case.

My uncle continues. "We knew the old lady had to be directly connected to the attack on Annabelle, because it happened right after their visit. So we began looking into Nurse Mary McGuire's background, to see if she was closely associated with anyone named Mike or Michael. The name Mike turned up right away because he's her son. He worked at the hospital in 1986, at the time it got closed down for good, too. We ran a background check, to see if he has a sheet and we found out that he doesn't have a criminal record. However, he's been fired from several jobs over the past twenty years since he worked at Wild Wood. He has no special training or degrees in the health field, but he's always worked at hospitals and other healthcare facilities. We made a few calls to his former places of employment and it turns out that wherever he worked, the medication inventory never came out right. No one could prove anything, but his last few employers were suspicious that he was stealing drugs and they let him go because of it.

"He's a difficult guy to locate, because he has no permanent address. His mother's address is the one on his driver's license, but he hasn't lived there in years. The old lady isn't being helpful at all. She denies any involvement in the shooting and claims she thought Annabelle was a charming young lady. She wishes she'd visit again."

"I bet she does." Nathaniel raises his eyebrows and presses his lips into a thin line.

I think about what kind of ambush would be waiting for me if I ever showed up at Nurse Mary McGuire's house again.

Uncle Johnny continues. "She has no memory of Annabelle asking about a hospital employee named Mike. She claims her son has been staying with some friends down the Cape in an off-season rental and she thinks he's working in a restaurant, but she can't remember the name of it or his temporary address, not even the town."

"You wouldn't believe the details she remembers about things that happened over twenty years ago."

Nathaniel looks disgusted. "She very conveniently becomes a confused and forgetful senior citizen whenever it suits her purpose."

"She can stonewall us all she wants. We're going to find him soon and bring him in. Don't worry, Annabelle. He knows we're watching you closely, so he had to make do with writing on your car when you weren't around. But he'll slip up soon and we'll catch him. He'll make a false move out of desperation and we'll be there. Meanwhile, you keep a low profile and either Wyatt, Nathaniel or I will stick with you whenever you're not at home."

I'm reluctant to admit it, but I do anyway. "Today at practice, when we were running through the Town Forest, I knew you were there, but I got really spooked anyway."

"He's less likely to come near you when you're in a group. There had to be what, forty kids in the woods on those trails?"

"More like seventy altogether. But we were spread out."

"That's why I was there. I know you couldn't see me, honey, but I never lost sight of you. I can't remember the last time I ran five miles. I'm gonna be sore tomorrow."

"Thanks for having my back, Uncle Johnny. Sorry you had to run five miles."

"Five miles silently, sprinting in a low crouch, from tree to tree."

I smile at him. "Wow! You really are gonna be sore. Better ask my mom for one of her salves or poultices. She makes a nice concoction for aching muscles."

"Good idea. By the way, our story about the coyotes stays the same. If anyone expresses any curiosity about Wyatt and Nathaniel sticking close to Annabelle, just say she's been getting some weird anonymous calls on her cell. She's worried so you guys are hanging around to reassure her. And don't worry about me sticking close. No one will ever see me." He winks. "Outside of a few cops and the people already involved in the case, no one needs to know the truth."

Nathan nods. "Gotcha. Good plan, John."

"Now get her out of here, Nathaniel. I'll talk to you later, honey." He bends and kisses my cheek. "Stay safe and get some rest. You look exhausted."

I'm damned tired of everyone telling me how awful I look. Nathaniel, Jeff and I get in his van to head over to my house so I can get my desperately needed beauty rest. My mother's going to be furious when she hears about the threatening message on the car. I wouldn't want to be Mike Donahue if she ever gets her hands on him.

When we arrive she fusses over me, changes the bandage on my shoulder and does the whole poultice thing which seems to take forever. Then she makes me drink two different kinds of tea and a Gatorade and puts together enough homemade pizzas to feed all seventy members of the cross country team if they should show up unexpectedly. Nathaniel and Jeff stick around to eat. Then Wyatt, Oliver and Jackson show up, too. Oliver has a huge pasta salad with him and a delicious brown rice and root vegetable casserole. My dad arrives home from work with two gallons of my favorite ice cream: chocolate chip cookie dough.

If food and love can keep evil away, Mike Donahue will never show up at my house again. Uncle Johnny arrives with my car at around at seven thirty and fills us in on the lack of evidence at our most recent crime scene, which is now parked in our driveway.

He cracks a few jokes about my vehicle. "Hey, Annabelle, that car of yours isn't a very smooth ride. You ought to get your old man to buy you something newer. I had to roll down the window with the little handle. I haven't driven a car like that in so long I forgot which direction to turn the handle for up and down. The passenger side window doesn't even open at all."

My dad laughs. "For a while, when Clement was driving it, the passenger side *door* didn't open at all. Everyone had to climb out the driver's side. We got it fixed for Annabelle, though. She's lucky she has a car to drive. We're paying two college tuitions and next fall she'll be in college, too. Hell, *I'm* lucky to have a car to drive." He actually has a truck because of his construction business.

Wyatt has his own opinion of what I should be driving—nothing. "I think I should pick up Annabelle and bring her home from school every day until we catch this guy. She'll be safe with me. He's a coward, obviously, picking on hospital patients and sleeping girls in the middle of the night. Oh, and one decrepit old vehicle, big brave man! He isn't going to bother her if she's with me."

"He certainly ran away pretty fast when he saw me with the rifle," my dad adds.

Uncle Johnny agrees and it's decided without any input from me; Wyatt will be my bodyguard until the police arrest Mike Donahue. If Wyatt's too busy, or he gets tied up at a late soccer practice, Nathaniel will fill in.

There's someone present, however, who's deeply involved in our mystery and everyone's forgotten about him but me. He makes his presence known, but even though two mediums and one very intuitive not-quite-a-witch are in our cozy, golden-lit kitchen, I'm the only one who notices him. Jeff's sound asleep across the room. Still, he pricks up his ears for a second and lets out a low growl, but then doesn't lift his head or open his eyes. Maybe he's getting used to Anthony.

My mother's candles flicker as if a breeze is blowing through the middle of the kitchen, but all the windows are closed. Everyone keeps on talking and eating and drinking. Then the candles fizzle quietly and grow a touch brighter. I catch an image in my peripheral vision, a reflection on the shiny, night-black surface of the big window overlooking the backyard. I'm not seeing through the window into the dark acres beyond the house, but back into the cheerful kitchen. A serious, pale figure appears for less than a second: only to me. Anthony's letting me know that he's here and he cares.

I excuse myself to go up to bed and everyone understands, because as they've all reminded me numerous times throughout the day, I look like crap and must be extremely tired, in order to look so ugly. Wyatt stands up and steps away from the table so he can hug me before I leave. My mother comments on how cold it's gotten in the kitchen. "Maybe the warm weather's finally ending. Bill, will you close the window? It's getting chilly out."

"Susannah, none of the windows are open."

I know exactly why it feels cold in the kitchen. He always brings the winter with him. As I leave my little circle of friends and family and climb the stairs to my room, Uncle Johnny calls out, "I'm gonna have a look around the property before your dad drives me home, honey." He intends to make me feel safer, but I'm not worried. No living person will be interrupting my sleep tonight and I'm not afraid of my supernatural visitor anymore. Wyatt's right. Mike Donahue has proven himself a coward and will never approach me with so many people around, especially when one's a cop and another keeps a loaded rifle close by.

I can sleep soundly and be safe. I brush my teeth and change into a t-shirt and some baggy, drawstring cotton pajama pants with pandas on them. Meg left them at my house one time after a sleep-over. I never returned them. I cozy up under my puffy soft quilt and sigh, waiting to hear Anthony's voice whisper in the darkness. He doesn't disappoint me.

"I want to come to school."

"What?"

"I want to see what school's *like*, not just see it, actually experience it. I want to talk to other students and eat lunch and walk to class through the crowded hallway when the bell rings. I want to carry your books like Wyatt did today."

Wyatt insisted because of my stupid shoulder wound.

"You want Wyatt to channel you during school?"

"Yes. I've never gotten to do anything like that. I spent my whole life locked up."

"Wyatt has to agree to it."

"He will, no problem."

"How can you be so sure?"

"I know him. He has a big heart; a generous spirit. I want a turn protecting you from the bad guy. I hope he comes at you when I'm there."

"He won't."

"Probably not. He's an evil coward, but I can wish he'll show up just the same."

"Okay, I'll talk to Wyatt about it."

"Everyone will think it's a great idea."

"How can you be so sure?"

"I'm the only one who's seen Mike Donahue before. He may be twenty years older, but I'd recognize him. I can be your best protection from him. You'll see."

"You're right. This could be interesting, hanging around with you in the real world, for a whole day. If anything weird comes up, though, you'll have to make a quick exit."

"Don't worry. You can count on me. I'm good at that. You're safe now. Sleep well, Annabelle."

The room grows gradually warmer, and I do, too.

Chapter 29

Anthony Goes to School

When I come downstairs for breakfast, Mom's sitting at the kitchen table, drinking tea. She announces she thinks it's a great idea for Anthony to come to school with me. Last night, he visited Wyatt after he left here and they discussed his plan. Wyatt asked Oliver what he thought and then he called both my mother and Nathaniel.

Anthony's our best chance of spotting Mike Donahue if the culprit comes near me. Uncle Johnny showed us Donahue's license photo but you can't always get a good feel for what someone looks like from those sorts of pictures. Anthony saw him move, heard him speak and observed the villain close up, even if it was over twenty years ago. Anthony's perceptions at the time were confused even on a good day, but my ghost is determined to help out by coming to school with me. So we're going to let him.

Enter If You Dare

Wyatt was a little hesitant to agree to let Anthony take over for a whole school day. He's worried about what'll happen if Anthony's controlling his body while he's going to classes and talking to his friends. Anthony has never taken over while Wyatt's been out in public before, but we convince Wyatt that it'll work. Anthony promises him he'll make a quick exit and Wyatt can take over again if anything weird happens. So Wyatt finally caves. Oliver arranges for Nathaniel to visit his History class as a guest lecturer who's an authority on supernatural legends, so he can hang around the hallways in between classes and keep an eye on things. Both Oliver and Nathaniel will be close by at all times and available by cell phone.

Wyatt picks me up in the morning and drives me to school. No one thinks Anthony's ready to try driving. Nathaniel meets us in the parking lot and goes over a few things with Wyatt. Then Wyatt becomes Anthony, just like that. His appearance undergoes a few subtle changes. He has dark shadows under his eyes and he's thinner with more prominent cheekbones. He looks like Wyatt might if he wasn't sleeping well or was coming down with a cold.

While the three of us are standing around talking, Meg drives up in her car and gestures out the window for me to join her. I jog over to her parking space, two rows away from where we're parked, to see what she wants. Glancing over my shoulder, I notice that Nathaniel and Anthony are still engrossed in their conversation. Meg tells me to hop in and I climb into the passenger seat. Then she looks down at her hands, resting on the steering wheel.

Her voice is quiet in the closed-up vehicle. "Ryan and I are going to take our relationship to the next level."

"Whoa! Are you sure you're ready?"

"He's been ready since day one. And I think I'm ready now. We've been together for almost a year."

I actually thought they'd already *taken their relationship to the next level*. They're always with each other and they look at each other in *that* way. Meg and I haven't hung out together for a while, though, so I'm obviously out of the loop.

"What does Jen think?"

"I haven't told her."

"But you're telling me?"

"I remember how Matt Riley pressured you sometimes because you two were together for almost a year. It turns out you did the right thing by not giving in. I wonder if I'll be doing the right thing when I *do* give in."

"Ryan isn't at all like Matt. He never even looks at another girl. He adores you."

"So you think we should?"

"Meg, I can't tell you what you should do. I'm not exactly experienced in that department. I'm experienced at saying no, not saying yes. If you do say yes, though, be careful."

"Obviously. We both know we have to be really careful. We're not idiots."

"Sorry. I know you're not an idiot and neither is Ryan. You two'll make the right decision."

"Thanks, Annabelle. I'll let you know how it works out."

I'm not sure I want to know, so I do what I often do when I'm nervous or uncomfortable about something. I make a joke. "T. M. I. Remember. I don't want Too. Much. Information."

She laughs. "Hey, we should get together soon, do something fun and girlie. Watch a chick flick or make s'mores over at Jen's fire pit again."

As if on cue, Jen shows up and taps on Meg's window. We both get out of the car. Meg invites us all over to Jen's house.

"Hey, Jen, Annabelle and I want to come over and toast marshmallows at your house. What night's good for you?"

"Friday's good. Hey! I forgot! That was so much fun last time! Meg, remember how you got melted marshmallow in your hair? That was hilarious! We should do it," Jen agrees. We did have a lot of fun the last time we used the fire pit.

"You might not have thought it was so funny if it was your hair." Meg has beautiful long, blonde hair and it was sticky for a week afterward. She sounds kind of annoyed, but she's laughing at the same time. "I had to wear it in a ponytail for like a month almost."

"And you guys made me call my mother to see if she could make some kind of an herbal concoction that would get marshmallow out of hair." Even my mother thought it was pretty funny.

Jen finalizes our plans. "Okay, that settles it. We'll meet Friday behind my house at about eight o'clock. I'll supply the graham crackers, chocolate and marshmallows."

"I'll bring the shampoo, Blondie." I giggle.

"Oh, I forgot. The only thing is, I promised Ryan we could hang out on Friday night. Can we invite guys?" Meg asks.

"Sure, Wyatt will want to come and he can bring someone from the soccer team. Maybe we can fix you up, Jen."

"Hell no, I want to be single. It's senior year. I'm not getting serious about anyone so don't try to set me up with a soccer player, even if there are some hot guys on the team. I'm gonna just have fun."

"I know," Meg says, "we can ask Connor."

It's the perfect solution. Connor's a guy so it won't be awkward with two couples and Jen. And we're all really good friends. At the beginning of sophomore year, Jen put the moves on Connor, but when he didn't respond to her flirting she gave up and moved on. There were no hard feelings and we're all still close. Fortunately, Connor's not a major threat to Jen's plans to stay single. So it's settled. The six of us will get together Friday at her house, build a fire and make s'mores.

It's exactly what I need to help me forget about Mike Donahue and his threats. I start to run back to my car to get my books and tell Wyatt about our plan, forgetting that he isn't Wyatt at the moment. As soon as I see his brooding, serious face, still deep in conversation with Nathaniel, I remember I'm spending the day with Anthony.

I call back over my shoulder to the girls. "Maybe we can tell ghost stories around the campfire!"

I know I could win a contest with mine.

Anthony's ready to go, so I reach into the car to get my books. He rests his hand gently on my shoulder and I look up.

"Oh, no, Annabelle, I'll get those." My self-appointed guardian angel lifts the books out of my hands and stacks them on top of his own. He manages to carry all of them easily under one arm. Wrapping his free arm around my waist, he pulls me toward him; then kisses the top of my head. This day is going to be even weirder than I thought.

"Hey, what the hell, Anthony?"

"Annabelle, I have to act like Wyatt. I've watched you two together. He's always touching you and kissing you. What would he do if he saw you standing in the morning sun with your beautiful face looking carefree and happy for the first time in days? And your hair smells like wildflowers. Mmmmm. You smell so good." He kisses my cheek and hugs me close to his side again.

Nathaniel smiles. "You're on your own with that one, Annabelle. The kid has a point. He did what Wyatt would do. He did what I'd do. He has pretty good instincts. He did what any guy would do under the circumstances."

"Thanks," I mutter. "Where's Jeff?"

"I know. I feel naked without him, but he can't come to school. Oliver has only so much influence. He got me in the door, but Jeff has to stay home. Anyway, he'd be barking his head off every time he came close to Anthony. You know how he hates ghosts. No offense, Anthony, don't take it personally. He hates all ghosts, not just you."

"No offense taken. I'm glad he's at home. I've been on the receiving end before when Jeff gets going with his hostility toward anyone who's in the least bit ghostly. I'll keep my distance from him, thank you."

"Let's go. We don't want to be late for History class and I still have to go to my locker first."

Anthony places an all-too-comfortable and familiar hand on my shoulder and ambles along beside me. He seems relaxed to the point of cockiness. I look up at his satisfied face and can't help but feel happy for him. The kid lived a miserable life and is getting a chance to experience a regular teenaged day in the twenty-first century. I smile at him and our eyes connect. His are darker than Wyatt's ever turn, but no one will notice except me. Even if they do, they'd never suspect what's really happening. It's way too farfetched.

We grin at each other like two people who share an unimaginable secret, because we do. As I look into his brilliant dark eyes, sparkling with eagerness, I think about how during his short, miserable life, Anthony was always restrained and locked up. Now he's free.

I whisper, "This was a really good idea," and my grin spreads into a full-blown, mile-wide smile.

My coconspirator smiles back.

Everyone else in History class looks bored and sleepy, but Anthony doesn't. When he isn't staring at me, he's soaking up every word Mrs. Fowler speaks, as if she's the most fascinating person on the planet. He looks in his text book. He looks down at his hand-writing in Wyatt's History notebook. He looks up at the teacher again and then he looks at me and smiles.

As I watch him write in Wyatt's notebook it dawns on me that he's never written a word before. During his life, he couldn't speak or read or write. Every letter he forms, every word he hears, every sight he observes today is new. He gives me a whole new appreciation for what a privileged life I lead.

He remains a model of self-control. But when he looks my way, even for an instant, his electric glances remind me he's in awe of this whole experience. I'm seeing the world through the eyes of a boy who was deprived, during his own brief and tragic life, of everything I take for granted every day. When I think about Anthony, even the air feels new on my skin.

He's awakening all my senses and I feel like a newborn in a teenager's body. When our eyes meet, we're born again together; the mute, neglected child who raged at the world around him and the girl who offered him love and true friendship.

After History, we have to separate and follow our individual schedules until noon. Later, Anthony and I meet at Wyatt's locker before lunch and walk into the cafeteria together. When he bites into the school lunch pizza, which is pretty good for cafeteria food, I stare at his face and feel like I'm tasting pizza for the first time. The stretchy cheese tastes salty, the tomato sauce tangy with just the right hint of sweetness and the crust is like fresh-baked, homemade bread, crunchy on the outside, warm and soft and chewy on the inside—delicious. He chews, swallows and takes another bite. I've never experienced anything so precious with another person before and it feels phenomenal.

I cover his hand with mine and tell him, "Wait until you try the cookies. They're my favorite."

I want to show him the world, to introduce him to life. I never want this day to end, mostly because I know he doesn't either. To hell with Mike Donahue, even thinking about him can't ruin today for Anthony and me.

He rests his forehead against mine and we stare into each other's eyes and chuckle softly. Both of us are reluctant to end the physical contact, but we know our unseen connection can never end. That's something Anthony has proven to everyone who's met him since his soul escaped from the hospital.

Just by being here, he's answering a question which has burned in the minds of humans for centuries, down through the tunnels of time and inside the castles built above those tunnels by the collective imaginations of millions of us.

Yes, Annabelle, there is *life after death: life and love and all the confusion and elation one soul can feel. It doesn't matter whether you welcome it or dread it; it's a fact.*

He never says these words out loud to me, but I hear them nonetheless and their eloquence stuns me, moves me and pleases me like no other gift I've ever received. And in this moment Anthony and I both know it.

I'm giving him affection, sympathy, companionship, communication: all of the essential things that were tragically missing during his brief and miserable time on earth. He's giving me a glimpse into one small part of the afterlife which awaits us all and even though there's a lot more to it than he can show me right now, he assures me that an afterlife *does* exist despite countless and ancient debates. I'll live on after my body deteriorates into dust and so will everyone I love and care about.

But we can't forget that without Wyatt, Anthony wouldn't be walking around in our world right now, as a free man, breathing and touching and tasting commonplace things as if they were miracles sent to us by the gods. Whoever would think of the school's lunchroom pizza as an amazing sensual experience?

Anthony tucks our books under one arm and then interlocks the fingers on his free hand with mine. Palm-to-palm, we walk out of the cafeteria, up the stairs to my English class. At the door of the classroom, he lets go of my hand and as I turn to walk into English, he whacks me on the butt.

I spin around and glare at him. "That's not cool."

"I know, but I had to. I might never get another chance. There it was, right in front of me, at hand level. Sorry, it won't happen again." He covers his mouth with one hand; probably so I won't realize he's grinning. But one side of his smile peeks out, despite his efforts to hide it. "Plus, it's the best butt in the whole school. Just ask the golf team."

"I'll see you after school at my locker. And keep those hands to yourself."

"I will. I promise." He tries to look sorry and serious, but fails.

"And stay away from the golf team. They're obviously a bad influence." I back into the classroom, frowning up at him the whole way until he turns and hustles off toward Wyatt's AP Biology class.

"Always with the boyfriend troubles, Miss Blake. I don't

know how you manage such an impressive academic performance every term," Ms. Coffman teases.

"It's cuz I'm always thinking about stuff like Hamlet; wondering if he's going to make up his mind to be or not to be within the next five centuries."

"Did you finish memorizing the soliloquy?"

"Yes, I did, British accent and all, mum. Alas, is poor Yorick ready? Because, you know, I knew him, Horatio." I do my best to sound like Cate Blanchett in *Elizabeth: the Golden Age*, but I sound more like Bruce, the shark in *Finding Nemo*.

Ms. Coffman cracks up. "That accent needs a lot more work, Annabelle. You sound more like the Crocodile Hunter than Hamlet." Ms. Coffman's a tough grader, but she appreciates my ability to make an idiot out of myself with very little effort.

Because my last name is at the beginning of the alphabet, I get called up first to recite. Fortunately, I worked hard to memorize the "To be or not to be" speech in between all the dramatic episodes of my own life. And even though my accent comes from down under and not from anywhere near Stratford-on-Avon, I speak with sincere anguish to that plastic skull and don't forget one word. She gives me an A plus. The A is for knowing the whole speech cold and the plus is for making her laugh so hard she almost peed, because my accent sounded ridiculous.

After school, on my way to cross-country practice, I walk up to Wyatt's locker and Anthony's leaning against it, crunching Doritos out of a bright blue bag, a delirious smile on his shadowy face.

"Look at this chip, Annabelle! It has so much good-tasting powdery stuff on it. What a bonus!" He pops the corn chip into his mouth and bites down.

After about a minute of crunching and swallowing, he licks his lips. "Mmmmm. Here, do you want one?"

He tips the open bag toward me.

"No thanks, if I eat anything too close to when I go running, I'll throw up. You might, too. Watch how many of those you woof down."

"It'll be worth it. These are great." He chomps down a couple more chips, tips the bag up and spills the crumbs from the bottom directly into his mouth. Then he smooshes up the empty bag and throws it into Wyatt's open locker where it will probably attract mice. Reaching into the locker, he pulls out a red Gatorade, twists it open, chugs down a few swigs and passes it to me. I drink half of it in three fast gulps and hand it back.

"Hey, slow down! That's mine!"

I laugh and hiccup. "I left you a little."

"Your lips are all red." He wipes his thumb across my lips and grins. "Do you know what was the best thing about today, besides being with you?"

"No idea. What was the best thing?"

"Geometry."

"I hate Geometry. If my dad hadn't helped me, when I was in ninth grade, I would've failed it. Even with his help I got a C for the year."

Wyatt actually takes AP Calculus for his real Math class. But for his Community Service requirement, he helps out the teacher in a freshman Geometry class. He's that good at math. Anthony obviously shares Wyatt's talent for math, probably because he's sharing Wyatt's brain at the moment.

"How can you hate Geometry? It's so beautiful. It clarifies everything. I love it."

Not even Wyatt feels Anthony's reverence for the subject.

"How can you love it? It's boring. And how can it clarify anything? It's confusing."

"Annabelle, geometry is the most logical thing on earth. But instead of words, it's shapes. Every physical object can be defined with shapes and lines and their relationships to each other. Everything in the visible world is made up of these shapes and lines. It's logic that you can see. And it's incredible to look at and think about."

"I've never thought of it that way before. My dad's good at geometry because he's a builder. It makes so much sense now." How can I be learning so much from Anthony when everything's all new to him? "I can't believe it. I'm having a conversation about math and I'm not bored to death."

Anthony grins and he looks so beautiful when he smiles that I want to stay with him and keep talking, but we can't. I take out my cell phone and check the time. "You'll be late for practice and you'll get yelled at."

"You'll miss the bus to Town Forest," he warns.

"Whoa!" I spin around and head down the corridor, toward the exit to the parking lot.

"'Bye, Annabelle. Thanks for everything!" he yells out.

I know what he means. Everything from Geometry to pizza.

Soon he'll have to leave Wyatt's body and his day here on Earth will be over.

Mike Donahue hasn't come near us. I'm safe and Anthony's big chance to be a regular high school student is just about done, but he remembered to say "thank you." I turn around. He's standing by the open door; watching me. Running backwards across the parking lot, I wave to him. He lifts his hand and smiles.

Then I turn and climb into the waiting bus. I feel so grateful to have been a part of his experience. I'm the one who should be thanking him.

My feelings for Anthony grow wings that lift me up and send me soaring high, past the roofs of the nearby houses and above the telephone poles with the singing wires stretched between them in the dazzling sunlight of this perfect, clear-skied afternoon. In my imagination I soar up, above the tree tops and then the clouds, into the endless blue of the sky and beyond, where Anthony will find me one day and keep me close to him forever.

Chapter 30

Anthony and Wyatt

The rest of the week passes by uneventfully. Mike Donahue doesn't make any more attempts on my life, or any threats against it. Wyatt recuperated quickly from his out-of-body experience, but the whole thing has left me feeling weird and unsettled. We end up spending time together midweek which is unusual, but Wyatt, Anthony and I are growing more and more inseparable. Dangerous circumstances have drawn us together into a quivering huddle and we give each other strength.

"My grip's weakening. It weakens every time I let him in." Wyatt sounds worried, despite the warmth and coziness of our surroundings.

Oliver and Jackson went out to dinner so just Wyatt and I are sitting on the couch in his living room. In the fireplace tall flames char the native fieldstones and the thick logs are disintegrating fast. Wyatt gets up to feed the fire periodically. As I snuggle deeper into his embrace I feel the heat and strength of his arms and my mood grows soft and sweet, like a fresh-baked cookie.

We're supposed to be studying for a History test, but Wyatt turned the lights off which makes it difficult to do schoolwork. Through a haze of cozy feelings, my brain finally engages and I find my voice. "What grip? Are you talking about Anthony?"

He caught me by surprise. I thought he wanted to make out, but now he's starting a serious conversation.

"Yes. Anthony. Every time I let him in, he grows more powerful and I grow weaker. It's scary. I asked Nathaniel and we had a long talk. He said he's never experienced anything like it."

"You talked about channeling? With Nathaniel?" I'm having trouble focusing on our conversation. I rub my palm over his chest and feel his muscles through his t-shirt. His hand closes around my wrist and he holds my hand over his heart. It's beating slow and strong.

"Mmmmm." He smiles and kisses the top of my head. "Your hair's so sparkly in the firelight; I can practically see my reflection. And what's that smell? It's not strong enough to be perfume. Is it your shampoo?"

"It's a rinse my mother makes from rainwater, flowers and herbs. I can't be more specific because it's a secret. You have to dunk your hair in a bucket of the icy cold liquid and hold it in there until your scalp tingles. Then your hair comes out all shiny. My mom invented the concoction. You'll never smell another girl's hair that will smell like mine."

"I'll never smell another girl's hair."

He's the sweetest guy ever.

Wyatt buries his face in my hair and breathes in deep. "Pine forest and a whole meadow full of wild flowers."

This isn't far from the truth. Rosemary's an evergreen and lavender and chamomile are flowers; those are some of my mother's secret ingredients.

"I love you, Annabelle."

Whoa. This conversation's taking a really serious turn.

Now I'm focused. The last time a boy said that to me he was lying. I stare into Wyatt's eyes and see the truth. I also see a question. Do I love him, too?

"I love you, too, Wyatt." It's out there now. I can't take it back.

"I've always loved you, Annabelle. Before I met you I loved you. I don't just love you; I *know* you. I *knew* you. I recognized you the second I looked into your beautiful, mismatched eyes, even though I'd never seen you before."

"You've never mentioned that about my eyes. I thought maybe you hadn't noticed."

"I noticed them first before I even looked at the rest of you. One's darker than the other. And they're green and brown, like a forest. You've had those eyes for centuries. Woodland eyes. When I look into them I can see the past, the present and the future. Together, long ago, you and I created this civilization. We live in it now and in the years to come, we'll inherit it from ourselves. You and me, Annabelle. We're different from the others."

Removing his arms from around me, he sinks both hands into my hair and gently holds my head, tilting it up as he lowers his mouth to mine. He deepens the kiss and a low murmur rumbles deep in his throat, like purring. We lie down, stretched out beside each other on the couch. Feeling his warmth everywhere, I press up against him, as I kiss him back. His hands move all over me, trailing delicious warmth everywhere they go. I've never kissed anyone like I'm kissing him right now. I can't seem to get close enough to Wyatt; from my lips down to my toes. Then he shifts his whole body until it's on top of mine and his weight sinks me down into the soft couch cushions.

He whispers, "Let's go up to my room."

Panicking, I pull my hands away from the back of his neck then push against his shoulders. Prying my mouth away from his, I heave him off me. He blinks and shakes his head. When I sit up, he sits up, too.

"C'mon, Annabelle." He moves in to kiss me again and when our lips connect, he nudges me down onto my back.

His lips move from my mouth to my neck where they make my whole body tingle even though they're only touching one small place under my ear. I push him away again and pop up into a sitting position. He gives up.

"Annabelle, Annabelle, Annabelle, how long have we been going out now?"

"Officially, not even two months. Not long enough."

"But I feel like I've known you forever."

"You have, in a way. But here, in Eastfield, in high school, it hasn't even been two months."

"Annabelle, I feel like I've waited forever for you. And I'm tired of waiting."

"Waiting for what?"

"To fall in love. I've never even had a girlfriend before."

"No way. You're eighteen, Wyatt. Lots of girls here in Eastfield think you're hot."

"I've had opportunities. But I always knew."

"Knew what?"

"I always knew that if I waited long enough, someone who was worth waiting for would come along. I trusted that feeling and I was right. I fell in love the second I saw you. Hell bent, running to class so you wouldn't be late, with your hair dripping down your back. Your books and stuff falling all over the place. I thought to myself, 'That's the girl I've been waiting for.'"

"Still, it happened only two months ago. I need more time."

"What would I do without you to bring me back to reality?"

"You know what you'd do and I know what you'd do, but I'm not going to say it." My face grows redder and it's not just from the heat of the fire. "Besides, I always worry that Anthony's going to jump in and take over when we're making out."

"Anthony and I have an agreement."

"What kind of agreement?"

"Like college roommates, you know, in a dormitory. I saw it in a movie once. If one roommate's with a girl, in their dorm room, he hangs a sock on the doorknob, on the outside of the door. Then the other roommate knows not to come in. Kind of like a do-not-disturb sign. If you and I are making out, Anthony has agreed to give us some privacy."

"I don't have to worry?"

"Nope. He won't take over. It's all good. It's just you and me and the fire, here tonight in this room. So, come on, Annabelle. I've waited a long time for you. I love you. Relax." He puts his arms around me and tries to nudge me back down again, but I refuse even though I want to.

"There are too many serious things to talk about and if we're kissing it's too distracting. You were saying earlier that your grip's weakening and Anthony's getting stronger. That doesn't fit with the whole sock thing."

I scoot down the couch on the seat of my jeans, putting a couple of feet between us and move a pillow from the corner of the couch to the middle of it, creating a physical boundary.

Wyatt shakes his hair out of his eyes and then continues. "It's true. Anthony gets stronger and I feel drained every time we switch places. The last time was too long. Thanks to Nathaniel and much to Oliver's horror, I ate practically a whole cow's worth of cheeseburgers. Nathaniel cooked them on the grill at his house and brought them over. He kept me awake to make me eat. Once I started, I couldn't stop. You should try his burgers. He's a great cook. After I ate I slept for sixteen hours straight."

"But you feel okay now?"

"Yeah, I feel strong and I have energy."

I'm very aware of that.

Wyatt continues. "But I'm closely connected to Anthony all the time. We know each other's thoughts and we could easily trade places. What if we changed places for good? I don't think that could happen, but it scares me. What if Anthony and I switched places and I couldn't come back?"

"Does Nathaniel ever feel that way when he's channeling?"

"No, never, he always feels in control. In the beginning, Nathaniel told me that Anthony couldn't take over unless I let him, which sounded reassuring at the time, but now he *can* take over. Nathaniel was wrong. When he's channeling, he's never formed that strong of a bond with a spirit, like the one Anthony and I have. Sometimes, when I don't consciously allow Anthony in, he pushes his way in. I might have let him in anyway, but he gets impatient. He surprises me. I don't realize what's happening until it's too late. He's in control and I can't reclaim my own body."

"Maybe it's because you care so much about him."

"You're right. We both feel an incredible empathy toward one another. Sometimes I feel like he *is* me. And I'm him. Once he's inside me, he doesn't want to leave. After he's left my body, he gets nervous that he won't be able to get in again. I know what that's like for him, because when he's in control, I worry that I'll never get back in again. It scares the crap out of me but how can I not feel sorry for him? I feel his sadness in my core. I've never felt that way toward anyone before. His pain is my pain and it's twice as intense because there are two of us."

"Two souls."

"Yes. But only one body. Mine."

This doesn't sound to me like a situation that can be controlled by hanging a sock over a doorknob. Perched for flight, at the opposite end of the big overstuffed sofa, I turn my head and meet his eyes. "What does Nathaniel think?"

"That's another thing that scares me, because Nathaniel's my mentor, but how can he mentor me when what's happening's beyond his experience? Like the cold; we always feel so cold around Anthony. Nathaniel said that he's felt cold spots before. It's common, when a ghost is nearby, to feel cold, but the chill that surrounds Anthony is way colder and much deeper and it lasts longer than anything Nathaniel's ever felt before."

"He brings the winter with him. It's a clue to the way Anthony died." The words tumble out of my mouth before I'm even aware that I thought them up.

"How do you know that?"

"I just do. It isn't some kind of psychic revelation. It makes sense on a conscious level. Daniel died on February 10th and we think Anthony died that night too, even though there's no official record of his life or his death. February's usually the coldest month of the year."

I don't explain to Wyatt that my intuition, which has grown stronger and more intense since my encounter with Anthony in the abandoned hospital a year ago, confirms what logic tells me is true.

My logic announced to me a long time ago that the extreme cold of February must factor into the mystery surrounding Anthony's death. But now I'm certain the deep freeze encircling everyone in his presence is a clue to the way he died. I'm almost ready to tell Wyatt about my beyond-normal intuition, its dawn and its progression, but not quite yet. So I continue to pass on knowledge gained through leaps of unexplainable understanding, letting it masquerade as conscious thought, born of normal, natural and earthly imaginings. Psychic ability is only a small jump beyond this type of thinking anyway; therefore I'm almost telling the whole truth.

"I have a theory. Nathaniel often feels sympathy for the souls he's channeling, but he never comes close to the level of your feelings for Anthony. You don't feel *for* Anthony, you feel *with* him."

"Anthony and I have so many things connecting us, the first and most obvious being you, Annabelle. We both love you. It binds us together and pisses me off. I hate sharing you with him, but it's like sharing you with myself. When he touches you, I hate it, but he touches you with my hands. It's hard to explain and even harder to deal with."

"No one we know has ever been through anything like this before, just you and me and Anthony. Not even Nathaniel knows what it's like."

"He's talked to a couple of other mediums about it, too, and they've never experienced anything like it."

"We're explorers on a new frontier."

"Yes. But my body is the frontier and I like this body. I'd like to stay here in it for a lot more years. I'm excited about the whole supernatural experience and I feel close to Anthony, like no one else will ever know. I don't have a brother, but I think I love him like one. Except sometimes it's horrifying."

"I think we need to hold onto the fact that my mother senses no evil from him. She'd never let him near me if she did."

"You're right."

"He'd never harm us."

"Okay, I'll hang onto that. That's good. He isn't evil. His intentions aren't evil. He means us no harm." Wyatt's gaze grows unfocused and he says it again. "He wouldn't harm me. He wouldn't harm you."

"Plus, I know stuff."

"What are you talking about?"

"It's because I have some unusual ancestors."

"I know you look like a girl from another century whose name was also Annabelle Blake. And I know about the curse and the Wampanoag tribe and the witches."

"It turns out I'm just beginning to discover and develop my paranormal talents. I never knew for sure that they existed until recently. My mother thought I'd start coming into my own around my eighteenth birthday, so she was going to wait to share the family stories with me until then, but stumbling into Anthony, up in room 209 last fall, rushed things along before anyone was ready. Everything came raining down on me: the dreams when he kept opening my door and then meeting you. The three of us connected, like pelting rain, bolts of lightning and earth-shaking thunder."

Wyatt continues with the weather analogy. "Like a funnel cloud begins and then a tornado forms and then it touches down and sucks up houses and roofs and cars."

"And this tornado has sucked up the three of us. We're stuck in the epicenter of this incredible situation and we're tumbling around; out-of-control."

"There must be somebody somewhere who can help us."

"I don't think there is. We have to do it ourselves."

"Maybe if we try harder, Annabelle."

"We know Anthony's a ghost and you're a medium, but what am I?"

"What are you, Annabelle? You're something. Is there a name for it?"

"I'm not sure yet, but I know I can do one thing. And it's different from what everyone else does; different than your talent or Nathaniel's. I know stuff and I don't know how I know it. I know things no one taught me or showed me or explained to me. I never observed these things. I just know them. I've always been a little bit aware of this and it's made me feel different, separate and alone. Then you came along and now I don't feel so alone anymore. But this above normal awareness is getting stronger and it will get way stronger before I've reached my full potential. I'm not nearly there yet."

"So, what do you know that might help us out?"

"I know that you and Anthony are inseparable because your parents abandoned you. He felt your loneliness immediately and it was a lot like his. Your warm front met his cold front and 'Boom!' Thunder and lightning. You crashed into each other and then connected because you're so much alike."

"Yes. What else?"

"He was your age when he died. He was eighteen."

"How do you know that?"

"I just do. It makes sense and I know it. It's part logic and evidence and then a leap built on an intuitive feeling. The rain and the wind part of the storm started with me and Anthony, last year, but the true forces of nature collided when you stepped into the picture. And that's because Anthony's parents left him at Wild Wood. They felt repulsed by him and he frightened them. So they abandoned him, even though he had no control over his condition. Your mother wanted to lock you up in a residential psychiatric facility, too. Only Oliver saved you.

"Jackson says that Anthony was severely autistic and he might have been schizophrenic. His inability to communicate frustrated him and he had violent outbursts. The people who were supposed to be caring for him at the hospital made his behavior worse with the way they treated him. So he became more violent out of frustration and anger. The poor kid couldn't help it, though. He couldn't interpret facial expressions or language. He was born that way and his parents rejected him because of it.

"Your mother did the same thing when you began having paranormal experiences, even though you couldn't help it. You're a medium. You were programmed at birth to become one, just like Nathaniel. Adolescence arrived and so did your paranormal talent."

"Exactly."

"Nathaniel's talent emerged under different circumstances, but it was just as inevitable. His mother accepted him and loved him when he discovered his paranormal abilities. When your talent became evident, your parents turned on you. Your father moved out shortly after your first encounter with a ghost and when your supernatural experiences became more dramatic and your mother couldn't ignore them, she wanted to lock you up in a psychiatric hospital."

"My dad moved out because he met someone twenty years younger than my mother and they hooked up."

"He left first and then he met her. He left because you saw ghosts and these experiences fascinated you. As soon as that happened he was out the door."

"Oh my god, you're right. It's true, but I never thought of it that way. He left right after we found the ghost at Jackson's church. My mother was mad that I saw Mariah's spirit, so I didn't talk about it much in front of her. But I talked to my dad. He seemed interested and supportive, but shortly after that, our family started falling apart."

"Can you remember exactly what happened?"

"I went to Eastfield with Oliver and we helped Jackson with the ghost of Mariah, the crying bride. After I came back, my mom got mad whenever I mentioned it. Dad didn't get mad or anything. He just left. He packed his stuff and got on a plane and we haven't seen him since. He got married right after he moved to California, so I assumed he dumped my mother for somebody he'd met before."

"Nope, he met her in California and then they fell in love and got married. He left because of you. He moved across the whole United States to get away from you."

"Thanks for pointing that out to me. I feel so much better."

How could I be so stupid? I could've phrased it in a less hurtful way. I try to make it up to Wyatt. "I love you and Oliver loves you, along with your paranormal talents and because of them, too. We love and accept the whole beautiful package that's you. Your parents are a couple of idiots who are missing out big time, but that's their loss."

"If you love me so much, come over here." He pats the couch beside him and moves the pillow that was lying between us.

I grab the pillow and push it down into its important position in the middle of the couch. "Leave that pillow alone. I'm not coming over there. It's too distracting. We need to talk. This is really important."

"It's important that I hold you. Just one hug. A little one. I promise."

"Nope. I don't trust you."

"Maybe you're just saying you love me. Maybe you don't really mean it. Oliver loves me. He would let me hug him right now if he were here and I asked him for a hug."

"And then you'd both stand aside and continue the conversation. I won't say he loves you like a father loves a son, because your own father doesn't love you that way. Oliver loves you much more than your father or your mother does."

"I know it. And I'm grateful for it. Now come over here. Cuz the way I feel about you is way different, just as intense, even more so, but really different, so please come here. I need to hold you."

If Wyatt turns his puppy-dog face on me, with those sad, changeable eyes, I'll be a goner, but he doesn't. He lunges for the pillow instead. I'm too quick for him, though, and his move is way too predatory; not cute or cuddly at all.

I sit up straight, with the pillow still between us, and keep my distance. "Anthony never had anyone like Oliver or me. He had Daniel, but it wasn't the same. They lived together in that awful room, but neither one could communicate with the other. Daniel had selective mutism and Anthony couldn't even think in language. The physical world bombarded his senses and he couldn't tune out any of it or control his reaction to the chaos that constantly tumbled around him and inside of him."

"But Anthony's not like that anymore. He's not violent."

"No, he isn't. When Anthony lost his living, breathing place in the physical world, all that ended, but he still felt lost and alone. It's why when I found him and then you found both of us, we formed an instant bond. The first night, when Meg and I were filming in the hospital, we both heard him crying. We both saw the blankets on the bed move on their own and we both felt Anthony's presence, but only I saw him. In one brilliant, speedy flash, I saw him. Meg didn't and the camera didn't either."

"Everything changed for you."

"Yes. And Anthony knew it too, from the second that he spotted me, standing in the doorway of room 209. After that, I figured out that the door opening by itself in my bedroom had something to do with what happened at Wild Wood. I didn't admit it to myself, though, until you came along."

"Then everything grew clearer."

"Gradually I accepted who I was and what was happening. I not only accepted it, I sought it. I'm obsessed with it now. I need to know how it's going to end. What happened to Anthony that night?"

"How did he die? What happened to Daniel?"

"What did Mike Donahue do to them?"

"How will we find the answers to those questions?"

"I don't know everything, but I do know that the answers will come from both worlds; this world and the next: the unknown world, the one where Anthony exists."

"So in this world, people like Oliver and Jackson can help us find answers and in the other world it's up to your mother, Nathaniel, you and me."

"Yes. But mostly you and me. And Anthony. You'll have to let him in again, not now, not tonight, but again. And we have to trust it'll turn out all right."

"Because he means us no harm."

"He isn't evil."

"Just lonely and scared."

"Except when he's with us."

"You mean except when he's me and he gets to be with you."

Chapter 31

The Fire Pit

Wyatt picks me up at eight o'clock on Friday night and the drive to Jen's house only takes a minute because I live a mile away from her, on the same street. Connor's car is parked in Jen's driveway, up close to the garage. Ryan's is behind his.

A centuries-old forest stands next to the right side of Jen's garage. The primeval woods are dense, scary and dark, even during the day. This New England version of a jungle goes back for miles, and like most of the heavily-wooded areas in Eastfield, the trees thin out gradually to reveal part of the great Hockomock Swamp.

On the opposite side of Jen's house there's another house close to hers. If she doesn't pull down the shades at night, her neighbors can see into her living room.

She has a big backyard with a ramshackled wooden

swing set that her parents haven't taken down yet, even though Jen's eighteen and an only child. She also has a tree house where we still have sleepovers in the warm weather and there's an old above-ground pool but it's closed for the winter now. The large half-oval of her yard is surrounded by woods three-quarters of the way around, across the back and on the right. On the left stands a section of wooden fence separating her yard from the too-close neighbor's.

In the center of this outdoor space sits a large, round iron fire pit, ablaze with thick logs. The smell is heavenly. Wyatt and I join the other two couples, who're sitting down in the white plastic lawn chairs circling the fire. Our front sides stay all toasty and our backs are cool. Before the four of us arrived, Jen and Connor collected six long, thin sticks and stripped the bark off the ends of them, for toasting marshmallows. The sticks' bare ends are still greenish, the best kind for cooking over a fire.

"Hey, great sticks! Thanks you, guys!" Wyatt grabs two of nature's cooking utensils and hands one to me.

"I brought some hotdogs and rolls over, too." Connor thought of everything. Even though we've all had dinner already, everyone plays a fall sport and consequently none of us can ever get enough food. Jen and Meg are on the volleyball team and Connor's on the golf team. They never ride in the carts, either, so they're out walking around in the fresh air every day.

We start with a first course of hotdogs on rolls and sodas and then move on to marshmallows and chocolate on graham crackers. Even Wyatt feels stuffed after about an hour. We gossip and tell jokes and stories about pranks and other stuff.

Ryan has a great story about making a submarine sandwich with cat food and leaving it in the refrigerator:

"I wrapped the sandwich up in the same kind of white waxy paper sub shops use, so it looked like real take-out. Next, I put a sign on it that said, 'Glen, do not eat!' Then I waited for my older brother to get home from football practice. Sure enough, Glen took the sign for a personal invitation, like he always does. He woofed down half the sandwich in three bites before I told him he had just eaten Fancy Feast."

Connor cracks up. "What did he say?"

"He didn't say anything. He finished the sandwich."

We laugh our asses off.

My brothers have played so many pranks on me throughout the years; it's hard to choose one. I'm not proud to admit that I fell for every one of their stupid tricks, too. If I was squeamish about reptiles or insects, my life would've been a living hell. Clem and Joe were always putting some poor turtle that crawled up from the swamp, under the blankets on my bed, along with a frog or two.

I tell everyone about the time my mother punished my brothers for putting two praying mantises into a box of my favorite cereal:

"Joe found them in my mother's garden and they were doing it. He brought them in and showed them to Clement."

"Ew!" Jen yells.

"It was Clem's idea to put them in the cereal box. I

poured the poor things out into a bowl and my mom started screaming about endangered species."

Wyatt smiles. "Hey, praying mantises are very beneficial to the environment. They eat harmful insects. I can just picture your mom."

"Her hair got really wild 'cuz she was shaking her head and her glasses slipped down to the end of her nose. Joe and Clem got screamed at for ten minutes straight. Clem put those poor bugs back outside in her garden and we snuck out and watched them for a while, to see if the female really bites the male's head off when they're done. It never happened. We kept going out back to check, but they just hung around on the same plant all day, doing what they were doing. The next day they were both gone."

Finally, Wyatt starts in with the ghost stories. He tells a disturbing tale about a young girl who committed suicide.

"She became this shrieking ghost who could shatter windows with her loud, high-pitched voice. Once the window was broken, she'd float into your bedroom and smother you unless someone heard your cries for help and came in to turn on the lights. Then she'd disappear, blow herself out through the broken window in a howling wind, and go looking for her next victim."

Right as Wyatt finishes telling the story a cold wind blows out of the dark forest at our backs and sends sparks and flames flying out of the fire pit. All three of us girls scream, but Ryan screams louder than anyone and jumps out of his chair. We laugh like idiots for about five minutes straight.

"Okay, now no one can say that Ryan screams like a girl, because none of us girls screamed that loud," Meg announces.

Jumping into her lap, he complains that he's scared and needs a hug. She groans because he's too heavy, so he switches places with her.

Our laughter dies down and Connor starts to say something, but I warn, "Shh."

Then I look around the semicircle, with my finger placed against my lips to signal the others. Wyatt makes eye contact with me. His eyebrows scrunch together in a silent question.

Keeping my voice low, I warn, "I heard something."

"What?" He mouths the word.

"A branch snapped, like someone walked on it."

No one here but Wyatt knows the whole truth about what's been going on in my life. They might've heard rumors about my dad shooting at coyotes in the middle of the night or prank phone calls to my cell phone. Maybe they've noticed that Wyatt's sticking closer to me than he normally does, but they don't know about Mike Donahue. Meg closed the door on the whole Wild Wood incident right after we presented our movie in class last year. We haven't mentioned what happened in room 209 to each other since then.

So only Wyatt goes on high alert because I heard a noise. Everyone else thinks the ghost story has affected my nerves.

Jen teases me. "Maybe you should crawl up in Wyatt's lap if you're that scared, Annabelle."

Wyatt doesn't laugh; he just turns to face the deep, untamed forest and peers into the darkness. I hold my breath and listen as hard as I can. Silence there and nothing more. Then an owl hoots soft and mournful. The New England woods are never completely quiet for long.

The weather's been pretty cold, so we can't hear any insects chirping or frogs croaking. But other nocturnal creatures are creeping around, uttering sporadic howls and screeches.

After the first frost, the evenings grow quieter, sometimes perfectly silent for short verses of time. Only random noises here and there puncture the stillness, usually announcing an encounter between a predator and its prey.

Tonight, it's cool and quiet, but not silent. The owl's call drifts on the night breeze again and then fades. A car cruises by out front. The fire crackles. The wood on the top shifts and falls lower. Connor gets up and puts another hefty log on top. I feel grateful for the warmth. Then I hear leaves shuffle behind me. I meet Wyatt's eyes to see if he heard it too. He did. He stands and looks at Ryan.

"Did you bring a flashlight, Ry?"

"Nope, why?"

"I heard some leaves rustling. I want to go back there, into the woods, and have a look around."

"It was probably a rodent scurrying away from that owl we keep hearing."

"Yeah, but I want to be sure."

Then he throws me under the bus.

"Annabelle's getting spooked. I want to go back there; make sure there are no coyotes or anything."

Jen speaks up. "I have two flashlights right here." She reaches down between her chair and Connor's. Wyatt takes the flashlight out of her outstretched hand, turns it on and heads into the deep dark woods.

"C'mon, Ryan, we can't let Silver play the hero alone. Let's go." Connor grabs the other flashlight off the ground and he and Ryan head into the woods together, a few steps behind Wyatt.

Jen and Meg get up and we three move our chairs around to the other side of the fire, so we can face the woods. We settle in close together, with me in the middle. As we stare quietly into the fire and listen to the rustle of the boys in the woods, Jen grips my right hand and Meg clutches my left. The owl hoots again, louder this time.

Meg whimpers and tightens her grip on my hand. Someone screams. We jump out of our chairs. Mine falls over; onto the ground behind me. Standing stock still, we huddle together, with our arms around each other, and look toward the woods. Connor barges out of the dark; a shaft of light bobs in front of him as he sprints toward the fire still holding the flashlight. Ryan's close behind.

"Where's Wyatt?" I'm almost crying.

Suddenly, he comes crashing out of the woods.

"Annabelle! Are you all right?" he shouts and rushes toward me.

"I'm fine. Someone screamed, though. What happened?"

"I thought it was you." Wyatt pulls me into his arms.

Connor owns up. "I was looking around, pointing the flashlight into the woods when two green eyes glowed at me, in the pitch dark, from only about two feet away."

"Yeah, I saw it too. So we both ran, but only Connor yelled. I knew it was probably just a raccoon or something." Ryan has no right to brag about not screaming. He came barreling out of the woods, looking just as panicked as Connor.

I can tell that Wyatt's fuming, so I warn him with my eyes to chill out. No one needs to know why he's so concerned for my safety.

* * * *

Finally the last of the logs glows orange before it fades into ashes and crumbles. The lingering scent of wood smoke does nothing to calm my fears. It's almost eleven o'clock and I'm shivering with cold and nervousness. I can't shake off the feeling there's a human pair of eyes out there in the woods and the owner of those eyes intends to harm me. I grab Wyatt's hand and pull. We stand up from our lawn chairs.

Wyatt drapes his arm across my shoulders and thanks Jen for having us over.

Jen wishes us a goodnight and then says to the others, "Let's all go inside and play video games for a while."

I've had enough and can't wait to get home. The four of them will be up until at least one in the morning, probably, and I could never last that long. I'm exhausted. Plus, I'll feel safer at home. The woods behind Jen's house are seriously creeping me out.

Wyatt and I head over to the Land Rover and the other two couples walk toward Jen's house. Ryan has his arm around Meg as they hurry to get out of the cold and Jen looks like she's getting pretty cozy with Connor for someone who has big plans to stay single. She's clutching his right arm and Connor looks happy to have it clutched.

Wyatt opens the door of the car for me, and after I climb up and in, I kiss him. He leans in and fastens my seat belt for me, kissing me back as he clicks the buckle into its slot. Then he dashes around to the driver's side, jumps in and backs out of Jen's driveway. We're at my house within a minute.

Neither one of us wants to say goodnight, but I *do* have an early practice and I can tell by looking at the house that my parents have already gone to bed. Only the kitchen windows glow yellow. All of the other windows, upstairs and down, are black. Outside, the lamp over the door closest to our driveway illuminates the short walkway. I hop out of the Land Rover and stand still, in the driveway, breathing in the cold air and looking up at the night sky. Wyatt gets out and wraps me up in a big, warm hug.

It's a clear night and the dark sky looks infinitely deep. Zillions of stars upstage the curved slice of new moon with their brilliance. Awed into silence, Wyatt and I stand locked together. He nuzzles me and murmurs into my neck, "Do you think anyone was in the woods tonight? Do you think it was him?"

"I don't know. Maybe I was spooked by your story. Maybe I did hear something, but it could've been a raccoon, the same one that scared Connor and Ryan."

"Yeah, I suppose so, but I want Mike Donahue caught. I want him gone, locked up. I'm sick of worrying that he's going to hurt you."

"He won't get a chance. You guys have got me covered every step I take. No one can come near me."

Wyatt insists on coming inside and double-checking all the locks on the doors that lead into my house. Finally, he goes down to the cellar to make sure the door to the bulkhead's locked, while I stay in the kitchen and gulp a glass of ice water. The salty hot dogs and super sweet s'mores made me thirsty. He emerges from the basement and announces that everything's locked up tight.

I remind him, "I told you my dad would never leave anything unlocked. He's as paranoid as you are about my safety."

Wyatt gives me one more kiss goodnight at the door and then leaves. Standing outside for a second, he makes sure I lock the door behind him. I turn off the light in the kitchen and leave the outside light burning so Wyatt can turn his car around without hitting the Prizm. Our driveway's long and hard to back out of, especially in the dark. After he's gone, I click off the light, tiptoe upstairs, brush my teeth, set my alarm and lay my tired head down on the pillow. Soon I fall into a deep sleep.

Chapter 32

What Do You See When You Look in the Mirror?

Out of a dead sleep, the cold wakes me up. When I went to bed the heat was on, but the house isn't toasty anymore. Blinking my sleepy eyes, I sit up.

"Anthony, leave me alone. I have to get up early."

The cold drifts away and I glance around before lying back down again. Suddenly, I bolt wide awake. Through the gloom, a pair of human eyes is staring straight at me.

Straining the seams of a butterfly chair, Wyatt's sitting a few feet away from my bed. The fashionable chair was designed to hold thirteen-year-old girls during slumber parties, not one hundred and eighty-pound guys, built of solid muscle.

"Hey, sleepyhead," he whispers.

"What the hell are you doing here?"

"Shh! Watching you sleep."

"How did you get in?'

"I knew I couldn't leave you tonight. I was too afraid that something might happen and I wouldn't be here to protect you. When I went down to the cellar I unlocked the door. Then after we said goodnight, I didn't go home. I drove back up your driveway, snuck around the back and came in through the basement. I waited long enough for you to fall asleep, then tiptoed up here to keep watch."

"That's insane; and obsessive."

"Thank you."

As he stands up and walks toward my bed, I can barely make out his features in the dark. But then he gets close enough so I can see his eyes more clearly. He looks surprised. The whites of his eyes form a startling ring around his pupils and his mouth is hanging open. Suddenly, I realize what's happening. Anthony's taking over. And Wyatt didn't invite him. When he reaches down to grab my hand, his palm and fingers feel cold.

"Come with me," he says.

"Where are we going?"

"Just into the bathroom."

I get up out of bed and walk with Anthony, wondering what he's up to.

"I want to look in the mirror with you." He pulls me toward the bathroom where there's a huge mirror over the double sinks. It stretches all the way across the whole wall and up from the counter top to the ceiling.

"Don't turn the lights on; just light that candle over there." Anthony points to a large white pillar candle on the bathroom countertop.

I open a drawer and grab a box of wooden matches. After lifting the glass cylinder off of the candle, I light it and replace the glass, with a delicate clink. Anthony grabs my hand again and we look into the mirror, side by side, palm to palm. The silent glow from the flame lights our features from beneath.

"Oh my god! It's you!" I'm not looking at Wyatt's reflection. I'm looking at Anthony's.

I drop his hand and stare at the boy in the mirror. "Pull your hair back so I can see your face better."

He puts both hands on the sides of his head and pushes back his long, tangled, black curls. His beautiful dark eyes connect with mine in the mirror. He smiles a real smile, the kind that starts in your soul before it reaches your face and shines out through your eyes.

"You're so beautiful! I can't believe it." I'm looking at the real Anthony; the way he looked when he was alive. Except now he's beautiful and peaceful and happy.

He beams back at me. His Adam's apple moves in his strong throat when he speaks. "Thank you." Tears shine in his eyes, but don't fall.

He's thinner than Wyatt, wirier, but still muscular and just as tall.

The irises of his eyes are almost black.

"How did you know about the mirror?" I ask.

"Haven't you ever heard the old ghost story about Bloody Mary?"

"The one where you turn the lights out, look in the mirror and chant her name; then her ghost appears?"

"Yes. That one. There's often an element of truth in every legend." In the mirror he stares into my eyes and reaches down to hold my hand again.

"We used to try it late at night, during slumber parties. Nothing ever appeared, but we scared ourselves silly, anyway."

"You're lucky nothing ever appeared. People who don't know what they're doing shouldn't fool around like that. You can invite a lot of trouble into your life when you experiment with the supernatural."

"Tell me about it. Look what happened to me." As soon as I speak these words I regret them, because his smile disappears and his dark brows come down low over his remarkable eyes.

"Annabelle, you know I'd rather die than harm you in any way."

"Except you're already dead."

Then he does something he's never done before. He laughs really loud. At first it's a husky, experimental sound. Then it grows into a full-on, fling your head back laugh. Anthony's laughter echoes through the bathroom and through the decades, back to the miserable boy who grew into a young man behind locked doors and barred windows. He lets go of my hand and puts his arm around my waist, hugging me close to his chilly side. As I hug him back, I can feel how solid he is. I move my hand up and touch his ribs through what feels like the thin fabric of an old pair of pajamas. Wyatt was wearing a thick, hooded sweatshirt tonight.

I stare into the mirror and he looks three-dimensional, real and alive, not transparent and ghostly. And he doesn't look at all like Wyatt. He looks like Anthony. In the mirror, he *is* Anthony.

"I want to face you and look into your eyes, Annabelle, with my own eyes, but I can't. You'll see Wyatt again if I do. The connection will break." Then he grins. "I didn't know about the legend until Nathaniel told me. He tried looking in the mirror once, when he'd formed a strong link with a spirit he was channeling, and he didn't see himself in the mirror. He saw the dead boy as if he were alive again, but only for a couple of seconds, not like this."

"When did Nathaniel tell you about the mirror?"

"He warned me that day in the parking lot, before I went into the school with you. He didn't want me going into the boys' bathroom or the locker room at school and surprising someone by looking into the mirror. They would've seen the real me, not Wyatt."

"Ah, Nathaniel, I don't know whether to thank him or pull out a hunk of his lovely hair."

"Do you know what else?"

"No. Because you haven't told me what else and I'm kind of afraid to hear it."

He smiles, baring his white teeth. "It works without the candle. You can turn on the light. I just thought we would achieve a more dramatic effect this way."

Then I get to hear his laugh again and I don't care if I'm the butt of his silly joke. He's been waiting for over twenty years to unleash his sense of humor. Who am I to ruin his fun? I smile at his reflection and he glows back at me from our shiny glass doorway into another world. When my gaze meets his, I want to turn toward him, to share this moment face to face, but we can't.

"I know," he says, as if reading my thoughts. "Turn this way. Turn your body toward me, but keep your face turned toward the mirror."

I do it and so does he. His arms go around me, pulling me against him, as we stare into the mirror. I reach up with both arms and circle his neck. He has to stoop down to let me and then he lowers his face so his right cheek rests against my left. His face is cool and a little rough from the prickles of his beard. I watch myself blush in the mirror, with one hand on the back of his neck and the other on his collar bone. We stay there in that weird position, like a pair of tango dancers, caught up in the spell of the moment.

"Annabelle, you're so warm. I can feel the blood come into your cheek through mine. I can feel your heart beating against my chest." He presses his face even closer to mine, so the corners of our lips touch. I fight off the urge to turn toward him. I don't want to break the link.

"What do you see when you look in the mirror, Anthony?"

"I see myself when I'm with you, like I never was in life, like I never have been before or will be again."

I look into the mirror and see two dark-haired teenagers, one girl and one boy. What are we when we're together? I can't think of a word that describes us. "You're more than just the ghost of the Lonesome Boy."

"I'm not lonesome anymore. I'm here with you."

"Yes. Tonight you're here with me."

"Not just tonight, Annabelle. I'll hold you close, in my heart, forever."

I step back and Anthony extinguishes the candle without blowing it out or touching it.

"That's unnerving." I flick up the light switch and blink, because of the glare. When my eyes finally adjust to the brightness, I'm staring up into my father's face. And he looks pretty pissed off.

Anthony flees like a coward, leaving Wyatt to deal with the situation. My boyfriend stretches his mouth into the widest, most rigid grin anyone has ever grinned. His parted lips reveal a wall of shiny white teeth and his face looks paralyzed. We three stand there for a full minute in silence and Wyatt continues to smile stiffly, like he has rigor mortis.

My dad speaks first, calling out to my mother. "Susannah, come into the bathroom. There's something you need to see in here."

My mom tiptoes up behind him, barefoot in her pale nightgown. "Wyatt! What the hell are you doing here?"

"Just making sure Annabelle's safe," he reassures her through gritted teeth, still grinning.

"We can do that just fine without your help," my dad counters. "Maybe you've forgotten about the night when I scared the bad guy off with a loaded rifle."

"No, sir, I haven't forgotten. I suppose she *will* be just fine without me. You're right, sir. I'll be going now." He keeps rambling. "If Oliver wakes up and realizes I'm not home yet he'll be worried."

"Here, let me show you out and lock up behind you." My dad gestures toward the stairs and Wyatt exits the scene of our little drama, with my father following in his wake.

Mom turns to me. "Annabelle, what were you two thinking?" She blushes. "Never mind. I know what you were thinking and so does your father. We were young once, too. Now go back to bed and no more late night visits."

Red-faced and flustered I stumble back to my room, creep back into bed and bundle the covers up around my ears. It's freezing.

"Oh no, you've caused enough trouble tonight. I need to get some sleep so I can get up early tomorrow and run."

The room begins to warm up again. As Anthony backs away I can hear his beautiful laugh, diminishing by degrees and finally fading completely away, into the night.

Chapter 33

He's Not Himself Today

A couple of days later, Wyatt finally gets up the courage to come over and face my parents again. He apologizes for intruding during the middle of the night and they accept his apology. They know I'm not completely innocent; I didn't kick him out after he snuck in. We share the blame for the whole debacle and Wyatt once again feels comfortable dropping by unannounced and coming over when I invite him, which is almost every day. Sometimes we go out for pizza or ice cream together. Sometimes we go to his house instead of mine. The days pass by pretty uneventfully and we spend a lot of time with one another.

During these times, Anthony often opens the door to Wyatt's soul and steps through it, so we can be together, fooling around, watching TV, eating and doing other stuff that friends do when they're hanging out. We try ping pong, but Anthony stinks at it; worse than Wyatt. Maybe because he never got to play any games when he was alive, or maybe because he's in Wyatt's body which possesses absolutely no ping pong skills. Anyway, Anthony and I have fun. The newness of everyday experiences never wears off for him. He always expresses his astonishment and amazement, even when something ordinary happens; something I take for granted.

He loves goofy comedies on TV, the stupider the better—shows where people fall or trip and crash into things. Someone landing unexpectedly on his butt sends him into high-pitched giggles. And he has the most unrestrained belly laugh I've ever heard. Wyatt has a loud, kind of obnoxious, laugh, which I love to hear. But Anthony's laugh is even more ridiculous than Wyatt's. It's a big, repetitive howl. Maybe it comes from the bottom of two souls, his own and Wyatt's; maybe Anthony lets loose so loudly because he never laughed when he was alive. For whatever reason, his laugh sounds outrageous and uninhibited and beautiful to me.

Sunday I'm out raking leaves for my parents and Wyatt stops by. Naturally, he offers to help, so I can be done faster and we can hang out. Then Anthony takes over. *Boom.* Wyatt's gone. Anthony and I rake the leaves into a huge pile and run and jump in it like six year olds. I have leaves tangled in my hair and tons of leaf crumbs all the way down my pants and in my underwear. It itches, too.

"We're going to have to rake all of this up again!" I fake yell at Anthony. I'm not mad, even though we've made more work for ourselves. I don't care because we're having so much fun.

Instead of grabbing the rakes and starting up again, we both flop down onto the ground, still giggling. I stretch out on my back in the leaves to catch my breath and stare up at the dazzling blue infinity. Anthony lies down beside me and grins.

A small, brown and orange-faced, blue-eyed dragonfly lands on my bent knee. Anthony rolls over onto his side, crooks his elbow and props his head up on one hand. Pointing at the insect, he zeroes in on it slowly and nudges it with the tip of his index finger. The dragonfly climbs onto Anthony's finger and allows itself to be carried up close to his face.

"Dragonfly," Anthony pronounces. I know he found the word in Wyatt's brain, somewhere, filed away.

"We usually have tons of them in the summer. They fly over from the swamp. Their larvae feed on mosquitoes and the adults, like this one, snatch small insects in flight and eat them."

"You know a lot about the creatures that live in this area."

"I love the creatures. I love the forests and the meadows. The swamp fascinates me."

"Me too." The dragonfly stares one more time at Anthony's face, rubs his tiny mandibles together and then takes off.

"Weird. He's flying solo and it's so late in the season for dragonflies, even if it's warmer than usual for this time of year," I wonder out loud.

"Will he be okay through the winter?"

"I hope so. He's called a Bog Haunter. They're on the endangered list. We don't see too many of them, even in the summer."

"Up from the swampland, the Bog Haunter, daring to venture close to civilization on a beautiful, warm autumn afternoon," Anthony says and chuckles.

"He's flying over that way." I point toward the woods. "Going back to haunt the bogs. He'll return when it gets warm again." I stare upward and follow the dragonfly's brave path, through the air, higher and higher, until he fades out of view, up above the treetops at the edge of the woods.

As I lie on my back in the leaves, Anthony leans over me. His head blocks the sun and I gaze into Wyatt's face, but Anthony's soul is behind those dark eyes now. We stare at each other for a whole minute, at least. Then he says, "You look perplexed."

I answer him back. "You look mystified."

"Are you rattled?"

"Are you stumped?" I love this game we've just invented.

"You've become unhinged."

"No, I'm just ruffled." It's like ping pong but with words.

"Befogged."

"Flabbergasted."

"Befuddled?"

"Maybe bemused."

"No, completely confounded."

"Discombobulated."

"Flustered."

"Nonplussed."

"Muddled, addle-pated and bewildered out of my mind."

"I give up." I don't know anymore words that mean "confused". He can't beat me at the real game of ping pong, but he wins our first match of word ping pong easily.

"I love saying words. I want to speak them forever, back and forth, with you, Annabelle."

"They're Wyatt's words. It's his mind and his voice." I'm starting to worry about Anthony's conscience. He doesn't seem to have one when it comes to taking over Wyatt's body so he can be with me.

"But they're my words right now, even if it's not for long. Do you want to know how I feel?"

He rolls over onto his back and lies there, with his head turned sideways, looking at me. I look back at his now serious face.

"Yes, I want to know how you feel, Anthony."

"I feel angry at anyone who would hurt you. I feel a treacherous kind of rage."

"Do you mean that you'd like to hurt Mike Donahue?"

"Yes, I'd do anything to protect you from him."

"Thank you."

"It's okay. You don't need to thank me. Good intentions have nothing to do with it. I don't feel that way by choice. I can't help it. If Mike Donahue was here right now, while I'm in Wyatt's body, I wouldn't be able to control the violence. It would erupt. I think I'd kill him. It's that kind of anger."

"Scary. Especially for Wyatt because he'd have to deal with the consequences, even though he didn't kill anyone."

"I think he'd do the same thing, though. He hates Donahue as much as I do and he wants to protect you like I do."

"So it would be okay, because you and Wyatt feel the same way toward him?"

"Yes. But we don't always feel the same way. I don't get jealous, like Wyatt does. I'm happy that Wyatt and you love each other. I don't feel jealous or angry. You deserve to be loved and kept safe."

"So do you, Anthony. Everyone let you down when you were at Wild Wood."

"I'm beginning to see that now. I'm starting to feel like I deserve love. I love you, Annabelle. Do you love me?"

"Yes, but not like I love Wyatt. I love you like I love my friends. Maybe I love you more than I love my friends, but not the way I love Wyatt."

"Wyatt feels angry if another boy tries to be close to you or touch you."

"Yes, he does."

"He gets mad when I touch you, even though I touch you with his hands."

"It's normal when two people are together, like Wyatt and I are, for them to feel jealous if someone else gets too close to the other person. He's not controlling his hands when you take over. You're controlling his hands and you're touching me and Wyatt doesn't like it. He's only human."

"And I'm not."

"Sorry, but that isn't a bad thing. It's like you're above it. You're too spiritual to feel jealous. Your soul has moved beyond those kinds of feelings."

"But still, I love you. That's a human feeling."

I turn my face away first because I can't keep looking into his eyes. I can tell that he wants to kiss me. And then we'd both be cheating on Wyatt. Anthony's a guest in Wyatt's body and it would be rude to kiss the host's girlfriend. I'm glad he doesn't try. I'm not sure how I'd respond if he did.

No one ever showed Anthony any affection when he was alive. This moment with me in the leaves is his only chance, but he knows he shouldn't kiss me. Even though the lips are Wyatt's lips, it's different. The decision to act wouldn't be Wyatt's decision. It would be Anthony's.

I can tell when Wyatt isn't Wyatt in a couple of ways. His skin feels cold and his smile is different, newer-looking, like he's learning how to smile but hasn't mastered it yet. He's experimenting with different eye crinkles and smile widths but hasn't found the ones that suit him best. As I'm thinking about this, I mull over why it took so long for Anthony to learn to smile. He never experienced happiness. No one ever loved him. He had no reason to smile, ever, when he was alive.

His parents abandoned him when he was too young to even form any thoughts that could later become memories.

At Wild Wood they locked him away, in a room with only one small window. The doctors restrained him so they could control him. His caretakers strapped him onto one of those horrifying tables we saw. They force-fed him medication. He never, in his lifetime, experienced friendship. He never felt even a casual, friendly connection, like when a cashier at a store is nice to you. He never shared a laugh or even a smile with another human being.

The depth of this realization pulls me down into a black hole, a vacuum; everything good in this world was denied to Anthony. He truly was the Lonesome Boy. Until now, he had no happiness in his poor abandoned soul.

I care about him because he needs me. How can I let Anthony leave this earth not knowing what it feels like to connect with another soul? He needs to see love in my eyes, hear it in my voice and sense it when I touch him.

I know if I kiss Wyatt when he isn't himself, when he's Anthony, everything will be different. Wyatt smells like the soap and the shampoo he uses, but underneath that, when we kiss, he smells like peppermint leaves and clover; green and alive. What if Anthony kisses me and he smells dusty and old, like a crypt that hasn't been opened in years? I don't want to risk it. But even if I'm offering Anthony only the deep affection of a true friend, he feels loved for the first time ever. That will have to be enough, for now.

Chapter 34

I Long for Freedom

The next few weeks pass uneventfully and I hate this feeling of boredom. The waiting and watching start to seem worse than my fear of Mike Donahue's next attack. Mom and Dad have me on a very short leash and I long for the freedom I took for granted before. The bad guy holds me prisoner even though he's nowhere near me. I'm dying for my captivity to end. For my mother to bend the rules, just a little.

It's late Friday afternoon and the last track practice of the season has just ended. Nathaniel drops me off in the driveway and Jeff walks me to the door. No one in my life, not even the dog, is willing to leave my safety to chance. I kiss Jeff's cold wet nose and look up to wave goodbye to Nathaniel. He grins and waves from the driver's seat. As I walk into the kitchen, I'm disappointed that no food smells float out to greet me. I'm starving. My mom pokes her head out of the pantry where she has obviously been working on one of her herbal concoctions. She looks disheveled and comforting. A few stray flower petals decorate her chaotic curls and her reading glasses are sliding down her nose. She looks like home.

"Everything okay, Annabelle?"

Her seemingly harmless question irritates me right out of feeling pleased to see her. I resist the temptation to complain about how I'm sick of everyone asking me if everything's okay, tired of being escorted everywhere I go and hankering for freedom. Wyatt's latest big fat genius idea is to have the two biggest guys on the cross-country team flank me every time I head down the trails for practice runs, kind of like how the secret service guards the president everywhere he goes. It's nice that my boyfriend's branching out and making new friends. Until recently he mostly hung out with his soccer teammates, but lately he's been making an effort to get to know some of the kids on my team. He told them I'd been getting prank calls on my cell and they said they'd be happy to help him out by keeping an eye on me and making sure I stayed safe.

I never get to be alone anymore, ever. Either Wyatt or Nathaniel shuffles me back and forth to school like I'm a prisoner going from jail to the courtroom. The soccer team made the playoffs, so I haven't seen much of Wyatt lately. There are a lot of practices. I've been to every game and they're intense. The Eastfield team has eliminated two rival towns so far. If they keep going they could end up in the final game for the state championship. The next game is this weekend in Somerset and Meg and I want to drive down together. I'm hoping my parents say it's okay. I want to hop into the old Prizm and drive somewhere—anywhere, as long as it's with no bodyguards.

Anthony checks up on me now and then, in between visits with Wyatt, but the case is at a standstill and even the ghost is bored by my monotonous existence. Our earthbound investigation is stagnating.

The cops can't find Mike Donahue. Oliver and Jackson questioned Dr. Peterson and Dr. Summers, but the psychiatrist and the pediatrician said they knew nothing about the death of Daniel Warren or his nonexistent roommate. The three people we've found who worked at the hospital in the mid 1980's claimed both ignorance and forgetfulness when questioned about Daniel Warren and a mysterious patient named Anthony. Everyone refuses to acknowledge Anthony ever existed, except Nurse Mary McGuire in her secret note and Daniel in his journal. Unfortunately, neither of these documents can be authenticated. They were written over twenty years ago and left to rot; hidden at Wild Wood. Plus, even in the journal and the letter, the Lonesome Boy remains nameless.

Also, we acquired both of these secret documents through illegal and unofficial means, while we were trespassing on government property. So the police could never use them to prove anything in court. Only Uncle Johnny knows the source of most of our clues has been dead for more than two decades. The rest of the Eastfield police force would never believe us. All this adds up to frustration.

Even Anthony can't tell us anything new. He wants to know what happened on that night in February of 1986 more than anyone, but can't remember. He can only think coherently now because he's been inside of Wyatt's mind. Back in the 80's his thoughts were chaotic. He wants to help with the investigation but he's stuck in the same holding pattern that's frustrating the hell out of me.

The state of absolute safety which I'm forced to live in has become a boring place to be, especially in contrast to the excitement I got used to in the beginning.

Boredom deadens my every thought and move.

The good guys are continuing their fruitless quest for clues and waiting for the bad guy to make his next move.

Although neither side can see each other, we're in a staring contest. I wonder who'll blink first.

"What's for dinner? I'm starved," I whine at my mother.

"It's early and I'm kind of busy. Look in the fridge. You can heat up some lasagna in the microwave. I made an extra pan the other night so we'd have plenty of leftovers." She's yelling to me from inside the pantry because she's working on one of her concoctions and doesn't even want to come out into the kitchen.

"Is there any good bread?" I yell back.

"I picked up a loaf of whole wheat fresh this morning."

I butter up a slice of bread and stick my lasagna in the microwave. It's hot in no time and I start in on it right away, scorching my tongue only a little. What did hungry people do before microwaves? I could barely wait the two or three minutes it took to get my food hot. I was practically drooling. If I couldn't heat everything up so fast, I'd be starving to death right now.

I yell to my mom. "Can you heat up leftovers in a regular oven?"

She pokes her head into the kitchen and laughs. "That's what we did back in the day. Either that or we ate them cold."

"How long would it take to heat up something like this lasagna in the oven?"

"Maybe fifteen or twenty minutes."

"How could you stand waiting that long when you were really hungry?"

My cell phone starts vibrating before my mom can answer. It's sitting on the countertop and the polished granite surface sends the sound reverberating around the room. Dashing over, I snatch it up and look at the screen.

It's a text from Jen. *Can U come ovr right now? We need 2 talk.*

I tick out my reply on the miniature keyboard. *What's up? R U okay?*

Guy trouble.

What guy, Connor?

Can we talk in person? I need U now.

Come 2 my house. We have lasagna.

Something's wrong with my car. Can U give me a ride 2 school 2morrow? PLZ come over.

I look longingly at the plate of steaming lasagna. Jen's always there for me, though, plus I'm curious. Nothing like guy trouble to perk up my interest. I decide to join Jen at her house. My next challenge is to get Mom to agree that I can drive a mile down the road, alone.

We argue for a few minutes, but she finally caves. I promise to text her as soon as I arrive safely and also when I leave. With a whoop, I spring free from the house and jump into my car. I'm flying solo for the first time in weeks.

The second I pull into Jen's driveway, shift into park and turn off the engine I text my mom. *Safe :)*

She sends back her thank you and I emerge from the car and head up Jen's back steps to her kitchen door. The door's locked. Usually I barge right in without knocking. Why did she lock the door if she knew I was coming over? I knock and get no answer. Then I pound and get no answer. Perplexed, I head back down the steps to the driveway. I look in the garage window. No cars. Where's her car? She said she had car trouble. Did it break down somewhere else?

I pull my phone out of my pocket so I can text Jen a *WTF*.

Suddenly someone grabs me from behind, pins my arms to my body and lifts my feet off the driveway.

My cell phone crashes to the pavement.

Chapter 35

The Attack

Squirming and wriggling, I kick my feet backwards. Wishing I was wearing heavy boots, not sneakers, I try to connect. He grunts as my heel hits his shin. Loosens his grip for a second. Snatches up my left wrist and twists. Reaching back with my right hand, I claw at his neck. He flicks open a knife. Flashes the blade in my face.

I freeze and he twists my arm harder, sets my feet on the ground and pushes me toward the woods. Large, full pine trees and dense brush lurk at the edge of Jen's driveway. Soon the forest will swallow us whole.

My attacker has obviously scouted out the setting carefully and he chose the wooded side of Jen's yard for his attack. No one will hear if I call out. Everyone's doors and windows are closed tight against the crisp cold of the late autumn afternoon. And we're pretty far away from Jen's neighbors, anyway. Even if they were outside, I'd have to scream really loud. But I can't. That's what the knife's for.

He's going to slit my throat. I can feel his hatred. And it doesn't feel good. I've been in arguments before. I don't like everyone and not everyone likes me. I've been the victim of cruel comments because I'm different. A few people called me "Ghost Girl" for a while last year, because of the film. They didn't mean it as a compliment. One time during a cross-country meet, we were running through the woods and a girl shoved me off the path so she could pass me. But no one's ever tried to slit my throat. This level of hatred dives deep inside of you and holds on tight, twisting painfully the whole time.

His hatred feels much more personal than it did the time he tried to shoot me.

Nauseating waves of hatred roll off of him, along with his body odor. He's fogging up the air with his disgusting stench. Clutching me close to him, he wrenches my arm harder, up against my back.

Only a fragile layer of tender skin protects my jugular from his knife. The pulse in my neck beats hard and fast as his blade hovers, razor-sharp, above it. The first warm trickle of blood slips down the cool flesh of my neck.

If he slices open my jugular, will the blood pour out too fast? Will I bleed to death before the wound can heal? I try to remember the stuff I was supposed to pay attention to in Biology. I know that an artery's worse. It spurts. There's one on the inside of your upper thigh. But what about the jugular? It's really a vein, right? I think I have a better chance with a vein. And how close is it to the surface? How deep will he have to cut? Where's the carotid? Shit! The carotid's an artery and I think it's on the neck. Damn. I wish I'd listened more in class.

I slide a sideways glance back to the driveway, which I can still see pretty clearly from here and spot my cell phone lying on the asphalt. It's vibrating and lighting up, which gives me hope. If it's Wyatt, he'll be worried that I'm not answering. He might not get completely freaked out, but he'll be concerned enough to contact my mother, to make sure I'm okay. Whoever's calling me will have to act fast, though. I don't have much time. This guy's hurting me and he smells bad.

I feel like gangrenous slugs on skateboards are using the walls of my stomach for ramps and jumps. Maybe if I puke on him he'll let me go. I focus on the undigested mash of bread and lasagna that I just ate as it oozes up toward my esophagus.

Mike Donahue twists my arm so hard that I see black for a second or two from the pain, distracting me from the nausea. Another thin stream of blood trickles down my neck. The sharp pain in my shoulder eases to a persistent throb. He pushes me forward, holding the blade against my throat, just beneath my jaw. I stumble along, blinded by tears.

"Where are we going?"

"Shh! Unless you wanna die right now. It might be easier to drag your corpse, so don't tempt me."

He tightens his death grip again and I wince.

Dear god he's evil smelling!

My knees fold under me. And the knife slices into my flesh. I yelp as I feel the sting. A stream of blood flows down my neck and starts seeping into my sweatshirt.

"I need to get you far enough into the woods so I can finish you off. Don't want anyone to find your body right away. No guns this time, too noisy. Besides, I'm enjoying the close connection. So young, so sweet, so pretty…"

Those squirmy, skateboarding slugs reactivate in my stomach, but I force them to stay still so I can think. If I scream someone jogging by or riding a bike might hear me, but the road's pretty far away. Also, if he thinks someone heard me, he might have to kill me fast and split. I decide to wait quietly and cooperate—someone might already be on their way.

Who called my cell? I keep hoping that if it was my mother she'll have the good sense to send Uncle Johnny and not come here alone.

A creepy thought invades my fear-rattled brain. Was it really Jen who texted me earlier? A new fear slams through my panicked mind. What if he hurt Jen?

My voice is hoarse and I struggle to speak. "Where's my friend?"

"Which friend?"

"Jenna. She lives here. She texted me to meet her."

"Several cars got mysteriously broken into today, after school, in the parking lot over by the gym." His voice is gravelly and low and his breath and body odor stink so bad I wish I could faint just to avoid the stench.

He has such a tight and painful hold on me I can't budge to move away even a little.

"I took a couple of cell phones from different cars, because I needed to make sure no one would figure out which car I was targeting. I don't want anyone to connect the break-ins to me. Your pretty friend left her nice new phone charging in her car while she was at volleyball practice. Very careless. She's down at the police station now, reporting the crime."

"So you texted me on her phone?"

"I had to come up with something. You have better security than the president. I just stayed patient and hidden, hoping an idea would come to me and then bingo, it did."

It's true. My antsiness combined with my mother letting up for just a minute, allowed his simple scheme to succeed. He continues to repulse me with his claustrophobic body odor and rattle me with his gross, phlegmy voice.

"Your friend Jen won't be home for a while. Filing a report about the missing cell phone should take about an hour."

"She'll be gone for an hour?" I try not to sound scared.

"Yes. At least. Her mom met her down at the station, because poor Jen was so upset. Her life is on that phone and it's a brand new one, too, all shiny with a pretty blue cover and tons of apps, such a pity. From my hiding spot, behind a van in the school parking lot, I could see her tears. You know what was really hilarious?"

I don't answer his ridiculous question. Of course I don't know. How could I? Whatever it is, I'm sure I won't think it's funny.

He ignores my hostile silence and keeps talking. The only good thing about this situation is that I can't see his face. If he looks anything like he smells, his looks might paralyze me and I need to be able to react fast if I want to escape.

He taunts me again.

"The big, long-haired dude you're always with? The tall one who drives that old Land Rover?"

He means Wyatt. What if he hurt Wyatt? I hold my breath and wait for him to say more.

"He came to Jen's rescue. What a hero! He dried her tears and gave her a ride to the police station. She used his cell phone to call the cops and her mother. That's how I know that no one will be home for a while. I figure I have at least an hour with you while they fill out a report and answer the cops' questions."

"A whole hour." My hopes are sinking.

"Yes. Then Jen and her mom'll come home. See your car in the driveway. No sign of you around. They'll call your mother and she'll call the police. Unfortunately, it'll be too late. I wish I could hang around and watch all the excitement, but I have to get going. My car's on the other side of the woods, parked on a dirt road. If we keep heading this way, we'll be able to see it soon. I'm gonna finish up with you, jump into the car and head out. Leave this stinking state. Maybe go to Florida."

He pushes me forward, toward his intended destination. He seems so sure about where he's going. Suddenly it occurs to me that the night of the campfire, behind Jen's house, that was him. Out in the woods. Spying on us and planning my abduction. A raccoon didn't make those noises. Mike Donahue did. I shiver in his grasp.

"Are you cold, Annabelle?"

I hate the way he says my name, as if he's so clever to have found it out, as if knowing my name gives him more power over me. Then I notice something that I hadn't noticed before. I'm so busy feeling repulsed by him I didn't realize that it's grown much colder. Colder than when I got out of my car. About fifteen degrees colder.

"Anthony."

"What did you say?"

"Nothing."

I didn't realize I'd spoken his name out loud. Even if Anthony can't do anything to protect me from this pig, I feel better just knowing he's here.

"You were in the woods that night weren't you? The night when Wyatt went running out into the forest to see what was making the noise."

"He almost found me, too. Then those other two idiots went running back to the fire and he followed them. He turned around just in time."

"What would you have done?"

"I couldn't shoot him. That would make too much noise. But I had the knife with me."

I shudder, wishing I could control it more.

"There you go again, shivering. Poor little Annabelle, she's cold."

He taunts me and continues to shove me ahead of him down the overgrown path.

We flounder our way through the brambles because I'm trying to slow our progress down as much as I can. He's pressed close against my back; pushing me from behind with my painfully twisted arm. If I walk too slowly he twists my arm harder. If I quicken my pace, the knife presses into the skin on my throat. So I move carefully. I'm not in a hurry to discover what he has planned for me. Together, but not in sync, we edge closer and closer to my fate.

I step over an exposed tree root. My captor, however, trips on it and curses. I feel the knife blade at my throat and another hot trickle of blood. When he pauses, tightening his hold on my wrist again, I fight down a gasp of pain.

Suddenly, he halts our awkward progress through the woods. We both hold our breath and listen but hear nothing. He releases his held-in air with a hiss. I release mine, stifling a sob. No footsteps. No one's sneaking through the forest to rescue me.

A blast of music shatters the silence. I snap my head to the right, barely escaping another nick from his blade. Somewhere in this forest, Rihanna is singing her latest hit song. Then I realize it's Jen's ringtone, coming from inside the villain's pocket. He forgot to turn her phone off. Maybe there's a GPS that can be activated and traced.

In one quick motion, he lets go of my wrist and, with his left arm, he wraps me up close against his chest, pinning my arms to my body. My feet are off the ground again. His right hand flips the knife closed and dives into his pocket. He drops the knife in there and grabs Jen's phone.

"Forgot to turn her damn phone off."

After turning it off with his thumb, he whips Jen's precious new cell phone toward the sky. The shiny blue missile flies a few feet, in a high arc, for an impressive distance and then descends swiftly, bouncing off the bark of a soaring pine tree, slipping and crashing down through its branches in a shower of dry needles. Finally it lands with a soft thud on the forest floor.

"Hey, dumbass, you almost hit me with that stupid thing!" Uncle Johnny steps out from behind the ancient pine, his gun aimed at my abductor's head from about fifteen feet away.

"Put the gun down or I'll slice her open like a..." Mike Donahue grabs the knife out of his pocket in a flash. But never gets to flick it open. As hard as I can, I kick backwards and connect with his shin. When his hold on me loosens, I shove my elbow up into his right arm. Within a second the knife flies high into the air. Flipping end over end. And then I'm free. Sprinting away from him like a jackrabbit. Falling to my knees in a patch of scratchy wild blueberry bushes, I gag, wretch a couple of times and finally vomit. Wiping my mouth with my sweatshirt sleeve, I look over at the spot where Mike Donahue was standing about two seconds ago.

My captor's lying face down on a patch of leaves and pine needles. One of Wyatt's knees is on his back and the other one's on his neck. Uncle Johnny runs over and cuffs his wrists and ankles. As the last plasticuff is zipped shut, Wyatt leaps up and runs to me. Even though I'm sure I stink like puke, he hugs me. I wince from the pain in my left arm.

"Did he hurt you? What happened? You're all bloody."

"He twisted my arm; I'll be okay. The cut's just a small one. I want to go home."

"You're still bleeding. Officer Blake, I'm taking her to the hospital."

My uncle looks worried. "Do we need an ambulance?"

"Yes." Donahue's voice is muffled because his face is smashed into the ground.

Uncle Johnny nudges him in the ribs with the toe of his shoe. "Not for you, dirt-bag. Shut up." Wisely, the prisoner does so.

I try to bargain with Wyatt. "No ambulance, no hospital. Call my mother. She'll bring me to the doctor's. His office is probably still open. Look, I can move my arm. I don't need an x-ray and the bleeding's almost stopped. He barely nicked my neck. I don't need to go to the emergency room. I feel much better already."

It's true, too. My wrist, arm and shoulder feel all tingly and not very painful anymore. Also, the slices on my neck are hardly bleeding at all. If they call my mother, my secret healing talent can stay a secret. Mom and I can pretend to go to the doctor's office, but we'll go home instead.

Uncle Johnny relents, but Wyatt insists on carrying me to the Land Rover even though I can walk. He's pretty pissed off that I went to Jen's house alone.

"Annabelle, I don't know whether to hug you or scream at you. I'm relieved that you're alive. But I'm pissed off that you went out alone."

He sets my feet gently on the ground, but keeps

one arm around my waist.

"I thought it would be okay because her house is right down the street."

Wyatt points his thumb at Uncle Johnny and his prisoner, to illustrate why it wasn't okay.

"I called your cell and when you didn't answer, I called your house to make sure you were safe. The second your mother told me Jen had texted you I knew something was wrong because her phone had been stolen. When your mother said that you went to Jen's house, I hung up fast and called your Uncle. Then I felt the cold."

"Anthony."

"Yes, he confirmed that you were in danger."

Uncle Johnny walks over to us, pulling along his stumbling prisoner.

"I was on patrol in my black and white when I heard the news about the car break-ins at the high school. I thought Mike Donahue might be involved in some way. I was on my way to your house to check on you when I got Wyatt's call. Instead of stopping at your house, I drove past it to Jen's."

"Your uncle arrived two seconds behind me. I was standing in the driveway, looking at your cell phone. Officer Blake can move silently through the forest so he led the way. I followed right behind. We snuck up really close to you guys."

"I quietly found my way to a hiding place behind the huge tree. Wyatt snuck up behind you and Donahue. He crouched down, in the underbrush, waiting to spring out at the right time. Then he took his phone out of his pocket and called Jen's phone, hoping to startle Donahue when the ring tone went off. And it worked."

Wyatt's pissed. "Damn it, Annabelle. I'm so thankful you're alive. I love you, even though you're a stupid, reckless jackass."

I have a special talent for inspiring conflicting emotions in the people who care about me.

Suddenly, my mother arrives on the scene, slams her car into "Park," leaves it running and flies over to me. Flinging her arms around me, she starts crying.

"Get in the car. This is all my fault. I never should have let you talk me into this."

I climb into the passenger seat of her car and try to act frail and injured when all I really want is to get home, clean up and eat some lasagna. My injuries are pretty well healed already. And I'm not even nauseous anymore.

Mom tells Wyatt he can come over later after I get home from the doctor's. He leaves, and shortly after his Land Rover's out of sight, a few more cops arrive to help Uncle Johnny escort the prisoner to the station.

Mom and I head home. My arm still hurts, but not horribly and the cuts on my neck aren't bleeding anymore. We park in the driveway and my mother looks over at me.

Gently, she touches my chin and tilts it up so she can check out my neck. Even though the cuts are almost healed, she starts hyperventilating, which is so unlike her. It's my turn to calm her down.

"Open the car door, Mom. You need some air."

After climbing out of the car, she stands there, leaning against it, with her mouth open; gulping in cold air.

"Take it easy. I'm all right, Mom."

As soon as she can talk she says, "I'm fine. You were right. I needed some air."

Her breathing finally quiets to something resembling normal and I put my arm around her. "C'mon, let's go inside."

When we walk into the kitchen, she drags me into her pantry and gets to work with the herbs and flowers. She soaks some cotton balls in a solution made from herbal tea and washes my neck with it. Then she puts on some band aids. The cuts aren't bleeding and they don't hurt anymore, but I let her do all this because it's calming her down.

"I'm putting your arm in a sling, too."

I draw the line. "I'm not wearing a sling, Mom. I'll just say that my arm's wrenched or sprained or something; that it'll be kind of sore for a few days. You're known for your healing. You can say you fixed me up with the right herbs so I'm not in much pain."

She doesn't argue with me, which is good because she'd lose. I refuse to wear a stupid-ass sling. My arm's fine now.

"Wyatt looked about ready to die from worry."

"Well, I'm fine, so he can relax and I'll tell him as soon as I see him."

"You're fine no thanks to me."

"Mom, you're not allowed to feel guilty. I pressured you into letting me go."

"I should never have listened to you. I'm the parent and you're the child. I should've insisted."

"I'm not a child anymore. It's hard to tell a stubborn eighteen-year-old what to do."

"You're still only seventeen and I'm your mother. I could've stopped you. I forgot that for one moment of insanity and I never will again. You could've died out there in those woods." She's crying again and she never cries.

"But I didn't. Nothing even hurts anymore; except my stomach feels empty. I threw up. He scared me and he smelled horrible."

The queasiness caused by my close brush with death has disappeared and hunger has taken its place. All I want is a hot shower and some lasagna. I run upstairs to the bathroom, ripping the stupid band aids off my neck on the way. First I brush my teeth and gargle with really strong mouthwash. Then I hop into the steaming shower and, in a cocoon of fragrant suds, scrub the dirt of the forest and the stink of my captor out of my hair and off of my skin.

After, I towel dry and head downstairs for some food. My hair's still dripping, but I don't care. My dad, Oliver, Jackson, Nathaniel, Jeff and Wyatt are all waiting for me, gathered around the table in my mother's candle-lit kitchen. Mom heated up a whole pan of lasagna and my dad picked up some pizzas.

After I shovel down a ton of the warm food and sit back with a cup of hot chamomile tea in front of me, I relax and bask in the glow of friendship and love that surrounds me; safe at last. The bad guy's behind bars, caught in a horrendous act red-handed this time. All we need is to get a confession out of him about the night Daniel and Anthony died.

The dangerous part is over. I can go where ever I want, alone, whenever I want to go there. I feel exhausted, contented, thrilled to my bones and triumphant. After kissing my mom and dad, I excuse myself to go up to bed, shooting Wyatt a look that says *follow me*.

He walks over to the bottom of the stairs with me and we fall into each others' arms. Gently and carefully he kisses me over and over, lightly then deeply. Backing up to lean against the wall, he pulls me up against him. With his lips to my ear he whispers, "Good night, you dumbass."

"Sweet talker."

He's right, though. I'm an idiot.

However, we wouldn't have caught the bad guy, in the act of committing a crime, so quickly and effectively if I was more cautious. But this is probably the wrong time to point that out to him. So I keep my mouth shut and tip-toe up to bed.

Chapter 36

Questioning the Prisoner

The next day Uncle Johnny calls to tell us that they're going to question the prisoner down at the police station. He wants us all to be there for the interrogation. At my uncle's request, I extend the invitation to Wyatt, Oliver, Jackson and Nathaniel, also. I've been cold all morning so I know Anthony's nearby and will be coming along, too. Unfortunately, Jeff will have to wait in the car. We can't have him barking his head off at Anthony the whole time we're at the station.

My father drives my mom's car, with her riding shotgun and me in the back. It feels like the old days, when I was little. Before we bought the minivan, whenever we went somewhere as a family, Joe and Clement and I had to squish into the back seat of the car together. We always fought about who got to sit near the windows. My brothers are older and bigger so they always won and I had to sit scrunched in the middle between them with my skinny, scabby-kneed little legs humped up in front of me. I used to whine and complain for the whole ride. Today I have my pick of the window seats in the back, but I'd give anything to be crammed in between my two big brothers.

As soon as Dad parks the car in the police station parking lot, I jump out and run over to Nathaniel's van. He and Jeff are sitting outside waiting for us. I wrap my arms around Jeff's furry neck and apologize to him because he can't come in. He licks my cheek to show me he has no hard feelings. Oliver and Jackson pull up with Wyatt folded into the back seat. As I watch Wyatt extract himself from Oliver's car I want to rush over and throw myself into his arms but I use self-control.

Jeff settles down on his dog bed in the back of the van and perks up one ear to show us that he's alert just in case there's trouble and we need him. Nathaniel leaves the door open so his dog can get some air and see what's going on. No need to lock the van. It's parked at the police station, plus no one's going to mess with a dog Jeff's size. The seven of us move toward the entrance to the station together. Wyatt hugs me to him with one arm around my shoulders and kisses the top of my head.

"Are you okay?"

"Yeah, that weasel didn't hurt me. I feel fine, just tired."

"Are you sure you want to see him?"

"I'm dying to see him. I still haven't gotten a good look at his face. I need to know who this monster is. He probably killed Daniel and Anthony and he tried to kill me, more than once. I think if my nightmare has a face, he won't seem so terrifying."

A cold blast of air brushes my hair back from my face. Wyatt feels it too. We look at each other.

"Anthony." Wyatt says. "He's finally going to get his day in court."

"We caught Mike Donahue trying to kidnap and murder me, which should put him away for a long time. But I don't see how we're going to get him to tell us what happened over twenty years ago."

"We'll think of something."

"Like what?"

"If your Uncle Johnny gets to question him, the guy's a dead man."

"Even Uncle Johnny can't get away with that."

"Maybe not, but Mike Donahue doesn't know it."

"They had to read him his rights. He must have a lawyer by now."

"Doesn't matter. Officer Blake can do it. I have faith in him."

Nathaniel looks up from his wheelchair. "I hate Mike Donahue for what he tried to do to you, Annabelle."

"Get in line. We all want a piece of him," Wyatt adds.

"Yes. We do. Only the law's protecting him now. He spent all these years hiding from the law and now it's his only refuge. Otherwise, we'd destroy him; even your mom,

Annabelle. I've never seen her like this. She'll rip him apart, probably with her bare hands, if they let her near him."

As it turns out, though, Mike Donahue doesn't need to worry about my mother's violent wrath. As soon as we enter the police station, Uncle Johnny and another officer escort Mike Donahue into the interrogation room. The prisoner gives his shackles a noisy waggle and sneers in our direction. My poor mother staggers backwards as the first wave of evil hits her. She could gather her strength and send it right back in his face, but we need him to talk. It would be counterproductive if my mother used her talent to subdue him. We need Donahue to be cocky and confident so he'll reveal important information. Uncle Johnny will probably try to get him to brag about what he got away with. That would be a good strategy.

My mother pushes her hair back from her face and tells my dad, "Looks like Jeff's about to get some company in the van."

My dad hugs her protectively with one arm and walks her out of the station.

When I finally view my enemy for the first time, he looks remarkably average, kind of like Kevin Spacey in one of his less crazy roles. Then Donahue squints in my direction and snaps his teeth at me. Uncle Johnny shoves him and he stumbles and complains about police brutality.

"You ain't seen nothin' yet," my uncle says as he and another officer push my attacker into a room with a one-way mirror, just like they have on *Law and Order*.

My uncle stays in the room with the prisoner and the other officer leads us into the adjoining room. It's small and dark and there's a row of folding chairs lined up in front of the big window. After we've been seated for a couple of minutes, the door opens and my dad joins us; he slides his arm around my shoulders and gives them a squeeze.

With his mouth close to my ear he whispers, "Your mother's fine. As soon as she got outside, she perked right up. We can fill her in on all the details after. She's taking Jeff for a walk around the parking lot."

I smile up at him. "Mike Donahue looks pretty ordinary."

"But he's not. Thankfully you don't often meet people like him."

"Yes. Once is enough."

We watch the prisoner, sitting on the other side of the glass with his hands cuffed together and his feet shackled at the ankles. Uncle Johnny starts up the conversation that we all hope will lead to a confession.

First, my uncle invites Donahue to sit down on a metal chair and asks him if he wants to wait for his lawyer.

"Nope. I'm not gonna admit to anything. Ask whatever questions you want. I'm good at keeping quiet."

"I don't need to ask a lot of questions. We caught you with Annabelle and the knife, in the woods."

"Like I said, I'm not saying nothin' incriminating so ask away."

"At least you smell better, Mike. That stench was pretty disgusting."

"Yeah, I'd been living out of my car for weeks." Donahue chuckles. "It was hard to find a shower sometimes."

"I still have nightmares about the smell." I shudder and Dad pats my shoulder.

A couple of police officers are standing in the corners of the room we're in. One of them is the detective who'll question Donahue after Uncle Johnny's done with him.

He turns to my dad and explains, "We want to try to get him talking before his lawyer gets here and I start questioning him officially; if you have anything you'd like Johnny to ask him tell me now. I can pass him a note."

Wyatt speaks up, surprising us all. "I want to go in there with them."

The detective pauses to think for a second and then says, "You helped capture him. I suppose you've earned the right to face him man to man."

"Yes. I've earned it and I can't wait."

"Keep your hands to yourself, though. We don't want to give him a reason to complain about the way he's being treated. We've got an open and shut case. I don't want to screw it up."

"I can control myself; don't worry."

"Okay, then, come with me." The detective leads Wyatt into the interrogation room and then comes back to sit with us. We all focus our eyes intently on the one-way mirror.

Wyatt doesn't sit down. He hulks around, pacing and staring at the enemy, who looks like he could be anybody's next door neighbor, except for the handcuffs and chains.

Mike Donahue chuckles. "Look who's here, the big brave hero. Pull up a chair. I'm not gonna talk, so now at least he'll have somebody to talk to." He jerks his head in my uncle's direction.

"I'd rather stand." Wyatt towers over the prisoner. He's two inches taller than my uncle who's standing beside him. Donahue shoves his own chair back and rises to face them.

I pull my chair close to Nathaniel's wheelchair and he smiles at me, which doesn't calm me down even a little.

Breaking his promise to stay silent, Donahue taunts Wyatt. "Where's the girl?"

"What girl?" my uncle counters.

Wyatt's face turns red and his eyes darken.

Uncle Johnny quietly tells him, "Stand down."

"You know what girl," Donahue jeers. "The one everyone's willing to fight and die for."

"What about her?" Uncle Johnny asks.

The criminal sneers at them. "Where is she? I'd rather see her than this guy."

"But I'm the one who has some questions for you." My boyfriend is speaking from between clenched teeth.

"I told you. I'm not talking."

"They aren't questions about yesterday, when you tried to kill my girlfriend. They're questions about the past."

"I refuse to talk about the past. I'm waiting until my lawyer gets here."

"Maybe you'll change your mind."

Nathaniel reaches for my hand and holds it, warm in his

own. In the small, spare room with the one-way mirror, I can feel everyone's mood intensify as we watch.

Wyatt continues. "I want to ask you about a winter night in 1986."

"I don't remember anything about 1986. That was a long time ago."

"This was a very memorable night, though. I'd appreciate it if you'd tell me about the night of February 10th, in 1986. You were working at the Wild Wood Psychiatric Hospital."

"I'm not admitting to anything."

"Maybe I can jog your memory. Right around midnight you paid a visit to room 209. You had a violent confrontation with a patient. His name was Daniel Warren."

"The name doesn't ring a bell."

"Maybe this name will. His cell mate was called Anthony."

"I don't remember anyone at Wild Wood named Anthony."

Mike Donahue starts shuffling his feet. One of his shoulders twitches up and then quickly twitches back down again. He seems agitated. Maybe he's wondering how Wyatt came up with the name Anthony. Maybe he's worried because he just inadvertently admitted he worked at the hospital.

Wyatt pushes the same emotional button again. "Anthony. He died that night, too. You murdered him and Daniel Warren."

"I didn't murder anyone. You can't even prove I worked there."

"I know someone who can."

"Who?"

"The girl. She's sitting out there. Watching us right now." Wyatt points to the mirror.

I let go of Nathaniel's hand, rise out of my chair and take a step closer to the window side of the mirror.

"Would you like to wave to the girl?" Wyatt smiles a thin smile, barely showing his even, white teeth.

With my uncle's help, Donahue turns and takes a step toward the mirror. His ankle cuffs and chains clink and jingle as he moves. He grins, probably because he thinks his presence will scare me, even through the glass. My uncle shivers and I know why the interrogation room has grown cold.

Then things happen fast. Wyatt's eyes grow even darker and gray half circles appear under them. His cheekbones become more pronounced and hollow-looking. Anthony's taken over his body.

The dead boy moves over to stand next to Mike Donahue, close enough so their arms touch. Anthony stares into the mirror and the prisoner does, too. Then Mike shakes his head like a dog with a flea crawling around in its ear. He blinks twice and lets out a horrific scream, a scream that could wake the dead. Except the dead are already awake.

Donahue sputters and spittle sprays from his pathetic mouth as he begs. "Get him outta here! Get that monster away from me!"

The whole time he's screaming and pleading,

Donahue's eyes are glued to the mirror because he can't believe what he sees. Anthony's face. The face of someone who died over twenty years ago. The prisoner's hair grows whiter as we watch. His mouth forms a black oval and he screams again. He grabs onto Uncle Johnny's shirt sleeve and begs, "Please, please. I'll tell you anything. Send it back to Hell. Get it away from me!"

Anthony smiles at me through the glass, a ghoulish imitation of a human smile. No warmth, no humor. A smile born from the cold satisfaction of revenge. A smile with all the charm of a skull's toothy grin.

"What's the matter, Mike? Don't you remember me?" The dead boy's voice slides up and out of Wyatt's throat like a vampire creeps out of his coffin at dusk. Slow and pale, but strong and bloodthirsty.

"If I never existed then why are you so afraid? Maybe you should scream louder. I don't think *the girl* heard you."

Mike Donahue lets go of my uncle's sleeve and stares into the glass with his eyes bugging out and mouth slack. It's a horrible sight. He's gasping for breath. If Anthony doesn't leave the room soon Donahue will have a heart attack and the paramedics will have to come in from the fire station next door. They'll have to use the paddles to revive him.

"I tell you what, Mike. Let's make a deal. Officer Blake is going to bring a detective in here and I want you to tell him everything that happened on February 10th, 1986. Then I'll leave you alone. I won't return."

"Okay. Okay." Donahue bobs his head a few times. He's shaking.

"But if you leave out even one tiny detail, I'm coming back. When it's dark and you're alone in your cell. We'll have a long talk. Just you and me." Anthony looms; large and threatening, as he takes a step backward, toward the door and lets loose a cold and hollow laugh.

"I'll talk. I promise. I'll tell him everything that happened. I won't leave anything out. Just go. Leave me alone. Please." Mike Donahue quivers and begs and still his tortured eyes stay riveted to the mirror. I stare into the hell that lies within them, while behind him Anthony leaves. Uncle Johnny unlocks the door and Wyatt walks out and closes it behind him. When the door to our little room opens, Wyatt stumbles in and falls into my arms. I stagger under his weight and my dad and Oliver jump up to help us. We get him into a chair and resume watching the drama inside the room with the one-way mirror. Uncle Johnny helps the prisoner back to his chair and the badly shaken man collapses into it.

"What the hell just happened in there?" The detective, who's sitting next to Nathaniel looks mystified.

"Beats the hell out of me." My dad shakes his head. "Maybe Donahue's guilty conscience is causing him to hallucinate."

"Crazy bastard." The detective shakes his head.

Inside the interrogation room, my uncle beckons for the detective to replace him. The detective leaves us and enters the room on the other side of the window.

Donahue's lawyer finally arrives. The lawyer sits down next to his client and opens a laptop. He glances up at the video camera in the corner. The green light's blinking. What will everyone see when they review the film?

The prisoner crumples and lays his cheek on the cold surface of the gray metal table in front of him. Through the dim window I can see the goose flesh on Mike Donahue's bare arms.

Chapter 37

The Last Race

My dad texts my mother and she comes back into the police station. He drags over a chair for her and she sinks into it. Some of us are sitting; some standing. We're a tired, ragged bunch and we've been on an unbelievable journey together. A journey that's about to end. I'm too agitated to sit down, so I rest my hand on Wyatt's shoulder and keep wiggling from one foot to another. Wyatt's still slumped in his chair, exhausted. I study the faces surrounding me. If the road ends here what will happen next?

The look on Mike Donahue's face makes it clear to us why my mother is able to join us again. His eyes look empty and his face is gray and more wrinkled than it was when he entered the interrogation room. Like an empty plastic bag blowing around in a parking lot, he has no direction, no confidence, no strength and no definite shape. He can't properly fill any defined space in this world. Anthony stole all of the villain's power, destroyed his cockiness and shifted his reality. The subdued prisoner waits for his lawyer to tell him what to do.

Someone brings in a tray of coffee. Even I don't begrudge my would-be murderer this small favor. In fact, I doubt he'll have the energy to tell his story without at least one cup of coffee. And we all want to hear what he has to say.

The detective unlocks Donahue's handcuffs. Observing the way his pale hands shake as they grip the cardboard cup and the way he sinks his bedraggled face to the lip of it, I figure it's the right thing to do. Mike's hands can safely be freed from the cuffs. The main character in my waking nightmares looks like he no longer has the strength or the will to harm anyone. Donahue inhales the steam and takes several sips before he begins to talk.

He speaks in a monotone at first, but as he gets going, he gains some emotional momentum. All his confidence deserted him the moment he looked into the mirror and saw the boy who'd spent most of his life imprisoned in room 209 at the Wild Wood Psychiatric Hospital. Now Donahue's fear is also fading. A little humanity enters his expression and his tone of voice as he begins to talk.

"I didn't kill those boys on purpose. You have to believe me."

His lawyer interrupts. "Don't say anything more, Mike."

Donahue gestures for him to be quiet. "It's okay. I need to talk about it. Just keep that monster away from me, please. You have to keep him away from me."

Donahue's lawyer looks puzzled. "What's he talking about?"

The detective shrugs and shivers. "Damned if I know." Then he nods at the prisoner and says, "Drink your coffee, Mike. We all need to warm up. It's freezing in here."

"Not as cold as it was on that horrible night. The night that Anthony died."

"Who's Anthony?"

"A patient at Wild Wood Hospital. He couldn't talk. He screamed and yelled but he never spoke a word. When he had a melt-down, things could get scary. He was pretty violent sometimes. We often put him in a straitjacket or sedated him. He was always restrained or drugged. The kid was tall and strong, but pathetic and retarded."

I cringe at the sound of Donahue's words. My heart breaks for Anthony.

"So tell us what happened," the detective prompts him.

Uncle Johnny's on the other side of Nathaniel and he moves forward, until he's perched on the edge of his chair. He's sipping on a cup of coffee, shivering and staring at Mike Donahue. My poor uncle looks worn out and confused. Like he's seen a ghost and is trying to reconcile what he saw with his former ideas about reality. Mike Donahue starts telling his story.

"One night we caught Daniel, this kid who had epilepsy, out in the parking lot. I suspected he saw me stealing some drugs from the locked medication room."

"And did you steal drugs from the locked medication room?" The detective interrupts.

"Yes, sir, I did. And Daniel saw me do it and followed me outside. In the parking lot he watched me put the stolen drugs into the trunk of the dealer's car. Then Daniel collapsed and had a seizure right there on the ground."

"And did you help him?"

"Yes. Another orderly who was in the parking lot heard Daniel go down and we both ran over. After that night, Dr. Summers moved Daniel into the same room with Anthony, the most violent patient at the hospital. We hoped Anthony would scare him, make him nervous, or even hurt him. Daniel couldn't talk, so I figured I might be safe. I didn't think he'd be able to tell anybody about what he saw, but I needed to make sure."

"And how did you 'make sure'?"

"Dr. Summers told me that he hoped Daniel would die in room 209. He hoped Anthony would kill him. Then no one would find out about us and we could keep making money off the drugs."

"So Summers was involved in the drug business?"

"The whole thing was his idea, but he didn't want to steal or move the drugs himself, so he asked me. I found him a street connection. Summers made sure I got the key to the locked medication room and I stole the drugs and put them in the dealer's car."

"What was your mother's part in all of this?"

Mike Donahue sighs. "Summers gave my mother a shift working in the medication room. He put her in charge of giving out the early evening meds and locking up afterwards. She handed off the keys to me on the nights when I'd be making a run out to the parking lot to meet the dealer. That's all. We needed the money. My stepfather was sick. He couldn't work anymore. My mother changed the drug inventory records so no one would know anything was missing and she gave me the keys. You can't put a woman in her eighties in jail for something she did over twenty years ago. Can you?"

"It all depends, Mike. It depends on how much helpful information you give us. If you cooperate, your mother will be safe. Just keep talking."

"Like I said, Dr. Summers and I were making good money. The whole thing was his idea. He was young. I think he had student loans to pay off; from medical school. Maybe he was just greedy. He covered up for me whenever I needed him to and I did all the rest of the work. I made the connection, with an old friend, this guy I knew in high school. He had a group of kids who sold the stuff on the streets, in colleges, wherever people would buy it: sedatives, pain meds, behavioral meds, you name it. Nothing ever changes; you'll always be able to sell drugs. People are willing to pay big bucks, too. I didn't use anything myself. I was just the middleman. It was fast and simple. Summers and I split the cash. My family needed the extra money. Dr. Summers was helping us out."

"Helping you out by enlisting you to sell illegal prescription drugs."

"Like I said, we were poor. It was an easy way to make some extra cash. But then Daniel caught me in the act. He must've been hiding somewhere near the medication room.

He followed me out to the parking lot and saw me loading the drugs into the trunk of a car. For a while I stalked him, just to scare him. He started to have seizures more often and they got worse. The doctor probably should've increased his meds, but we wanted him to get worse. We would've been better off if he died of natural causes. Then we wouldn't have to worry about him telling someone I was messing with the drugs in the locked room."

"So the doctor withheld the medication that he knew Daniel needed."

"I never thought of it that way but I guess he did. Sometimes, if I was near Daniel, he'd drop. It was kinda scary. His face would turn blue. Once when another orderly was with me, he revived Daniel with mouth-to-mouth because he stopped breathing. If I had been alone, that would've been the end of him. I wouldn't have revived him. We were supposed to give him a shot of Phenobarbital as soon as he started seizing. That would relax him enough so he'd stop jerking around and start breathing again. Then we were supposed to roll him onto his side. If I was alone with him when he had a seizure, I never bothered with any of those procedures."

It makes me feel sick to hear Mike Donahue speak so coldly about a child whose safety was his responsibility and I start shaking a little. Wyatt puts his arm around me. The prisoner continues to tell us everything he remembers.

"Part of the doctor's plan was for Anthony to make Daniel nervous, so his seizures would get worse. If Anthony saw Daniel seizing, maybe he'd get over-excited and hurt

Daniel. But when we put them together in room 209, those two mental cases seemed to calm each other down."

"Anthony never tried to hurt Daniel?"

"Not that I know of. Daniel was a few years younger and much smaller than Anthony. We were hoping for a violent attack, but nothing ever happened. The doc didn't give up hope, though; he kept them together, thinking that Anthony was so violent and unpredictable, he'd turn on Daniel and mess him up. But Anthony didn't and we began to get nervous. Summers and I started worrying that Daniel would find a way to tell someone about the drug deals."

"What about the night of February 10th, 1986?" The detective steers Donahue toward talking about the night the boys died. Uncle Johnny takes out his cell phone and asks for someone to get a warrant so they can bring in Dr. Summers. No one mentions Mary McGuire, though. The detective keeps his word. He promised Mike Donahue and she *is* in her eighties.

The subdued villain takes a huge gulp of coffee, shudders and begins to speak again. "I was working the night shift on February 10th, 1986 and I decided to try something new. I was sick of always having to worry that Daniel would find a way to tell someone about the drug deals. I dunno, sign language, pointing to stuff. I was afraid he'd figure out a way to communicate. I thought about it all the time. I wanted him dead, so he could never tell anybody anything."

"Exactly what occurred on that night, Mike? Take us through it step-by-step."

"Sometime a little before midnight, I visited the boys in room 209. I brought a syringe of Phenobarbital with me. I wanted it to look like I was trying to save Daniel during a seizure. But really, I wasn't gonna give him the medication until it was too late. I figured that Daniel would be scared when I walked into his room. He'd have a seizure and turn blue, stop breathing. If he did, I wouldn't give him the sedative and I wouldn't revive him."

Whoa! We all look at each other. Donahue just admitted he planned to kill Daniel and everything he says is being recorded by the video cam in the corner of the ceiling. Whoever watches it will see what an ordinary face Evil wears.

"Sure enough, as soon as I opened the door to the room, Daniel got hysterical. Then something unbelievable happened. He yelled, 'Anthony!' and suddenly, I knew he could talk. I knew for sure, right then, that Daniel had to die; the sooner, the better."

"Then what happened?" The detective leans toward him.

"Anthony was sleeping on his cot, but he woke up when Daniel yelled. Daniel was lying on his bed and I was leaning over him. He was scared out of his mind and he started having a grand mal seizure. Before I knew it, Anthony jumped on my back and I fell on top of Daniel. That crazy bastard was strong. I remember how hard and sharp-edged he felt, all muscle and bone, wrestling with me from behind. I stood up and tried to shake Anthony off my back. Suddenly he let go. He was looking down at the cot.

Daniel's face was blue and he wasn't moving. He was completely still and his mouth was open wide and there was no doubt in my mind. He died like that, seizing and scared to death, underneath me and Anthony."

"What did Anthony do then?" the detective asks.

"He came at me like some skinny, crazed wild animal. He clawed at me and kicked me. He bit me; you can still see the mark." Donahue yanks aside the collar on his jail uniform to show the detective his shoulder. We can all see two rows of dark pink indentations: the imprints Anthony's teeth made in his flesh over twenty years ago. "The bastard drew blood!"

I wish Anthony had bitten him harder and left a worse scar.

"While his teeth were still imbedded in my shoulder, I stabbed him in the thigh with the syringe. I stuck it in hard. Everything else happened fast. Anthony felt the stab of the needle and staggered backwards. Then he looked at the open door and ran like hell. I didn't follow him. I left the door open and hurried to the nearest nurses' station. Nobody was on duty because of the budget cuts. I was the only one working on the second floor that night. I reached under the desk and pulled the emergency lever to unlock all of the exits and then I raced down to the control room and turned off the alarm system. Anthony did exactly what I wanted him to do. He found a way out and ran as fast as he could, into the sub-zero February night, barefoot, wearing only his pajamas. Then I called Dr. Summers and told him everything."

"What did Summers say?"

"He told me to lock the doors back up and reset the alarms. He said not to say anything to anybody and to wait for him to arrive. We were really understaffed, so no one heard Daniel yell and no one saw Anthony leave. I knew he wouldn't survive on such a cold night, so I waited for daybreak. That's when Dr. Summers would be getting to the hospital."

"What did Summers do when he arrived?" The detective wants to find out as much as he can about the pediatrician's role in the deaths of the two young patients.

"The next morning Summers came in early, like he said he would. He told me to go outside and look for Anthony. He'd take care of Daniel and he did. He pronounced him dead due to complications resulting from a seizure and then he signed the death certificate."

"What about Anthony?"

"Hardly anybody even knew Anthony existed anyway. He was so violent he stayed locked up in his room most of the time. A few orderlies and maybe some nurses had restrained him once or twice. Some of the nurses might've sedated him here and there, but a lot of them were let go because of the budget cuts. Most of the time, I was in charge of Anthony. That morning, nobody even noticed he was gone. Nobody asked about him."

"How did his name disappear from the hospital records?"

"Dr. Summers convinced Dr. Peterson, the boys' shrink, to destroy any records proving Anthony ever existed, for the good of the hospital and so we could all hang onto our jobs a little longer. We told Peterson that Anthony caused Daniel's death and the hospital would be shut down for sure if the state authorities figured out we kept a nonviolent patient like Daniel locked up in the same room with Anthony. Peterson agreed and just like that, Anthony never even existed at all. I think Peterson might've suspected that there was more to the story, but he wasn't gonna talk. I think he was a little afraid of Summers and me. He might've suspected we committed a double murder."

"A double murder, Mike! Did you commit a double murder?"

"I more or less just set things up and then let them die. I didn't deliberately kill those boys. But my mother was afraid that somebody would think I did. She made a crazy anonymous phone call to a newspaper reporter, telling them about the violent roommate who caused Daniel's death. She thought it would take the suspicion away from me. She didn't want me to get arrested or fired and she didn't want anyone figuring out that someone had been stealing drugs, because she was involved and so was I. But, by the time the authorities started their investigation, Dr. Peterson and Dr. Summers had already destroyed all of the evidence. There was no patient named Anthony mentioned in any of the paperwork in any of the files at the hospital. And Daniel wouldn't be telling anybody about the stolen drugs."

"Did you ever find Anthony that morning?"

I feel tears building up in the corners of my eyes as I wait to hear Mike Donahue's answer.

"Yes. I walked out and saw the beginning of the trail he left. So I followed it. When I got to the fence I could tell he'd climbed it. I saw his blood on some of the chain links. The metal was so cold his flesh must've stuck to it and then peeled off when he pulled his hands away. He was bleeding. I unlocked the gate and followed his footprints into the woods for almost two miles before I found him. I can't believe how far he got."

"And why can't you believe it, Mike?"

We all know why, but I guess he needs to say it out loud so it'll be recorded on the video.

"It was below zero out there and the wind was howling. I remember feeling exhausted from being up all night. I had a coat, a hat and my gloves on and I was still freezing. Anthony was only wearing his pajamas and he was shot full of Phenobarbital."

"So, even though he was freezing and drugged, Anthony managed to travel almost two miles away from the hospital. And you were able to find him?"

"Yes. It had snowed a little during the night and the snow made it easy to follow the trail left by Anthony's bare feet. The blood was especially noticeable. I remember how red his blood looked, on the white snow."

At this point in his story, my tears start to fall faster than I can wipe them away. Mom hands me a tissue.

"After about a mile and a half, his footprints turned to drag marks in the snow. He must've fallen to his knees and crawled along the ground. The sedative kicked in big time but Anthony still didn't give up. Finally I saw him. He looked more peaceful than he ever had when he was alive. He was lying on his side, frozen solid. His skin was as gray as granite. He looked like a statue that had toppled over."

Now we know. Anthony fought to escape as far away from Wild Wood as possible. When he could no longer stand or walk, he dragged himself across the frozen ground. In the end, he fell over and died; alone in the dark and the cold.

The Last Chapter

We all bend our heads in silent prayer for Anthony. The Lonesome Boy. Who tried to save Daniel and failed.

Mike Donahue begins the final chapter of his tragic story.

"I carried him back to the hospital. He was skinny, but kinda tall, so he felt pretty heavy after a while. Plus his body was stiff, so it was hard to keep moving with him in my arms."

Horrified, I look at Wyatt and he wraps me up in a big hug. Even though the prisoner can't see me he stares straight into the mirror and we make eye contact. Only he doesn't realize it because he's looking at his own reflection. As Donahue continues his horrible tale, I experience a different kind of chill than the one Anthony always brings with him. The criminal's voice is empty of compassion. It contains no trace of self-awareness or empathy. Wyatt hugs me tighter as I shiver in his arms.

"I half-dragged him and half-carried him back to the hospital, almost two whole miles. I felt exhausted and colder than I'd ever been before in my life. Summers let me in one of the back doors. We put both boys into the same coffin, sealed it up and left it in the hospital crypt. As soon as the ground thawed out enough, the grave diggers buried them. No one noticed the coffin weighed enough to contain two boys. They were both pretty thin."

How can these men live with themselves? Summers is a doctor; a pediatrician! And what about Daniel's and Anthony's parents? These were their children. This happened in 1986, not the dark ages. The prisoner continues to explain why he, Summers and Peterson will rot in hell one day.

"Dr. Peterson called Daniel's family, but they didn't want a funeral or anything. The staff at Wild Wood was left with the responsibility of burying him, which was the way Peterson and Summers wanted it to be."

"Why?"

"The less anyone interfered, the better. Summers signed the death certificate for Daniel. I think it said something like 'due to complications resulting from a seizure.' We destroyed all of the documents and records that mentioned Anthony. We made it look like he was never a patient at Wild Wood. The doctors and I searched for and got rid of any paperwork that had his name on it. We made it seem like he'd never been born. He didn't exist anymore."

"What about his parents?"

"When Anthony was a baby, his parents brought him to the hospital and never visited him after. Because he was so violent, almost nobody at the hospital had any contact with him. Sometimes a couple of us would get called in to restrain him and give him a shot; usually me and whoever else happened to be on duty. If any of the hospital workers knew him or remembered him, they didn't ask about him. There were way too many patients in that hospital and not enough staff. Nobody even noticed Anthony was missing. Nobody knew he was dead except me, Peterson and Summers."

Uncle Johnny makes a quick call on his cell phone, for someone to pick up Doctor Peterson.

"My mother might've suspected something, but she kept her mouth shut. She was smart enough to figure out she was better off not knowing all the details about the night of February 10th."

"There's one more important detail we need to know, Mike," the detective reminds him.

"Yes. I know. I remember exactly where they're buried. The grave's unmarked, but I'll never forget where it is. We can go over there as soon as you're ready."

Two officers enter the interrogation room and escort the prisoner back to his cell. After asking to be kept informed about any new developments in the case, Donahue's lawyer says goodbye.

Gray-faced and shaken, the detective comes in to talk to us. "What you observed was a full and legally-obtained confession. The rest is up to the district attorney."

"I need to be kept in the loop. I want to stay involved every step of the way." My uncle has never sounded more serious.

The detective puts his hand on Uncle Johnny's shoulder. "Of course, John. I know he kidnapped your niece."

Wyatt walks me out to my parents' car and then leaves with Oliver and Jackson. Dad, Mom and I ride in silence. We're thinking about Daniel Warren and his only friend, Anthony. When I get home I stretch out on the couch to read a magazine article, but fall asleep after about three paragraphs. I dream that Wyatt's lost in the forest behind Wild Wood during a blizzard. I keep trying to find him but an endless wall of white snow surrounds me, blinding me so that I walk into trees and trip over rocks. The vibrating of my cell phone in my jeans pocket wakes me up at about four o'clock in the afternoon.

It's Uncle Johnny. "Annabelle, honey, how are you?"

"I'm okay, just tired."

Then he tells me the news. "After we got a court order from a judge, a team went down to Wild Wood and excavated the grave. They found the remains of both boys. Anthony and Daniel will finally get justice."

As soon as I call Wyatt, he races over to my house.

Ten minutes after I hang up, I hear his tires squeal in the driveway. He bursts into the kitchen, wearing only a t-shirt and jeans despite the cold weather. He didn't even pause to put on a jacket before he left. Opening his arms wide, he stops in the middle of the kitchen. I rush over to him and bury my face on his shoulder. After a couple of minutes, he threads his fingers through my hair and tilts my head up.

"I promised Anthony he could say goodbye." While he's still speaking these words, the temperature surrounding us drops and Wyatt morphs into a darker, hungrier version of himself. Anthony spins toward the door and races outside. I stop to grab a sweatshirt and pull it over my head as I run after him.

He's standing where our backyard ends, in the tall, dead grass at the edge of the forest. An army of huge green-needled pines, bare-branched oaks, maples and birches, marches on forever behind him. To the west the cheerless sun squints weakly through a thick dome of pale gray clouds. It's due to sink from sight in half an hour.

Slouching up against a thick-trunked oak, with his hands in his pockets and the woods at his back, Anthony waits. Our old tire swing still dangles from the sturdiest limb of the tree he's leaning against. A feeble wind moves the frazzled rope back and forth. The tire twists weakly once or twice then stops. Grabbing both his wrists, I pull his hands out of his pockets. Wrapping his cold arms around me, he rests his cheek against my hair.

"I killed Daniel. He needed my help and I killed him."

"No, Anthony. You tried to save him."

"I attacked Donahue and he fell on Daniel. If that hadn't happened, Daniel wouldn't have died."

"Mike Donahue went into your room intending to kill him. Daniel knew that and he had a seizure. He might already have been dead when you two fell on him. We'll never know for sure."

"I need to know."

I think back to Nathaniel's story and borrow his words. "We have to make split-second decisions all the time and as long as they're made with good intentions, we can't blame ourselves for the outcome. Sometimes you're in the wrong place at the wrong time and something horrible goes down. Sometimes you're trying to be a hero and circumstances make it impossible. Sometimes you try to help when someone needs you and everything goes tragically wrong."

He pushes back my hair with one cool hand and holds his palm against my cheek. "Annabelle, how did you get so wise?"

I shrug. "I'm not wise. I stole that from Nathaniel."

"You were wise enough to listen to him, then."

"You need to forgive yourself, Anthony. Mike Donahue's the one who wanted to hurt Daniel, not you. There's no reason to feel guilty."

"I want to believe you."

"You *need* to believe me."

"I'll try. What you're saying makes sense. I think that you're right about many things, Annabelle."

"I can't take credit for any of it. Basically I'm an idiot. People have given me a lot of good advice. That's all. I should remember to follow it myself more often."

"I want to remember forever how you look right now. With your beautiful face shining up at me."

"Anthony, don't go."

"I have to."

"I'll miss you so much."

"Annabelle, you have been my light in the darkness. Together we uncovered the truth. And now you've given me the strength to forgive myself. And the power to leave."

"I'll never forget you."

"I'll love you forever, with all my heart."

"I wish we had a mirror so I could see the real you one last time."

"Close your eyes and picture how I looked when I was alive."

I close my eyes. For the first and the last time, Anthony bends and touches his lips to mine.

His kiss doesn't feel the way I was afraid it would feel. There's no hint of death or decay. No taste of the grave corrupts this moment. His lips are cold, but the warmth from mine melts the chill quickly.

Fragile like a snowflake, Anthony's kiss disappears the second his lips press harder against mine; like each moment in time disappears while you're thinking about it. Like the present becomes the past; instantaneously.

When his arms tighten around me and grow warm, I know that he's gone and will never come back.

Wyatt ends the kiss before I'm ready to let go.

"In the end Anthony got what he wanted most, Annabelle. Your love." His frown ruins the moment.

I need to make him understand that Anthony had to experience love before he could let go. "If I didn't want him to stay, he could never have left."

A tear slips slowly down my cheek and Wyatt stops it with a kiss as gentle as the first drop of rain from a spring shower. When you have to look up and reach out your palm to see if it's really beginning to rain or not. I look at Wyatt's face, to see if he really wants to kiss away my tears and I can tell that he does because he's smiling a small, close-lipped, sad smile.

Then his face darkens again. The corners of his mouth turn down. His eyebrows pull together and cast a shadow over his eyes.

"You kissed him."

"Only once." I could argue and say I was really kissing Wyatt's lips, but it would be a lie. I wanted Anthony to kiss me and he did.

Someone had to love him. He waited for more than twenty years in that god-forsaken dungeon of a room, with the door to his soul slammed shut and locked, until someone came along to save him. When he saw me standing in the doorway, he knew I was the one earth-bound person who could set his lonely soul free.

Wyatt was an essential part of it, too. We needed his body, his mind, his voice and his heart, which beat so hard and so strong that I could feel it through his chest when he held me. Together, we opened the door for Anthony.

Wyatt takes a step back. And pries himself away from me.

Damn it!

He's being such a typical, stubborn guy. If I could blast his stupid jealousy into another universe, I would, but he insists on torturing us both with it. I want him to hold me and ease away my sadness with his kisses, but he has too many doubts.

I grab him by the arms; my hands don't even reach half way around his biceps. He lets me hold him still. The cold has raised his skin into hundreds of tiny goose bumps. They prickle against my palms as I rub Wyatt's arms, to warm him.

"Annabelle, I'll never get this out of my mind until I know the answer."

"Go ahead. Ask."

I'm afraid to hear his question. I'm dreading it.

"Who's a better kisser? Him or me?"

Ugh, why are boys such douche bags? Even this one and I love him so much.

I say the first thing that occurs to me because it's true. "You've had a lot more practice."

"Don't make jokes. I'm not in the mood."

"I'm not joking. It's true. Anthony lived a miserable life. Your life hasn't been easy, but Oliver loves you and so do I. The people who care about you have shown you a lot of affection. You have friends and the promise of a great future. Anthony never experienced any of that."

I try to explain so that Wyatt will understand and forgive me, even though I'm not sure there's anything to forgive.

"I loved Anthony, even though I knew he had to leave. Forever. And I'll miss him every minute of every day. It's hard to be so completely selfless. I don't have to be that way with you, Wyatt. I can be human and selfish and flawed. I can be myself and love you. We can love each other for as long as we want. I don't have to let go of you. I'll never feel depressed and miserable because you're gone."

I move closer to him and touch my lips to the pulse in his throat. He sighs. My lips press harder against the spot that's causing his stubbornness to weaken. I can feel his pulse speed up, so I keep kissing his neck. He pushes me away and looks into my face.

"He loved you so much, Annabelle."

"He loved you, too. We all loved each other. The three of us. But he's gone."

"Now it's only you and me."

"And that's the way this had to end, Wyatt."

"I already miss him."

"So do I."

Wyatt's strong arms reach around me and he backs me up against a nearby tree until I can feel the roughness of its bark through the layers of my clothing.

"Promise we'll stay together forever, Annabelle. I never want to share you again."

He kisses me before I can reply. His chest presses against mine and I can feel the tireless rhythm of his beating heart. Finally, we're alone.

ABOUT THE AUTHOR

Alyson Larrabee lives in Easton, Massachusetts, near the epicenter of the infamous Bridgewater Triangle. When she's not skulking around the many graveyards of her hometown at midnight and exploring the deep, dark depths of the Hockomock Swamp with her adventurous husband, Raymond, she teaches English at Easton Middle School.

A graduate of Oliver Ames High School, Emerson College and Bridgewater State University, Alyson is an avid reader of mysteries, ghost stories, historical fiction and many ridiculous but fascinating internet articles filled with unfounded rumours.

Alyson is also the proud mother of three young adults and one very poorly behaved but loveable redbone coonhound named Nigel.

*For your reading pleasure,
we invite you to visit our
web bookstore*

WHISKEY CREEK PRESS

www.whiskeycreekpress.com